Dances with Pucks

by

Debbie Charles

Texas Tornadoes
Book 1

Trade Paperback ISBN 979-8-89044-410-3
Digital ISBN 979-8-89044-409-7
Cover by Wicked Smart Designs

Dedication

To Julie (again!) and Gene
I could not have even started this without you

&

To Stephen Meserve
I could not have finished this without you

Dances with Pucks Playlist

Just The Way You Are – Bruno Mars
Save the Last Dance for Me – Harry Connick, Jr.
Moves Like Jagger – Maroon 5 featuring Christina Aguilera
A Whole New World - Tanz Orchester Klaus Hallen
You're the Boss – Brian Setzer Orchestra
Harder Better Faster Stronger – Daft Punk
There's Nothing Holdin' Me Back – Shawn Mendes
Don't Stop the Music – Rihanna
Iqual Que un Angel – Kali Uchis, featuring Peso Pluma
Winner – Jamie Foxx, featuring T.I. and Justin Timberlake
Texas Hold 'Em (Pony Up) Remix – Beyoncé
Take My Breath Away – Berlin
Señorita – Shawn Mendes, Camila Cabello
All The Small Things – Blink 182
This Will Be (An Everlasting Love) – Natalie Cole
we can't be friends (wait for your love) – Ariana Grande
Espresso – Sabrina Carpenter
Million Dollar Baby – Tommy Richman
Birds of a Feather – Billie Eilish
Gonna Make You Sweat (Everybody Dance Now) – C&C Music Factory, featuring Freedom Williams
Beautiful Things – Benson Boone

Chapter One

Cam

The sliding glass doors of the terminal open to a wall of heat, and I stagger back a step. Friends and even management of my new team warned me Austin was hot. However, they'd failed to divulge the blanketing of humid oven-like temperatures or the resulting total body sweat. Even the points of my elbows were damp.

Sheesh.

Dragging my suitcase and backpack, I scan for rideshares, delighted when signs point me into the shade of the short-term parking garage. The heat snakes in behind me, rising from the floor of the concrete structure.

Not wanting to complain to a local, I silently settle into the back of the rideshare. The driver might be a hockey fan, and an expansion team and its players need only positive PR. The city skyline zooms past on my left as we zip up the highway to my new rented home. How does anyone live here? More importantly, how do they keep the ice solid?

It isn't as though hockey is new to Austin. I like to think of it as the city upgrading. Team owners Greg Donovan and his sisters won the bid for this expansion NHL team by offering financial support for Dallas's AHL team, the Texas Ice Spurs, to relocate to Oklahoma City.

We'll play in a whole new compound in the northeastern corner of the city, which is supposed to be finished within a week.

Hopping out at the rental, I zap the driver a tip and wave thanks before wresting my bags up the walk. The new Tornadoes organization created an online community for the incoming players, connecting us with a few handpicked realtors and leasing agents to help us find living spaces.

A woman pops out the front door and skips down the front walkway with a smile so wide her perfectly veneered teeth shine in the sunlight. Us hockey players know a thing or two about restorative dental work. I recognize her as my leasing agent from her thumbnail profile online.

Oh boy. A ready-made puck bunny before our inaugural season even starts. The signs are all there. The few people I met face to face and on Zoom during the draft and signing process all dressed pretty casually. This woman is in a tight white top with a red lace bra peeking out from the deep vee which leaves nothing to the imagination. And despite the heat, she has heavy makeup with her long hair worn down. I cringe at her fitted skirt and stiletto heels. She's going to twist an ankle on the uneven concrete path that is broken up with tree roots.

She stumbles and I leap forward to catch her as I roll my eyes. Her sigh at my hand on her arm sounds happy rather than the normal reaction of embarrassed.

"Mr. Hill? I'm Lisa. Welcome to Austin."

"Cam. Thanks." I'd told her I preferred to use the lockbox and familiarize myself with the house on my own. As I hadn't given her my flight information, I have to wonder if she's been staking out the place all day, probably after she checked my roster photo and contract, all of which are public information. At least the air conditioning will be running full steam.

We step inside the mid-twentieth century bungalow. As always, everything seems smaller in person.

Sure, that may be because I'm 6'3" and weigh 210 pounds, but leasing agents are experts with photographing places to look their best.

She's walking around the space waving her arms and exclaiming about the quaintness and extra touches I could add like colorful throw pillows. Know your audience, bunny.

At least the furniture looks clean and isn't too miniature for me and my roommate, Jack Landry. Given my modest salary in the AHL these past two years and college before that, I hadn't been in a position to invest in furniture I'd want for the long term, so I searched for furnished rentals. I'm one step closer to not needing that though, thanks to following the plan I set for myself in college—NHL, multi-year, multi-million-dollar contract, meet the right woman, get married. Figure out a post-NHL source of income as needed and then kids timed to retirement from hockey so I'll never be the unsupportive workaholic father mine was.

Jack will arrive in a few days with his dog. Why he'd get a dog when he'll be on the road more than he's home, I don't know. But he's had two years in the NHL already as a defenseman with the Las Vegas Desert Kings, so he can afford the vet bills, food, and pet sitter fees. Because of the dog, he'll have the master at the back of the house with its own door to the backyard.

We're both on a one-year contract with the Tornadoes. He's supporting his family financially, and I save every penny I can. My mother had to hide money for my hockey gear from my father, and when she died just before my last year of high school, my coach had to step in. My father was more focused on providing food and a roof over our head to be willing to "waste" money on after-school activities. He regularly told me to focus on learning "marketable skills" rather than playing games, and never acknowledged my hockey scholarship or my placement in the draft, or even my entry level contract with the league as proof hockey could be more than a game. My scholarship didn't cover more than the essentials, so for a while I was always hungry and always worried about money. Now, I'm determined never to feel that way again.

Austin rent rates are way higher than Peoria where my team played. So I posted in the team forum that I was looking for a housemate. When Jack responded and we chatted online, we found we both like company but some private space. And Jack wanted a house with a yard for the dog, which sounded appealing. When we chose this house, we decided to keep the smallest middle bedroom as a computer room and privacy buffer so I'm in the third bedroom. That means my bathroom will be the one shared with our teammates when they're over, but I don't care. My priority was negotiating a lower portion of the rent.

I roll my suitcase to my bedroom and bunny, aka Lisa, says, "Your stuff was delivered the other day, and I asked the guys to go ahead and set up your bed."

Ick. The team had arranged movers for all of us, and I'd asked her to be on hand for the delivery of the few boxes and bed that encompassed all my worldly belongings. Meanwhile, I couch surfed with a friend for the last week to avoid the cost of a hotel. I draw the line at renting a bed, for obvious reasons, so I'm not thrilled the movers were handling it.

I step into the doorway and stop, turning my head to glare at her.

She flaps. The air fluctuates against my shirt. "What is it? Do you not like the placement? I wasn't sure how else it would fit."

Which is exactly the problem. A lot of rental places don't have the room for a king bed. So despite my size, I own a queen and sleep diagonal. Based on the measurements of the room and those damned realtor-style photos online, my queen bed, bedside table, and a tallboy dresser should have fit just fine. I mean, I have a plain wood frame which doesn't add more than a few inches of depth to the bed.

But there's about a foot between the end of the bed and the opposite wall. And barely a foot of space on the far side between it and the wall with a window.

In front of the bed there is maybe a three-by-five area with the dresser and bedside table almost touching corners as they sit at a right angle to one another. I'll never be able to do my goalie stretches in this room, that's for sure. Also, while it's unlikely, if I wanted to hook up—not with you, bunny—I'd be embarrassed to bring them here.

"Isn't it cozy?" Lisa asks.

"No. It's cramped." I turn to her, my mouth a flat line and my finger pointing to my bed. "The listing said the room was ten by fourteen. That bed is five by eight. Clearly the room dimensions were false."

She flaps again, elbows at her sides, forearms and wrists moving wildly. "Really? Are you sure? Is that a king?"

"No." I fold my arms and of course her gaze goes to the bulge of my biceps against my ribs. That's the only bulge she'll be seeing. I'm pissed. "It's a queen. Shall we walk it off, or do you have a measuring tape? This won't do."

"But-but-you signed——"

"The lessor signed off on the specs they provided. And that's what we agreed to rent."

"Um." Her eyes were wide at the possible loss of a placement fee. She whipped out her phone and held up a finger, stepping back into the hall. "Let me see what I can do."

As she whispers furtively into her cell, I test the space. Holding my arms out at shoulder height, I have less than ten inches on either side. Given that my wingspan is seventy-seven inches, five inches wider than the goal I tend, this room is nine feet wide.

Lisa reappears in the doorway. "I remember now. When the owner added central air conditioning a few years ago, he had to bring the walls in between this room and the garage for ductwork. The measurements must not have been changed in the listing. But I've talked with my office and we're able to reduce your rent by a hundred dollars a month."

It's a good thing I'm not claustrophobic and can see through her bullshit. But with a savings of $1200 a year, I can splurge on a hotel room if I don't want to bring someone back here, or they can damn well take me to their house. I nod. "I need that in writing by day's end."

I'm pretty even keeled most of the time. But having experienced her bait and switch, doe-eyed flappy act, I choose to err on the side of sounding less flexible.

"Shall I show you the backyard?"

"No, thank you. You mentioned there's a Google doc with the basic directions for pool care and a weekly service?"

She nods.

"And the movers brought my car?"

"Yes, it's in the garage, and your keys are on the kitchen table."

"Then we'll call with any other questions." I head for the front door to show her out. She dawdles for a minute, but I haven't left room for excuses, holding the door for her and giving her hand a brusque shake. I don't wait to see how she navigates the walkway, closing the door firmly the minute her tightly-clad ass clears it.

Strolling back down the short hall to the kitchen, I take it in. Functional, with more space than my bedroom. I go out the kitchen door and the heat smacks me again. I step back inside and peruse the backyard and the small pool from the door's window. Now that I've felt the temperature, the splurge on a house with a pool feels justified.

And assuming I stay on the roster for at least ten games without being sent down, my salary will be more than thirteen times what it was these past two years in the AHL. Which would be a big enough goal. But I really want the starting goalie position, and given the youth of this team and my stats from Peoria, I think I have a shot.

I return to my bedroom and take one step in, throwing myself on the bed and twisting to land on my back. Well, that's expeditious, I guess.

Sitting up, I grab my backpack off the top of my suitcase, barely stretching to do so. I fish out my laptop and pull up the pic of the Wi-Fi login information on my phone that I'd snapped from the welcome information on the kitchen table.

I need to unpack sheets, find a grocery store, a yoga studio and a coffee shop, not necessarily in that order. But my most urgent need is a pair of shorts and fresh t-shirt. The jeans I wore on the plane may never be worn again in this town, given the heat.

Being careful to avoid anything with hockey-related emblems on it, I change. I heard that college sports and the soccer team are bigger draws here than hockey, but I'd prefer to get the lay of the land before outing myself as part of the new team in town.

Research and the drive from the airport have taught me that coffee houses fight breweries for dominance in this town. At three p.m. in August, it's 103F and the sidewalks are shimmering. A beer would go down too quickly, and I want that starting goalie position more than anything. Iced coffee it is, then. I open my laptop and locate what I hope will be my local coffee shop.

* * * *

Walking the six blocks is torture. I'm practically wading through the air as I hit the café door, and I'm sweating like I just finished a five-mile run. I step in and sigh in relief at the blast of air conditioning. It's surprisingly busy for mid-afternoon, with more than half the tables occupied by solitary tattooed twenty-somethings, with a few scattered polo-shirted corporate types on the periphery. Most people have at least one part of their head shaved and wear earbuds as they tap their laptop keyboard in time to their overcaffeinated leg bounces. So this is working remotely in Austin. I just hope they all like hockey.

Iced coffee in hand, I head home. A dance instructor and studio are next on my agenda. My mom and I would watch the reality TV dance competitions together before she died. Then I read a news article about my hockey idol, retired for five years at that point, competing in one of those shows where various celebrities were paired with professional dancers. I was drawn by the fluidity and beauty of the movements and the dance styles. They mimic hockey in intricacies that an uneducated eye might not see, the partnership—or teamwork—required, and the speed and agility of it all, which make me a better athlete.

Conveniently, Indiana University had ballroom dance as an elective, and I became hooked. After I exhausted the university's offerings, I negotiated private lessons from one of the instructors. It stressed me out financially, but I craved it as a connection to my mom and excused it as less than most of my peers spent on beer. Even better, once I hit the AHL, I found out I could deduct it as a job-related expense.

I'll need someone with time in the morning and some flexibility to their schedule if I want to continue lessons during the season. Almost as important, I hate dancing with petite women, and so many dancers are tiny. The stretch between their height and mine makes hand placement, stride length, and even some turns awkward. Some men like smaller partners for the sake of the lifts, but I'm fit enough that isn't a concern.

Back at the bungalow, I notice that the covered patio has a ceiling fan. After trying three switches, I finally find the correct one on the wall and grab a lounge chair to sit and check that the Wi-Fi stretches this far out. I settle in with my laptop.

Skimming the web search for ballroom dance classes in Austin, I pass the top listings of national studios achieved by paid placements. Come Dancing is listed on the bottom of the second page, with an address near mine.

Their About Us page tells me it's a year old, and gives me a headshot of the owner, Maria Garcia. They have a social dance hour scheduled for tomorrow morning, but Maria isn't listed as the instructor. Someone named Christina is, and the studio's site doesn't include a photo or bio for her.

I call.

"Come Dancing, this is Maria. How may I help you jig?"

Catchy. "Hi. I've had social-style ballroom lessons for about six years, and I'm looking for private instruction. I'm over six feet tall, so I'd prefer a taller— female—instructor please." Never hurts to specify.

"Great! We're happy to help. We'll need to evaluate your skill and you'll of course want to check us out…" After outlining the rules of the studio, she takes my name and directs me to come by the studio tomorrow.

* * * *

In the morning, I plug my phone into my car and follow GPS to a single storefront in the middle of an L-shaped strip mall. Only the check-in area is visible from the sidewalk which means the studio must be behind it. I'd wanted to observe the social hour with the instructor who would be evaluating me, but the endless strip malls in Texas are challenging, and it had taken me longer to find than I'd expected, so I'll only get to watch for a few minutes.

Stepping in, I find an empty desk and vestibule. To the left there are cubbies for people's street shoes and belongings, and a hanging area for…what? Jackets? It's already 85F at nine a.m., and I cannot fathom ever wanting to wear a coat again. I scribble my name on the sign-in sheet as the big band music coming through the open studio door winds to a close.

A woman's voice announces a change of style to the cha cha.

I cross the lobby to the bench provided and set my bag down. My dance shoes, each encased in its own velvet bag to protect their soles, replace the slides on my feet. I tuck my gym bag and sandals into an empty spot in the wall cubbies before I step through the doorway. The sounds of dancers' feet on a wood floor under the music are as familiar as the scrape of skates on ice, and I smile in anticipation.

In the next moment, my mouth goes dry. I swallow.

In the front of the room, a woman in a leotard and dancer's wrap skirt is demonstrating a pivot to a pair of dancers. She's my perfect…everything. I'd guess she is five-nine or -ten, wearing dance shoes with straps across the inset and a two-inch heel that would bring her to nose height on me. Her chestnut hair is in a high ponytail that trails to her shoulder blades in thick waves. She's lean but not whip thin like many dancers, with a luscious curve of hips under her skirt and breasts that would be a handful even for my size hands.

What would her ass feel like when I hold her for a lift? Dammit, I know better than to lust after an instructor. The dance world has strict no-fraternization rules, and while Maria didn't mention that yesterday on the phone, it was on their website, and likely the reason

Christina's last name isn't listed.

I take one step farther into the room, and her gaze meets mine as her voice trails off.

Chapter Two

Christina

I've been off-balance all morning. My meeting with Maria had taken longer than I hoped, so I was late opening the studio.

The group that attends this session are some of my favorites. I know their names, preferred styles, and strengths and weaknesses. They're part of what I hope will be a relaxing summer before my brother's latest business venture opens in the fall.

We warm up with some stretches and then I play Bruno Mars's *Just the Way You Are* for some slower-paced swing dancing before I take requests. The tempo picks up, and I circle the room, gently adjusting form, suggesting a spin, or clapping for more elaborate steps. In between, I linger near the front and allow them to do their thing or come and ask for assistance as they'd like as I ignore the micro-bent knees and droopy elbows here and there.

The Smythes come over and ask me to refresh their memory on a turn. I talk through the counts as I move, acting first in his part then in hers.

Movement at the door catches my eye and I look over, nearly trampling Mr. Smythe's toes and stopping mid-count.

Holy smoke. That is the hottest man I've ever seen in person.

His t-shirt clings to him, and his nylon track pants encase long, strong legs. An image of them wrapped around me whips through my head before I shake it off.

He's wearing dance shoes. *Yes, please. Dance with me.*

But social hour is almost over. Clearing my throat, I step toward him. "Can I help you?"

"I hope so. Christina?" He holds out a bear-paw-sized hand. At my nod, he adds, "I'm Cam."

I shake his hand, my breath stuttering at the warm dry calloused skin engulfing mine. Tilting my head, I try to place his name, but my thoughts are jumbled and my heart's beating a mile a minute.

"I, uh, spoke to Maria yesterday, and she said I should come by now for an evaluation." He shrugs.

Oh, right. Maria had asked me to do a new student review after this social hour. I'd pictured another retiree as most people work during the day. According to the schedule, his name is Cameron Hill.

My gaze drops to his shoulders and the perfectly formed traps, dent, and deltoids are outlined through his shirt. He doesn't have the basketball "ball" shoulders, but he clearly does more for his workouts than dance. This is way better than a retiree. I bet he could handle my height and weight for tricks better than any of my competition partners. I've missed the rush of flying through the air with the help of a partner, and the few extra pounds I've added since my days competing wouldn't matter with those muscles.

"Is that still okay? I can wait over there." He gestures with his chin toward the chairs on the back wall.

My synapses fire. "Mr. Hill. Yes. Sorry, I had forgotten about you." *Nice, Christina. Way to make a good first impression for the studio.*

He turns and strolls over to the row of seats. The rear view is just as biteable as the front one. A student catches me staring. The seventy-year-old winks and wiggles her eyebrows. Huffing a laugh, I check the time.

"Last dance, everyone. What'll it be?" I always have them pick the last style of the day. Putting on Harry Connick, Jr.'s version of *Save the Last Dance for Me*, I toss my phone down on the sound system and go perch on a chair next to the newcomer, slipping my hands between my knees to hide their tremors. At least the seats are side by side. I might drool if I look at him head-on.

"Sorry I spaced earlier."

"Don't worry about it. It's nice to meet you."

"Tell me what you're looking for and a bit of your dance history?"

"Sure." He kicks a leg up over his other knee and leans an elbow on it to support his head so he can look at me. "I started in college. I'm a social dancer, no competitions. But I love trying as many dances as we have time for. I've dabbled in swing, salsa, tango, a little foxtrot, and rumba."

I conjure him tangoing, or his hips twisting to the rumba. I blink, unable to form a response, and swallow the saliva pooling in my mouth.

Look away; give a girl a chance, dammit.

Glancing down, I focus on his dance shoes. Black lace ups, they're soft with wear and have a half-inch heel.

They are also significantly larger than my competition partners'.

Oh my. Maria would have a field day checking out his hands and feet and extrapolating all sorts of mouth-watering conjectures.

We met as competitive dancers, and she's the wildest and most outspoken of my friends. When I dropped out of competing to attend college, she continued, but we stayed in touch. I used a small portion of my trust fund to invest in Maria's studio as a silent partner with an agreement that I'd have studio space for my dream, a nonprofit offering dance lessons to kids who can't afford it, once I get it up and running. As she ramps up the studio this year and continues to train for competitions, she asked me to teach a few classes. For now, she needs to continue working part-time elsewhere to pay the rent on her apartment and the studio.

The music winds down and I mumble an excuse. If my hips sway a little more than usual in my saunter—*walk*—to the stereo, it's purely coincidental. Clapping, I call out, "Thank you everyone. I'll see you later this week, I hope."

Out of the corner of my eye I catch Cam doing side lunges so low his magnificent ass is on his heel for a second before he effortlessly lifts and sinks to the other heel. His range of motion and flexibility rivals any dancer's. The gym can produce muscles like his, but not that level of elasticity. I'm curious to find out how such a large man, both height and muscle-wise, stays so flexible.

I gulp.

One of my students comes over to say goodbye and nudges me. With a snicker, she says, "More interesting view than we were, eh?"

Heat climbs my throat and face.

As the last students meander out, still chatting, I gesture him over.

"Rather than walking through the steps you've learned, I like to start with a dance when a student feels comfortable." At his nod, I ask, "Shall we start with a basic swing?"

"I prefer the rumba if that's okay." His voice is a rumble echoing the beat of that music.

My eyes and memory flash to his hips. Watching them shimmy in the Latin dance will be amazing, and the rumba has a more open stance with less touching, so I have a chance of controlling my libido and not climbing him like a monkey on a tree.

"Right. How about…" I scroll through my phone for an appropriate song.

"That one." He's suddenly right behind me, his body heat a visceral touch, his big hand coming around me to point to Maroon 5's *Moves Like Jagger*.

I bite my lip to stifle a gasp as my butt strains to lean back against him for a second. A beat later, his choice registers and I snicker. "Confident, are we?"

He laughs. "I just like it, and it's the right speed. You can decide after if the choice was ironic or not."

The rumba is a one-handed connection for most of the steps, and he'll need to be a strong lead to manage it well with a new partner, but I withhold judgment. He chose it and this song, and frankly if his dance moves are half as well-formed as his body, he has reason to be self-confident.

As the music starts, he takes my hand and leads me to the center of the room, already using the four-count basic step of the dance.

I'm using my peripheral vision so hard I'm going to give myself a headache, but it'll be worth it. His exaggerated hip rolls in the classic figure eight motion are drool-worthy.

We dance through the steps: the New York turning at a right angle and stepping forward, a fan, and even an Alemana which is basically a twirl for the follower in Latin dances. A small secret smile blooms on his lips, and he takes me through another fan, then pulls me past him into a Hockey Stick step.

I check his form as I step past and feel the expected tug on my hand over my head, to bring it down and around my body and pivot me to face him. Near perfect.

I relax into the rest of the dance, no longer concerned about his skill level. The sublime pleasure of dancing with a partner several inches taller than me is worth relishing. So often my partners are close to my height or even a bit shorter. This is a treat I mean to enjoy, even though I'll hand him off to Maria for his lessons so I can refocus on setting up my nonprofit.

Cam seems to gain confidence once he becomes accustomed to my style and stride. I step up my game, adding a touch more flare to my own steps, my wrap skirt flapping.

He pulls my arm, stepping into a close hold and circling us in a tight rotation.

I lose my breath at the sensation of his length against me. And I do mean his length.

New dancers are often shocked at the lack of personal space in ballroom dancing. Hips often brush, thighs pivot to end between each other's legs, and hands skim breasts on close turns. And that's without lifts.

He seems annoyingly unaffected by our physical contact. Meanwhile, I worry I'll stumble and embarrass myself. After all these years, intertwined legs shouldn't even be a blip on my radar, but my blood surges at every sweep of nylon track pant and each push and pull of his arm frame.

My gaze latches on to his flexing biceps as he leads us around the wooden floor. When we twirl, my hair slithers along his arm, and I catch a whiff of soap and laundry detergent. The scent gets interrupted by the hint of a fragrance when he turns his head, making me want to sniff his shampoo bottle. Or conditioner, given the lustre of those thick golden waves.

He brings us back to center and spins me out then back in, then out. I only realize the song is drawing to a close when he releases me to bow.

I draw a cleansing, Cam-free breath and his gaze drops for a millisecond. I pace over to fiddle with the music, willing my nipples into submission. Leotards are great for range of motion, but they hide nothing. It's gonna be a long hour.

For the rest of the evaluation, I test him in several dances. As we get more comfortable, he adds confidence into his directions with his arm pushes and pulls becoming smoother as he trusts I'll go where he leads me, and I'm left in no doubt where he wants me next. But in the last dance, when he brings me into a close hold and twirls us again, which means stepping between each others' legs to circle multiple times, I struggle to spot. That's definitely the reason I end the song dizzy. Never mind the Cam-shaped brand along my whole right side. My hip still holds the imprint of the bulge in his pants and my skin won't stop tingling.

Cam returns to the front to change his shoes, giving me a chance to recover. I quickly turn the equipment and the lights off, trying to regain the mantle of professionalism and calm my breath. I'm starting to understand those bodice rippers' references to heaving bosoms. Snorting at myself, I join him.

A bead of sweat rolls down my sternum and is caught by my leotard, but his only sign of exertion is sweat-darkened hair at his temples. Any doubt as to his fitness level is obliterated. I stifle resentment. Now I'm not only self-conscious of my visible perspiration, but I'd have liked to see his shirt cling to those pecs. Forcing myself not to stare, I say, "I'll tell Maria your level of experience and she'll call you to set up a schedule of lessons."

"With her?" At my nod, he asks, "How tall is she?"

"5'3"." His face falls. "Maria is a pro. She'll make it work."

"It's just a lot less fun. I feel like I'm prancing. Also, I need someone available in the mornings, and given that you're here and she's not, I'm wondering if she can do that. I have some flexibility this month, but I won't after Labor Day."

Dang it. I don't want this distraction. After graduating from UT, I became certified as a CFA, a Chartered Financial Analyst, to manage my family's considerable wealth. Most of the time, that consists of a few hours every day checking our investments and answering questions or authorizing spend requests from our three accountants. My plan was to use the rest of my days to get my dance program off the ground. However, my brother immediately roped me into his dog and pony show to get investors to back his newest business project. Between that and Maria needing help to get the studio up and running, I haven't had the time I want for my own dream…admittedly my fault for saying yes to things. But I want to support the people I love and I have the time and means to do so.

The financial markets open early given Austin's time zone, and I should be monitoring them, although most of my trades are scheduled ahead based on a stock hitting a certain value. "You can't do afternoons?"

He shakes his head.

I admit, "She has a second job to help fund her competitions and the studio, as it's still in its infancy. And she's the only instructor for now."

"What about you?"

"I'm just helping her get started."

"Wouldn't more private lessons do that?"

"I'm not always available in the mornings, either."

"I'll take what I can get. Please?"

I waffle. Maria will kill me if I decline this. It'll be the additional funds she needs to enter an upcoming competition, which would be a credit to the studio.

"I'll pay a premium."

I blink. Apparently, waffling is good. What on earth does this gorgeous creature do that he can offer more money for lessons during hours when the rest of the world works? I scan him again. Perhaps he's a model, but Austin seems like an odd place for that.

I guess my brother could do that, too, so maybe family money, like ours. It's none of my business, anyway. But the studio definitely is. And I don't like the idea of disappointing Maria.

My libido is dancing inside as I anticipate the press of that cock against my hip for weeks, while my brain wonders where my professionalism has hidden.

"Fine. We can try it for the month."

Chapter Three

Cam

I'd pulled out as many tricks as I dared with a new-to-me partner for my evaluation dance to impress my smoking hot instructor and make her beg to work with me—or beg for anything.

I hardly slept last night in anticipation of my first private lesson today. She's everything I could ask for in a dance partner, so this will be both the best lesson ever and complete torture as our bodies brush and jostle in the intimacy of ballroom dancing.

I've had dozens of partners in my years of training. After the initial strangeness, we all got used to focusing on form and steps and not on the incidental contact of body parts. Yesterday, I couldn't find that perspective; I'd fought a boner from the first swish of her hips.

When I walk in, she's in the vestibule waiting for me to sign in, wearing another leotard and filmy scarf/skirt thing tied around her hips. When she steps around me to lock the door, my cock leaps in eagerness. We have total privacy, and that knot in her skirt looks easy to untie. I turn away and try to refocus on dance, sitting to change my shoes and discussing the most benign topic I can think of. "Phew. I'm guessing you got here early or have this place on a timed thermostat? I was worried I'd come out of one oven into another."

She snickers. "You must be new to town. You'll get used to it."

"They keep telling me that, but it's hard to believe."

"Why didn't you wear shorts then?"

"Track pants are closer to pants that I'd actually dance in, and I wasn't sure of the studio dress code. But if you're okay with shorts, I will."

I'm grateful she didn't ask for more proper dance clothes. She doesn't need to know that all my pants have to be tailored or custom made to fit my hockey thighs and glutes. I only have a few suits and a couple pairs of pants with stretch in them for dancing, having been on a tight budget the past two years. While even entry-level minor league salaries are more than many people earn, including my father, they're not the stuff of bespoke suits, or even extensive tailoring. I made dance clothes and shoes a priority, but I'm glad the rules changed for Austin's expansion draft, allowing anyone with a year left on their entry-level contract to be eligible.

I'll make an eye-popping amount if I stay on the roster, ideally as the starting goalie. The team owners and coaches decided to aim for younger players. Our average age runs almost two years below the overall NHL average. Out of the three goalies selected, I have the strongest save percentage so I hope to shine.

Christina asks, "What got you into dance?"

"I wanted a way to maintain flexibility, not just fitness. I enjoy yoga, but this is more fun and gives me a better workout." I'm oversimplifying, but I prefer not to out myself as a professional athlete yet, much less explain the extreme flexibility that a goalie needs to someone who may not even like the sport. I smile, remembering my old teammates' freakout whenever I drop into a split or firefly pose.

I lace my second shoe. Men's ballroom dance shoes don't come in my size. Most competitive dancers are a lot smaller than me, both in height and bulk. So I had to have my thirteen-and-a-halfs custom made, which is almost as pricey as bespoke suits. Thus, I own one pair at a time. Dance studios require that shoes worn on their floors have only been worn indoors on dance surfaces. Not that most people want to wear suede-soled shoes anywhere else.

"And what are you looking to work on now?"

"The Latin dances provide more stretches for the men, on average. It's also why I stick with social and showcase style dancing. Well, that and it's more fun than regulation."

She laughs. "Yes, competition judges are very strict. People are always surprised it's not full of lifts and fun props like the reality TV shows."

Before I can ask if she's competed, she says, "Why don't you choose a song, then? We can pick a dance based on the song and your mood. Do you have suitable music on your phone? The stereo we have has phone connectors or I can give you the Wi-Fi. Or you can peruse my phone again."

"Uh, I don't want to second guess the expert, but shouldn't we warm up first?"

"Yes. But I tailor warmups based on the style of dance you pick." She arches a brow.

"Oh." I duck my head to scroll through my phone as

my cheeks warm. *Way to alienate the pretty instructor, dumbass.*

"You know what?" she interrupts my perusal. "Many students come in with a specific plan—wanting to learn the tango, or something like that. As you don't have one, and you know several dances, let's stick with a general warmup, and we'll run through a few songs and styles again. I'll reinforce form today, then together we can plan for the next few lessons. I could also choreograph us something aiming at flexibility, once I have a better knowledge of your abilities."

As she walks away to get her phone and start some music, I'm laser-focused on her swaying hips and ass. I'd like to show her my abilities beyond dance, and I don't care who choreographs that demonstration.

Damn. These pants make reactions like that visible.

A Whole New World starts playing. I nod. Disney aside, this song fits my life right now. We flow through some basic stretches, some yoga-based, before she leads me to the barre along the back wall. Facing me, she drops into a squat, one hand on the bar.

I grin. I can hold a squat for two hours—most of my game time is spent in that pose. I widen my feet and drop low.

Standing, she rotates one leg from the hip in a circle, toe pointed and knee straight. Her foot is on par with her head at the top.

I mirror it, my foot also even with my considerably higher head at the top.

Her mouth drops open.

I arch a cocky brow.

A slow smile spreads across her face. "I see what you mean about flexibility. I'll have to think of some steps and particular dances to take advantage of your limberness."

We run through short versions of the samba, tango, salsa, and West Coast swing. My brain is only half-focused and I stumble out of step twice. The other half is cataloging her attributes—silky hair, long legs that could wrap around my large frame easily, high perky tits, and incredibly full lips, the lower one plumping from her chewing on it. Her butt is nicely rounded and my palms itch wanting to test how it would fit them. My lizard brain keeps wanting to lift her and let her slide down my body or tug her up against me on the end of a spin.

She chooses the slow foxtrot for our warm down, putting on a song from years before either of us started dancing, *You're the Boss*.

I'm in agony. While a locked arm frame and torso is supposed to lead my partner, the stance for this style requires our hips to be arched toward one another, so our lower abdomens brush with every step. The teasing, light friction tortures my cock. By the end, I'm panting and sweating like I raced our fastest player, who per the stats is our center, Drew Busbee. I only hope Christina doesn't notice.

As the music ends, I twirl her out and bow, receiving a responding curtsy. When she turns away to power down the stereo and unplug her phone, I surreptitiously adjust myself.

Sitting on a chair along the back wall, I feel ridiculous. I haven't had an uncontrollable public reaction like this to a woman since my first year of college. Bending over to unlace my shoes, I ask, "Same time tomorrow then? Shall we pick a dance to focus on for a week then switch it up?"

She nods and says, "Swing will give me the most choreography to play to your agility. Shall we start there?"

"Sure. Thank you again." I nod goodbye and let myself out, already impatient to see what she comes up with.

* * * *

I check my email while my car cools down enough that I can touch the steering wheel. I'm waiting for an all access pass from the Tornadoes Operations Manager, Kayla Morrison. Nothing yet, which likely means the compound hasn't passed all the required inspections.

As I drive home, my phone buzzes with a text. The display shows it's from Jack so I play it.

"ETA 30 min. I hope you're home."

Gotta love the amount of notice. He's lucky I wasn't still at the studio, or my phone would have been on Do Not Disturb.

Ah well, such are the joys of roommates. We'll figure out how best to work with each other.

Pulling into the driveway, I leave my car outside in case he wants to stage stuff in the garage. Like me, he travels light, but he rented a truck and brought bedroom furniture he owns as well as his hockey stuff and personal belongings. He's going to buy a car here—he gave his to his younger brother.

I reply to the text with a thumbs up emoji and head inside to stay cool until he needs me to help unload. He's been living in Las Vegas, so at least he's used to the heat, if not the humidity. A couple years older than me, he was second line defense there, and he's hoping to make top six here.

As he's been making NHL money for a couple years, I'd asked him why he wanted to share a small rental.

He told me he'd just bought his parents' house and is paying for his brother's college. As we all get one-year contracts with a new team, he'd rather wait to buy until he knows what his salary—and location—look like beyond this year. He also likes having a built-in friend and wingman.

I'd laughed with him, but I hadn't understood. I could drop into any environment and get along fine, but I found it hard to make close friends.

The doorbell rings. Weird. No one knows I'm here, except Kayla and the leasing agent bunny.

I check the peephole. That's a hockey player. If I hadn't studied the roster sent to us after the draft, I'd know just from the height and build. And this player's reputation precedes him. Drew Busbee. Why the Tampa Bay Storm gave him up, I don't know. Well, I can guess. He won a big contract last year, but he'd underperformed—or they didn't surround him with the right players—and they wanted to reclaim some room under the salary cap. I have high hopes for him, as I'm guessing the owners and coaches do.

I swing the door wide and offer my hand. "Drew. Good to meet you. I'm Cam. When'd you hit town?"

"Uh," he seems at a loss, and glances down. A large suitcase sits at his feet. "Did Jack not mention I'm crashing here for a few days?"

I raise my brows. "Hmm. Roommate breakdown in communication. Not the first time or the last time. Come on in out of the heat. At least you're in time to help me unload Jack's truck. He should be here any minute."

"This weather isn't bad. You'll get used to it."

I roll my eyes. If one more person tells me that, I might lose my shit. His Florida days must have acclimated him. I'm excited that hockey has finally spread south and west so much in my lifetime.

He looks around the living room and kitchen, then spies the pool through the window in the kitchen door. "Sweet. You guys will be party central."

"I hope Jack's dog is friendly, then."

A car horn sounds outside. I check the front window and Jack is waving at me.

"We're up." I gesture to Drew to follow me to the garage, where one bay is clear for us to stage Jack's belongings as we unload the truck.

The garage door slides up to reveal a six-foot-one hockey player with his blond hair up in a man bun bouncing on his toes holding a leash. A medium-sized mutt with definite shades of Australian shepherd is on the other end panting. "Cam! Buzz! Great to see ya! Hey, give us a minute, it's been a long last leg with too much iced tea."

Drew and I exchange smirks as Jack rushes by us to find a bathroom.

"Oh yeah, call me Buzz if you'd like," Drew comments.

We unlock the back of the moving truck and shove the rear panel up. We groan in unison at the contents. There won't be a need to find a gym to work out today, this will cover it. Jack's bedroom furniture is only a third of what's in there. He owns enough stuff to fill the whole house and then some.

Chapter Four

Christina

I grab the first parking spot I find and glide in. As I shut my car off and grab my purse, I check the time. I have twenty minutes before I need to head for the bar to meet my friends for our monthly girls' night out. I meander through the tunnel between shops that offers an easy pedestrian path from the parking garage to the main drag of the upscale outdoor shopping mall.

Terroir, the wine bar we almost always meet in, is directly across the street, but the two shops on the left of the tunnel are some of my favorite boutiques, and I browse the windows before heading across to claim a high-top table.

As I'm sitting, Maria walks in.

"Hey, you," I say as I hug her.

The waitress approaches, but behind her Lauren is weaving her way through the high-top tables to reach us so I ask her to give us a minute. The bar has a garden theme for both its indoor and outdoor space. But even with misters, summer is a stretch to sit outside, particularly for those of us in business casual clothes, rather than Maria's dance apparel, so we're inside, where it will get noisy as it fills up.

We order the usual three dip trio with vegetables and pita chips, and select a bottle to share. Lauren consults the Google doc that Nicole, the project manager of the group who couldn't make it tonight, created for us to work our way through the wine menu.

I was the one who picked a wine bar. We all love trying new wines, but I'm a bit obsessive about it. I'm also enough of a wine snob to live in the pool house on the family estate, with Greg in the big house. It's enough personal space but also enough closeness to my brother, and I have a pool and the big house's wine cellar at hand with no responsibility for maintenance. It's perfect.

Ordering done, I lean in. "How's the dance studio?"

"Still not busy enough to open another day or hire another instructor, but the classes are starting to fill up. I need more privates. Especially at the rate you're getting."

Lauren raises her brows. "What is this? Chris pulls a special rate?"

I slant Maria an aggrieved look, but she grins at me, unrepentant. I decide to tease her with a version of the truth. "The rate is based on size."

They both fall out laughing, although Maria sticks her tongue out at me as she does. The waitress returns with our wine, giving them a minute to catch their breath.

"He's over six feet and wanted a tall instructor. When I declined, he upped his offer and I couldn't say no when it would help the studio."

"How old is he?" Maria asks. "He sounded young on the phone."

"He is. Younger than me. Mid-twenties, I'd guess."

"Hmm. Tall, dark and handsome did you say?" Lauren propped her chin on her hand.

"No, actually. Tall, golden-haired, and…," I stop before I finish my thought of *built like a brick shithouse*. Heat creeps up my face.

"And handsome!" Lauren claps her hands. "Tell us more!"

I give in to temptation and gossip. "Y'all. He is the most fit of any human ever. It's crazy. I'm not even sure I could pinch him. I'd bet even his ass is a rock. And holy smoke, what an ass it is." I fan myself. "And he's flexible. Like, as flexible as I am."

Maria leans in, mouth open. "Dayum. I'm going to need to catch up on administrative work at the studio one of these mornings when I'm not working."

"The most fit? Ever? You who have danced competitively are saying this? And since when is any guy, even a dancer, as flexible as you? What the hell does he do with his time?"

"I have no idea honestly. He schedules lessons during office work hours. And frankly, he must need hours in a gym to keep that body, so who knows when he'd have time for work."

"Ohh, maybe he's a construction worker. With a tool belt." Lauren smacks her lips.

Maria rolls her eyes and smacks her arm lightly. "Girl, you read too many romance books."

"There's no such thing. Please—can you ask him if he has a tool belt?"

Maria throws out, "He could have family money like you. And you two can roam the world together having dirty pretzel sex everywhere."

That throws a bucket of cold water on my libido.

"We know that's not happening."

Lauren reaches over to squeeze my hand before sipping her wine again. She leans in so we aren't overheard, but the bar has become busy enough that's unlikely. "I know you go for older men who are less likely to want children, but a guy in his mid-twenties will be all about casual. If he's that hot, it's worth a fling. The doctor and therapist both told you that after surgery, the pain during sex should be resolved, and the birth control should keep the endometriosis under control."

I'd quit dance when pain in my lower abdomen had sent me to a doctor who found extensive endometriosis that required surgery. Since then, medication has thus far kept it at bay. I didn't mind giving up dance at that point, as it had taken its toll and I wanted to attend university while I was still close to the other students' ages.

"Sex wasn't all that interesting before the endometriosis interfered."

My friends have all the details of my life. Maria says, "You had two partners when you and they were teens. No one knew what they were doing. And some of that was the endo. It'd be different now, especially with someone you're this attracted to."

"I just haven't wanted to try, given the all pain and no gain. And the longer I go, the more I worry fear will stop me from becoming aroused because I'll get in my head."

"And as I tell you every time you say that, you'll never know if you don't try," Maria admonishes me with a smile.

The other part of my diagnosis is that I'll probably never be able to have children. To stop taking birth control would be a huge risk given how extensive the tissue spread was. I went to therapy about that, as I'd hoped for a family one day, but I'm adjusting. That's why I target older men who have children or made the decision against having them. I've also bowed out of every relationship the minute they start pressing to add physical intimacy, as I haven't been ready to have a conversation about my condition.

For now, I answer Lauren with other advice from the doctors she is ignoring. "They also said it would be best to have sex in a committed, trusting relationship, so I could share my concerns and be certain my partner would be supportive. That doesn't lend itself to crazy monkey sex with a client of the studio, which is also against the rules."

"Oh, please. That's standard industry practice. Special dispensation could be made once I determine how attractive he is." Maria wiggles her brows.

"Seriously, though," Lauren says, "maybe you take the approach that casual sex can be more relaxing because less is riding on it. Then you're less likely to tense up, but if you do, it won't matter because you're not planning on bringing him home to meet the family…?"

"Yeah," Maria chimes in. "If you can get yourself to relax it could be a breakthrough. You're already attracted to him. Build on that. Don't plan anything, but let it happen if there's an opportunity." She winks and adds, "Then you'll have less time to stress and talk yourself out of it."

I nod. It's excellent advice, if I can keep it in front of my fears.

* * * *

As Cam is more advanced than I'd expected of a young man walking into the studio, I've introduced faster songs and bolder moves than I normally would this early into private lessons. It also helps that he's taller, broader, and stronger than any past partners.

With that in mind, after our warmup today I choose *Harder Better Faster Stronger* by Daft Punk for us, and snicker at Maria and Lauren's imagined reaction to that pick.

As we swing, I admire his form. It looks so natural. He's well-trained, but beyond that, even the best-trained amateurs drop their elbows, their shoulder muscles tiring at the unnatural activity. The one thing Cam seems to struggle with is straightening his leg fully. He says it's an old habit. Experience has taught me that form is harder and more visible in a female dancer. A man can hide that micro knee bend under pants.

Wondering whether it's worth being hyper-vigilant to correct, I ask him, "Have you considered competitive ballroom dancing?"

Even though my competition days are done, jealousy claws at me as I conjure an image of him in a form-fitting suit brushing hips with a dainty woman in a flowy dress, twirling around a competition floor.

He shrugs. "Maybe someday, but not right now."

Relief washes over me. Stupid brain. I have no right to be jealous or relieved.

"Do you want me to correct little things about your form, or are you more interested in dancing for fun?"

He purses those lush lips as he tilts his head in thought.

Heat arrows down to my belly and beyond. This man is hot without even trying.

Studio rules, I remind myself.

I consider asking him what he does, but I'm not quite brave enough. I don't want to explain why I'm available, that my days are flexible. Most days, managing my family's varied investments only takes part of my day. The remaining hours are divided between setting up my dream project and staying in dance instructor condition.

That'll change in the fall, as my brother decided to build a championship NHL team here in Austin and has pulled out all the stops. I spent a bunch of time helping him get backers, and he's asked me to help in the first part of each season. But after that, my own passion project will have to take precedence. Dance had been an outlet growing up, but I learned early on that it was an expensive pursuit. Lessons cost a lot of money, never mind travel and costumes if they choose to pursue it competitively. Many friends dropped out because of that. Everyone focuses on sports subsidies, with no attention on dance lessons for students who couldn't afford them. That's where my nonprofit after-school program would come in. But my ideas aren't formed enough yet to share with a near-stranger.

So instead of talking, I abandon myself to the dance.

The next morning, Cam tells me about his latest discoveries of Austin and his neighborhood as we stretch, something that has become a routine.

Finally, I give in to curiosity. "What prompted your move to Austin?"

We flow from warrior two to warrior one then down to a high lunge.

"A new job that starts in a few weeks. That's why my schedule will change in September."

Ah. That explains how he has so much free time as

well as why he's new in town.

"Where are you from?"

"Outside of Chicago."

I snicker. "And you moved to Texas in the summer? I bet that was a shock to your system."

He laughs and nods as we rise to switch directions and repeat our flow on the other side.

I press a little further. "Where?"

"A few different places. Most recently, Peoria."

Given my family's love of hockey, my thoughts jump to the AHL team there, but I shouldn't assume every Northerner is a hockey fiend. His vagueness signals that he doesn't want to discuss it further, so I let it go.

Changing the subject, I say, "I've added in some kicks for flare. Things that I'd normally do but can be incorporated into the lead dancer's routine as well."

"Sounds good. Let's spend an extra few minutes at the barre then. Any chance we can do some lifts?" He has asked that every lesson after the first few.

I'm selfishly resisting because his hands on more parts of my body might be more tempting than I dare until I either get my thoughts straight or my libido under control. But that isn't fair to a client, and I need to determine what lifts might make sense. He hasn't done any with other partners. He claimed it was no fun when he could tuck them under an arm like a football. There was also the risk he'd toss them too hard and break them.

"I'll bring an idea or two tomorrow."

"Really?" His wide grin and eager tone drag a reluctant answering smile from me.

"Look up the fish lift on YouTube and I'll find a spot to incorporate it." Although lifts are not part of competition ballroom, every dancer plays around with them when they have time and a partner they trust. The fish is a beginner level lift and one of the few that don't put my head near his crotch, his hands near mine, or anything else that might cause me to fall from distraction.

I hardly sleep that night, worried about how I'll react to his hands on me. *Come on, Chris, you're supposed to be a professional.* There is nothing professional about my body's reaction to him, though. Every single lesson, I've had to wear pantyliners so my bodysuit won't show a wet spot from my reaction to him. Thank goodness for wrap skirts which act as extra insurance.

In the years since my surgery, I haven't missed sex. But getting to see and touch Cam's naked body might be worth the potential physical pain. Plus, my friends are right. The doctor had said that was far less likely after surgery, especially if my partner and I prepared my body. It's prepared, all right. Holy smoke. He might be the perfect test subject.

The next day, Cam is bouncing on the balls of his feet like a kid on Christmas morning.

The damn man is even cuter when he's excited. Perhaps he'd bounce like that if I invited him back to my place. "Full warm up. Let's go."

After we're warm, especially his upper body and my inner leg muscles, I talk him through the swing routine we've been practicing, to the spot which makes sense to incorporate the lift.

He's walking through it with me, his form still strong despite the casual pace and lack of music.

He spins me away to his right, and I talk him through the new steps as I take two circling steps back in still holding his hand so it wraps around my waist with me facing away from him.

I kick my left leg out to the side in front of him and release his hand to wrap my left arm around his neck and shoulders. "Press your hand to my abdomen, centered on my belly button. Your other hand comes to my lifted leg midway up the thigh."

In this lift, I help raise myself using my shoulders and arm pressing down on Cam's shoulders. My leg muscles are tightened so I can hold its extension and angle to my body and am not yanked into a super split when he lifts me.

He's already flattened his palm on my stomach where I'd conveniently positioned our hands as I spun, and I worry I'll need burn treatment after this lesson from the sear. His other hand slithers around my thigh just as I'm tightening my core and leg muscles to hold my position.

My swallow is audible because my throat has gone tight. I should have put background music on. His hands are so huge that they brush the edges of my sex. His pinky finger on my belly reaches my small patch of trimmed pubic hair, and the thumb of his hand on my leg is brushing the leg seam of my leotard. Molten liquid rolls through me and my stomach muscles loosen. That pantyliner may not be enough to counter the deliciousness that is Cam.

He tightens his grip and lifts me. I bend the knee of the leg he's not holding to get into the pose. I didn't even need to press my left arm on his shoulders to help. It's just lying there, his muscles bunching and rolling under me.

Without prompting, he spins, and I neglect to spot.

The room whirls around me. When he lowers me, I need a moment before I can unwind my arm from his neck. I choose not to spin back out to show him where we'd continue the dance steps. "Well done."

"Seems a bit too easy. Is that really the whole lift? What about on those competition shows?"

"We have to start somewhere. I have no desire to fall, so we'll build up to more complex moves, just as you did learning the steps."

"I'd never drop you, Christina." His voice rumbles with offense.

"Says every dancer ever," I reply lightly and step back into place. "Let's do it twice more on my count and then we'll put it to music."

I tell myself I'm mentally prepared for his hands on my body, pointing at my swollen pussy from two directions. I'm not. I gasp again and almost stutter on the count. I tighten my arm muscles to press, but again I'm up before I can use them.

At the end of the hour, he's unable to stop grinning. "This was so fun. Please, let's learn another one later this week?"

"We'll see."

"Hey, can I buy you coffee or lunch? I'd love to see a local's favorite spot."

I shake my head.

"Come on. I don't usually put my hands on a woman without at least buying her a drink." He winks.

Whew, his smile is lethal. My body is thrumming with need, and I swear I might be panting like I'm outside in the Texas heat. My brain has just enough blood flow to remind me that I'm into my third decade of life and this man-boy is too young for me.

"Sorry, against studio policy." I shrug. "I can text you a few suggestions."

"Dang. Okay. Any other lifts I should YouTube?"

I shake my head. I'd been considering the assisted cartwheel, but my head goes directly in front of his groin as he turns me in the cartwheel with his arms, my arms on him rather than the floor. I have no idea how I'll get through that without either embarrassing myself or dragging him into a horizontal tango, or both.

Chapter Five

Cam

I might need to start wearing compression shorts under my dance clothes. I leave every lesson with a hard-on, and the lift in the last session, as simple as it was, made it worse.

My fingers tingled knowing how close they were to her pussy. I can't decide if I hope we're going to repeat that or not. The dance steps have enough groin rubbing to make me crazy already. This might put me over the edge.

I've never been a fan of casual sex, indulging only when I needed a release and didn't have a girlfriend. And being single happened more often than I'd like, given how brutal a professional hockey player's schedule is.

And that's part of the problem. The few glimpses I have of her—her professionalism, her poise, her humor—make me want more than her body. I'd much prefer to take Christina out, get to know her brain first and then her body, but she shot me down after I asked her for coffee. That's all right, I didn't make it to the NHL by giving up at the first sign of resistance. So yeah, hard-on or not, lifts need to continue, cuz I swear she twitched when my thumb came to rest on her inner thigh.

After our warmup today, Christina puts music on. We tried the lift with music at the end of yesterday's hour, so I'm ready.

I spin her out then in. When I place my right palm on her belly, I feel as much as hear a small gasp. My heart begins to pound and my cock is already coming to life. Hopefully, my touch made her catch her breath, so I'm not alone in my reaction.

She swings her arm over me and her left breast is close enough for me to bend my head and bite. Aanndd that thought did not help the rising issue in my pants, dammit.

We do one turn and I set her down as we did yesterday, finishing the dance.

"Great. You remembered all the details," she says with a smile.

Yesterday, the set down was a little harder than it should have been at first. I was so distracted, I'd lost my perspective on the length of her legs. But it's fixed now. "Cool. Can we add to it or try something new? Please?"

"Let's adjust it a little and add to it," Christina replies, stopping the music. She brings up a short video that shows a male dancer sliding his arm under his partner's leg to lift her using the crook of his elbow. "I figured since you can squat so low and were lifting me without any effort, you'd be comfortable trying this. What'dya think?"

"Yeah. Yeah, I can do that." The guy pliés, sliding his left leg out wide and then side lunging into it. The woman in his arms tilts down, holding one arm in front of her and the outside arm along her body in a flight pose, her lower knee still bent.

Christina stops the video there, though. "Let's try the different hand positions first."

"It looked like his hand on her core was a little higher, his arm wrapped around her more?"

"Yes, to use more arm and back muscles as I can't help with the lift, and to keep my body out of the way of your leg bends. It goes here"—she gestures—"but we'll get into it by raising our hands together then I'll keep mine up as you slide yours down to position."

We're facing the mirror, with her in front of me. She holds my hand at her waist as though she's just spun back into this position, and raises our arms overhead. Releasing my hand, she keeps hers there and with her other hand, lowers mine to where it should be.

My hand is over her left ribcage, her breast in that space between my thumb and forefinger. I gulp at the simultaneous impact of the proximity of her soft mound to my digits, visible in the mirror, and the feel of her ribs under my hand. My knees bend into a squat.

"I probably don't need to say this, but keep your head up so I don't hit you when you raise me," she says, watching us in the mirror.

I force myself to keep my gaze on hers in the mirror. Holy shit this is hot, and not just physically. She competed, sure. But not everyone can then find a way to teach it to a wide variety of students in an understandable way. With a nod, I slide my arm under her raised leg, bending my elbow against her taut adductors along her inner thigh.

"Remember, don't squeeze, just lift. You're using your arms to lift so your hands can be gentle."

I do it.

She daintily points her toe as her standing leg leaves the floor and then bends her knee to touch her other leg with the tip of her shoe.

We run through it a few more times before I hold her mid-air and ask, "What about the next step? The side lunge?"

"Okay—"

Excited, I step out and bend my knee, keeping my hold on her. Her weight shifts and my position angles her more steeply toward the floor.

She shrieks and grabs my arm under her ribs.

There is zero possibility of me dropping her, so I'm confused, but I quickly straighten both of us and let her down. "I'm sorry, Christina. Are you alright? Did I hurt you?"

"No, but you scared me. Let me talk you through moves before you try them. There are micro-adjustments that are important, and I really don't want to break my face."

"There was no threat of that. I promised I wouldn't drop you. I'd sooner take the fall myself."

"You can't promise that," she starts.

Yes I can, and I do. Hockey players have incredibly fast reflexes, and none more so than a goalie.

"Besides, you can still injure one or both of us not knowing how to adjust a hold, or scare the crap out of your partner." She steps away and takes a few breaths.

"I'm sorry. It won't happen again. What did I do wrong? Can I see the video again please?"

She plays it and points out where my right elbow needs to raise to keep her horizontal. When she lets it play further, he makes a three-step turn then lifts her to lie face up on his shoulder. She swings her bent leg up and out in front of them both in a straight-legged fan.

Christina continues playing the video, but all I notice is the position of the man's face at that point. Holy crap, my face will be in the crook of her waist staring at her pussy as she makes that fan. *Fuck yeah.* Except then I might have to excuse myself from the rest of the lesson. My voice is hoarse when I ask, "Do you want to do that whole sequence?"

"Not right now. Let's get the first swing right without me feeling as though I'm going to faceplant, then we'll move on."

I wince. "Fair."

We go through it a few times. On the last, I warn her, having learned my lesson, "I'm going to try the three-step turn, okay?"

"Okay." She apparently feels secure up there.

Her vanilla and coconut scent tantalizes me. Hoping my cock doesn't block her path down to the floor, I step around before lowering her carefully.

"Nice. Let's do it at speed with music a few times."

Her body sliding against mine again might kill me. I turn away, but this studio has way too many mirrors. I fake a need to walk around and shake my arms, just to surreptitiously adjust the steel rod in my pants. At least dance clothes have stretch.

"Am I too heavy?" she calls. "Do you want a break?"

Shit. Shaking my arms sent her the wrong signal. Well, at least she'll be looking at them and not my dick. I turn and smile, shaking my head. "I'm fine. Let's do this."

I'm for sure going to have to rub one out after this, though.

* * * *

I haven't skated in over a week and am itching to be on blade and ice. The email indicating the main arena and training facility are open encouraged us to try any and all aspects of the complex. The coaches won't be there until closer to training camp, but they want us to test things and we're happy to play guinea pigs. The note also reminds me of the dates we received in our original welcome/move packages, and I check I have all the dates in my phone calendar. There's a Fan Day and charity ball coming up on Labor Day weekend, followed by an extended training camp to get us ready as a new team, then into pre-season. The attached map of the facility shows a separate fieldhouse on the property that houses a practice rink and physical therapy rooms, and of course the main ice in the arena. Both buildings have gyms and showers, although the fieldhouse gym is more extensive, according to the email.

Jack and I grab our bags and head over to check out our new team digs—a place that will be home more than any rental house could be. We go to the main building to test out the arena equipment and rink as we'll spend most of our time in the fieldhouse when training camp and official practices start.

The dressing room is as fancy as any of the league's. Built-in fans at every player's spot, carpet, dimmable lighting, and a giant screen at the end of the "U" of seats for game prep all will make it comfortable long after we've stunk it up. Overhead, our backlit logo, a purple "TX" split by a stylized gray tornado keeps us centered. I can't wait to dirty it up with pads and tape balls.

Buzz and a few other guys arrive as we're unpacking at our assigned lockers, and I recognize Gabriel St. John. He's been a top performer in the league at right wing and has taken two teams to the Stanley Cup Final, but never won. He was injured on and off most of the past two years and is thirty, which is the only reason the Tornadoes got an opportunity to sign him. Someone like St. John, who has been that close to the Cup and has a limited number of years left to win it, is going to be hungry. I shake his hand eagerly, trying to minimize my fanboying. He's truly one of the greats.

Buzz and I finish stowing our bags and head to the gym, the others trickling in behind us, still getting to know one another. Like the dressing room, this is state of the art. Top of the line equipment, racks of dumbbells at four spots throughout so no one has to wait, and two rows of bikes for warmups. The carpet is purple and the ceiling is white for better light. Our logo is painted on the ceiling, probably so there's no bad luck with someone walking over it on the floor. There is a stereo system, but every cardio machine also has a USB port to play your own audio or video. This is a far cry from the stinky, decades old gym in Peoria that was more worn than a chain gym. After wandering around and trying to act cool while silently oohing and aahing, I start my stretch routine. Others get on treadmills or bikes to warm up.

I always stretch because I never know what rotation I'll be on in net. Even though there aren't any coaches today, these guys are probably as eager as I am to shoot a puck around again and possibly scrimmage.

My ass almost touches the floor on each side lunge, and my quads bulge with how low I go. I move to pigeon pose to open my hips, lying flush along my bent leg, then rocking back into a calf stretch. Finally, I get to splits.

Gabriel looks over and asks, "Man, I took two weeks

off to grab some beach time and get my stuff here and I'm tight. How the hell do you stay so limber?"

Jack jumps in before I can. "Ballroom dancing. He's gone every day since I arrived. Can you believe it?"

"What the hell?" Gabe looks befuddled.

This won't be the first or the last time I'll need to defend my choice. I'm not bothered by it. Hell, I'm proud I chose this way to keep my mother's memory near and dear. I grin. "Hey, don't knock it until you try it."

"Is it to meet chicks?"

"Nah. Most are twice my age, other than the instructors, and they have no-frat rules. It's to maintain my flexibility and strength with a little fun added in."

He nods as I switch legs on my forward split. "It worked. You won't get any flack from me…" he trails off and looks around to catch the others' eyes, and the next word emerges at a much higher volume. "Prancer."

They all crack up. I shake my head with a one-sided grin, conceding the point. Apparently, I've already earned a team nickname. I suppose it could have been worse.

Eager to test out our home ice, we head out to the rink after warmups. This will likely be our only time to free skate here without coaches yelling at us rinkside. The TX tornado logo is emblazoned at center ice, and the goals are already in place. I pause for a moment and inhale. Nothing beats the smell of a hockey rink.

We start with speed drills and some shots on goal. I don't usually participate, and I'm terrible. I spend too long imagining where the goalie would be and how he'd react to aim properly. But after the summer, I need to limber up before training camp.

Buzz calls, "I hope you don't think that shooting is

what you'll have to defend against, Prancer. This ain't the AHL."

"Ha ha. You want to take shots on a protected goal? I'm happy to show you what I got."

"Let's do it."

I'm certain either Buzz or Gabe will be our Captain, and I want to impress them. I tug on my protective pads and switch sticks. As I do, I sneak a glance up at the suites. A couple are lit, and I can only hope members of management or even one of the owners—preferably the guy, Greg Donovan, who seems to be the face of the Donovan family owners—are watching, so I can impress them too. I'm determined to have the starting goalie position by the end of training camp.

Chapter Six

Christina

My Prius rolls slowly down the winding driveway to my brother's new venture. My siblings make fun of me for having a bargain car given our wealth, but I'm trying to balance caring for the environment without the inconvenience of a plug-in electric car. Our parents were older and passed over ten years ago. Their siblings are gone as well, so it's just the three of us now—my older brother Greg, me, and my younger sister Amy. We each have trust funds, but the majority of the family's wealth is in a holding company that Greg manages. I help oversee the investments for our portfolios but don't get involved in the day-to-day operations. Amy stays as far away from all of it as she can, choosing to use her time and money to help those less fortunate.

The facility is still a construction site and I worry about nails or other debris puncturing a tire on my little car. Greg wouldn't have thought about that as one of the fifty percent of Texans who drive pickup trucks. Why he chose that I have no idea. It's not as though he's handy; he probably doesn't know what DIY stands for.

Certainly, none of us has ever needed to move our own furniture, even for college.

He invited Amy and I, along with the rest of management, because the buildings and campus are finally finished enough he can show them off, including offices we'll each have onsite. At least he's bringing in lunch for us.

Amy negotiated her team ownership portion to include leadership of the Tornadoes Foundation and therefore the funding to pursue her dream of helping the homeless. So she'll likely be spending much of her workdays in these offices getting that up and running.

I, on the other hand, am dreading this meeting—it's a precursor to a temporary end of having free time, given Greg's plan for me to meet with players to offer personal investment advice. I fell into the financial advisory role when my uncle retired and I showed an aptitude and affinity for the markets, and I was happy to take over. Numbers are steady and predictable.

I'm glad Greg is offering this benefit after hearing the stories of professional athletes blowing their huge salaries within a few years of retirement. I just wish he hadn't thrown me to the wolves, rather than hiring someone else. Most hockey players don't have a college education, for several English is a second language, and few to none will care about saving their money. As much as I enjoy watching hockey, I know enough to be wary of trying to offer hockey players advice on anything. They are kings of their world, young and healthy—and superstitious. While that attitude is well-deserved confidence rather than conceit, it means most won't be ready to view themselves as fragile or their career as short-lived, much less plan for the next phase of their life.

I make a mental note to peruse the team roster to learn who is married and especially who has kids. If I can get early meetings with those, they might put in a good word with the others. Otherwise, it's going to be a complete waste of my time when I could be spending time planning my after-school dance program. Plus, meeting more than twenty new testosterone-laden egomaniacs in rapid succession is torture, even one at a time. I was never an extrovert or good at meeting people, but after my surgery I stopped trying. If Lauren and Nicole hadn't adopted me at UT, Maria would likely be my only friend. I'm much more comfortable with my spreadsheets or teaching dance to a handful of students ready to have fun. Even helping Maria with classes is outside my comfort zone, with the exception of Cam. He makes me uncomfortable for different reasons.

Following the signs for the VIP parking, I pull up next to Greg's truck and Amy's sedan. I approach the entrance to headquarters, located at one end of the massive arena. Off to my right a paved path winds through lush greenspace to a fieldhouse.

If I remember the digital mockup we used to woo investors, the players' areas are on the bottom two floors. The next two floors house the arena's food courts and retail spaces. And finally, the two above that are the offices. The executive offices occupy the fourth floor and are connected to the luxury boxes overlooking the rink for easy access on game days.

As I get off the elevator, I smell my favorite taco place, and my stomach rumbles. In the conference room, I grab Amy for a hug and kiss as she heads to the piles of individually wrapped tacos with various fillings set out on a counter at one end of the room. I lean in to peck Greg on the cheek as he talks to the Director of Public Relations, Saylet Young, and wave to a few other members of management as I grab two tacos and plop down next to Amy.

"How is the Foundation world?" As jealous as I am of my sister's ability to get started on her dream, I don't want my nonprofit tied to my brother's organization. Sibling relations work best when we keep family and business separate, and I thank the heavens that neither of them are the least interested in finances beyond knowing they have the money they need for their passions.

Greg and I are still recovering from my stint helping him secure investors for the team and getting through the approval process with the NHL. He's constantly getting wild hairs about some new venture, and I thought he was nuts to want to bring hockey to Austin. So I looked into it and saw that the AHL team here sold out every game, and soccer and Formula One racing have also done well. An NHL team made sense, and could be exciting. His joy when I agreed to help was overwhelming; I hadn't realized how passionate he'd felt about this particular idea or how much he loves hockey. We joined forces and made it happen, but it's been a long road and a lot more together time than I prefer with my domineering, CEO-type older brother. That aside, the three of us are close. We'd lay down our lives for one another.

"The usual balancing act. Not having enough money to solve all the problems we see, not wanting to suck the benefactor well dry." Amy's smile denies her words of frustration. Running the Tornadoes' non-profit arm is where she belongs. Setting up a community to help the chronically unhoused and provide a supportive community with health care and dignified work opportunities of their choosing is all she's ever talked about.

Greg claps his hands at the front of the room. "Does everyone have food? I'd like to run through a few things with you before we take a quick tour of the facility."

His fanatical focus has kept the organization and construction from any major delays, but it's exhausting sometimes. At thirty-five, he has the maturity of more than a decade running the family's conglomerate and the enthusiasm and energy of youth. He'll make a great leader for a bunch of alpha male hockey players. I was like that about dancing and hope to be again about my nonprofit. Amy is equally passionate about her work, so I guess it's a family trait.

"We have one final walk-through by the city to sign off for full occupancy, at which point we'll open it fully to staff and to players as they arrive." He looks at our Operations Manager. "I think a few are already here?"

Kayla nods.

Greg continues, "We have the grand opening on Labor Day weekend, then the training camp with some quick decisions needed to get us to preseason play. Let's go around the room and report where everyone's at and if they need anything from the team."

I zone out, enjoying my tacos.

Before Saylet begins her report, Greg interrupts to say, "By the way, I've said it before, but I'm saying it again now. I expect everyone in this room to attend the ball. Yes, it's a holiday weekend, but please plan to be there this Saturday. Hopefully we'll avoid that timing in future years."

I give a tiny negative shake of my head when he

catches my gaze. Way too much peopling. I prefer a Merlin role to Greg's King Arthur.

He returns the gesture with a firm nod, insisting. "Owner," he mouths silently.

"Ugh," I mutter.

When Saylet wraps up, he claps his hands and rises to his feet. "Alright, let's check this place out!" We all follow him for the inaugural tour.

I had seen the plans. Heck, I had estimated the cost of the plans. But seeing the state-of-the-art facility is a whole different ballgame. Or hockey game, as the case may be. He'd wanted to include everything possible to lure the best players and staff here. So, as he points out in each room we tour, everything has the best equipment—the gym, the PT rooms, the portable X-ray machine, even the locker room is fancy. My guess is it'll still stink by the fifth game, if not before, but whatever. Onsite daycare is offered for employees with children.

After seeing the back areas on the rink level, we step into the arena. I stare at the ice from behind the goal, as well as the handful of players running drills. Greg explains that three layers of ice had been laid, with white paint going between the second and third application of purified water. At that point, it was a blank oval as though for figure skating, although it's colder—he calls it "fast ice"—which figure skaters would hate. In the fourth layer, the blue and red markings that make it a hockey rink were painted, then ten more layers of ice had been laid, and it was finally ready for the few early arrivals to test out. Standing against the boards, smelling that faint ice odor that is as much cold as it is smell, I begin to feel Greg's excitement. Our team logo, a bold purple circle containing "TX" with a stylized tornado between the letters, at center ice proclaims our readiness to take the NHL by storm. I can almost hear the drum thumps as the team is announced.

We circle up through the food court with vendor signs already up—all spots were filled months ago by eager restaurants. Greg is only allowing locally owned companies to sell here.

By each outside entrance to the arena, team store skeletons sit waiting for merch to be stocked. As starters are identified, named apparel and stuffed…what? tornadoes? I don't know and don't ask…will be ordered. As various players gain popularity, the rest will be filled in.

The last stop before returning to the executive suite is the box level, via keyed elevator. The owner's suite is over center ice, of course, with a standing bar and buffet area in the back half, and stadium-style tiered seats in the front. There are four TVs, just in case visitors are too busy wining and dining and forging business deals to watch the live action. I shake my head, memories of my short dating history with Greg's friend, Travis, intruding. He was all about wheeling and dealing. Still is.

Amy catches my head shake and leans in, tilting her head toward a door in the side wall. "The private restroom might be worth it, though."

I snort.

Greg and Saylet are standing in the front row of the stadium seating watching a few players practice. With no jumbotron and DJ, we catch wordless sounds of their muted chirping and the incredibly fast scrapes of their skate blades on the new ice.

I blink. I've only seen a handful of games in person since Greg played in college, and they were nothing like this. Even in a few man practice, these guys are *fast*, seeming faster than on TV. And the puck is even faster, flying at the goalie after the loud thwack of a stick against it. I lose track of it for a microsecond, but despite all odds the goalie blocks it and laughs at his teammate.

His laugh sounds familiar. I frown. I can't place it. But all these guys have just arrived. I consider asking Greg if he played with any of them in college, but given his age, I'm pretty sure that's not the case. I drop it, as I'll meet all the players within a few weeks anyway.

* * * *

After the tour, I swing into the executive kitchen to grab a fancy coffee from the machine that has more buttons than my entire kitchen before heading to my office.

Now that I've seen the whole place, my plan is to go through my client list and figure out where to meet them. This floor screams management. The cubicles, offices, and conference rooms behind a fancy entry area with a reception desk with expensive flowers don't even make me comfortable. I want to partner with the players, offering advice rather than mandates. So that means meeting them on a more even playing field—or rink, I suppose. My hope is to take my laptop down to an empty room on the players' floor that has a table and chairs. There are a few such rooms for agent meetings and phone calls along the hall where the PT rooms and coaches' offices sit.

But for now, I enter my office and pull my laptop out of the bag I dropped here before the walkthrough. My office is small by request—I hope my visits will be infrequent. In fact, I attempted to decline having a dedicated office, but Greg was having none of it. But it does have a beautiful view of the green area and fieldhouse behind it. I made sure my desk was positioned so I get to enjoy that view, not just have it as a backdrop to impress or intimidate visitors. Thus, I sit perpendicular to the door and the window, able to keep my eye on comings and goings on both sides. My sister's office is right next door. As we're less involved in the daily operations of the team, there are several other members of management between us and Greg, which works fine for me.

As we're closer to the elevators than his corner office, I'll get to see who gets called up here. Just because I don't want to date them doesn't mean I don't recognize that hockey player physique is amazing, and I haven't yet seen one at the NHL level.

My thoughts drift to another amazing body—Cam's. With his high, round butt and thick thighs, he could give a hockey player a run for his money.

Focus. I'm here to focus. I need to start putting names with faces, as I hadn't paid attention to who Greg selected from the expansion draft beyond the guys already playing at a level to make sports news highlights.

In addition to starting with the married players, I'd like to identify who's emerging as a team leader so I can schedule them early as well. I make a note to ask the GM and head coach who they're considering for the Captaincy. No, first I should ask Greg who owns that decision so I don't step on any toes before the season even starts.

I open up Excel and start my spreadsheet. Name, age, marital status, and salary. Halfway through the HR files, I move the mouse over the next name, preparing to click.

Cameron Hill. The unique name leaps out at me. To have my dance student and a player, both new in town, share it seems more than coincidental. *Please no*. My friends have all but convinced me to have a brief affair with my sexy student, and this could ruin it.

I don't remember my dance student's last name. Maria handles the scheduling and billings. Swallowing hard, I click. There he is, as sexy and delicious as ever, that one dark blonde wave hanging over his forehead, the dimple in one cheek where his mouth curls a bit higher. The warm brown eyes smile as much as his mouth does.

Holy smoke. That's why the goaltender's laugh sounded familiar. It was—*is*—my Cam.

Unable to look away, I scrabble blindly for my phone and dial Maria.

"Hey, what's up?" she says. The background noise is one of her preferred dance pieces so she's not at the café and is practicing solo, or she wouldn't have answered.

"He's-he's—" I can't say the words out loud. If I do, it'll be real. My most fun dance partner ever would be an employee, which means a double no fraternization rule. Greg had the standard corporate no frat rule instituted for the Tornadoes org. Even without it, an owner dating a player would be incredibly awkward. And Greg would be worried and annoyed especially after my breakup with Travis. As Greg's best friend and five years older than me, he'd seemed glamorous when I first graduated a few years ago. At that time my entire focus was on learning the management of our family's finances. He helped me make connections and find new investment opportunities. But as I learned the responsibilities that came with our family's wealth, and began to focus on how to put that to good use, his attitude of "you can never have enough money" became tiresome. He hadn't understood, and even went so far as to complain about how intense Amy was about helping the homeless. As soon as he criticized my sister's philanthropic efforts, I was done. Now, things are awkward when we're in the same room together.

"Um, Chris? Who and what is he? Can you give me a hint at least? Sounds like…?" she jokes, referencing Charades.

I take a huge breath and whoosh it out. "A hockey player."

"Oh yeah? You met one? How was his ass?" I can hear the smile in her voice.

"Cam. Cameron."

"Your student? Is a player for the Tornadoes?"

"A goalie. Yes."

"Dayum. I bet Lauren's not even going to be pissed he doesn't have a toolbelt." Then she asks, "You were considering hitting that, huh? And now you can't because he works for you."

"Not really. And especially not given his age. He's twenty-four. I guess it was all a pipe dream. He's such a great dancer, it makes it harder."

She snorts.

"Girl, stop being dirty." I roll my eyes. "Anyway, it would have only been a short-term thing. Now it's a non-existent fling. It's just a shock."

"And disappointing. I get it. I'm sorry. It did sound like an excellent end to your dry spell." She snorts again.

I groan.

"Can you get the PR Director to do a calendar of the team shirtless, and at least use it for your spank bank?"

"You're not helping. I'm sorry I called you."

"You love me."

"I do. Ah well, I'll get over it. Thanks for listening."

Until I saw that photo, I hadn't admitted to myself how much thought I was giving to the idea of taking him for a test drive to see how sex felt with a dance god. I guess it's back to the drawing board. I'd worry about the next dance lesson and whether to tell him or not, but the secret will be out in a few nights anyway, when he sees me at our charity ball. It's not even worth skipping it, since I'll be offering him financial advice within the next few weeks anyway. And for the sake of the team, we'll hopefully have a long and profitable business relationship.

Damn shame I didn't take him up on the meal invitation, though. I might have if I'd known that was my last shot at socializing with him.

Chapter Seven

Cam

Generally, the first time players are required to show for a team event is training camp. However, given that we're an expansion team, the Donovans scheduled a Fan Day with a few of the better-known players and a charity ball to introduce the whole team to Austin (or at least those who could afford the tickets) and kick off the Tornadoes Foundation.

I ramp up personal ice time to hone my skills for training camp and to meet the rest of my team before the formal setting. That meant I needed to skip a couple of days dance practice. I hate not seeing her, and worse, I'll need a week for training camp soon enough. On the other hand, I thought I caught a glimpse of disappointment in her face when I told her, which means I might have a chance at dinner—or more—one of these days. Feelings aside, hockey comes first. It's my golden ticket to financial freedom.

The guys and I play a friendly scrimmage the morning of the dinner. Some of us head to the gym afterward while others leave to continue unpacking their new homes. Jack and I hit the gym after lunch. Afterwards I introduce him to a local juice and smoothie chain that makes delicious snack drinks with all sorts of protein-centric add-ins. At home, we lounge by the pool and throw the ball for his dog, King, until it's time to go to the event.

"Tux?" he asks.

"Nah. Dark suit. Unless it's required?"

"The invitation didn't say black tie, and Austin is pretty casual by all accounts."

"Cool. My suits are cut looser and have some give. You never know when there might be an opportunity to show off my dancing skills." I figure I might as well lean into my ridiculous reindeer nickname.

"Man, I'd pay to see that," he says with a grin.

We ride together, as he still hasn't bought a car. I don't mind playing chauffeur given that Texas is the oil and gas capital of the country, and gas is cheaper here than anywhere I've lived.

As we enter the ballroom, I spy a third of the team already clustered at one end of the bar. The PR Director whose name tag reads "Saylet" intercepts us and calls over her social media analyst. "Walk these two around please, make sure they don't huddle with the other players in a corner?"

I schmooze with local elite, meeting University of Texas administrators, several members of the state congress, and a bunch of doctors, bankers, and lawyers.

I nod and answer the same questions over and over. I grew up in Indiana, I've played in the AHL but am definitely ready for the NHL. My save percentage is 0.920, highest in the AHL both seasons. I'm single.

That last one I try to avoid, and most are polite

enough not to ask outright. They'll resort to scanning my ring finger instead. But one woman, who I swear resembles a shark with silver hair and a pointy nose, kneads my bicep like it's dough then asks the question as she presses her surgically enhanced boob against said bicep.

If my mother were still alive, she'd be within five years of this woman's age, and I'm not sure whether she'd be younger or older. I repress a shudder and look over her shoulder and wave.

"Sorry, ma'am"—I've also noticed Austonians go with ma'am for anyone over thirty so I should be safe using that moniker—"one of my teammates is gesturing me over. If you'll excuse me, it was great to meet you."

Escaping to the bar, I sigh as Buzz and Gabe—unimaginatively dubbed Saint because of his last name—snicker at my expression.

I ask them, "Did you have to run the gauntlet, too?"

"Oh yeah, Saylet is lying in wait for everyone." Saint shrugs. "You get used to it. It's part of the deal."

"I suppose." I lean toward the bartender and ask for a local bourbon I'd found driving around. He doesn't have it but he seems pleased I requested it, pouring me something he said would be similar enough. It'll be my one and only drink for the evening. No way am I getting drunk in front of the owners and management, especially until they pick the first line and starting goalie.

Kyle Scott, a defenseman acquired from the Anaheim Admirals, nudges Buzz and jerks his chin toward a woman across the room. "Do you know who that is? She's hot AF."

Buzz glances over. "Yeah. Her name is *Off Limits*. She's a Donovan, dumbass. Didn't you even Google the owners so you'd recognize them?"

"I was more focused on the coaches. And I met Greg Donovan via Zoom. He was involved in the interviews, although I'm not sure why," Kyle admits.

I stay quiet, unwilling to admit that I had only Googled Greg Donovan as well. I figured the sisters were silent investors. But I guess if they live here, they might attend functions. Especially as the three are all under thirty-five and I heard at least one of them works for the organization as well.

"Shit. Can't she be ugly or something then. I already hate this no fraternization rule and I haven't even glimpsed the rest of the back office ladies," Kyle jokes.

Jack replies, "Never fear. Austin is full of hot chicks waiting to become puck bunnies. You'll be rolling in pussy in no time."

Kyle rubs his hands together. "That's what I like to hear."

Greg Donovan ascends to the raised dais. He uses the microphone and podium to ask everyone to take their places at the tables.

Praying I don't end up with Ms. Shark, I head toward my assigned table. My name card is at an eight-top with a French-Canadian left winger, Mathieu du Près, along with an assistant coach, our physical therapist, and six bigwigs. *Thank fuck.* The table is full.

Buzz and the other goalie, Dan somebody-or-other, who I've been avoiding, sit at the table behind us, choosing the seats closest to us.

Thankfully, Ms. Shark is at neither of our tables and instead sitting at Saint's table. He's married so he won't have any trouble fending her off. Or not. Come to think of it, his wife isn't here tonight. Although I'd never cheat, I try not to judge, and I'm still learning my teammates so I'm unable to guess what they'll do.

We make it through Greg's speech welcoming us and the three course meal with the required small talk. Then Saylet introduces our head coach, Michael Steele. He played before my time then coached college when the Tornadoes tagged him for this role.

"I hope everyone has had a chance to meet our players." He pauses as everyone applauds. I calculate quickly: even if tickets were a hundred and fifty bucks a seat, and most season ticket holders would go for higher priced spots, then these folks are spending over six thousand dollars to attend our inaugural season. *Sheesh.*

Coach continues. "They're young—two years younger than the NHL average. And they're hungry." Ever the goof, Jack holds his empty plate up. Ignoring him, Coach Steele continues, "We have guys on the team who've had a taste of the playoffs and want that Cup, and other guys who are eager to prove themselves coming up from the minors. In management's view, this is the perfect combination to get a cohesive team in short order, and make a run for the Stanley Cup right from the start."

The crowd stomps and roars, louder than I'd have expected from a bunch of big wigs. That's promising.

As far as I'm concerned, my team is a contender for the Cup every damn game we're out there, so I don't need the pep talk. When my agent called me with the offer and told me their plan, I leaped at the chance to come here. Sure, getting to the NHL means better endorsements and more income sources, but every hockey player's holy grail is the Stanley Cup. The trick will be getting the lines set and ensuring they gel as quickly as possible, like Coach said. As a goalie, I'll offer pointers where I see gaps from my position.

A DJ starts playing music, starting with older stuff for the whales. He then shifts to country music and a number of couples take the floor to two-step. The four of us lounge in our seats, turned toward one another.

A woman with her back to me standing in a small cluster with Greg catches my eye. She looks familiar, but I can't place the long medium-dark hair or what I can see of her figure in a dress with a flared skirt. Her legs are fantastic, though, long and toned.

She turns to smile at Greg when he says something and I almost fall off my chair.

Christina.

"Holy crap." The other three guys turn around at my shocked tone. "My dance instructor is here."

"Really? At a hockey-sponsored event?" Mathieu's accent makes it "reeelly."

"Where?" Buzz leans forward.

"Over there," I say, gesturing with a tilt of my head. "In the gold dress in Greg's group."

He looks and his eyes go wide. "Dude. Are you serious? Am I the only one who knows who anyone is?"

"Who is she? A skater? A local celebrity or something?"

"Wait, your dance instructor?" Kyle interjects.

"Yeah, Prancer here ballroom dances in his spare time." Buzz is snickering so hard he can barely speak. "Hey, Prancer. Go ask her to dance."

"Who is she?"

"Apparently, your dance teacher. Come on. We want to see you strut your stuff. Hey guys," he calls to a few more players lingering at the bar and gestures them over. "Prancer's instructor is over there. Shouldn't they dance for us?"

"Hell, yeah."

"No question."

"Abso-fucking-lutely."

I roll my eyes. This is not going to go away. I have no idea what I was thinking saying that out loud. But dancing could be an effective way to distinguish myself, maybe show Mr. Donovan I'm more than just a pretty face and good goalie statistics. Not that he necessarily cares about anything beyond my performance on the ice.

I stand.

The guys cheer, and Christina turns to face us.

I stride toward her.

Chapter Eight

Christina

I've been avoiding Cam all night, but it seems like that's about to end. A burst of laughter comes from the cluster of guys at the two tables closest to the bar and I look over without thinking.

He's standing and starts toward me as soon as we lock eyes, eating up the dance floor with his long-legged gait.

Does he know who I am now? Does it matter?

Greg is chatting to someone beside me but I can't focus on anything but Cam. His intense gaze, the dimple brought out with his grin, those broad shoulders.

He stops in front of me and nods. "Christina. Fancy meeting you here."

Greg looks over, surprised. "Oh, you two know each other?"

I'm stumped as to how to answer that.

Cam turns so half his face is hidden from Greg's view and winks at me then says easily, "Yes. In fact, I was coming over to ask her to dance."

I start to shake my head but Greg answers, making

me grit my teeth and fist my hands to avoid thumping him. "Oh, Christina was a dancer on the competitive circuit. She loves to dance, but you'd better be sure you can lead."

Cam holds out a hand. "I'm ready to try. How about it, Christina?"

My brother is chuckling, and I swear I'm going to pummel him later in private.

Knowing appearances are key for this inaugural event, I acquiesce. He leads me to the edge of the dance floor and asks me to wait while he confers with the DJ.

He arrives back as the first notes of *There's Nothing Holdin' Me Back* by Shawn Mendes begin, with a smirk at his teammates. Apparently, he's taking the lyrics to heart.

"You ready? We don't have to do the lift," he asks.

"We absolutely should not do a lift when we haven't even warmed up. But yes, let's dance, then."

And he swings me out onto the floor.

Greg hoots and comes to stand at the edge, as do Cam's teammates. Although he's a conscientious dancer and keeps us in an open area, other dancers soon step back or stop to watch. We've suddenly become the evening's entertainment. Fortunately, the press was limited to the red carpet with only a hired photographer in the event, and Saylet's approval on all released images. The Donovans have been in the public eye enough that I'm immune to publicity in the instances I can't avoid it, but it's a relief to not have to worry about any extra gossip about my connection to one of our players. Saylet will be able to control the narrative should anyone raise a question.

I dip, twirl out from Cam's extended arms, pirouette

under his hand, and everything else he leads me through for just over three minutes. We end with our arms extended, side by side, to applause. He sweeps a hand to me. After I curtsy, he bows then sweeps his arm back toward me.

This has apparently been a team bonding opportunity as the guys are stamping their feet, clapping and calling for another.

Saylet hurries up to the microphone and thanks us, introducing us to the crowd in case people didn't know our names.

As she says my last name, Cam's jaw goes slack and he whips his head around to stare.

Apparently no one told him I was one of the team owners. I sigh.

A few of the players start howling with laughter, bending over. He shoots them an angry look, then blinks twice and sends a furtive glance to where Greg stands on the other side of the floor. His shoulders drop a smidge when he sees my brother clapping.

Saylet is still at the mike, talking over the hooting and hollering players. "No way, folks. If you want another performance by Christina and Cam, you'll have to ante up. We're here to raise money for the Tornadoes Foundation, and you only get one free show tonight. So what'll it be?"

I frown. She hasn't even asked us, and she's auctioning us off to the highest bidder.

Cam tugs me in. "Are you okay with another dance?"

Well, at least someone cares if I am. He skipped over his own reaction to me being a Donovan to check if I'm all right. I try to ignore the little twist my heart gives at his thoughtfulness, which is another reason I shouldn't try for anything casual with him. As if the rules of the org weren't enough, it would be too easy to fall for this kind man who probably wants children, when those aren't in my future. I nod.

"Phew," he says, nodding over to his team.

They're waving dollar bills. Hundreds if I'm not mistaken.

He calls, "Yo, Jack, didn't you say this afternoon you'd pay to see me dance? Ante up, roomie!"

I roll my eyes at him. "Hockey players."

He shrugs with that oh-shucks grin that might kill me one day. That dimple is a weapon if ever I saw one.

"Guilty," he replies.

The guys are talking among themselves. Buzz has a hand up in the air with his first finger raised as to ask Saylet to wait. They break and he calls out, "$5,000 from this group. Who else is in?"

He looks over directly at Greg. *Ballsy.*

My brother probably has no idea what he's gotten himself into. He laughs. "Matched!"

And it's on. The testosterone in here might yet poison me.

Cam tugs me toward a door. "Come on, let's plan it a bit if we're going to have to put on a show."

As we leave, Greg is at the mike saying, "No one else has to shout out their bid, but if you come sign up with Saylet—or heck, bring a check—I will personally match every one of these particular donations."

Cam snickers. "Ah, brothers. He's egging them on."

"Do you have brothers?"

He raises a shoulder. "Not really."

I frown. One either has brothers or they don't. But now is not the time to talk about it, and Cam's response makes it clear it isn't a favorite subject anyway. I shift into choreography mode, still unsure how the night unraveled so quickly.

He's already on it, scanning his phone. "How about the rumba? To this?"

"That's fast for a rumba."

"The DJ could step it down a hair. But we can handle it. I was thinking…" He plays the first few seconds of Rihanna's *Don't Stop the Music*. A hard drumbeat comes in halfway through the first line. "We walk out to this, getting people clapping to the beat. It drops off after a few dance steps, which will work for the crowd."

When he glances up at me from the phone, I nod.

"I'd like to incorporate our lift." When I open my mouth to respond, he adds, "Please?"

I balk. We have only practiced it for a week. Wanting to fairly evaluate his request, I ask, "Why?"

"Look, the guys put me up to asking you to dance, obviously without telling me who you were."

Growing up, Greg's friends would make him do all sorts of stupid stuff, but Greg would shrug and say that's what guys do. I'll never understand it. "I should probably explain—"

Cam interrupts me. "You can tell me how the owner of a team ends up teaching in a dance studio another time, but I took their challenge to make sure the owners and coaches know who I am. Anything I can do to stand out and get the nod as starting goalie is worth an effort. This isn't only a great way to stay flexible but can also show my new team both my suppleness and my team spirit by raising money."

I can understand his logic. Heck, I might have done the same thing. Warmed from the dance and his proximity, my body is primed for closer touches and ready to ignore the fact that this is a work event. But I still have one worry. "Are you sure? I've fallen in competitions. But"—I tilt my head back toward the ballroom—"you'll never hear the end of it if that happens tonight."

He jerks straighter. "I meant what I told you. I'll never drop you. Fumble, maybe, and I'll deal with the fallout if that happens. But hockey players have fast reflexes, goalies especially. I promise you're safe with me."

Ha! If only he knew how much I wanted him to be dangerous rather than safe. But not on a dance floor. Refocusing, I listen to the song, talking us through the steps, and point. "After she references your hands around my waist and chest to chest, you swing me out, then I step back in and on that third round of not stopping the music, I'm up. Let's not try the second part of what you saw. Instead, you're taking me high with the elbow grip. When you bring me back down, loosen your elbow a little as you straighten, allowing my leg to straighten. Then do your plié, aka side lunge Mr. Hockey Player, and I'll go into the slanted split."

He's squinting as if trying to picture it, so I bring my phone out and show him the last part of the move again from the video.

He nods.

"Let's do the whole routine a couple of times. I'll find an empty room for us to warm up and practice. You go in and make sure the DJ has the music, can adjust the pace down a notch, and tell them we'll be in in…fifteen minutes?" I ask.

He nods again and we turn in different directions.

After we run through it a couple times and he's nailed the second part of the fish combination, Cam pauses it when the singer starts referencing Michael Jackson. "We should get the crowd involved again at this point. And then do a last twirl or something and end it on her next refrain, as it's a quieter point and the DJ can fade it down."

"Yeah. That sounds good," I reply. "It's almost a five-minute song otherwise. I'm not sure they've earned that long a show."

"Oh, I don't know. They were at $30,000 when I was in there."

My eyes go wide. "Before my brother's matching donation?"

"I don't know. Does it matter?" he asks with a little laugh.

I wave a hand, my mind elsewhere. "I still don't want to go too long after the lift, as that should be the high point of the dance. But I do have one idea. How stretchy are those pants?"

His brows shoot up. "I have them tailored to dance in, so they're fine for most things. What do you have in mind? Because I really will never hear the end of it if I split my pants."

I giggle at that image. "If we warm up a bit more, could you do a split in them? Forward split, not side."

"I think so, but I confess I haven't tried. Let's do the warmups anyway. If I injure myself tonight, it's all for nothing—aside from the good cause, of course," he adds quickly, glancing at me with a hint of fear in his eyes.

And that's a perfect example of why I can no longer pursue the idea of even a casual fling with him, delicious though he may be. While I have little to no input into the

Tornadoes organization, it remains an unbalanced power dynamic.

In short order, we're on the edge of the dance floor again, and the pop song's first line and beats boom out. The players have assorted reactions, from raised brows of appreciation, to elbows in each others' ribs.

With our encouragement, they clap along, and we rumba. My skirt swishes with the hip movements as Cam's hand directs me. We do a couple tight turns and I want to moan at his leg between mine, his hips and cock brushing me. It's maddening. But I won't embarrass him in front of his teammates, so I refocus. He tugs me out then in, his hand hot against my belly and on my thigh as he lifts me. Thankfully, my skirt is not only flared but knee length and allows for all these movements without showing anything untoward.

The guys are hooting and hollering again when I'm airborne, but their shouts sound like praise and perhaps surprise at their teammate, rather than jeers. Saylet looks on with an open mouth.

Cam takes his three-step turn with my lower leg bent, toe touching the shin in his grip. He lowers me and takes me into the tilted split.

Applause breaks out as he takes me down to standing and out. I'd forgotten how fun it can be to dance in front of an audience. The crowd changes to rhythmic clapping the repeated mantra at the song's end comes on, and a rush goes through me.

He grabs me and twirls me then supports my waist as I drop into a split on the second-to-last line. He is lined up behind my forward thigh when he does one last spin and drops into his own split behind me. The music fades to silence.

For a beat, there is only quiet, then a whispered, "That was fucking hot as hell," from the back of the group of players. Rowdy applause and cheers break out.

Saylet hurries to the podium. "Give it up for Cam and Christina! Thank you both, you helped us raise over $50,000 more for the Foundation." My mouth goes dry at that figure. Greg really didn't know what he was getting himself into.

Saylet gives the clapping a minute to die down again and then says into the mike, "The bar is open for another hour, but that concludes our entertainment for the evening. Frankly, I don't think anything could top that. Thank you to everyone who attended tonight. Go Tornadoes!"

Cam has risen and tugged me up with what seems like zero effort on his part.

He's placed his foot in front of mine to provide a stop so I don't slide when he tugs me up, and I come up flush against him.

In the instant before I step back, my eyes flutter shut and I catalog every inch of where we touch for later. His arms encircle me ensuring I don't fall back, and my hands rest on his mouth-watering biceps under his shirt, his jacket long ago discarded. My breasts brush his shirt on either side of his tie, providing the most delicious friction, and his impressive bulge is nestled between my hips on my lower stomach. This might be the first time in my life that I've wished I was taller, because even in heels our groins don't quite align.

He steps back and sketches a shallow bow to me, saying, "Thank you, ma'am."

I narrow my eyes at him. "No ma'ams, please."

"You're like my boss's boss's boss's boss or

something."

"So, no more lessons?"

"Oh no, definitely more lessons."

"Not if you call me ma'am again."

"Sheesh. Okay, I'll do my best. Christina. Thank you and good night." With a grin, he saunters back toward the bar.

I collect my purse and head toward the exit with a very specific plan for what I'll be doing within the hour. My body is so primed I'll never sleep without some release.

* * * *

The next morning I'm in my home office enjoying my herbal tea and a good day on the stock market when my phone buzzes with an incoming text from my sister.

Amy

Are you coming into the
Tornadoes offices today?

Wasn't planning on it. Why,
what's up?

Saylet is looking for you.

??

I dunno, but I figured I'd give you a heads up

You gonna be there long enough to grab lunch with me?

Yeah, I'll be here for a bit. The community site walkthrough has been delayed again.

You should get Greg on that. I have no idea how he kept the facility construction on time.

No thanks. I prefer to do this on my own.

I get it. <heart emoji> cya in a couple hrs.

I wrap up a few trades I've been mulling over, look over the quarterly reports from two REITs, then talk myself out of going to the office in yoga pants and force myself to change.

I text Amy when I'm downstairs for lunch and we head to Torchy's Tacos to feed my ongoing addiction.

She waits until we've ordered before bringing me up to date on the gossip. "Everyone in the office is talking about your performance last night."

I groan around a mouthful of taco al pastor.

"How did that all happen, anyway? You disappeared right after that second dance. But even you can't dance like that with a partner you don't know."

I explain how I know Cam, trying to keep it innocuous, but something in my voice or words must give me away.

She arches a brow. "You do recall how awkward things are with Travis, right? And the company policy regarding relationships?"

"I do." I'm not going to tell her we broke up in part because of him sneering at my "flower child" sister.

"But…a quiet fling never hurt anyone, if you wanted to ride that cowboy."

I snort. "Like a bull. But I'm not going to. Until I have a clearer picture of what my future involvement in the team looks like, I need to steer clear."

Back at the new building, I pull up my notes and the roster again to continue my evaluation of who might be most open to accepting financial advice.

Saylet pops her head in my door. "There you are!"

Her energy is always so much bigger than her five-foot-three frame. And too much for my introverted self to be comfortable in one-on-one interactions. I brace myself and give a half-hearted wave. "Here I am. In my office."

She makes herself comfortable in one of my visitor chairs.

I don't ask why she's here. I'm too busy wishing she'd forget why she wanted to meet me and go away.

Or maybe she just wants to chat. I can do that. But I'm not going to start it off.

"So, that dance." She fans herself.

Oh no.

"Yeah, um. You knew I danced competitively, right? And Cam—" I clear my throat. "Mr. Hill has apparently been dancing since college."

"Y'all earned us over a hundred-k last night. The fifty I announced was before the match, as I wanted to give Greg an out given how quickly it had escalated. He didn't take it." She looks smug.

"You're welcome?" I say as a half-question.

"No, no." She waves off my thanks. It's a bad sign. "You don't get off that easy. If we could raise that much in twenty minutes last night, imagine what we could raise with some promotion around it? One of our players and an owner doing a spotlight dance at the Holiday Ball? I was going to wait to create posters for a few key on-ice plays along with the team photos, but I asked the photographer to send me a couple shots of your dances, and they're brilliant."

I sigh. She wouldn't be good at her job if she didn't think like this, but as soon as Amy told me she was looking for me, I feared she'd push for more dancing. I hadn't wanted to breech Cam's privacy by confessing the dance lessons, but now she believes we put that together in a quick huddle last night.

"This is not to be shared as I don't know what he is comfortable with—" I give her a stern look. "But Cam took some private lessons from me at Maria's studio." She knows Maria from social gatherings we had as we built our staff.

"Even better. So with time, you could do something

even more showy." Saylet somehow makes every statement sound like it ends in an exclamation point.

I'm already tired and looking for a reason to excuse myself from my own office. "No. I have my financial meetings with the team, and Cam obviously won't have free time once the season starts. To say nothing of Greg's and Coach's comfort with him throwing me around and risking injury."

"You do have enough time. You already told us you'll continue to help Maria at the studio until she gets it on its feet."

She's grabbing her phone and scrolling. Her pointer finger stabs the screen triumphantly before I can tell her she hasn't addressed my other statements.

An indistinct male voice answers the phone as she brings it to her ear.

Saylet holds my gaze and grins as she says, "Hey Cam, how are you?"

I set my jaw. Dammit. Before last night, he'd mentioned continuing lessons as his schedule allowed, stating only that he'd be traveling a lot for his new job. It all makes sense to me now. The NHL travel schedule can be brutal. His statements last night about ensuring management saw him as a team player mean he'll likely agree to Saylet's publicity scheme.

"Oh, sorry. You have to get back to training. I'm lucky I caught you in a break. My question is quick—would you be willing to perform another fancy dance with Christina to raise more charity funds at the Holiday Ball mid-season?…Yes?…I know it's in the contracts, but to confirm, it's ok to use a photo of your dance last night to promote the event?…Great! Thank you so much."

She hangs up and drops her phone in her lap, looking at me expectantly.

"Alright. I get approval over any shots used for promo." As an owner of the team, I won't have one with me in a split, my skirt half up my legs. Nor do I want one where my desire to suck him like a Slurpee is apparent. It's bad enough I'm going to be in close contact with our goalie with the godlike body and the flexibility of Gumby for the next four months.

I have no idea how I'll keep my hands and lips off him now. A fling is starting to look inevitable, even though it's still a terrible idea. Heat zings through me at the thought.

Chapter Nine

Cam

Sweet. I have team-sanctioned time with Christina which will give me time to get to know her better and maybe get her to go out with me.

I lay awake for hours after the ball trying to talk myself out of pursuing her. Lusting after a team owner is the epitome of a career-limiting move for sure. But she's so much fun to dance with, and she's smoking hot besides. I haven't been interested in dating in ages, and after those sleepless hours of reflection, I know my interest isn't just physical. We'll just have to be careful. Even though it can't go anywhere, I'm determined to get more time with her.

Coach Steele claps several times walking through the locker room indicating our break is over so I shut all thoughts of her down. My head has to be one hundred and ten percent on training right now to win that starter position.

This first morning of training camp we have full-team drills to shake the summer off. After lunch, the teams will work with their skill coaches. That means endless T-pushes, shuffles, and butterflies. I have no idea how older goalies deal with the impact of the ice on their knees, even with all our pads, but hopefully I'll have the opportunity to find out in a decade or so. Meanwhile, the intensity of training camp is always a reality check. Fortunately, pro teams employ the best sports physical therapists, and the Tornadoes are no exception.

Later today, they'll give the rest of the team an opportunity to take shots on goal with each of us in the net. I'll be able to assess my teammates and figure out who I'd want on my first line if it was up to me.

Chirping is low-key as the friendships aren't cemented yet. Buzz and Jack are tight, and welcome everyone. The rest of us are keeping a close eye on our teammates. Until the roster is finalized, we're all competitors. My perspective in the net lets me assess everyone, but I'm especially interested in my rivals for the starting position.

After a long day and hot showers, management has catered dinner so we can continue to get to learn more about each other off the ice. Jack is still getting food when I sit down.

"What's your story, Prancer?" a French-Canadian wingman asks. I think his name is Boulanger.

"No story. Just hockey. Indiana U then Peoria Wild."

"That's your resume, not your story. Why goalie?"

"So I can see the whole board. I like knowing where everyone is on the ice, their strengths and weaknesses."

"You let fewer in than Murphy or Wayman. Keep going like that and you'll be starting goalie, eh?"

"That's the plan."

Talk moves around the table and I relax back against my chair. I have no desire to spill my childhood woes to these guys, especially on night one. Let them see my past as my draft placement and my AHL stats. That's all they need to respect me. No one needs to know about my dickhead father or the fact that I have a half-brother I've never met.

"Yo, Petrovksy," Jack calls as he joins the table. "Prancer here shut you out. You're gonna have to do better than that if you want to play with the big boys."

"Et voilà, the trash talk begins," mutters might-be-Boulanger.

The Czech player narrows his eyes. "I'll do better tomorrow. I'm not worried."

I murmur, "If you keep hunching your right shoulder just before you shoot, you should stay worried."

Jack hears me and whistles. "Ooohhhh, burn. Milo, you have a tell."

"No way."

I shrug. "I guess we'll find out tomorrow, won't we?"

Boulanger catches my eye and gives me a small nod. He's seen it too, apparently. Still, Milo Petrovsky is fast, and can manage the puck on a breakaway like no one else except Buzz or Saint. Boulanger is slow, or at least slower. It'll be interesting to see who'll make first and second offensive line.

Petrovsky is pouting, so I keep my head down and eat.

* * * *

The next day, we're doing drills in the morning and scrimmaging in the afternoon.

Us goalies go to a separate rink and do some extra stretching on-ice before refreshing our muscles with a shorter version of the T-push and shuffles.

Coach has us line up and do five back-to-back reverse vertical horizontals. I excel at RVH's with my flexibility so hopefully this will win me points toward that starting spot. A goalie has to drop one knee to the ice, while keeping the other vertical. Usually the leg closest to the post goes flat to the ice. After the first five, the coach and trainers see that I'm the fastest in and out. They turn the line so that the other two are behind me and tell them to keep pace with me.

My heart pounds with hope from that gesture. Another sign that I'm being seen as a leader and will be a strong consideration for starter. This is why I chose yoga and dance as off-season focuses.

Bonus clauses in my contract aside, I want this. I've worked too damn hard my whole life to let this opportunity pass, or even be delayed. If my closed-minded asshole of a father had even an inkling of the injuries, the swollen knees and quads, the bruises, and the sheer amount of sweat I've poured into this, maybe he'd begin to understand that this is a job. It's work. Work I love. More than just a game. We bring thousands of people together over a shared passion. We give them a break from work they may not enjoy. And we entertain millions around the world, crossing boundaries in a way that only food and art and entertainment can.

Whatever. I don't even know why I still let him in my head. I'm over it. I'll build my own family, and every member, right down to a damned pet, will be loved harder than they could ever dream.

A long whistle blow brings me back to the ice. I was going through the ups and downs alternating legs by rote, lost in my thoughts. The trainers, along with Murphy and

Wayman, are all staring at me.

Murphy says only, "Dude. You're a machine."

The trainer asks, "Didn't you hear the whistle?"

I shrug. "Guess not. I was in the zone."

I look behind me at the ice as we skate off to return to the main rink. I've practically filled a Sno Cone machine with what I've chocked up, whereas the other two sets of marks are significantly neater. Turning back, I shake my head. As far as I'm concerned, that's what it takes to win, and I'll make a mess if I must.

Just before lunch, the coaches call for another round of players shooting on goal with each of us manning it.

When Petrovsky gets the puck, he looks determined. He's my teammate and I try to help him fix it. When his shoulder curls up, I yell, "Hunch!"

He startles and shoots wide so I don't have to worry about blocking the shot. He stomps off the ice as soon as he can.

Over lunch, I find out he's won the nickname "Quasi" for the hunchback of Notre Dame because of my chirping. *Oops*. I duck my head to hide my grin.

We get ready for the afternoon scrimmage. Jack told me in the car this morning that he's going to test some of the European players to ensure they're ready for the physicality of the NHL. I feel a little sorry for the wingmen. Maybe I should warn the trainers more ice baths might be needed tonight. But I don't want to get in trouble for inciting more physical play; the goal of training camp is to evaluate players while avoiding injuries.

Jack heads for any player by the boards, careening into them and grabbing the puck away with his stick that I swear bends at will, he's so good. They all shake it off.

A few take precious extra seconds to get their heads back in the game, whereas others immediately chase after him, and that difference is what he's watching for.

No one says anything in the locker room with the coaches around, but afterward a group of us go to dinner. The complaints start with the first round of drinks.

Jack laughs. Clapping me on the shoulder, he says, "Gotta support my goalie and keep you guys out of our zone."

"That's probably how he lets so few goals in," grumbles one of the players from the other "team."

I've had enough. Us roommates have to stick together. "First, that's the very definition of the defensive line—to help me defend against goals. What hockey have you been playing?" I don't give them time to answer. "Second, I let so few goals in because I'm that good. And you have tells."

Emil Bergstrom, a winger, is barely twenty-two, over from the Swedish Hockey League. He's been super quiet throughout training camp, but now he pipes up. "What is my tell, please? I'd like to fix it."

"You look left and right before you decide to shoot, even if you're by the boards." I smirk, recalling Jack plowing into him at least once. "When you're passing, you only look to the person you want to send the puck to."

He nods, thoughtful. "Thank you."

"Dude, I've been playing in the NHL, not the peewee league. And scoring. There's no way," another guy says while shaking his head.

I lift a shoulder. "Not against me."

Jack flicks a glance at me and shakes his head once.

I twist my lips but subside. It ain't bragging if you

can back it up.

Chapter Ten

Christina

After more than a week of no lessons following the ball, Cam texts on what I now realize is the second-to-last night of training camp.

Cam

> I might need one more day before we get back to lessons. Can we do dinner tomorrow to talk about the holiday gig Saylet asked me about? I assume she's also talked to you.

> Yes.

I'm typing the rest of my response when his next text comes in.

Cool, where to?

Damn. I meant yes to his assumption. Oh well, it's just dinner. I evaluate my favorite restaurants on the east side of the city for some place cool to introduce him to.

Salty Sow.

<laughing face> Seriously?

<link to restaurant> 7:30?

<thumbs up>

Reservation under my name.

Damn. Does this mean you're buying, boss?

...

Too soon? <rolling crying laughing face> Cya tomorrow Christina.

The irritating man is cute even via text, damn him. I squeeze the phone so hard it creaks. I firm my resolve. I need to keep reminding myself of how stilted my interactions with Travis are now. No hanky panky. Aanndd now I sound like a grandmother.

* * * *

The next day I have a scheduled call with my old dance instructor. I contacted her as soon as the ink was dry on the agreement with the NHL, to start designing classes that could be fun and inclusive for my nonprofit.

"Hi Brenda! How have you been?" I ask when she joins the video call.

"Same aches, same pains. You know how dancers age…"

"With arthritis," we say in unison. I don't think it's actually a thing, but she warned every dancer who went on to compete about the increased likelihood of that, so it's our little joke. That aside, she's aged well. Her face may have a few more wrinkles and her hair may be gray, but her skin is youthful and her eyes are bright. Each visit with her brings back the joy of dance. I'm excited to carry that joy on to as many new dancers as possible.

"Did you get the revisions I sent over that you suggested during our last call?" I ask.

"Yes. The cadence of learning looks much better for middle schoolers and up, but I'm still concerned if elementary school age dancers are in the class."

"Me, too. I'm wondering if I only offer it as a junior high and high school program to start with. Otherwise, we'll need to break the class up for attention spans and muscle strength, not just beginners versus more advanced. I don't want to get ahead of myself on engaging instructors until I can gage interest."

"I see. That makes sense. Do you want to have a program ready for younger students in case? It's been decades since I taught anyone that young, though," she says doubtfully.

"My thought was to hire a dance instructor who's taught that age group recently, or get advice closer to when I'm ready for it. Do you know anyone who can help, rather than us trying to figure it out ourselves?"

"Actually, I do, if she's still at the same phone number. She passed promising students on to me back in the day." Brenda taps her chin and scribbles a note.

"Great, thank you. Now tell me how you're doing, and your grandchildren's latest antics."

After sharing stories and catching up, we end the call. I check the financial markets and when they appear quiet, I put CNBC on the living room TV and sit at my kitchen table to make progress on the logistics of setting up the charity.

Amy is the family expert so I'll need her to verify the project plan I'm putting together so she can check the lead times I'll need. Until I know my path to opening classes, I can't announce it to schools and start accepting students. But the non-profit sector is a world apart from corporate pacing and I'm stuck.

I call my sister. "It's me. Do you have a minute please?"

"Of course."

I quickly set up a screenshare and talk her through the various decisions and actions I need to make. "How long does it take you to hire?"

"Our organizations are really different. You should probably ask Maria that."

I nod, leaping to the next thing. "I need to balance instructor resources with student interest. So looking ahead, after all the paperwork is filed, if I leave three months to get a couple instructors to help, it seems like this could be up and running by next summer…?"

"Yep."

"Ok, thank you. I'll assume two instructors plus me, and two locations for the first round of classes. I flip flop between fear we won't have enough interest and worry we'll have to turn kids away."

"You're doing the best you can. The first year will be the hardest, and it won't necessarily all balance out perfectly. But it's still worth doing."

"How did you get to be the wise one, younger sister?"

"I didn't dance my way through my late teens," she responds with a laugh.

"Ah, but that was training for this, my real career." I glance at the time and add, "I have to go, but thank you. I'll work on paperwork for the state and federal filings of organization next, and draft some job postings and letters to schools."

"Oh, and you should think about buying a list of contacts."

"Huh?"

"Like from another nonprofit in a similar space— really any after-school program would be a decent fit.

You buy their mailing list."

"I had no idea that was a thing. Okay, I'll add it. Thank you!"

"Why do you have to go? Don't say my hermit of a sister is actually venturing out into the world? Or is this one of your girls' wine nights?"

"No." I sigh. "I'm meeting with Cam Hill regarding the Holiday Ball dance."

"Dinner with the hot hockey player slash dance partner. I like."

"It's a meeting."

"So are dates."

"It's not a date."

"Okay." Her voice holds laughter.

I'm not going to win this so I say my goodbyes and go get ready for my *dinner meeting*. My insistence that it's not a date and reminder to myself that there can be no dalliance, casual or otherwise, doesn't stop me from picking out one of my favorite dresses. A halter top in a fun pattern of hot pinks against white, it shows off my tan and makes the most of my boobs. Knee length with a flared skirt, as almost every dress and skirt I own is. As the charity ball proved, you never know when an opportunity to dance might present itself, and I can't dance the way I want in a pencil skirt or bodycon dress.

Heeled sandals, dangly earrings, and a brighter lipstick than normal complete the look. I don't even stop to assess my overall image in the mirror after applying the lip color. If I did that, I'd have to acknowledge that I've dressed and primped as though this is a date.

It can't be a date. I repeat the mantra as I slide behind the wheel of my Prius and roll toward the estate's gate. It can't be a date.

Chapter Eleven

Cam

I hear Jack in the kitchen making dinner—for King. For himself, he'll order something and go pick it up while we still can. Both of us can fly under the radar right now, but if our team gets the fans Greg Donovan hopes to, and depending on how well each of us does, our mobility could become more limited. Austin's only other professional sports team is soccer, and I don't know anyone in that club yet, but I suspect it'll be a bit before either they or we have to worry about crowd control.

I duck into the hall bathroom to check my hair again and Jack pokes his head out of the kitchen and catches me.

"Dude, I thought you said this was a meeting with Christina Donovan?"

"Yeah. I want to put my best foot forward with an owner. So sue me."

"Or else you're hoping to bang her. I don't think an owner will care about your hair." He arches a brow.

I don't take the bait, in part because he's right.

He shrugs. "Not that I'd blame you. Go get 'er."

He's such a manwhore. And a bad influence on the other young, single guys. I debate the over/under of when I'll cross paths with some puck bunny of his in the kitchen.

I call a rideshare to take me to dinner. Despite its crazy name, Salty Sow seems like a cool place with a fantastic food and drinks menu. If only I could have gotten her there during the off season so I could enjoy more of the menu. But the last three days of training camp have earned me a cheat meal to some extent. The driver tells me he ate there once and loved it. He drops me at the door and I thank him. He was a cool dude and I tap on my app to give him a generous tip.

Christina comes in a minute after me, in a pretty print dress that shows off her toned shoulders, arms, and those fantastic dancer's legs. She looks as gorgeous in this as she did in her fancy dress for the ball and her dance clothes.

I hope my golf shirt and neatest pair of khakis are dressy enough. Austin may be casual but Christina Donovan appears not to be, and I am here for it. I want to take her dancing in a club, show her off on a red carpet, or spend a night in cuddling on the couch. I stifle an urge to check my hair again. To make any of those wishes come true, I first have to make this date—ok, dinner—a success.

She sees me and hurries over. "Sorry, the parking lot here is tiny. I hope you found a spot."

"I ordered a ride. I might splurge and have a drink, although we're back to practice tomorrow morning."

She replies, "I imagine the extended training camp was rough, and pre-season starts soon. I was just as careful when I danced competitively."

I'd never given much thought to professional dancing, but any competitive sport requires a similar level of discipline. Yet another thing we have in common. "Will you attend the games?"

"Absolutely. I watched my brother play in college and loved it. Then I traveled for dance and didn't have the time, so I'm looking forward to refreshing my knowledge and passion for the game."

My heart thumps. She's gorgeous, a dancer, and loves hockey. Three key things I require in a girlfriend and potential wife. But crap, my goal here is to shine this last year on my entry-level contract and earn a multi-million, multiple year contract with a team. My assumption was always that whoever I met would make less than me and be willing to move. And that is without the whole can't-date-an-owner rule. I need to avoid being sent down this year more than I need to continue dating her, despite how well this first evening is going.

We negotiate our order to share appetizers and a couple entrees she recommends I try. She orders a glass of red wine, but I decide to stick with the bottled Mexican seltzer water available everywhere in Austin.

"Before we talk dance, tell me a bit more about yourself. Didn't your brother say in one of his welcome speeches that the family's been here twenty years?" I genuinely want to get to know this fascinating woman.

"We moved when I was a kid. I went to UT and stayed here because I help with the family businesses." Her posture is dance perfect, shoulders back and spine straight, but when she reaches for her glass of wine, her breasts jiggle under her dress.

Damn. She's not wearing a bra. But my interest in learning more about her is genuine and I refocus on the conversation.

"How did you end up working at the studio?"

She shakes her head. "I'm helping Maria get started for her first six months."

"Ah. So what do you do otherwise? Your sister is heading the Foundation, right?"

"Yes. Do you remember your comp package including financial advice?"

"Yes. That's very cool. I mean, I save pretty well on my own, but I suspect a lot of players need it."

"That's me. I'm a CFA, and I manage the family's investment portfolio."

"Oh." That's impressive and even a little intimidating. It also adds another layer to my attraction. Nothing is sexier than a smart woman.

After the server brings our appetizers and drinks, she asks, "Why do you believe you save better than most players, if you don't mind me asking?"

I laugh, thinking of the Honda Civic I bought used with seventy thousand miles on it. "If you saw my car, you'd understand. You realize I share a rental house with Jack Landry, right?"

"No, I didn't." She purses her lips, a small furrow between her brows, as though she'd like to ask a question but doesn't want to pry.

"I'm not quite ready to count on the NHL salary until I get a multi-year deal." I shrug. "Besides, my mother struggled to find money for me to play hockey. Later, my scholarship at Indiana didn't cover living expenses, so I have loans. I don't want to ever have to worry about money again, and if I play hard these early years, I can avoid that."

"Was she a single parent, then?"

My mouth twists and I nearly deflect like I always do when my old man comes up, but there is something about the way she asks that has me answering. She's leaning toward me and her voice has gone softer. Like she genuinely cares to know. "No. My father didn't see the point of wasting money on a 'game.'" I do air quotes. "He worked long hours just to put a roof over our heads and food on the table. My mom worked too, but she managed to hide the funds for my hockey gear and dues."

"What about when you got the scholarship?"

I shrug. "It wasn't like he had planned to pay for my college anyway. He'd wanted me to go get a job, but bottom line, he didn't care as long as I was out of the house. My mom died the year before and I couch surfed at friends' while the coach helped me find sponsors. My old man wanted a clean slate. He started all over again after I left by marrying someone new within a year."

I'm shocked at myself. I never share this much, even with girls I'm dating. Then again, they don't ask. They're all about hockey and where I want to play and how much I'll make. Christina is different. Older and more mature.

Her mouth drops open at my revelation, then she shakes her head. "That's terrible, Cam."

"Yeah, well, I'm over it." Mostly. Other than a mild obsession about his new family. I'd still prefer a subject change. "So, this dance…?"

She takes the hint. "Saylet will want more than one. We might as well plan for that."

Our entrees arrive. As we eat, we discuss dance styles and possible routines we can prepare.

Damn, she's tempting. She's got her shit together, she's smart and compassionate, and she's downright gorgeous. There's no way I can risk my career by dating management, much less an owner, but if anyone could tempt me, it would be her.

* * * *

Jack swings into the living room where I'm lounging on the couch surfing Instagram, King dozing at my feet. Thankfully, Buzz had only needed to crash for a few days until his furniture arrived so our living room is back to its former dubious rental glory.

"Yo, Prancer. What'rya up to?" He slings himself into a chair. King lifts his head at his father's voice, but doesn't move.

"Just chilling. Why?" I'd been scrolling through my stepmother's feed, although since I've never met her, I'm not sure it makes sense to call her that. She posts tons of pictures of my stepsister and half-brother. I'm kinda surprised she never locked down her profile, but it works for me. My half-brother plays hockey and I was trying to determine if my dickhead dad is there to watch him play, unlike me. He's not in the pictures, but now I can't decide if that's better or worse. I never want a child to be ignored like I was, but my heart twists thinking I was the issue.

"How about we do a spur-of-the-moment backyard barbeque and invite the team?"

"Jack, there are *fifty* people on the team right now, until they announce the roster."

"Yeah, but I bet not all of them can make it on short notice, and we have the backyard and the pool."

I knew this would happen when we found this house. I might as well get used to it now. "Fine, but you're getting the food."

"Cool—you get the beer."

"Hell, no. Have them bring beer. Not all of us are on NHL contract pay yet."

"Oh, yeah. Good point."

He pulls up a local grocery store on his phone. "OK, whadda we need?" I toss my phone on the coffee table and he glances over at it and adds, "Wait, who are they?"

I glance down. I'd left my phone open to Instagram. They're strangers to me, no need to explain. I'd had enough verbal diarrhea last night. "No one. It just came up on my feed."

"Ah. Ok, burgers?"

"Chicken. Some of us are trying to eat healthy."

"Let's do both."

Ah, the joys of making close to a million a year. But even then, I wouldn't spend my hard-earned money on fifty guys, half of whom are headed to the minor league team within a week. I shrug to myself. It's generous of Jack, and it's not my money, so I'll sit back and enjoy it. Or man the grill and enjoy it, whatever.

The guys roll in within two hours, bringing beer as promised. We got iced tea, although not that syrupy sweet tea everyone seems to drink down here. It's almost pre-season, after all.

Coleslaw is as close to salad as we get, but there's a ton of fresh fruit, both whole and cut, and we'd both brought high-end blenders. Someone will likely commandeer one for margaritas, but every athlete has their own smoothie recipe and ours run at least once a day. So that fruit will get used.

I throw chicken and burgers on the grill. At least I managed to talk him out of the processed meat that is hot dogs, as I was not about to deal with those farts in the locker room tomorrow. Jack sets out the various sides and condiments in the kitchen. There's a corn and black bean salad which looks delicious and vaguely healthy, so he did listen to me regarding the food.

After two rounds at the grill, Drew volunteers to take over and I accept gratefully. Grabbing a flavored seltzer water after making sure it isn't one of the hard seltzers that are like an invasive species taking over the beer section in stores, I throw myself down on a lounger in the shade.

"Prancer, come in the pool!" One of the twenty guys in the small blue kidney calls.

"Give me a few." I have no desire to be in that tight a crowd. I'll go take a cold shower to cool down if need be.

Du Près perches sideways on the chaise next to me. "Heard you're expected to whirl and twirl again at the holiday shindig."

It never ceases to amaze me that people see women as gossipers. They have nothing on a hockey team. "What the hell? How'd you hear that?"

"So it's true. I was at the bar getting a drink between your performances and two women were talking behind me. One said she'd never seen Christina dance like that before. When the other asked about competitions, she said those are stilted and formal, and this was free and fun, and Christina had never flowed so smoothly or looked so happy." He watches me closely as he adds, "As I turned to go, I saw the speaker was Amy Donovan."

Christina's younger sister. Who we both knew would have seen plenty of her performances. A thrill shoots through me—she had fun with me. I play it off. "Yeah, social dancing has a lot less restrictions, which is how I talked her into a couple easy lifts."

"Hmm."

I frown. "What?"

"So you aren't thinking of hitting that?"

"Shut the fuck up, du Près. We have a no fraternization policy. *No one* should be thinking that." Geez, first Jack and now Mattie. Hockey players really are players.

"When has that ever stopped a hockey player?" he says, confirming my thought.

"Are the guys talking about her? Who do I have to kill?"

"Nah," he says, the American slang sounding strange with his French accent. He laughs. "Just testing. Everyone should get their starting role on merit."

I groan. He has a point. If I'm chosen as the starting goalie, I wouldn't want anyone to assume it was because I was sleeping with an owner. Something I should have thought of before committing to the encore show. "I'm not breaking any rules. I need a big contract, so I need to keep my nose clean and my save percentage up and show them what I can do these next few months."

But damn, I'd like to hit that. Beyond that, the more I learn about her the more fascinated I am. And putting my hands on her for dancing and lifts for the next couple months is going to be hell if I can't get her naked, despite the fact that we can't be more to each other.

Chapter Twelve

Christina

A few days later, I unlock the studio a half hour before Cam is due to arrive and crank up the cool air. We're meeting in the afternoon just before Maria's evening classes begin, and while she keeps the air conditioning on, she puts it ten degrees higher when we're not there. It takes longer to cool down in the afternoons, so here I am, unwilling to admit that my concern over Cam's adjustment to Texas is the reason I'm catering to a student more than I would otherwise.

I've stayed out of the office the past two days because the coaching staff were arguing loudly from the conference room, shuffling names around on the white board and debating their active roster, and which players they'd start for the first pre-season game.

I looked at the stats because not only do I love the game and am an owner, but I adore numbers and how they tell a story. Cam is much stronger on paper than Dan Murphy, although the coaches would also be assessing during training how each player worked with the rest of the team. I may have told myself that my interest in the goalies was because a strong goalie leads to wins.

The roster is due to be published today, but I'm not sure what time. I'm equal parts excited and nervous to see how it unfolds.

Cam's nerves have been visible as well. He's been increasingly tight over the past couple practices, his steps smaller, his arms not extending to full stretch. I hope most of that will subside when—if—he is named as the starter. Of course, some of it is from the extended training camp and may or may not change with exhibition games, travel, and an eighty-two-game season.

So instead of trying to nail down form, I've kept our focus on trying different music with various dances to determine what feels right. We tried a couple of Christmas songs, but I worried that was exclusionary and he agreed. I'm scrolling through my playlist to find the next ones I want to try when Cam bursts into the studio.

His shoes are off and his bag is still closed, hanging over his shoulder. He takes a few quick steps then slides along the hardwood floor toward me, stopping in front of me like he would on the ice.

Before I can even ask, he says through a huge grin, "Guess who got starting goalie?"

I squeal, "Yes! Cam, that's awesome." Without thinking, I throw my arms around him in a hug.

He stills. Then his arms come up without dislodging mine around his biceps, and he holds my waist, pressing me to him as he bends his head to envelop me.

I've never been full-length against him like this. I close my eyes and enjoy his post-practice soap and deodorant scent. Under my hands, his back muscles shift and flex. His pecs are like steel against my cheek and I want to bite them, but they're so hard I probably couldn't get purchase.

He sucks in a huge breath, and his shirt and muscles rasp against my leotard-covered breasts. My nipples pebble, showing through despite the lining.

He steps back, blinking twice, and I know he's seen them. His voice husky, he says, "Thank you. It's only the first step, but thank you."

Not sure whether I want him to take advantage of my arousal or ignore it, I bluster, "You'll do great. I've seen your stats."

"Yeah, but at this level? Even against my own team in training, it's a constant challenge."

I turn away to start music for our warmup. "That's what practice and pre-season are for. I have confidence in yo—the team."

He nods, and we flow through a shortened warmup. As he's come from practice, his muscles are already looser.

But when we start to dance, he's distracted and misses a couple of steps.

"Sorry, sorry," he mutters for the third time.

The song is on repeat, so we restart at the top. A minute in, he twirls me out to extended arms. His frustration seeps into his movements, and he tugs me back in too hard. My feet tangle at the unexpected force, and I begin to tip forward.

Before I can even worry about falling, he's there holding me. But instead of being my support to get to standing, he bends his knee and takes us both down in a graceful slide. His hand reaches for the floor while the other holds me against him, and I end up sprawled on top of him staring into his eyes. A half-grin crooks the corner of his mouth. "I told you I'd never drop you."

"So far. I still say you can't promise that." I put my hands to his chest to give us some space. My legs are offset with his and I try to put a knee to the floor to take some weight off him.

He tugs me upward, dragging my core over his hip, then grasps my thigh that's between his and draws it out so I'm straddling him. "There, that's safer."

Oh my god, my knee had been nudging his junk. *Oops*. I gasp, "Sorry."

"Clearly, I'm too distracted to dance. I apologize, I thought this might be a good outlet and didn't want to cancel last minute. I should have gotten on the treadmill in the gym but I needed to get out and celebrate, and it's too damn hot to run outside." Cam props himself up on his elbows shifting me down back to his pelvis. "Got any other suggestions to work off some excess energy?"

I drop my gaze to his lips. His tongue emerges, licking just the right corner of his top lip and suddenly there's a growing hardness against my pubic bone. His pectoral muscles twitch under my hands. The craving to scrape my nails down his chest while licking that now-damp corner of his mouth overwhelms me.

His cock burns me through my clothes causing my blood to pulse and contract my muscles. I wonder if he can feel it.

He stares at my chest before he blinks his gaze back to my face. I'm sure my nipples are again sharing their own ideas for activities.

His chest rises under my hands as he asks, "Yeah?"

"Yeah," I reply with a quiet breath even though my body has already answered his question.

His abs crunch under me and I want to swoon. I've

always been a sucker for core strength and a six-pack, and I suspect he's hiding a couple spare under there.

He raises his head and brings one hand to cup the back of my head. His gaze is zeroed in on my mouth and I'm transfixed, ready and willing to be dragged under the deluge. His breath against my lips is a drum brush under the song still on repeat. He flicks a glance up to my eyes, checking again.

I nod, and he refocuses on my mouth, tilting my head to the angle he wants me as he closes the gap between us.

I can't remember a single one of the many reasons I thought this was a bad idea. All I can process is this magnificent mountain of muscle under me.

I sigh against his lips. They're lush and plush and I really, really need to stop with the rhyming.

He drags them against mine in short swipes before twisting a little, his tongue coming to lick at me.

I open and press forward, following him down so he's flat on the floor, my hands roaming his shoulders before playing in his thick hair. I need to consume him.

But I'm not given the chance. His hand fists in my hair over my ponytail, the other sweeping the line of my back to cup my butt and rock me against him gently.

I pull away briefly to gasp before he tugs me forward again and his lips slant under mine, our tongues twining and starving for a taste of every corner of each other's mouth.

I circle my hips once and we both groan in our chests through the kiss.

I pull my knees up to get better leverage so they're beside his hips.

"Christina?" Maria's voice calls from the front room.

"Shit! Shit shit shit shit shit." I scramble off Cam, covering my mouth with one hand, and race for the stereo in the corner of the room so she can't see my guilt written on my face.

All the reasons—two no frat rules, he sort of works for me, he's a damn player on the road half the time, and I don't even know if he wants kids—come rushing back into my head, and I'm appalled. I yell, "In here, Maria. We're almost done."

In my peripheral vision, Cam vaults to his feet and adjusts himself as he joins me.

"I'm sorry."

"I'm sorry."

We both apologize at the same time, then both shake our heads to dismiss the other's statement.

"Look," I say, still out of breath from the kiss. "I was more wrong, given our positions"—he snickers, and I roll my eyes and continue—"in both places. It won't happen again."

In the mirror, Maria's head pokes around the door, and she scans him from top to toe, making googly eyes at me. I shoo her away.

He glances around but she's gone. In an undertone, he says, "Would it be so terrible if it did?"

I don't answer because the truth is that no, no, it would not.

* * * *

"He's a total smoke show," Maria is saying as I perch on a barstool at our usual table in Terroir.

Lauren and Nicole are grinning.

I had texted both of them when I'd found him on the roster for the team. They'd agreed being a hockey player explained his extreme flexibility and availability during the business day and immediately demanded a full-length photo, which I ignored. They could make do with the head shot on the team's website.

Lauren sighs and says, "I suppose I can live without the tool belt in this case. What about Maria's idea of a shirtless—no, naked—calendar? Please? For us?"

Maria waves a hand. "Don't worry, I'll talk to Amy about it as a fundraiser."

I glare at all of them.

Maria asks, "So what was going on in the studio when I came in yesterday?"

The other two prop their chin in their hands and lean in, elbows on the table, like sponges ready to absorb all the gossip they could get.

"Nothing. Why do you ask?"

"I could see feet on the floor from the door. That's why I called out." When Lauren and Nicole frown, trying to follow, she adds, "I saw the bottom of their shoes, the owners clearly lying on top of one another on the floor. By the way, he has really big shoes."

The other two hoot.

"I tripped. He was, ah, a little overeager on a spin. He caught me on the way down and cushioned my fall."

The non-dancers ooh and ahh but Maria raises one eyebrow and says, "I doubt that body was much of a cushion…?"

My face heats. "It was enough."

"Has that happened a lot? I thought you said he was an excellent dancer for an amateur."

"No, he was distracted. He got the news that he's starting goalie for at least the pre-season." When they all straighten and stare at me, I realize my voice has risen in excitement. Oh no.

"Girl." Maria's voice is firm. "We talked about hitting that. We did not talk about catching feelings. I can ignore the studio policy, especially if you can please attempt not to violate it *right in the damned studio*. But you need to consider his career as well as your involvement with the team before you get emotionally involved. And have the conversation about children."

"I know, I know. I'm trying."

"Did the horizontal part of the 'lesson' help allay some of your fears about sex being painful? And were you able to check if other body parts are similar in size to his feet?"

Heat spreads up my neck to my face.

They all grin at me.

"Yes. He also has very large—" I raise a brow, and they lean in—"hands."

They boo. Maria balls up her napkin and tosses it at me, and the others follow suit.

I continue. "I definitely wasn't in my head."

Nicole groans. "Come on, we're gonna need more than that!"

I inhale. On the exhale, I rush out, "I was more aroused from his kiss than I was the last time I had sex. How's that?"

"Yay!" Nicole yells.

Maria raises her glass, and Lauren claps.

My besties are all excited, but I'm still nervous. "You talked me off the ledge about this after my surgery, but I never got to that point with Travis so it's been a while. Can we run through it again now please?"

"Of course," they chorus.

"Ok, for all the reasons Maria mentioned, this would

have to be casual and secret. I don't want to overshare about my condition. But should I tell him that sex has been painful in the past?"

"Not necessarily." Nicole answers. "That could spark questions and ruin the mood."

"So what do I do if it hurts?"

Maria jumps in. "You just said you were more turned on than ever. Hopefully that means you won't get in your head. But if you want him to slow down or do something different, just ask. We women are still afraid to advocate for ourselves, whether it's for orgasms, a haircut, or a raise."

Lauren has her glass halfway to her mouth, but sticks her first finger out to point at Maria. "She's not wrong."

"I rarely am," Maria says with a smirk.

I roll my eyes, but move on. "Doesn't that ruin the mood too?"

"If you're not having fun, there is no mood to ruin." She raises a brow. "*That's* what you need to remember. And before you ask about his mood, think about this. Any guy you'd want to get naked with should also be the type whose goal would be for you to have as much fun as he does. Hasn't a guy ever asked—"

"—or told," Lauren says through a cough.

Maria slides her a look and curls her lip. "Or told, if you like that sort of thing—you to squeeze a little more, go a little deeper, whatever?"

"No."

"Well, that explains a lot." Maria's lips press together in exasperation at the men in my past.

Nicole nearly snorts her wine.

"Probably, but here I am. I only have my own experiences to go on."

"Nah, you have ours as well," Lauren says, reaching across to squeeze my clenched fist.

"You can say it nonchalantly. A good lover will sometimes know when you're not into it, but it's hard to do that in the beginning. So if something twinges or hurts, or hell just isn't doing it for you, suggest something else or direct him. 'Oh, can you do that a little higher please?' or 'Oh, you're so big, give me a minute to adjust?'" Maria goes into a breathy girly voice for the examples, and we all crack up.

Nicole adds, "Yeah, it's always good to reward good behavior, too. 'Yes, right there, keep doing that.' You can do the same for positions. If one isn't working, ask for another."

"Whew. I never knew there was so much conversation during sex."

Lauren reaches across for my hand again. "Hon, the key to any good relationship is communication. That goes for naked time as well as clothed."

"And for casual as well as serious," Nicole says with a nod.

Maria adds, "Sometimes the pretty ones don't care enough, because it's all come too easy for them their whole life. But if he's got you that excited from fully-clothed kissing, it's a good sign."

I nod. "Ok. I keep reminding myself that the doctor did say nothing should hurt now, too."

Maria voices the words running through my conscience. "He's a cowboy to ride, a means to an orgasm or four. Besides, he's young. I'm sure he's not looking for anything serious."

My friends are excellent enablers. It's against policy, but I rarely break rules. Cam seems interested and worth a few broken rules, based on that hotter than hell kiss.

* * * *

The team's first pre-season game was on the road, but they're home tonight.

I'd always planned to attend despite Travis likely being in the owner's box frequently. Now, I'm more determined than ever to make as many home games as possible to see Cam in goal.

When I enter the suite, Travis and Greg are talking at the bar so I head over to greet my brother. I won't let my ex-boyfriend deter me. My lip curls for a moment when he does his usual sweep of the room, cataloging who he should talk to next. Amy will be here tonight, and for a moment, I worry about him saying something rude to her. But he's never been overtly dismissive to her directly. Their paths shouldn't cross much anyway. I prefer to be in the stadium seating to watch the game uninterrupted, and she'll hang with me. Travis will be negotiating…whatever it is he negotiates at these things, as though it was a corporate meeting.

I've never paid attention to the goalies other than their stats. But now I have a personal connection—a *dance* connection, I remind myself—and I watch the warmups like they're the main event. I'm in the first row of suite seats so I lean forward to see better over the rail.

As the teams set up for the faceoff, Cam chonks the ice so he has the perfect amount of traction for his stance. He lowers into a crouch.

He's nearly unrecognizable from this distance. His warm brown eyes are hidden by the goalie mask, and his trim, tight physique is encased in thick pads. It needs to be with puck speeds over eighty miles an hour.

I salivate, thinking of his quads. How did I not figure out he's a professional athlete when he easily held such a deep squat for so long in the studio?

At some point, Amy slides in next to me and we trade one-armed hugs.

I mutter under my breath at the D-men to help Cam more. They're spending way too much time trying to score and not enough back in their own zone. This should be more like soccer where they hang back. Ugh.

I relax when the Tornadoes get control of the puck, even going so far as to grab food from the buffet. When the buzzer goes and everyone around me cheers, I'm lackadaisical in turning to watch the replay, but I rush back to my seat for the faceoff. My attention is centered on Cam in goal.

The St. Louis Sentinels pass and their right wing takes a shot at goal, but it's slow enough Cam sees it coming a mile away. He catches the puck in his huge glove, and the ref whistle blows. A glove save as his first move in the home opener is a good way to get management's attention.

I'm inordinately proud, ignoring the fact that I should be equally proud of our goal that took first blood a couple minutes ago. As an owner, I should be—I mean, I am, should Greg ask—invested in all our successes and all our players. I'd like one particular player to be invested—inside me.

I snicker at my own joke.

Amy, who has been sitting beside me, frowns.

She asks, "What on earth are you thinking about? First, you were muttering. Then, you go up and get food while we have control of the puck and miss the first goal, now you're laughing at nothing. Are you even watching this game?"

"Absolutely. I got distracted. Excuse me, little sister."

She rolls her eyes and turns back to the game. After a minute, she asks in a casual voice, "So how are the dance practices going with our goalie?"

My eyes dart sideways, but she's studiously focused on the ice. "Between training camp and the start of play, we haven't done much yet."

"Do you know what style you're aiming for?"

"We'll work that out in practice." If I tell her about the kiss, I'll never hear the end of it. She wants me to get back out there as much as my friends do. "I want to choose a few songs and try different things with them. And Cam should have a say."

A Sentinels team player crowds Jack Landry and jabs an elbow in his gut without the ref seeing.

"Dammit." We swear in unison and lean forward.

As other players rush forward, the Sentinel flicks the puck to his center. There's no way Cam can see the puck with all the skates and sticks in the way. And yet, when their center slaps a one-timer, Cam's already adjusted his angle, skating a foot further out to block the angles to the goal. He deflects the shot with an outstretched leg, and Jack is there to get the puck directed toward the other end of the ice.

I unclench my fists from the seat arms and lean back with a sigh of relief.

Amy's spine relaxes against her chair also. "Yeah, I guess you're watching at least half the game."

Dammit. I have to stop being this obvious about my obsession with Cameron. At most, he can be a secret fling, and even that is a bad idea.

Chapter Thirteen

Cam

We won on the road, but this—our first home win, even if it's only pre-season—feels different. We're riding high and the locker room is boisterous.

Coach comes in and we pipe down a bit, but his victory speech praising us for finding our jam and working together so soon only makes us more raucous.

We head to Chasers, a new bar that's opened a few blocks away from the arena. With the tornado- and drink-related name, the owner's intention of being *the* after-party location is clear.

Saylet has a poll going on Instagram for fans to choose our team song. As we walk in, the one with the most votes to date plays. The poll will close before the season starts and the players will get to vote on their favorite of the top three. I can't see anything wrong with picking *Winner* by Jamie Foxx with T.I. and Justin Timberlake, even if we have to adapt the basketball reference for ourselves.

The front-line guys' hands are over their heads and they're yelling along with the song as they enter. I shake my head. There's no need to be flashy. When the hostess extends a hand to direct me, I beeline to the corner roped off for us. Jack will buy me a beer and I'll return the favor before I go, although my limit is still one and will be until hopefully June when we win the Stanley Cup Finals.

Emil Bergstrom, the young rookie, trails me. Third line in Saint's position, he's been quiet and doesn't strike me as the rowdy bar celebration guy, but at least he came out with us. His performance in training camp was solid if unexciting, but tonight he looked shaky. On the other hand, it had been my second game at the NHL level, and I was hyper-focused on making a good impression, so maybe my perception is skewed. Or worse, I looked shaky to others.

Nah. I know my stats. I had a strong game. As a goalie, I take a degree more pride in our wins and a degree more guilt about our losses. Hockey is one hundred percent a team sport and we need every player on the ice to be their best, but the puck stops with me.

I ask the youngster, "Do you want a drink? I can get Jack's attention. I think."

"Buzz is getting me one, thanks."

"What's the drinking age in Sweden?" I ask, as much to make conversation as from curiosity.

"Our rules are complicated, so sort of eighteen to twenty-one. I don't drink much, though. I prefer to stay focused on hockey."

"Me, too. One beer's my limit, even when I was in the AHL."

Other players join us, trickling in from the arena. A few had caught rides with their teammates, leaving their cars at the arena to be safe, which I respect.

The guys at the bar come over as they receive their drinks and in no time, we fill the tables saved for us.

Jack makes sure he's facing the rest of the bar, as does Drew.

Drew starts counting Tornadoes jerseys. "This is awesome. Look at the support for us even before the regular season. And the arena was sold out."

Drew's name and number is already on jerseys. The team had identified several seasoned players they were investing in with big contracts and had ordered jerseys with their names printed, knowing they were going to be popular.

Others, like me and Bergstrom, who are new to the league, have to earn our place in the team store. My personal goal is to have my name hanging in that store by Halloween.

Jack's focus is on counting puck bunnies. He nudges me. "Whatdya think? Shall we take down the ropes?"

"No. We have practice tomorrow afternoon and a game the following day. And management is still making decisions about the season. Pace yourself."

"Overrated. I have no doubt Austin can keep me entertained throughout the season. Now's as good a time to start as any." He gestures me up. "Come on. I need a wingman."

"No."

"Emil? I'll show you how it's done, just like I do on the ice." He winks at the younger guy.

Emil gives a good-natured smile but shakes his head. "I, uh, I have someone back home, thank you."

He sounds unsure, which is odd. With someone older or who he knew better, Jack would joke around about keeping his bed warm when Sweden is so far away. But the kid is so serious and so reserved, he leaves it alone, grabbing Buzz to go chat up the women lingering along the ropes pseudo-casually sipping their drinks with their arms squeezing their cleavage higher.

None of them can compare to Christina. I can't stop thinking what she's doing right now. She's probably in bed. I picture her in various sleepwear—a tank and shorts, a slinky nightgown, naked…my jersey. My cock hardens in my suit pants and I'm glad I'm sitting at a table rather than standing at the bar.

My need to pursue her is starting to override my worries about the organization's rules. After all, she said that as the person in the position of power, the fault would fall to her. On the other hand, she's an owner. There is only one person who would leave the team if Greg or management has an issue, and that's me.

However, our dance practices give us cover and no one's thought anything of our meetings so far. Ok, well maybe Jack and du Près. But if we keep it on the down low, perhaps I can talk her into a fling. She tasted of vanilla and coconut. My mouth waters at the memory. I'd love to find out if that's her shampoo or bodywash. All I know is that I need to taste her again.

* * * *

Several members of the team have met with Christina to discuss their "financial health." The few married guys like Saint were impressed and happy with the meeting. He even said privately to Jack and Buzz and me that he was relieved, knowing his rudimentary plan for the future was now being shepherded by a pro.

I glowed with pride in Christina at that, then reminded myself that not only did I have nothing to do with her skill, but I also wasn't even in a position to associate myself with her publicly.

It's my turn now. She already knows I have a plan in place, so I expect the finance part of this will be quick and perhaps we can sneak in a snog. Snog. I love that word. My mom used it and I've adopted it as my own in her memory. It's more fun than "kiss," and encompasses some fooling around, which I'd love to do.

I get to her office doorway and she looks up. Fuck, she's gorgeous. All serious now, with a silky printed top with cap sleeves. I should ask if we can walk and talk so I can check out her dancer legs again. Then again, that could be distracting. I can't help picturing them on either side of my hips on the studio floor.

"Hi." Her voice is breathy. Hopefully that means she's as affected as I am. "Have a seat. Thank you for meeting with me."

"I thought it was mandatory?" I joke, but immediately shake my head. "I like spending time with you, Chris. I'm happy to have this additional lesson."

She waves me to a chair then folds her hands in front of her laptop.

"Here's what I like to do. Everyone has a different comfort level with how much information they want to share about their expense burdens. So I'll ask you a few questions, but feel free to decline to answer. Then I can talk about saving options and investment choices." She stands. "But first, let me close the door for your privacy. My certifications and the fact that I'm not actively involved in Tornadoes management, nor using Tornado equipment"—she gestures at the sleek laptop—"means any details we discuss here remain between you and me. Also, you will be responsible for making all transactions on your account, although I can help you today and at any time going forward, or we can set them up to be automatic after each paycheck. I won't earn any income from any choices you make."

"Why are you doing this then?"

She shrugs. "To help my brother attract and retain the best players he can. And because I hate to see people hobble themselves by mismanaging money."

She stands and comes around the desk. Damn, she's in a pencil skirt. My cock tries to get to her through my joggers. I'm surprised she doesn't hear the rustle of cloth as it springs to attention.

My mouth goes dry as her luscious peach of an ass passes my head. I want to bite it. Then I want to lay her on the desk and worship her with my lips and tongue. Or play teacher and naughty student who she takes to his knees. Or—

She's back around the desk and tilting her head. "You seem flushed. Are you warm? This office gets some sun in the afternoons, and we're still getting the A/C right for everyone."

"I'm fine, thanks. If I can't handle a little sweat, I'm in the wrong business." I dismiss her concerns with a smile. "Hit me with your questions."

We go through my expenses. She's amazed at how little I spend and how much of my previous salary I had saved.

She asks, "What are your plans now you're making NHL money?"

"I'll continue to live on the same amount and funnel everything else into savings."

"Wow. Not a single splurge?" She raises her brows.

"No. I was serious at dinner when I said I want to

save as much as possible. I hate debt and I want to buy a house."

"You mean you want to buy it for cash?" She's aghast.

"Yeah."

She starts to say something and swallows it back, instead stating, "We should talk about that before you make that decision. For now, though, how did you invest what you've saved?"

"It's mostly in savings, but once I had a year's worth of expenses, I started putting amounts in high yield money market accounts for a higher return."

"That is an excellent start, Cam. You're more financially savvy than many. So let's talk about increasing your return even further. Did you know that the stock market outperforms savings accounts by about three times?"

I've looked at the stock market, but there have been some huge downturns. Recessions can last years and the prospect of losing much of what I've saved makes me ill. "I prefer to avoid risk. Doesn't that depend on the years?"

"Yes. But reviewing the last twenty years, which are arguably the most relevant, if you invested $10,000 in a high-yield savings account you'd end up with about $16,000. If you had put it into a diversified mutual fund—the stock market, but a collection of stocks rather than an individual company—you'd have $65,000 right now." She pushes two charts toward me.

I peer down at the curve with the sharp upturn in the last five years and point to an earlier period. "But look at these market dips. That's over a decade of negative returns. What if I wanted to buy a house during that time?"

"Well, yes. I wouldn't recommend putting all your savings into one security, even when it's a fund holding many positions."

I push the charts back to her. "I want to focus on—what's the term I read?—'capital preservation.'"

Her eyes flare a little at my use of the word "capital," investor jargon. I'll have to remember that if I ever get her in bed.

I guess some good can come out of having told her about my sucky childhood, as she'll understand my reasoning. "I never want to have to worry about money again. That last year of high school and college sucked. Besides, I think you have short-term memory bias." I've done my homework. "You talk about the last twenty years, but I only see ten that are positive on that graph you showed me, and even the last five show a drop with a two-year recovery period."

"I agree. I'm happy to look at further diversification. Given your low risk tolerance, I'd propose a blend. My point is, you're young, you have many years ahead so you don't have to time the market—you're not likely to have to sell your positions urgently. That's what that year's worth of expenses in a bank account is for."

"I don't know." I shake my head. That's way outside my comfort zone, even with my new salary.

She presses her lips together, then inhales and tries again. "Cam, you're young, but this career is shorter than most. You want your money to work for you. I'm not suggesting high risk investments—"

"Isn't that defined in the eye of the beholder?" I ask gently. I don't want to argue with her. And geez, even her use of financial terms makes me want to kiss her.

"Yyeess." She sighs, then brightens. "Can we make a deal? Please?"

My brain is still focused on kissing her. Maybe she wants a kiss for every dollar earned. Or a new position. Hey, a guy can hope. I manage to keep my tone neutral when I ask, "Like what?"

"You give me control over $25,000. I'll show you what I can do with it between now and the end of the season."

I start to shake my head even as I smile at the passion in her voice.

She holds up a hand. "Wait, I'm not finished. I won't do anything overly risky to try to earn more, I'll avoid as much risk as possible without being too conservative. And…" she pauses for effect. "I'll reimburse you out of my own pocket for any losses. Off the record."

"Why would you do that?"

"Because I believe in this. This is my area of expertise, like goaltending is for you. If I wanted to improve my skating or hockey playing, I'd come to you as an authority on the subject. Will you trust me to help make your dreams come true while minimizing your risk?" Her voice rings with passion.

My fingers tap against my side underneath my crossed arms. She's watching me pleadingly. I can't imagine the Donovans' wealth, but if the family trusts her with their entire portfolio, then I can too. Besides, this is Christina. I'm already knee deep and I don't want to disappoint her. But twenty-five thousand is still a huge chunk of money. Finally, I compromise. "Fifteen."

"Done." She grins at me, making me suspect she expected me to counter. Either way, I'm locked in at this point. Fifteen-k won't kill me I guess, now that my salary has an extra zero on the end.

Chapter Fourteen

Christina

When Cam conceded that small amount of money to me to manage, I was beyond elated. Then the team practices accelerated so we've only had a couple in-person lessons this week and I've missed him. Maria's voice in my head keeps shouting the word "casual" at me, and I wonder how I'm going to feel when he's on the road for the upcoming two pre-season games.

We started discussing our routines for the holiday party over the phone. I had thrown out some ideas in text, but he responded by video calling me. Thrown off, I'd declined. I had no makeup on, my hair was up in a messy bun, and I wasn't sure what the area behind my desk looked like.

Sprinting into the bathroom, I'd cleaned up as best I could and moved to my spare bedroom which I'd converted to a mini dance studio. It has hardwood flooring, a barre and one mirrored wall. My stereo system is house-wide, so I use my phone and Wi-Fi for music.

He'd squinted when he first saw it and asked where

I was, shaking his head without further comment when I said my house. My friends know about my family's wealth, so I don't give it much thought until someone new reacts to it. But I might have broken the news of my personal studio to him differently had his video call not thrown me off my game.

Thankfully, we moved on to talk through songs and dance styles, and I used the video opportunity to show him a few showy steps we could add to the rumba.

Today is our third in-person practice, and as they have today off after traveling home yesterday from one win and one loss on the road, I blocked two hours on my schedule. Unfortunately, I forgot that Maria has a class that conflicts with the second hour.

Between that and the team's growing popularity, I debate inviting him to my house to work. If we go to the studio, he might be mobbed by dance/hockey fans, since there are already posters up in the studio about our holiday performance. Also, the word fling hovers in my mind, and not about dance lifts.

Before I can dither any longer, I text him my address.

> There are classes at the studio, if you want to come here we can work longer if you're not too tired.

I get a thumbs-up emoji. A stupid, needy part of me that should be squashed is hurt by the apparent lack of enthusiasm. I mean, I don't invite any other dance students or even partners into my house.

In our other studio sessions, we'd worked on adding a few showy touches to our rumba and reinforcing the lift that he has already nailed. I'm procrastinating because I'm working my way up to having his hands on me in other places. Every time he grabs my thigh, my body jolts. I hope he can't feel it, that it's just my heart thumping, but it's disconcerting.

I've used my battery-operated boyfriend more since I met Cam than I had in the prior two years, although I still haven't been brave enough to put it inside for fear of pain. Even so, the vivid images of his touch, the remembered sensation of him under me, our kiss, and the pulsing vibration on the highest setting work wonders.

The ecstasy and agony of our video chats are distracting. I love seeing his face light up when I suggest contrasting the slower rumba with a couple of showy steps with a second faster dance that could showcase bigger lifts because of momentum. But it also makes me miss him more somehow. I need to keep my emotions at bay. He's a student, and at most, an unlikely candidate for a casual fling. No matter what, after the holiday dance I must be able to walk away without either of us getting hurt.

I've already alerted the gate to a visitor, but I'm still shocked when the doorbell chimes. I jog over to let him in. "Hi."

"Hi," he mumbles, still looking around wide-eyed. I live in what was once a pool house on the family property ever since I was at UT. Greg now resides in the main house and Amy is off doing her own thing. She claims she needs space from Greg for her personal life since she spends her workday with him. I would too if I worked with him more. My brother can be intense but we both love him. We've got an amazing pool, but the real draw is the wine cellar Greg keeps stocked without anyone keeping regular inventory. Yes, I could find whatever place I wanted and build a studio, but I like being close to my family and I'm a teeny bit lazy about moving.

"Come on in. Can I get you a drink?"

"I brought one thanks. I came from the gym." Catching my glance, he adds, "I kept it light, but my weight training needs to be heavier than a buck ten or whatever you weigh."

I smile, not feeling the need to correct him. At five-nine, I weighed more than that even when I was dancing competitively.

"Great, it sounds like you're warm then. I was trying a few things out already, so I am, too. Come on back and I'll show you what I've been working on."

The front half of the house is open concept, keeping the original pool house design. One wall is all windows facing the pool. The front door is on the side wall of the living room, at the end of a path from the driveway.

The other half of the great room has an L-shaped kitchen with a deep island and barstools. There's a small dining area in front of the kitchen that faces the windows and pool. I don't entertain here for more than my girlfriends so I don't need a formal dining room.

There is a short hallway down the center with a bathroom and laundry room facing each other, and then the house splits into two rather large bedrooms. Both overlook Lake Austin. All the rear facing rooms in the big house do as well, which is why we kept this to one level when we expanded it to be my residence.

The bedroom closer to the main house is my studio

and has sheer curtains closed over the windows, both for climate control and privacy.

"Alright, let's get down to business," I say. Maria's dirty mind echoes a laugh in my head at my phrase. If only.

* * * *

We'd decided on *Take My Breath Away* for our rumba. I put it to play on repeat before he got there, the volume turned down so I'd hear the door. Now, I raise it only a little as we're going to talk through some lifts.

"How warm are you? Did you stretch as well as lift?"

"Of course. I wouldn't say it and risk injury—boss," he smirks.

"I was thinking about some options for both of us doing splits, that's the only reason I asked," I return mildly. Our working relationship is front and center in my internal debates between pursuing a delicious fling and staying out of trouble, and I am not yet ready to tip my hand one way or another.

"I'm good. What do you have in mind?"

I show him a snippet of a video, talking him through it. "Here. As you turn me, I do a high fan kick with my leg going to the outside. Given your unique-to-your-position flexibility, maybe we then do another fan. Close hold, but this time I push you out to side-by-side and *you* do the high fan kick."

"Cool." He's nodding. "What are my choices before we start, though?"

I show him two videos. One is more traditional, with the woman's back to the man's front where she bends a leg up around his butt, usually after a twirl into a close hold.

The other is something of an advanced hold, but some of that is because the man needs fine motor skills to balance her on his shoulder as well as the strength to get her up there. Both of which Cam has for his day job. On screen, the guy twirls his partner in to stand in front of him, then bends and grabs her inside leg, his other arm going around her waist. He lifts her to lay back over his shoulder so she is draped facing upwards. Her straight leg extends across his body at shoulder height, and her other leg curls around his side as she reaches both arms out in an upside-down arabesque.

"Slow it down and show me again?" His voice rumbles over my shoulder, and I suppress a shudder of want.

"Sure. I guessed you'd like this one so I can talk you through it, too. One thing to watch please—see how he brings her down, shifting his hold, and then they do some arm movements in a stationary close hold? That's to ensure she isn't dizzy from the rotations on her back."

"Oh. Thank you for clarifying. Okay, let me watch it all through at 50% speed."

Then we talk and step through it standing, music off so we don't rush anything. He tugs me in, my butt riding the top of one massive thigh until he slides a foot back and bends.

"You thread your hand between my legs"—I might die of need right here, or of embarrassment if I soak his hand—"and grab my left thigh. Make sure you can feel that I've engaged my leg muscles before you lift." I slide my arm around his neck and get his shoulder below my shoulder blades. He'd never be able to do this with a shorter person. Sure, he could get that low, but the balance would be off.

He lifts. Again, I hardly need to help with my arm across his back as he raises me effortlessly with a hand on my leg and the other around my waist. "Don't squeeze me quite so hard around my waist. Let me do some of it."

He puts me down. "I was scared to lessen my grip."

"Ok, that's understandable. Let's try it again, but keep it looser from the get-go. If you feel like I'm slipping you can always tighten. I prefer to breathe if we're going to keep dancing after it."

He chuckles. "You're asking for a lot."

"You're the one who said you won't drop me." I grin. "And until I'm over your shoulder I'd land on my feet anyway."

He grumbles, but gets into position. It goes super smoothly, and I'm up and draped to face the ceiling in no time, my left leg extended across his neck, my right bent at his side.

"Ok," I say, a little breathless. From the position, of course. "Do a three-step turn, then allow my leg to lower a little. As my weight shifts, you're going to tighten on my waist as my bent leg tightens around you. My straight leg will bend to also wrap around you and you're going to flip your grip to hold just below my knee so it's under my weight."

He turns, then starts to lower me.

"What are you doing?"

"I'm worried about you falling when I take my hand off."

"I won't fall. And didn't you say hockey guys have fast hands?" On the floor, I turn to face him.

He laughs, but shakes his head. "I needed a minute to get my head around it. I'm sure I could catch you. Or hold you tighter with my other arm, but I don't want to crush you."

After a minute I reply, "Tell ya what. You stay still. I'm going to lean hard on your shoulders and put one leg up to hoist myself to waist height facing you. Once I'm clinging to you like a monkey, you can bring your hands to just behind my knees." *Or I could give into temptation and rub myself up and down your muscles to take myself over the edge.* I'm halfway there already.

"That isn't the stance we're talking about, but okay," he says. Holding his hands out above his waist to keep them out of the way, he plants his feet.

I put one arm around his neck, the other on a shoulder, and hook a leg over his hipbone, then push upward. Oh lord. Even as I bring my other leg up, I realize what a bad idea this was. We're face to face, chest to chest. Groin to groin.

His hands are there, hovering, a frown of concern on his face. Once he's holding me, his brow smooths and his hands flex around my thighs.

I envision his hands sliding forward to cup my ass, thrusting me against his hardness. Then I imagine it without clothes and I nearly lose my grip.

His eyes flutter closed for a minute, before he opens them to stare unblinking at my face. His voice is full of gravel when he asks, "What next?"

"Lower your hands away from me by a couple inches."

He does.

"Now, I can hold in this direction for a while." Never mind that I wonder how long I could hold it if he's bringing me to orgasm. "We're going to do the same thing in the other direction."

I drop to my feet and turn, and he stands offset from me as we would for the move.

"Bring me up to your shoulder as you did. Turn if the momentum helps." From up there arched over him, I say, "Rotate to face the mirror so you have line of sight if I slip. Now bring me down a little, releasing my leg and putting that arm out straight to your side."

I'm horizontal in front of his neck now.

I continue. "Instead of coming back to your shoulder, my left hand will slide down your back to your side. Literally with each of us with one hand, we can do one turn like that. Then as I slide further and come upright, I bend the straight leg back around your waist, and your second hand goes under it to help stabilize, allowing me to lower gracefully. You're going to let go again after a turn as I slide to standing."

He's standing with me under his chin for the last part. In the mirror on the side wall I see his nostrils keep flaring and his eyelids flutter, making me realize what part of me is right under his chin.

His demonstration of strength aside, my already-damp core is almost within licking distance of his plush lips, and I'm here for it. If we were naked…a small shudder runs through me at the thought.

"You all right?" he asks, ever solicitous.

"Yes, but let's walk through it."

"Slow, please," he says, probably not realizing it's actually harder in slow motion.

He groans as I slide down him to standing, before I step around to twirl to a close hold.

Whoa. That was definitely harder. My butt slid over a steel rod on the way down.

And now I'm picturing that stance naked, with him

thrusting into me from behind. Perhaps not as much leverage as face to face, but he could reach my clit. My pulse thrums in my chest, my wrists, between my legs. This is why I worried about adding more lifts.

He's turned away, I'm guessing to will his cock into submission. But he's apparently a sucker for punishment because he asks, "Let's do it with music."

As am I. "Sure."

As he raises me to his shoulder, my leg extended, and begins to twirl, my only thought is how close his hand is to my pussy. I moan, and he inhales deeply. If he's smelling me, I'll be so embarrassed. That might be worse than if my arousal leaks down onto his hand.

He clutches me tight for an instant before allowing me to slide down. I wrap my arm around his back, the arch of my spine more pronounced than before. I've forgotten the move. My ass craves his cock against it and my legs are splayed wide to get maximum friction where I want it. I'm too high, though, so I'm splayed across his belly, his big hand inches above where I need it to be. He releases his left hand where it had moved under my knee and I slide down, leading with one tiptoe so I can slow my slide over his cock.

I am shameless and over this lesson almost before it's begun.

I don't spin around and instead shimmy my ass against him.

His hand tightens around my waist as he pulls me even closer. We breathe in unison. My back brushes his chest with every inhale.

"Christina?" he asks into my hair. I'm sweaty and horny and I don't care about resisting any more.

I whisper, "Cam. Please."

Spinning me around, he responds with a husky, "Thank fuck," as his hands go to my head and his lips meet mine.

He kisses far better than anyone I've ever experienced. I'm lost. My brain skitters along the hard floor under us before I remember that my bedroom is literally feet away. But I'm afraid to break the spell. I want to sink into these sensations, this pleasure, and wallow in it.

My hands roam his hard muscles. Arms, back, chest, shoulders are all explored as our lips and tongues play. I tunnel under his shirt, craving skin to skin, and he moans. I flick his nipple with a fingernail, and he shudders around me.

He also starts to explore. His fingers knead the muscles of my upper back, around the base of my spine, and my ass. He skims as far down my legs as he can reach and mutters against my mouth, "God, I want these wrapped around me."

I nod.

He raises his head, looking a little surprised. "Are you sure?"

"I'm sure. It's been a while, though, so please take it slow." I'm not ready to share my specific worries about penetration, angle, or position, but I'm safe with him. This is a man who worries he'll drop me a few feet from a simple lift.

Nor is this the time to talk about keeping this whole thing secret. Maybe I can get my fill of him today and then move on. I'll worry about all that later. Right now, I need the pleasure his body has been taunting mine with for weeks.

"If you need me to do something different, tell me."

He's done asking for permission, however, because he peels the straps of my leotard down to my hips in one move. Plucking the knot of my filmy wrap skirt open, he tosses it aside and gets me naked except my shoes in seconds.

I suck in a breath. The mirrors reflect a three-quarter view of the back of me, so he can see *all* of me at once. And while he's in his prime, both age-wise and being a professional athlete, I'm no longer the lithe competitive dancer I once was. I've filled out, although I stay fitter than most thirty-year-old women.

"God, you're gorgeous. Even more beautiful than I imagined." His voice is reverent, allaying the few worries my thoughts had room for. It's time to bask in this experience.

He lowers to his knees; I assume to take my shoes off. But no, he runs his hands up and down my legs, testing the muscles with light squeezes. "Your legs are my greatest fantasy."

Well, that's hot. And original. I brace my hands on his shoulders. Even with him kneeling before me, the power dynamic of me naked and him clothed is a little overwhelming. I tug on his shirt. "Off, please."

He does that young guy thing, grasping it behind his head with one hand and yanking it up and off, flinging it aside.

My hands return to his shoulders. Warm, smooth skin covers muscles that are hard even at rest. I could fondle him all day.

He has other ideas. Tucking a hand behind my knee, he braces me by holding my other hip and slides my knee over his shoulder, opening me to him.

I'm still wearing my dance shoes and it puts me at

the perfect height for him to nuzzle into my pussy.

"I need a taste," he mumbles as his thumbs spreads my outer lips and he licks up my center.

My nails dig into his trap and my other hand goes to his hair. Not for balance or direction, but just to clutch more of him to me. Maybe I can keep him there forever. Because his tongue is magic. He traces my folds and laps at my wetness. When he licks my opening right before sucking on my clit, I nearly collapse.

I lock my knee holding my weight and moan, bowing over him. He brings one hand to where his mouth was, circling my nub with one finger before sliding it slowly into me. He turns it, which spikes my pleasure, to make room for his mouth to work. His other hand is on my mons, pulling my skin to expose my clit.

The few men in my past who have done this gave a cursory effort, and then only at the start of our relationships. Cam, however, is devouring me. Slurping and licking and sucking. His hand is wet against my thigh, whether from his saliva or my body's reaction, I don't know and I don't care. His nose and cheeks are also damp, and he is humming and moving his hips like he's the one getting off.

He's definitely not. I clutch him tighter as ecstasy grows and spirals up my spine and outward along my limbs. I'm dizzy with it, and everything he touches tightens.

He twists his finger inside me a fraction, then bends it and shortens his pistons as his tongue speeds up.

"Cam!" My shout echoes off the glass and wood.

"Yes, baby. Let go for me," he hisses against me.

And I do. My knee buckles and he is literally holding me up with his hand under my convulsing sex, his finger still wiggling gently inside of me, his face still rubbing any way it can against my gyrating flesh.

Fireworks explode behind my eyelids as every muscle—except of course that damn knee—tightens. Even the other knee does, clutching him to me as I surf the crest of the wave, astounded at the length of the orgasm.

I open my eyes to see my hands digging into his shoulder and hair. I loosen them and release his back, bringing my leg off his shoulder to the floor.

He slides his finger slowly out of my oversensitive flesh. I shake with aftershocks, and he grips my hips. Staring up to me, he asks, "You good?"

My grin is a little drunk as I answer him. "I'm great."

"I meant to stand, but that works, too," he replies with a chuckle.

"Oh. Yes. Thanks. Come on," I tug on a forearm to raise him and lead him to my bedroom. Normally I want a nap after an orgasm, but I'm energized. For the first time in a long time, I want some dick in me. But I have no doubt that not just any dick would do. Only Cam makes me feel special and safe. My own personal Tornado creating a storm of pleasure and emotions.

Chapter Fifteen

Cam

Fuck, I hope she wants sex. I'll do whatever she's cool with, including leave now, but I might have to stop in the bathroom because I'm about three strokes from going off like a rocket.

That was the hottest thing I've done in forever, and I've had threesomes. (Come on, doesn't every college athlete? They're offered freely.)

She's smoking hot clothed. Sans clothing, she's a goddess I want to worship forever.

The hardwood was kinder to my knees than ice, but I'm happy she's heading toward her carpeted bedroom. I can still taste and smell her. Maybe I won't wash my face the rest of the day to enjoy this.

Hell, I need to aim higher. Maybe I'll get another taste.

She turns at her bedside and asks, "Do you have a condom?"

"Are you sure? I mean yes, please. I mean yes." I roll my eyes at myself mentally. I've reverted to a teenager in my eagerness.

She doesn't seem to notice replying, "Ah, good, because I don't actually have any. I, uh, haven't done this in a while and wasn't expecting this."

"Hey, you don't owe me anything. I loved that"—I gesture—"so no pressure." I even mostly mean it.

She rewards my good behavior with a smile, and says, "No pressure felt. It's a happy surprise, and we're here because I brought you here. Now, where were we?"

Closing the last gap between us, she reaches for my belt.

"Oh geez. You'd better let me do that this time, or I might embarrass myself." I twist my hips an inch to the side.

She grins. "Hey, you got to taste."

I groan and hold my cock through my clothes, squeezing it to stop it from spurting any more. I might need to run my pants through the wash to walk out of here as it is. "Don't say things like that until I've taken the edge off. It's been a while for me, too."

"Do you want to wash up at all?" She gestures to the bathroom and when my brow furrows, she circles her face.

I lick a circle around my mouth as far as I can get and grin. "Hell, no. I'm in pussy heaven right now. Your house smells even better than it did when I walked in."

She raises her brows. "Okay, then. I guess I'll take that as the strangest complement I've ever gotten."

I step out of my pants, unsure whether to remove my boxer briefs quite yet. I'm doing my damnedest to take it slow as she asked. Well, aside from devouring her once already.

She solves my dilemma, turning me and shoving me to bounce down on the bed before climbing atop me, knees outside of my hips.

"My turn." Her grin is evil.

She leans forward and kisses me, before trailing her lips down my neck, across my collarbone, and to my shoulder, where she sinks her teeth into my deltoid. Her other hand is trailing across my chest, through the light smattering of hair across my sternum.

My body bucks under her and my glutes tighten to lift me up in response to the contrasting sensations of soft lips, teeth, and fingertips. I'm on overload. My cock is begging for friction and needing to pump.

Her ass settles on my upper thighs, inches too low to do what I need it to. I moan and thrust once more.

She tsks. "Settle down. I want to savor this."

That word has me twisting under her again. "Savor later, please? I'm dying here."

As she slips her hands into my boxer briefs, her finger brushes my cock and I moan. She scoots back off the bed and yanks them down and off me. I lever myself backwards over the bed, lying sideways across it as she climbs back aboard.

She brushes her slit against me, her wetness and mine coating both of us. Sliding herself along the length of my cock, she shudders.

I've been running my hands up and down her back and along her legs, enjoying the feel of her everywhere I could reach. At her second slide, I reach one hand to her belly, thumb finding her clit again to circle gently.

"Ahh, you're good at that," she says, throwing her head back.

Has no one worshiped this woman the way she deserves? No matter, I'm here to remedy that.

I quickly grab the condom and roll it on, then notch

my cock at her opening, changing the angle of her hips with my hands.

She freezes, her face tight.

"Chris? You okay? Did I hurt you?" I ask, trying to keep my cock from pulsing against her and scaring her.

"No, you didn't. It's just—" she gulps. "Sex has been painful before, and you're…big."

"Oh." I wonder again about her past partners. I want to be angry but I'm too turned on at the moment. My hands fall away, by my shoulders as though I'm at gunpoint against the duvet. "You're in charge."

"I don't know that I can be." She seems nervous, maybe close to tears.

"Come here." I gather her down against my chest. "No pressure, remember? We do as much or as little as you want."

Her eyes well. "Thank you. I'm not sure that's really fair, but it's nice of you to say. I do want this. I do. I just—" She hides her face against my throat.

"Hey." I coax her up and slant my lips over hers. "Just relax. Enjoy what we're doing now."

Some of the tension leaves her and she settles more fully against me as our tongues explore one another. My cock slides along her seam and she moans.

She's still turned on. And she told me she wants it. An idea comes to me. I shift her an inch higher and palm a breast, still kissing her like I want to eat her up with my lips first. An infinitesimal twist of my hips aligns my cock with her opening. She's wet enough that I don't need to worry about hurting her. I'm big, but I'm not going to split anyone open if they're properly aroused.

And she is. It's her mind getting in her own way.

I hope this is all right. My hips tilt and I nudge into

her. As soon as I feel that, I plant my foot on the bed between hers and thrust in one more inch. Not deep, but far enough that she can test the sensations.

My cock is not thrilled with this. It is a heat seeking missile wanting to bury itself in her over and over until it empties itself.

She gasps against my mouth. I push her shoulders upward an inch. "How is that?"

"Oh my god." Her eyelids are half closed, and her mouth is slack. I can't read her expression.

I groan. "You're killing me, sweetheart. Does that mean good or bad?"

In answer, she sits up another few degrees and drops an inch, sinking me farther into her. "So good."

Phew. My cock pulses, and she flinches. "Sorry, that was unintentional. I can't help how hot you are." I say with a grin, but sober to ask, "Did that hurt then? Should we stop?"

"Don't you dare. It didn't hurt, it was just a surprise."

"I'm just full of happy surprises today, it seems." My head thunks down while my hands fist against the bed to stop myself from ramming up into her. "Do you want to be in charge now?"

"Um." She squirms and drops down. An inch away from actually resting her weight on me, she slides up then down again, experimenting. Her gaze is on me, but vague, her thoughts clearly centered where mine are. She slides that last inch and groans.

Hot, tight, wet heat surrounds me and I almost nut right there and then. Quickly I slide my thumb back to her clit, happy to find it still engorged. Her physical desire hasn't diminished and I think we've almost got her out of her head.

Her words nearly undo me. "You drive. Just—not too hard or deep, please. But fast. I need fast. I'm close."

Thank Christ. That makes two of us. I clutch her hips, tight at first but then looser so she doesn't wear handprints after this. She grabs my hand and brings it back to her nub, increasing my arousal. I'm relieved she's into this enough that she's directing me for her pleasure.

I clench and move against her, as she does against me, my thumb pressing and releasing in time to our thrusts.

She loses her rhythm so I know she's close. Her hands on my ribs tighten.

I hold her an inch away from me and piston my hips off the bed, never so thankful for hockey muscles.

She begins writhing and screaming through her teeth, "Cam!"

My name on her lips and her inner muscles gripping me are too much for my control. I grind up against her without going too hard or too deep, conscious still of her concerns. As my cock throbs and empties into her, my eyes shutter closed and I groan in pleasure and relief.

I have no idea what will happen going forward, but this is the best day of my life. I'm a starting goalie for the NHL, and I have an amazing dance partner who is also fantastic in the sack. The future can wait.

* * * *

We lounge and nap, then take turns in the shower. When my stomach rumbles as I re-enter the bedroom, Chris takes pity on me and gets up. We throw underwear and shirts on and head to the kitchen, where she makes a late lunch salad with hummus and chips. She snacks as I scarf, having eaten lunch at a normal time like most people.

"Do you want to continue to work on the lift?" I ask between bites. "Maybe show me a couple of the others?"

"I'd rather work on one at a time. But before we do that, we need to talk."

I swallow my bite of food and lay my fork down. Those words never bode well for a relationship. Or even a situationship, or whatever we've started here. I probably sound like I'm agreeing to have teeth pulled when I nod and say, "Shoot."

"We're both aware of the various reasons we don't fit together."

I raise my brows. "All recent evidence to the contrary aside."

She flashes me a wry look and continues, "But I'll repeat them to be clear. Both organizations I work for have rules forbidding a relationship between us. Not to mention the very real issue of owner/player."

Her words are a good reminder that my future is at stake if this goes wrong. The gate and security at her driveway plus the size of the main house, let alone hers, was a stark reminder of the gap between us. At the end of this year, I have a chance at a much bigger, long-term contract that I can't jeopardize. Still, I could use several more rounds of sex before I'll be happy walking away. At least on that level, we do indeed fit together perfectly.

She continues. "But I admit, I'd be interested in more of this afternoon's activities. And frankly, I'm not sure either of us could abstain if we're going to dance together and include lifts and tricks. Your hands on me are *potent*."

I almost fall off my barstool when she echoes my

thoughts.

I straighten my spine and smile. She'd been worried about pain before, and now she's all in for more sex.

"We have to keep it on the down low. No being together in public, no dates, no romance."

What the hell? I frown. Every girl I've ever known wants romance. Plus, I like spending time with her beyond dance. "I don't like the idea of not being together in public. We've already had dinner out once, and people know we're practicing dances for the charity gig. I get that you don't want me to hold your hand or make out. But I want more than a wham, bam, thank you ma'am. I enjoy your company."

Not meeting my eyes, she grimaces down at her kitchen counter.

Geez, maybe she's only interested in sex. I contemplate that. No, she likes my company, too. Given her fear of sex, she wouldn't have attempted it if there wasn't more upside. I don't understand why this disturbs me so much.

"I want to ensure we're both on the same page here. Quiet and casual. And it has to end after the Holiday Ball."

"*Secret* and casual I can do," I reply through laughter. "But can you yell my name quieter?"

She throws a dishtowel at me. "Let's get back to dance, unless you need time to digest."

The dance lesson leads to another round of sex, after which she kicks me out, citing concern that my car had been parked in their driveway for too many hours and Greg would be suspicious. I text Jack to grab a celebratory drink in our favorite neighborhood bar. He doesn't need to know what or even that I am celebrating.

* * * *

Christina and I split our practice time between Maria's studio when it is available, as it's midway between our homes, and her home studio when we want longer sessions.

She's trying to give Maria the business but having her bedroom right next to our practice room is super handy after practicing our two lifts. I'm hoping she'll introduce a new one after the team's road trip next week.

Since that first afternoon at her house, she seems to have dropped her guard. I've even talked her into breakfast or lunch out, depending on the times of my practices and the last pre-season game.

After today's session at Come Dancing, I tell her I've found a taco shop that is the best I've had. We've debated this several times, as she has yet to take me to her favorite. Torchy's is a chain, albeit a local one, and I've become an Austonian in loving one-of-a-kind local joints, so I continue to search for a new favorite Mexican restaurant for her.

I get there first as she had to turn things off and lock up. It's an odd hour for lunch, especially as people here seem to eat at 11:30 in the morning, which is my after-practice snack time. So at 1:45 I have my pick of tables and choose a back corner. I've become more visible and while I love what that means and adore all hockey fans—I couldn't play without them—I'm greedy with my Christina time.

Requesting a sparkling water, I lean against the wood paneling decorated with photos of the owners and scroll Instagram. There they are. My stepsister is almost a woman at her eighteenth birthday. She seems to have my science skills though, as she didn't quite make high school graduation, needing another semester to complete her diploma requirements. Her younger brother, my half-sibling, is in the birthday pictures, too, posing with his arm around his sister. At around age six, he looks like he hero worships her.

Last hockey season, I saw that he was in a youth league. I wonder if he trains in the off-season like I used to or if he loves it like I do. Is something like that hereditary? Pretty sure it's not. Although maybe my father's family had skating skills that went unused due to lack of funds.

Christina slides into the seat across from me, and I smile.

She returns it, then her gaze drops, and she asks, "Friends of yours?"

I realize the phone has tilted forward, still on the post of Zoe's birthday. "Oh, um."

Chris's brows rise.

Her question was casual, and the fact that I don't answer easily makes it more apparent that I'm stalking these kids, which is beyond weird. I find myself explaining. "I told you my father remarried. I haven't met his wife or kids, but I like to keep up on how they're growing up. The boy is Robbie, my half-brother."

"Oh." She tilts her head. "Why haven't you met them?"

I shake my head. "My father had better things to do than go to a single college hockey game, even though I was in state. When I called him with the NHL draft news and my contract, he asked when I was going to stop playing games and get a real job."

"Seriously? Does he not have any concept of how competitive a job this is, much less how much it pays?"

"He's always valued putting his head down and plowing ahead over figuring out how to find work-life balance." I shrug. "He never tried to know my schedule so his calls often came during games, after his work hours. One of his voicemails *informed* me of his upcoming nuptials. Not even a request for my address. So no invitation. Nothing. That was the last call I received."

"Cam, that sucks." She reaches across and squeezes my hand where it holds the phone on the table. "Does Robbie play hockey?"

"Yeah."

"Do you think he knows who you are?"

I've wondered about my father telling them about me. "I don't know. If he did, wouldn't he have pinged me on social media?"

"Depends. How old is he?"

"Six. I guess his parents and/or the social media companies might limit his interactions on there." I shrug.

"Who posted these?"

"Their mom."

"Has she messaged you about you following her?"

I duck my head, feeling my cheeks heat. "I do it under a separate account with an alias."

She nods.

Relieved that her questions seem to be at an end, for now at least, I sigh. Changing the subject, I ask, "When are you going to show me the next lift?"

Chapter Sixteen

Christina

Sitting at my kitchen table, Amy tries one last time, "Why would you want to have to spend all that extra time and effort meeting such strict regulations?"

And I say for the fourth time, "Because it beats spending all that time and effort asking others for money when a) I have it, and b) I hate peopling! Please, let's move on."

She's been trying to convince me to make my as-yet-nonexistent dance program a public charitable organization, which requires at least a third of its funding to come from public sources. But I can't see the point when I have plenty to fund it and several other charities. I want to spend my time helping underprivileged children learn to dance, not asking my family's rich friends for money, or worse, crowd-sourcing through social media or one of those funding platforms.

"Okay, okay. I suppose we can figure out how to change that if it becomes big enough or you get spread too thin."

"How would that happen?"

"Oh, maybe if you end up spending even more time with a hot hockey player who dances like a dream?"

"Don't make me sorry I told you that," I say with a grimace, dropping my hands from my laptop across my kitchen table from her.

"I'll change my response. Maybe if you fall in love one day."

I roll my eyes. I've already told her it's casual. But my sister is the ultimate romantic. I'm sure she's picturing him sweeping me off my feet. Which is a lovely theory, except that he may want children of his own. And I refuse to be the person stealing someone's dreams of his future from him like a selfish bitch.

"Let's start with potential email lists to buy."

We dive back into the operational logistics of getting this thing off the ground. I can handle the budget, the government filings, and the dance part. But for the management and worse, recruiting, I need her help. At least through my dance contacts, I have the curriculum, and Maria's and one other studio ready to donate blocks of time.

After another hour, she flicks her laptop closed and stands. "I have to run, but we've made good progress. Another few meetings and you should be in a good place to start getting teachers and students. I'll send you back my thoughts on the role descriptions."

"We still have to figure out how many students to start with." I scribble a note.

"Yeah, but that'll depend on how many instructors you can find, won't it?"

I stand and come around the table to hug her. "Have I said thank you yet?"

"Every time." She smiles against my shoulder.

"Thank you. You are so good at all of this."

"That's what sisters are for, silly." She squeezes me. "And now I'm off to help our brother."

"At least you get paid for that."

As she leaves, my phone dings with a text. It's Cam, as their season opener is on the road. He sends his usual greeting.

Cam

Whatcha doing?

Working on an idea I had.

A dance idea?

Yes, actually. But not for you.

<sad emoji with a tear>

It's not all about you.

<emoji with tears streaming down face>

> Sorry to burst your bubble.

I'm giggling out loud in my kitchen now. The man is cute even in text, damn him.

> Whatcha doing?

> Laying down for an hour before I go get ready for the game tonight. Will you be watching?

> Yes, up in the house with Greg as he has the satellite package that shows more games without commercials. Good luck.

> <thumbs up> K text me after. Gonna try to close my eyes for a few.

I put my phone down and go back to finish my notes from my meeting with Amy. A few minutes later, my phone dings again.

> BTW, I still want to know what the dance idea was. ;)

Damn him. How do I keep this casual when he craves family enough to stalk his step and half-sibling and wants to hear about my hopes and dreams?

* * * *

Cam was tired and disgruntled after their loss tonight, enough that I was able to divert the conversation when he asked me about the dance idea by promising to tell him in person after he's had some rest.

After the call, I lie awake curious if he has a post-loss routine or something to help him sleep. He'd told me at our first dinner that he only drinks one beer a night during hockey season.

I almost text him, picturing him in bed reliving the game. But if he did get to sleep, I'd hate to wake him.

Instead, I stare at the ceiling and relive it for him. Then I berate myself that this is supposed to be casual and have no business caring about his after-game routines. Finally, my brain stops circling enough to sleep and dream about strong thighs and bitable pecs.

The next day is a travel day for the team so we have only a brief text exchange, especially as he's getting pumped for his first regular season home game.

All three of us Donovans have been working toward tonight, the first game in our stadium, for a long time, and I'm nervous for both Greg and the team. I'll be in the owner's box with my siblings. Which I should not be sad about, dammit. It's the appropriate distance.

Travis is there, chatting up a couple investors Greg invited. What did I ever see in his fancy old-boy's-network suits? He's so cold, so contained. I doubt he could be passionate about anything other than money.

Sure, I work with money and get excited about investments and news and market trends. But that's my job. I don't associate my worth with it.

I smile. He annoys me a lot less now that I'm mellow from great sex with Cam. I'm so glad Travis and I never ended up in bed together, especially given his comments about Amy. He can fuck himself with his money for all I care. She and I have better things to do.

Travis is conceited enough that he'll undoubtedly think I'm smiling at him. I quickly grab a sparkling water and go down to the stadium seating to sit with Amy.

"You okay?"

"Sure." I smile.

"Huh. You really are. Your shoulders aren't up by your ears like they usually are around WhatsHisFace."

"I'm here for hockey."

The visitors are announced and skate out. Our fans are already invested in the Tornadoes and boo the other team, a division rival.

Before the announcer introduces the team, he thanks the crowd for their involvement in picking the team song. Saylet told me the social media poll had had great response rates, and then the team voted yesterday on the plane. This will be a nice change. They'd been playing the three in the poll on rotation for the six pre-season games.

Almost every seat is filled. And every last one has been bought, so I suspect a few of the corporate clients are just late. As they play each of the final contenders, the crowd cheers. Then on the Jumbotron fireworks show and a drumroll sounds as the announcer drawls, "And your Texas Tornadoes' team anthem is…" and trumpets start, leading into *Winner*.

Amy and I exchange grins. We love that a current song with an R&B vibe beat out the other classic rock options.

The sound technician turns the music up when the lyrics reference the stands, and the crowd roars. But when the word "ball" is rapped, she turns the volume all the way down and the announcer calls, "what are we passing?" and the crowd screams, "PUCK!"

I laugh. Ah, the power of social media.

The team is announced over the rest of the song, and the crowd is thunderous, cheering and stomping their feet. The better-known players we'd managed to snag as free agents gain extra noise from the crowd. The starters had been juggled a little based on pre-season performance, and will continue to be, but Cam's role as starting goalie remained fixed.

Between the enthusiastic adoption of the theme song and the crowd's energy, I have a new appreciation for how excited Greg has been about this whole venture for the past few years.

However, as play starts, I'm frustrated. What does Cam's game face look like? Is it anything like his "O" face? I want to see his fierce concentration on the action. I can't imagine having ten huge bodies in front of me and flashing blades and sticks, while trying to keep track of a three-inch rubber disk.

An opposing player takes a shot on goal. Jack might be in Cam's line of sight, I can't tell from here, but the puck gets by Jack, and Cam is toward the back of the crease. If he's slow to catch that, it'll be over the line and in the net. He pushes off with one skate to drop to a sliding butterfly and brings his glove down.

The goal light stays dark. The crowd is on its feet

roaring again and all of us in the box are frozen. Somewhere behind me I hear Travis droning on, but the rest of us are focused on what we're here for. The seconds until Cam opens his glove to display the puck are interminable.

Dammit. If I was down in the players' seats—or Greg's other set—I could have seen it happen.

I attended a few games of the Austin-based AHL team, the Texas Ice Spurs, as we sussed out their stadium. During high school, our family would attend UT games, as Greg was on the team for two seasons before admitting he'd never get regular ice time. I've never before cared where I sat, enjoyed the action from the various perspectives, even when Greg was on the ice.

So much for keeping things with Cam casual. I ignore that thought to pursue a solution for the more pressing problem of seeing the action. If I use Greg's ice level tickets, he'll not only ask why, but also might not always have them available as he uses them for whales he is wooing.

But Cam gets a pair. And I bet Maria, Lauren, and Nicole would be interested in joining me sometimes. Maybe Amy would come down with me, although she loves the food in the box.

Would it be weird to use his? Greg and others would notice, but perhaps I can play it off as one of the benefits of being his dance partner.

Ha, now I'm using the phrase friends with benefits. There, that should remind me that this needs to stay casual.

Chapter Seventeen

Cam

My first regular season game as a starting goalie in the NHL. My first home opener. My first time playing with these guys, some of the greatest in the league. Nerves have my heart thundering in my chest the whole afternoon through stretches, suiting up, and warmups.

I run through the bazillion things I want to keep track of. How the lines play together, any weaknesses I see from my perspective behind them, any tics or habits of the other team. The list goes on.

As I grind the ice around the goal to my preferred roughness, I breathe and take in the icy scent.

Tonight's ice smells different. Sure it's a new stadium but it seeps into my being with a different warmth. It wasn't like this for the last two pre-season games on the road. I flick a glance up at the owner's box. A tall, lithe figure stands against the balcony, backlit by the box's lights. The temperature of the stadium climbs another degree. The difference is Christina.

Smiling, I return to my routine, side lunging in place and staying warm while we get ready for faceoff.

As both teams skate into position, I get into my zone. My pulse slows, my focus narrows. Only the players, the puck, and the ice exist. We explode into action. The puck zings between sticks. Blades swoosh on the ice. Guys clash against the boards, the sound echoing in the arena. Meanwhile, I barely blink, ready in a micro-second should the puck be shot my way.

After the first shot on goal, an easy save, I call to Jack and Kyle that San Jose's right wing leaves an opening when he's receiving a pass too close to his skates. They nod and on the next loop in our territory they steal the puck away from him.

Calmer, I settle in to watch. The hits are a little harder, the puck is a little faster, but I've been training for more than a decade and I'm damned good. I've got this.

During the second intermission, I beat myself up about a stupid goal that whizzed through a cluster of players into the five hole a half second before I folded to my butterfly. But when the puck dropped for the third period, I was determined to be invincible. Goalies more than any other player have to be as cold as the ice. There's no time for distractions. Especially not doubt or anger.

We win handily with a final score of 3-1.

We're almost levitating off our skates on the path to the locker room, yelling and shoving in a frenzy of excess energy.

Coach needs three tries to quiet us. His speech is short and to the point. "You guys played fucking great hockey. We didn't look like an expansion team, we looked like an original six team. But this is only the second of eighty-two games, so keep doing what you're doing and try to pace your celebrating tonight."

Jack howls, sending us into a new fever pitch of

rowdiness.

Greg comes in, and we quiet for a minute. He keeps it short as well. All our muscles are clenched trying to contain our celebration. "Austin picked the perfect song for you guys. And you lived up to it. Well played. My sisters and I have been looking forward to this for more than two years. We've put together a fantastic team and organization for our hometown. I knew Austin was ready for the highest level of professional hockey. I wasn't sure they knew they were. We sold out, every seat filled. They love you already. You showed them—and me—your love tonight, too. And we're grateful. Congratulations, guys!"

We roar.

The unspoken plan at least for most of the team is to head to Chasers, and most of us shower and change in record time. A couple of the more seasoned guys are dragged in front of the press but the rest of us escape and head to our roped-off corner of the bar.

I check my phone as I close my locker. I've started thinking of Christina as Dancer to my Prancer, so I changed her name in my phone, which will also help keep our communications private.

Dancer

Congratulations! You looked great out there!

Surprised you could see me from those nosebleed seats.

Hey, I'll have you know they're supposed to be the best seats in the house.

I prefer to see the whites of their eyes.

LOL, that you do. What are you doing to celebrate?

Hmm, is that an invitation?

More a question. You know, with that thing? at the end?

Funny girl. The team needs to burn off a little adrenaline. We're headed to Chasers. Want to join us?

I don't think an owner showing up is going to vibe with the team's letting loose. Especially a woman...

She left that ellipse to torture me. Or else she's shy but thinking of a different sort of celebration. Damn, my cock has been hard since I saw her text. After a win, it doesn't take much anyway, which is why so many of the guys enjoy the puck bunny attention. I take the bait.

> I'd love to celebrate privately with you after a quick drink.

> Oh yeah? I was hoping you'd say that. Could you ride share to my house though, please? I don't want Greg to see your car here overnight.

My excitement flags, at least mentally. My cock doesn't care how the hell I get there and would prefer to skip the drink. I shove it aside. I'd agreed to casual and secret, and the benefits far outweigh the downsides. I reread the text. Sweet. She wants a full night. But if I go there now, I'll pound her, and especially given her comments the first time we had sex, I don't want to hurt her. I groan, but rein in my libido.

> It'll probably be an hour and a half. That ok?

Now I need to navigate a bar full of puck bunnies and randy teammates with a hard-on for an hour.

*   *   *   *

The estate is dark when the ride share pulls around the circular driveway. Christina believes her brother won't notice me staying the night, but they must have security cameras at the very least, if not onsite guards. Hopefully, they only report to Greg about intruders who weren't authorized for the gate.

I stride down the pathway, lit by short walkway lamps, and knock softly on her door before twisting the handle.

Leaning in, I see a dark living room and kitchen, with a nightlight in the hall and a low light coming from her bedroom. Placing my bag on the floor quietly, I toe off my shoes and pad down the short hall.

She's curled on a fancy half-backed, one-ended couch by her bedroom window. A chaise? I don't know what they're called and make a mental note to ask her later.

She's wearing a red filmy nightgown, bright against the dark gray velvet of the furniture. It gently holds her breasts then flows over her, probably to mid-thigh when she's standing, based on her stretched out bare leg. She has a lightweight fringed throw partially over one shoulder and her bent leg, one hand resting on a pool of blanket and one curled under her head.

I shuck my shirt, tossing it aside, and my socks. Clad only in jeans hiding boxer briefs, I glide forward, soundless on the thick carpet.

My shadow moves over her as I step in front of the bedside lamp, and her head twitches. Her eyes blink open and she starts.

I drop to my knees so she can see me. "Hey, it's me."

She smiles. "Hey, you."

When she starts to uncurl her legs as though to get up, I stop her. I slide my butt and a knee onto the odd couch to face her. I can't resist touching her nightwear, more negligee than actual sleeping apparel. I rub it between finger and thumb, and it's soft and lightweight. It's so sheer I can see my finger through it, which I guess is why they have three layers to the dress and why the bra cups are a different opaque shiny fabric. I want to turn on all the lights and have her pirouette for me.

She stretches her arms over her head, arching her back and drawing my eyes back to her breasts.

"Tell me you sleep in this." My voice is rusty with lust, as well as from shouting during the team celebrations.

"Sometimes, when I'm feeling sexy."

"You should always feel sexy, because you are." She snorts, but I double down. "It's true, it's not a line. So you felt sexy tonight, hmm?"

I trace the tops of her breasts along the line where the fabric meets her skin.

Her nipples harden and it's everything I can do to not

fall on her like a slavering animal. The win still thrums in my veins and heats my blood. "I don't know how slow I can be tonight. My first—"

"You don't need to be slow tonight. Seeing you play made me so hot I could barely wait the hour for you. Changing into this didn't help. The cool fabric sliding against me when I wanted the roughness and heat of your hands? Please, Cam." She puts her arms up to me and her words unleash my beast.

I lever to kneel between her legs on the chaise and slide the thin straps of her negligee down her arms. Her breasts pop free. I scoop one hand under her hips inside the fabric and lift her to tug the nightie to her knees. Setting her down, I bend one of her knees and she mimics the movement with her other leg, so I can draw off the garment and toss it in the direction of my t-shirt. I like the idea of our clothing being as intertwined as we're about to be.

She's biting her lip watching for what I'll do next with wide eyes in the dim light. I glance down. She's wearing the tiniest matching lace underwear.

"Pardon me for a moment," I mutter. "I need to see the back view."

Her laugh is low and throaty as I flip her over.

Yep, sure enough, it's a G-string. Palming her ass cheeks, I stroke then squeeze. She moans, then yelps when I snap the string against her tailbone, before dragging it down her legs. I flip her back, propping her against the slanted end of the couch again. Fuck me, she's still chewing on that lip.

"Only I get to gnaw on you tonight," I say, leaning in to kiss her thoroughly.

Her hands are at my waist, working the button and

fly of my jeans.

I'm too impatient to let her play so I stand to skim off my jeans and briefs together, grabbing a condom out of my wallet and returning to my kneeling position between her legs. With her reclining like this, half-sitting half-lying, I'll need to adjust something to fuck her. I grab her legs and lift them, scooting closer before lowering them to rest on my thighs. Now I have unfettered access to all of her. Craving another taste, I plant a hand by her hip and capture her lips again.

The kiss ratchets my desire higher, and I break it off to refocus on all her other delicious parts. No matter how fast my pulse races, Christina is normally tight, and I never want to hurt her. I run my fingers over her pussy lips, patting them a couple of times and eliciting a gasp from her. I part them and dip my middle finger inside testing her readiness. Dragging some wetness up, I circle her clit twice.

Her hand comes to grip my wrist.

I grin. "Ah, baby girl, it's cute you think you can stop me. If San Jose couldn't get by me, how are you going to?"

She snickers and lets go. "I wouldn't dream of trying. I was going to offer encouragement, but I see you don't need it. Just—hurry, please."

She thrusts her hips on the next circle. Her level of arousal clearly matches mine. The need, the craving, is almost uncontrollable. I spread her arousal around her opening, roll the condom on, and notch my cock against her.

She's watching me, and when her hands come to my hips to pull, I thrust halfway in. I retract a little, then thrust again. Then, as I have every time since she told me her concerns that first night, I check in. "All good?"

"Other than the fact that you're not moving, yes. I thought you weren't going to go slow?" she pants.

I laugh. "I'm not."

I lean forward, elbows locking me over her as she reclines on this weird couch that has turned out to be super convenient. And my hips power over hers, fast and furious.

She arches up. "Cam."

"What do you need?"

"I want to feel more of you." Her voice is throaty. "Scoot us down, please?"

Complying with her requests is one of my new favorite things, so I lift her and bring us down several inches. I spread my legs over the sides of the piece and sit, bringing her legs to the crook of my elbows and take them wide, hanging onto the sides of the furniture as I press forward to suck one of her furled nipples into my mouth.

"God, your goalie flexibility." Her eyes drift closed. She looks so innocent yet debauched lying with her hair spread around her, her lips and nipples rosy and wet from my mouth. A spurt of heat in my chest feels different than my normal lust.

Ignoring it, I succumb to her and my need for release. I don't have as much leverage in this position, so instead, I grab her hips and move both of us in counterpoint, our flesh slapping with the force of the movement.

She gasps and claws at my chest.

I pant through gritted teeth, "Tell me if it hurts. Or, please, tell me you're close."

"I'm close."

"Thank God." The couch thing moves an inch and I

readjust my feet. I can't stand it anymore and I raise my torso. Holding her still to thrust against with one hand on her hip, my other goes to thumb her clit because there is no holding back this maelstrom of an explosion I'm edging toward.

She cries out. Her body goes rigid, and everything under my hands vibrates. First her clit, then her whole pussy, inside and out, and her belly quivers next to my other thumb.

I jackhammer into her, chasing my own pleasure. My world whites out as I shoot my load, losing my rhythm but still making small thrusts for a long moment. Finally, I release her so I can support myself on my arms, no longer able to sit upright.

Chapter Eighteen

Christina

I guess my doctor was right. The combination of the surgery and having the right partner results in zero pain and maximum pleasure.

I never thought I would enjoy that hard a pounding. I snicker internally, knowing some of my friends would find our sexcapades tame. But holy hell that was the hottest thing I've experienced, waking up to a sex god who ensures my pleasure even when I can tell how amped he is by the hard line of his jaw.

After a moment for us both to catch our breath, Cam slides out of me and stands to straddle the chaise. Those quads, raising him up from a wide squat like it was nothing.

I sigh, and he glances at me. I wave him off, "Just enjoying the view. Pardon me, I need to see the back view."

He throws back his head and laughs at me parroting his words back to him. Swinging a leg over the chaise longue, he heads to the bathroom to clean up.

"Someday I want to bounce a quarter off that ass, for

real," I mutter as his glutes flex with each step. My mouth is dry with lust—I'm pretty sure all the moisture in my body is between my legs—and I wonder if he'd be up for another round. The man just played sixty minutes of hockey at the highest professional level and then pounded me for my pleasure, and I'm hoping for more? I need to stop being a greedy slut and let him rest, even if he is twenty-four and could rise to the challenge.

I wander toward the bathroom as he emerges, wrapping the soft throw around me in lieu of clothes. After a quick cleanup, I redon the red baby doll and underwear. When I turn, he's standing awkwardly halfway between the bed and his clothes.

"I wasn't sure what you wanted," he half asks.

I smile and offer him the choice. "I told you earlier I didn't want Greg to see your car overnight. But if you want to sleep in your own bed, especially after the game and all, I understand."

Leaving the decision to him, I crawl into my side of the bed. I have one knee down and am turning to plant my butt when the bed bounces hard, and he's there on his back grinning at me.

"Yes, please."

I shake my head and laugh at his antics. "Are you still wound up or are you going to be able to sleep?"

"I dunno. I've never done any of this before. If not, how do you feel about your sleep being interrupted for round two, or should I slip out if that happens?"

He needs to stop being so damned cute and sweet already. My heart won't be able to take it. Falling in love with him cannot be part of the equation. Ever.

Still smiling, I say, "Thank you for asking. I'm sure you can convince me, should the need arise." I draw out the last word with a grin. "I do have a question for you, since you don't seem like you're about to crash."

He scoots the covers out from under where he threw himself then tugs on my arm. "Sure, but come down here to ask it. I need to hold you."

Geez. More cuteness. I throw my hair up in a scrunchie so neither of us gets smothered by it in our sleep and arrange myself facing him on my side. That crook of his arm is as enticing as a pillow, but I want to see him to have this conversation.

"What's your question?" he asks, brushing a loose hair behind my ear.

"Could we get away with me using your tickets without arousing suspicion?" A grin starts to bloom on his face as I continue. "Would people believe you offered it to me as your dance partner, or be suspicious because I'm not using the owners' lower level seats?"

"Aw, you want to sit closer to me. How sweet," he teases.

"Ha ha. I want to sit closer to the action." I can't admit that he's right, it's too intimate, not at all casual. Anyway, I'm focused on the secrecy aspect. "Seriously, though, what are your thoughts?"

"It should be fine. But why *don't* you want to use your brother's?"

Thankfully, I anticipated this question. In bed with Cam is not the time to discuss Travis. "Because he likes to use them for sponsors and big wigs, and I don't want to have to schmooze. The whole point of being so close to the ice is to watch the game." To watch him.

"Ah, I getcha." He shrugs the shoulder he's not lying on. "Sure, I'll let the Ops team know."

"Of course, if you want them for anyone else ever,

just tell me."

"Who else would come? My teammates from Indiana are all on tight budgets, although a couple are coming to our games when we're on the road. And I don't know anyone here outside of the team."

His voice sounds sad, as though he might be thinking of his half-siblings, but I don't press. He's already had a long night, and now I've inadvertently reminded him that he has very few people to celebrate this huge career step with. Instead, I snuggle closer and enjoy his magnificent body pressed against mine as we fall asleep.

Cam wakes me at dawn with his hands roaming my body over the nightie. His cock pokes my butt as he spoons me, and I shimmy against him.

I can't tell him this, but I've only spent the night with a man a handful of times and that was years ago, before my endo diagnosis. This is new and thrilling, yet strangely comfortable because it's him.

My hip shake gives me away, and his caresses grow bolder. He skims the strap he can reach down my arm and pinches my nipple gently, then harder. He nuzzles behind my ear and asks again, "You cool with this?"

"This is delicious and totally okay, but you're a furnace. It's hard to be cool."

His shoulders shake behind me with a silent chuckle while his tongue traces a path from my neck along my shoulder.

I shiver, and reach behind me, grabbing his hip to grind myself harder against him.

I've never had morning sex, as there were always dance practices to get to, and later classes. Since the surgery, I've been too afraid to brave any sex, but perhaps I should have. My body feels more relaxed, either from sleep or the magnificent orgasm last night.

He kisses down my spine, pressing me forward to lie on my belly with one leg bent. When he helps himself to a quick bite of my ass cheek, I yelp and say, "If you need sustenance, I'll make breakfast."

"You *are* breakfast." His kisses trailing back along my spine to my neck reinforce his words, as does his nip of my neck tendon.

Then he freezes. "Fuck."

I try to roll to face him, but his arm holds me in place across the top of my ass.

"Don't move for a second. I need a minute to…I don't have another condom."

"Oh." My tone holds all the same disappointment his does. I consider what I know of him and the team policies and say slowly, "You got tested for the team. I haven't been with anyone in years and have a clean bill of health, and I'm on birth control."

At his silence, I try to figure out what's going through his mind. He or someone he knows has probably had a puck bunny or three say whatever he wanted to hear to claim him as a conquest. Or worse, there are horror stories of pinpricks in condoms and suing for parental support. My shoulders sag. "It's—"

"Yes, please." His voice is strangled. Cam releases me and fumbles against my butt.

"Are you sure? Can I turn over? Your voice sounds funny."

"I'm holding my dick to avoid jumping you right now. The thought of you bareback…Fuck, Chris."

"Oh." My cheek presses against the pillow as I smile in satisfaction.

He slaps my butt cheek with a snort of laughter and

rolls into me again. "I'm sure. Now, where were we?"

After another round, we manage to sneak him out of the house to the driveway. Just as I'm opening my front door, Greg opens the back door of the big house and calls over, "Have you eaten, or do you want to grab breakfast with me?"

I gulp. His timing is close enough I wonder if he saw me with Cam out front.

He doesn't bring it up and I can't ask, so I presume my secret is safe for now. But the whole encounter reinforces the risks to Cam in this short-term affair, to say nothing of the risks to my heart.

Chapter Nineteen

Cam

I roll up to the house after Jack has left, sprinting through to change and grab clothes for after practice.

Gym bag in hand, I head to the rink.

Jack greets me as I enter the locker room and says at top volume, "How was she?" I swear, he speaks at volume eleven on purpose all the damn time.

The guys' heads whip around. "What? Prancer got some last night?"

"For sure he didn't come home." Jack is laughing.

I glare at him. "Wow. I'd say I'll remember this for when you do something stupid, roommate, but as that's a daily occurrence, I won't bother."

"Come on, Prancer. Share. Some of us didn't get lucky, aside from our win," Boulanger calls out.

"First, I'm sure Jack did. He's deflecting. Second, if any of you didn't, it's by choice. I was at Chaser's with you, and there were unlimited options."

"Did you grab a bunny then?" Kyle asks.

I ignore them and change.

Behind me, someone whistles. "Jack, have you

checked his phone? Maybe he's on Tinder."

Another says, "Why do you guys assume it was just one? Prancer here's so flexible, he could handle at least two."

I roll my eyes.

"Come on, Prancer." Boulanger is almost whining. "Give us something. Blonde? Brunette? Wait, redhead! That'd be hot. Did the carpet match the curtains?"

"Shut the fuck up, Bakery Boy." No one gets to talk smack about Christina even if they don't know it's her. He wants to be derogatory toward women, I'll make sure he gets a new nickname based on his name. Fed up, I grab my skates and leave. I'll put them on rinkside after I do some preliminary stretches. As I'm exiting, I hear du Près say, "Eh, ferme ta gueule, Boulanger. Laisse-le." I've played with enough French-Canadians to know when someone is told to shut the fuck up and drop it. My respect for Mattie climbs up a notch. He and I are solid.

In goalie practice, Murphy is showing rapid improvement. That both scares and relieves me. While I don't want a threat to my starting role, the team needs to be in safe hands for the games I don't play.

The coaches then have us in net for more drills with the offensive lines.

Back in the locker room, Coach Steele breaks down what he saw. "Petrovsky, Dunbar, Gauthier. Work on your player awareness. Know where your teammates are to pass to them, and know where the enemy is in case he's sneaking up behind you. Same thing to the third line. We'll work on that tomorrow. Hill, Murphy, Wayman, I need a full day with you for the lines to practice shooting on you. I've already cleared it with Coach Murray."

The next morning as planned, we're on the ice with

the second and third lines. A goalie sees everything, and his job is to warn his teammates about on-ice threats as well as ensure they help him protect the goal. Coach's words yesterday emphasized that part of my job. So when the other team is coming at me, I call, "Behind," or "Look for the pass."

Their responses get steadily more acerbic and a few of them start getting sloppier with passes and shots, rather than cleaner.

Finally, Petrovsky skates right up to me so we're nearly touching when I straighten out of my crouch. He points to the coaches. "See them, Prancer? *They* are the coaches. See this?—" he points to the goal—"This is the goal. You are the goalie. Not a coach. Stay the fuck out of my business."

He breaks his stick over the crossbar, and tosses it at my feet, then storms off the ice.

Shit. What the hell kind of goalie has he played with in the past? We're a new team, but we still need to help each other, and my words may have been critical, but we're all on the same side for the actual games.

We're dismissed for a lunch break. The locker room is quiet and most guys opt to eat onsite. I sort of hope for Saint to step in and say something as captain to clear up my confusion, whether he backs me up or tells me to shut up. When he doesn't, I shower quickly and run out for a smoothie. I need space to try to get my head on straight, and they need a cool-down period.

I trust every single one of them to do their best work out there, to review game tape, and then to improve their best. But they don't seem to trust me. We're such a new team, I guess I understand. It's going to kill me to bite my tongue and not point out improvements that would make us a better team, but I guess that's what I need to do.

I'm trying not to wallow. Hockey has been my go-to family since my mother died. Without this team around me, I'd be lost. I flashback to being in my house with my father, then imagine Petrovsky speaking in Czech to me. I'm an island, alone in the ocean of this new world.

Goalies are always a little separate from the other players. But every single practice and game has felt like a team sport, with every player contributing their unique skill set.

I need this game, this job. And now, with Christina in the mix, and Jack and a few friendships I've started to build with players, I want this city. As I pull into the player parking area, I'm determined to do what I need to in order to remain a part of the team. I'll back off, stay quiet, and simply play the net as Petrovsky asked.

Back in the locker room, Saint checks in with me. "You good?"

I lift my chin. "Yeah. Thanks."

He wisely chooses not to use Petrovsky's nickname of "Quasi" that I caused. "Petrovsky?"

"Fine," he grumbles.

"Then let's play."

On the ice, I practically chew a hole through my mouthguard staying quiet. Petrovsky glares at me every time he's in blue paint. His shots on goal might be harder and faster than during games. I manage to avoid flinching when they hit my pads.

He still doesn't get one past me, though, nor do any of the second and third line players. There's some satisfaction to that, until I question whether they'll stay angry at me because of it. Hopefully the road trip will improve camaraderie.

Chapter Twenty

Christina

We have one more dance practice before Cam leaves for a week-long road trip tomorrow on a sweep of the eastern half of the Midwest, including Pittsburgh, Columbus, and Detroit. All are seasoned teams, and I suspect our Tornadoes are going to struggle against them as the guys are still learning to read each other.

Cam has been stressed after practice the past couple of days which is also affecting his dancing. He's strung so tight, his muscles are tighter and his spins are faster.

I chose songs with faster beats. Competition ballroom is performed to music with 98 to 120 beats per minute, depending on the dance style. But the reality dance show competitions are often performed to music with significantly higher speeds, over 140 BPM.

I plan on using a faster song for our second dance anyway, so I focus on that this week, allowing him to get some of his angst out on the hardwood and loosen his muscles up.

The last thing he or the team needs is for the starting goalie to have a groin pull this early in the season. He's done so well that Murphy only started two pre-season games and none since the regular season started.

Given the road trip, I'm hoping for more than dancing in this last practice so we're meeting at my house. A knock sounds before he enters, as we've agreed. He smiles when he sees me in the kitchen tidying and places a bag with the team logo on the bar to come kiss me. "Hey, Dancer."

I beam. I love that he's given me a nickname.

"I brought you something."

"Oh yeah?" I cock my head. He knows I can get team merch any time.

He goes back around the island and gestures to the bag, placing his hands on the counter, nearly vibrating with expectancy.

I tug it closer and peer inside, finding the heavy polyester of a jersey in a deep purple, our home color. Tugging it out, I hold it up, surprised to see "25" on it.

He'd told me he chose number twenty-five for several reasons. He'd been in Vegas on Spring Break when he saw a Vancouver goalie shutout. The guy's number was 25, which is unusual for a goalie; they often choose numbers thirty or higher. Then he'd decided twenty-five was the age by which he'd have a seven-figure savings account, which still makes me smile and caused me to change his ringtone to *Million Dollar Baby*. He is well on track for that—especially if he'd let me direct him on investing a bit more.

More importantly, I never knew marketing tagged Cam as a popular enough player to order jerseys with his name and number. This is huge. I flip it around. Sure enough, "Hill" is in large white letters across the shoulders. "Cam!"

His grin is so wide I swear it must hurt his face. He deserves this. Greg's team would only order this based on a combination of popularity and statistics. And his stats have been excellent so far.

"Congratulations!" I lean in to kiss him. "I'm surprised you didn't wear it here."

He shakes his head. "No, this is yours. I figured you could wear it to the games since you'll be in my seats."

My smile fades. We're already pushing the envelope by me sitting there. I can't wear his name on me. That would announce to the world that we're together. Only lovers and families wear named jerseys in the players' boxes.

When I say that to him, he scoffs. "Half the damn crowd is in Buzz's number."

"They aren't in players' seats."

"No, but who is? *Friends*"—he emphasizes the word—"and family. So it makes sense that they're the only people you'd see in the player's jersey. If I had a non-hockey guy friend here who came to the games, he'd wear it without worrying about people thinking we were lovers."

"I really love the gift. But I can't play favorites as an owner, just as Greg couldn't pick a player's jersey and wear it. I'm sorry, Cam."

He grimaces and turns toward the over-sink window, leaning his hands on the counter edge. "I don't understand why you're drawing this arbitrary line. You'll sit in my seats but won't wear my jersey."

"It's more…," I search for the right word. "Personal."

"My hands will be on you in personal places, in public, when we dance. What's a jersey?"

I tilt my head, surprised at the vehemence of his reaction. "I thought we agreed this would be casual as well as private? Why are you upset? It's not like we're in a relationship, planning marriage and kids."

He stiffens and turns his head to look at me. "What if we were? Would you wear it then?"

Is he thinking along those lines? I thought he had as much as risk as me, if not more. Dammit, I was hoping by keeping it casual and short-lived I wouldn't need to have the conversation about children. Although the more time I spend with him, the harder it'll be to move on after the ball. "We aren't."

He starts to say something, but I cut him off, needing to make this part clear. "And Cam, we won't be. This ends at the Holiday Ball. I don't plan to have children."

This shouldn't be a big deal as we've both agreed to the secret and casual thing. It feels big, though. I bite my lip waiting for his reaction.

"Wait, what?" He frowns.

I nod. "You heard me. This needs to remain secret and casual. I'm sorry I can't wear your jersey. I respect your frustration. And I *am* excited for you. You'll have a ton of women lining up to wear these." And doesn't that kill me to say or think about.

He's still staring at me in shock. Shit. I knew this was too good to be true.

Finally he asks, "How did I not know this?"

I shrug. "It never came up."

"Right. Secret and casual."

Ugh. It should be our mantra. I hate hearing it as much as he clearly hates saying it.

He waves a hand at the jersey. "Wear it to sleep in or use it to wash your car. I don't care. Oh, but of course you don't wash your own car, do you, Princess?"

I was enjoying the idea of sleeping with his name on me but he went and turned vicious. "Hey. That's not fair. I thanked you for the gift. I'm sorry I can't live up to your expectations. You have no right to be mean."

He sighs and drops his head, leaning back against the counter. "Sorry. Give me a minute."

I stay quiet, arms wrapped around my middle. That last shot hurt. I've never thrown my money in his face, and he'll make close to a million dollars this season so it's not like we live on completely different planes.

He straightens and comes over to me, putting a finger under my chin to bring my eyes to his. "I'm sorry. Really. And yeah, based on my reaction now, I realize that part of my desire to see you in my jersey was because I want to publicly declare you as mine. I'm in your bed. Hell, I'm in *you*. And I want to see me on you when I'm playing. But you're right—"

Wow. I can't remember another boyfriend admitting to being wrong, even the few times I'd received an apology. Much less one who had figured that out with a few minutes of introspection. If I hadn't seen Cam's records, I wouldn't believe he was only twenty-four. For that matter, his interest in marriage and children and his considerate nature demonstrate a maturity beyond his years.

"This can't be long term. We agreed this would be secret. So while I stand by my other arguments, I understand why you don't want to risk it."

He's being solicitous of my feelings even when we disagree, but I still flinch again at his reference of an end date. Which isn't at all fair to him when I insisted on it, but there it is.

Oh shit. I've been unconsciously evaluating the possibility of a real relationship. Dammit, I'm half in love with him. Of course, I figure this out in the same conversation I learn that he wants children. My luck with men sucks.

"Am I forgiven? Please?" he cajoles.

Still reeling from my self-discovery, I need a moment to gather myself. Slanting him a teasing look, I reply, "Mostly. I'll have to come up with an act of contrition later. In the meantime, we should get some dance practice in before your road trip."

"Lead on," he says with a sweep of his arm toward the hall.

I grab the bag and jersey and take them to my bedroom before joining him to warm up in the dance room.

* * * *

I hold it together until the next morning when Cam leaves for his road trip, then call Maria. When she doesn't answer, I check her schedule and realize she's working at the coffee shop. Lauren and Nicole will be at their offices or on their way.

I send a group text.

Nicole

Lauren

Woohoo!

Maria

<emoji with party hat and horn>

The subject of kids came up indirectly and he was really thrown when I said I don't plan to have any. He definitely wants them.

Maria

So? <cowboy emoji>

Yeah, yeah, she said to treat him as a cowboy to ride and nothing more, but that's easier said than done. He's so damned nice.

Lauren

How much did you talk about it? I mean, he's 24. He's probably not looking for them right now. You can still have fun.

Nicole

Yeah, Maria's advice was to use him for an orgasm or four, so unless you've already had four…

<blushing emoji>

Nicole

Congratulations! Go you!

Maria

You weren't supposed to fall for him. But your concern seems beyond a casual fling. So I'd repeat our theme of the last GNO - communication is key.

Lauren

What she said.

I don't want to put his career at risk. If this doesn't work out, he has far more to lose.

Nicole

> He's 24, not 4. Let him worry about that. And you can talk about that, too.

Maria

> Or just ride that ride until you can't and do your best to keep it secret and casual.

> Ok, I'll think about it. Thanks, y'all.

They all send me hug emojis. We'll figure the rest out at the next girls' night, but it helps just to vent. I can't decide if I want to talk to Cam about it or leave it be. After all, he repeated the idea of short-lived and secret. I need to guard my heart as best I can and enjoy this while it lasts.

Chapter Twenty-One

Cam

Every minute I'm not on the ice, I'm obsessing over Christina's declaration at our last practice session or the dysfunctional relationship I have with the second line.

On the surface, everything is fine.

I may text Chris a little less or take a little longer to respond to her texts, but I don't go dark on her. This isn't her fault. She's right, we'd only ever discussed this as a fling.

It's not her fault that simply snogging with her is better than sex with anyone else, or that her dancer's body can turn me on no matter what she's doing, to say nothing of her analytical brain.

I should be relieved. This should make it easier to walk away, which I need to do for my career. The last thing I want is for anyone to say my next contract wasn't based on merit. And I can only imagine the complications in a trade to another team with an attractive woman as part of the ownership or management team. I can almost write the additional clause in my contract.

Like with Christina, Petrovsky and his brethren still call to me when play requires it. But there's no chirping, no friendly locker room chat. We only end up eating together when Jack or du Près or Buzz invites both them and me. I've kept my own counsel since that practice, but they haven't forgotten or forgiven, which doesn't bode well for our cohesiveness as a team.

The jersey and kids debacle precluded an opportunity to talk out my on-ice woes with Christina. I'd broken the owner/player wall a couple times about small stuff and she'd been a good sounding board, so I would have liked to get her thoughts on this issue with Petrovsky. Instead, I'm strung tight, wondering if I'll fit in with the team, if the coaches will notice something is amiss, or if any of it will affect my play.

And it may have. We've struggled on this road trip so far. Enough that I'm sweating my starting position.

I swear Pittsburgh fans won the first away game as much as the team itself did. Although the Pioneers were on fire that night. The puck seemed to move faster than ever. The team constantly zigzagged it across the ice. Twice that zigzagging got past our D-men and me. I was so frustrated by the third period I wanted to rip the net apart, but the key to not allowing any more goals is to find one's Zen. So, for the most part, I did.

Our team became desperate to score and kept taking wild shots and creating more turnovers. I bit my tongue, but by the second intermission, I couldn't stop myself. If they're going to spend this much time at my end of the ice, they were going to get my opinion. "Keep that fucking puck out of my goddamn zone!"

"We're not crocheting out here, asshole!" Petrovsky muttered as he swept by me.

That exchange plus the loss had my stomach in knots, which was only exacerbated when Coach announced Murphy would have the net tonight. I couldn't help but wonder if one of the players talked to Coach about the friction between the second line and me.

Coach said it was that he didn't want me playing three in a row on the road. He wanted me rested for tomorrow's game in Detroit, against one of the fiercest teams in the league, the Michigan Cougars, on their home ice. I tried to take his statements at face value. Murphy does need ice time, and an easier opponent is the best opportunity for him to continue to grow in the NHL.

So here I sit on the bench. The Ohio Hammerheads' last two seasons were lackluster. If we could get our act together, they are eminently beatable. And would bolster our confidence going into the Michigan game.

None of us can get out of our heads, however. Too many passes are too hard, too fast, misplaced, or just plain missed. The stress of witnessing the mess and seeing Dan allow four goals to our one is as bad as if I had played and done the same.

The locker room is quiet. A few players are talking quietly about the game here and there, but most of us are thinking about errors made on the ice, or the future of the team, or both.

Coach comes in. We turn to face him, and he stands tall, taking time to look each of us in the eyes before saying, "The answer is no. To those of you wondering if you made a mistake coming to this team, starting from scratch. The answer is no. To those fuckers blaming others for tonight's loss. That answer is also no. There isn't a single Tornado out there who didn't make some shitty mistakes. Notice I say mistakes, plural. I see that you're all pretty introspective—for a bunch of fucking meatheads who have had too many pucks to the head." A few guys manage to chuckle, despite the doldrums we're all in. "That's good. Stick with that. Just make sure you're figuring out what *you* can do better. Tomorrow, we're going to examine the game tape and talk about it. Tonight, just think about it."

Heads are nodding, including mine.

"Then? After tomorrow?" he says. "We're going to take what we've learned and put it into practice and come back stronger than ever against those Cougars. I don't care how many Stanley Cups they have. They've also been around nearly a century." He raises his voice to a growl to finish, "We don't need that long to get to a Cup, do we?"

The guys perk up, saying, "No."

"I didn't hear you!"

We all stand and shout, "No!"

Re-energized, I head for the shower.

Saint swings into step with me. "Do you know what you did wrong?"

"I didn't play."

"So?"

"Okay, then, before tonight? I think so. I let myself get distracted."

"It's more than that, Prancer. Think beyond the ice." With that, he peels off to talk to another player coming our way, taking his role of team captain seriously.

Ugh, now I'm confused and depressed again.

I've hung out with every member of the team. Even before some guys were sent to our AHL affiliate, I was an equal opportunity socializer. Sure Jack and I have grown close, despite our yin and yang personalities.

Between him being one of my primary go-tos on the ice and living together, it was inevitable. But we both agreed that team bonding was essential, which was why we've had a couple more poolside cookouts at our little rental house.

On the ice, I ruffled a few feathers, but that's my job as goalie. I've got the best seat in the house—I'd argue better even than the coaches'—to see our strengths and weaknesses.

Just because I've played less than a dozen games at this level doesn't mean I don't know my shit.

Regardless, their snapbacks made it clear my voice wasn't welcome, and I've kept my mouth shut since then. So how did my more recent off-ice behavior have anything to do with our loss tonight?

* * * *

Hours of game tape later and a short flight to Detroit, we're on the ice again. My fear of the Cougars' longstanding reign as one of the best teams in the league wars with cautious hope as we bolster each other's courage in our brief morning skate. But those fears are still echoed in my teammates' faces.

To go home with three back-to-back losses always makes players nervous about the next road trip, which will in turn affect team performance. We could really use a win to reset our outlook.

It's not fatalism to say it seems unlikely, but that doesn't mean we can't play a fantastic game of hockey.

Saint echoes my thoughts. "Let's shake off the last few days and just play great hockey like we know we can."

Everyone cheers and we're out on the ice for

warmups. The NHL ice is always miked during warmups so we keep quiet in case our nerves come out on national TV.

Christina texted that she'd be watching tonight and "around" tomorrow night if I wanted to swing by when we land. I grin in anticipation wondering if she can see my face. I laugh at myself. I'm sure she has better things to do than watch hockey warmups a half hour before the puck drops.

Back in the locker room, Coach gives us another pep talk. I skate to my post and get into the zone chocking the ice and stretching my legs. My focus drills into the three-inch rubber disk. Let's do this.

Sixty game minutes later, we've lost. Michigan fans are beasts, yelling and trying to break our concentration, not allowing us to communicate much during play. More than that, though, the Cougars outplayed us. The biggest advantage of an older team—both members and team history—is the cohesiveness that we're still chasing.

On a positive note, we had way less nerves and tallied one goal, celebrating like we'd just won the Cup for a minute before the ref whistle blew for a faceoff.

I let in two goals. But that was out of what seemed like a hundred shots on goal. The Cougars are freaking fast, their sticks almost blurred in slapshots and passes. Most of their team has played together for the last several years, including their entire first line. They can read each other's slightest body language. Our team is still learning that, on and off the ice.

Coach says as much after the game, insisting that we played strong and we should be proud, loss aside. Saint adds, "We did what we set out to do. We played great hockey. We'll get them next time on our ice."

We change and head back to the hotel in our suits, changing again to hang in the hotel lounge to wind down after the game. Almost a week of being on the road has mellowed some of the players, even the player players. However, some are undeterred. Jack and a few others stand at the bar instead of sitting with us, emanating puck bunny magnetic waves.

Buzz catches my eye and does a chin lift toward them. "Aren't they around your age?"

I look over at Jack's entourage. There are a couple twenty-year-olds from Canada that came up from the junior leagues. I frown. They can't drink legally in the US, and there's a bigger gap in our ages than there is between Buzz and me. Jack and Buzz are the same age, only two years ahead of me. I answer, "No more so than you."

"Fair. Sometimes guys like them make me feel ancient."

Saint joins us, grumbling with a frown, "Who's ancient?"

"Well, now that you remind us…," Buzz plays along as though we've been talking about our captain.

"You know, I looked it up." My words come slowly. I don't want to piss anyone off, but I'm feeling a little defensive after his comments the other night. "This is a young team. The average age of our team is twenty-six, versus closer to twenty-eight. Our first line is younger. And the average age of team captains in the NHL is thirty-one."

"Yeah." Saint nods. "Coach said Mr. Donovan's vision was to aim young and have the team grow together, so we get stronger every year."

"Then what's the issue with me pointing out things

that I see can be improved, when I'm uniquely situated to do just that?"

"Ah," Saint says with a sigh, sitting back. "That's where you were going. You still haven't figured it out."

"I want this team to be the best it can be. Scratch that, the best, period. And the way I learned it, part of a goalie's training is to help fill holes when he sees them."

Saint sips his beer and nods. "I appreciate your enthusiasm, young Prancer."

I nearly snarl at him. "I thought we established that I'm not all that young, particularly on this team."

"Okay, okay, sorry. Here's the thing." He turns and nods at du Près, asking me, "What do you know of him, beyond the profile on the team's website?"

"Uh…he only drinks Canadian whisky, preferably Found North. His family is coming in for the next game. He left a girlfriend in Florida."

"Right. How about Scott?"

"He's a hound dog, he was happy to come here because he likes warm weather almost as much as he likes being on the ice, and um…he has an older sister who's an attorney."

He nods. "What about me?"

"You married your college sweetheart several years ago, you hate corn, and like me, you only have one drink a night during the season."

He turns to Buzz. "You've hung out with Prancer quite a bit. What do you know about him?"

I retract my head at his question, not expecting that turn. I thought he was quizzing me on bonding with the team and that I'd been doing well.

"He's from Indiana. He's as stretchy as Gumby and uses ballroom dancing and yoga to maintain that. And he eats super healthy." Buzz shrugs, not able to think of anything else.

"No one on the team knows anything about your family, your dating history, or even where you last went on vacation. You hold yourself apart. If you're committed to this team, then treat us like it. Hockey teams are families. We don't always get along with each other, but we always have each other's back, and we trust each other. Part of trusting is opening yourself up. But you haven't done that, so you haven't earned the right to criticize, even in private. Besides which, sometimes it's not what you say, it's how you say it. Be careful with new relationships, as you would with a girl. Or guy. See, I don't know if you're gay or straight," he says with a smile.

"Straight as a ruler, but totally cool with whatever. I've had teammates who were gay. As for the rest"—I sigh. It's hard to trust others, but regardless, he's right. I have to earn *their* trust, even if it means being vulnerable. "I'll work on it. Trust is a slow thing for me on the personal side. But I trust everyone here the second skates get laced up."

"It has to go beyond that."

"I'll try." The idea of opening myself up to more rejection or scorn is exhausting, particularly after this grueling road trip. I stand. "Thank you, Cap. I hear you. I'm tired, though, so I'd prefer to not boil this particular ocean tonight. I'm gonna head up."

He nods and takes his last sip of beer. "I'm right behind you."

I wave to Jack on my way by and pull out my phone as I stride to the elevators.

You up?

Chapter Twenty-Two

Christina

One more game, one more night, and one more day before Cam is home. All the color leached out of my world when the team plane took off, despite the knowledge that we want different things long-term.

The girls tried to cheer me up at our last happy hour, pointing out older men and talking about planning something for New Year's Eve. I told them Cam and I agreed to end things after the Holiday Ball in December.

I didn't tell them about the jersey argument. They'd side with Cam, and I'm not up to fighting them all. I've worn it every night to sleep. That polyester makes me feel sexier than any of my fancy lace and silk nightwear, to the point where I've had to masturbate on the nights we FaceTime. Not on the call, obviously, especially because he shares a hotel room and has to sneak in calls when Jack is in the shower or down at the bar. But afterward, there was no sleep without relief, with his smiling face so fresh in my mind.

Tonight's game was on ESPN, so I told Greg I was tired and wanted to view the game from my cottage rather than going up to the big house. Originally he'd planned to attend all the games everywhere, excited at watching his vision develop. But there's still some hiring and setup to do, as evidenced by the additional jerseys being added to the store, and I think he mentioned one food vendor had pulled out. So he hadn't been able to join them on this road trip. Some of the growing pains of an expansion team are better handled here in person with his staff, rather than via phone or videoconference in between flights and games.

I made a chef's salad so I could eat during commercials without worrying about it getting cold, but it didn't matter. I ended up eating less than half because I was on the edge of my seat for the whole game.

Our guys were shut out this trip – not a single win. However, this last game felt different than the first two. Our Tornadoes fought hard and played well. They looked more in tune with one another, like the kinks are being worked out.

I linger after the game reading in bed, one eye on the phone. I'd hear it buzz, but I check it every few minutes anyway. A few times, my fingers hover over the screen and I debate whether to send a message or not. This is supposed to be casual though, and he'll be home tomorrow.

Normally, I'd go over a new dance routine to settle my brain for the night, but picturing him dancing with me is not helping me relax.

Finally, the phone buzzes with a text.

Cam

> You up?

> Yes. You doing ok? That was a tough game, but you guys played really well.

> Yeah, Coach said the same. We were more cohesive tonight. Other guys just outplayed us <shrug emoji>

> ...

> ... Saint is on me about speaking up when I see things that can be fixed

I can tell even through text that he's down. Who wouldn't be after three losses in a row? I'm not sure how to cheer him up, but I'll try. I snap a picture of me in his jersey in bed and send it.

> Oh wow. You look good in my number

I do. He'll be back by dinnertime according to the team schedule that gets sent to all the back office. When I reissue my text invitation, he offers to pick up tacos for us. We are back on track.

* * * *

Cam brings tacos from my favorite spot, even though it's out of his way and his favorite is closer. I dismiss my unparalleled excitement at seeing him by telling myself I'm taking notes for when and if I do want a long-term relationship with someone not focused on having a family.

When he steps inside and draws me close, I feel like I'm home. His shower gel scent with a hint of starch from the dress shirt he's still wearing is better than any expensive cologne. His height, broad shoulders, and long arms enfold me in the sexiest cocoon possible.

I've tried to gain perspective on this relationship being short-lived while he was on the road but I failed. Despite multiple stern lectures to myself to not get emotionally involved, ending this supposedly casual relationship will hurt like nothing ever has.

Trying to regain my balance, I focus on dance. "Let's dance first and eat after so we don't have to wait to digest, unless you're starving?"

"I'm good." He nods. "That way we don't go too late. I have an early skate tomorrow."

He quickly changes into a dance outfit he left here.

Lifts are normally all about the woman's flexibility and the man's strength. But given his extreme flexibility and the fact that he has the higher profile as a player, I want to highlight him as much or more than me. It should garner more donations for the charity, which will make Amy happy, but it'll also help cement his reputation with the fans. My hope is that if he's a fan favorite, it'll smooth things with his team members. He's already popular, or they wouldn't have stocked jerseys with his name on them in the team store.

I try a few more songs that are faster paced than the first we've been practicing. The lift I want to try is an assisted cartwheel and momentum will help, as it's really two lifts. He'll hold both of my forearms, and twist me through the frame of his bent intertwined arms. Then, trickier will be him cartwheeling with my assistance. He'll have to have one hand on the floor as there's no way I can hold his weight even for a minute.

For this we're West Coast swinging, as it's much less structured and we can play around with it, creating a greater contrast to the slower, more formal rumba. We'll develop the routine together, based on a series of ad hoc steps and what feels best.

It's time to practice the cartwheel. He couldn't do this with a shorter partner, as I need to get my hip at the level of his bent arms, so I go up and over, rather than dragging him down. He needs to be able to use his shoulders and back to help me, not just arm strength.

He's strong enough that we're able to go through the

entrance to it slowly. The end of the lift is the same set of moves but in reverse and with his other arm. However, the slower speed is distracting as hell to me. I end up with my legs in a V under Cam's face, held there as I start to talk him through bringing me out. I'm almost certain a moan escapes his lips so at least it's not just me.

We do it faster and I try to ignore the flash of heat between my legs as though his gaze is burning me there. My hands start to sweat and I stop to dry them, my heartbeat pulsing between my legs and under my ribs.

Deciding it's time to move on, I say, "Alright, you know the basics of that. Let me show you the rest."

I play the video of the second version of the move, with the lifter churning the spinner as though they are turning a vertical dial with their connected arms, adding speed for the cartwheel.

He watches it once then frowns. "Why would we regress when we've already done the no hands version?"

"Picture *you* doing the cartwheeling," I say with a grin.

He flicks his gaze back to the frozen video, then up to meet mine, his lips forming a slow smile. "Ohh…Now I see. I like it. Sweet."

I talk him through the steps. This one has to be fast from the start, or he's basically doing a one-armed cartwheel without help. First, I have him do a couple of cartwheels across the floor so I can check his form.

I don't check his form at all. I should be ensuring he's properly aligned, but instead I follow his impressive bulge and his hockey bubble butt as he rotates, salivating. God, I love mirrored walls.

He cartwheels back to stand in front of me.

I lick my lips trying to find words, but something in

my face must give me away.

He steps in, sliding a hand under my ponytail to cup my head, and bends toward me. His mouth settles across mine and I clutch him, sliding forward that last inch to press my body flush against his.

He groans and deepens the kiss, his tongue undulating against mine. Half-lifting his mouth from mine, he mutters against my lips, "God, I missed you."

I'm too busy coaxing his tongue back into play while tugging on his shirt to answer.

He walks me backward a half dozen steps then stops me and raises his head, reaching behind him to yank his shirt off and toss it aside. I can't remember why I thought professional dancers were sexy, because this hockey player might set me and my studio on fire. He spins me with his hands on my hips.

We're at the barre, and I'm staring at us in the mirror.

He places my hands on the wood, then unties the filmy tie of my skirt and lets it drop away. His eyes are roving over me as he kicks my legs wide. His voice guttural, he growls, "Second position. Now wider."

I blink. He apparently has something specific in mind, and I'm here for it. I widen my stance, my leotard already damp with arousal.

I don't see him move, but his hand comes to my upper spine and smooths down. All the way down, over my butt and between my legs. Never has a man made my front tingle when he touches my back. With one hand no less. My nipples pebble, eager for him to smooth over them. Instead, he gently presses three fingers against my soft folds, sliding them backward and bringing all my nerves to life.

Needing more friction, I bend my knees an inch to

press down against those fingers. The spandex in my leotard makes it hard for him to touch my clitoris directly and the nylon makes the pressure too soft.

He squats with his legs behind mine to align our hips. Those delicious hockey quads allow him to hold me rather than the barre, pressing his naked chest to my back above the low scoop of the bodysuit. I stare at us in the mirror.

His eyes are hooded as his gaze roams over me, and his hand is massive over my lower ribcage and stomach. "You're gorgeous."

I'm sucking wind like I just tried to race him on skates. "Cam. Please. Your skin feels so good against mine. I need more."

"You'll get it," he promises. Standing, he grabs the straps of my leotard and peels them down, unbuckling my shoes and tossing them aside as well.

I snap my legs together and step out of it when he crouches to tug it off each leg. I'm naked now. His hair brushes my butt, and his gaze burns me as he rises again.

He toes his shoes off, then strips with the efficiency of an athlete. When he taps the inside of one of my ankles with his foot, I return to my wide stance and watch him through the mirror.

He mimics me, coming behind me again. His blonde waves brush my forehead and his breath gusts over my cheek as he leans in. His voice rumbles in my ear, "Now plié."

I lower myself, holding onto the barre for what I expect is going to be the longest and most pleasurable squat of my life.

He lowers himself with me and brings one oversized hand next to mine to hold the railing. With the other, he parts my labia and brushes my clit then dips lower to wet his fingers in the copious lubricant my body has already created for him. He circles. When I fidget, he presses his forearm down my back.

"Cam, I'm close. How am I close already?"

He grins in the mirror, pleased with himself.

My hand shifts to clutch his on the barre, needing that extra contact to ground me as I might splinter into a trillion pieces. It's soothing and unbearably arousing all at once.

He moves his other hand behind me and nudges his cock at my folds before sliding partly inside.

"Okay?" he asks. At my nod, he adds, "And you can hold this position?"

"I think so."

He shoves in another inch without further warning.

I gasp. His size had somehow been blurred by a few days apart. Now it feels like a battering ram if such a thing could be the best thing in the world while still carrying an element of scariness. Pleasure curls through me reaching every corner. Heat spikes, burning from my core to my fingertips and my back arches, ready for more.

He pinches a nipple—damn hockey player doesn't need to hang onto the barre to do this—and slides all the way in.

I explode. Never in my life has an orgasm snuck up on me like this, especially one so extreme. My muscles clamp down, pulsating around him, and my legs go taut. I rise and fall in tiny movements, seeking to prolong it. Cam's finger is back on my clit, pressing rhythmically. I mostly stifle a scream through my teeth, keening as the pleasure goes on and on until I'm limp.

Thankfully, he has one hand on the barre and I'm almost sitting on him, as I can't hold myself up at this point.

"My turn," he says.

I hold on tight as he starts to piston, tugging his hand away from my clit for a few minutes until it—I—recover from my first climax.

But as his thrusts get harder, jolting me upward each time, he says, "Come with me."

I'm mesmerized by the view in the mirror layered on top of the physical sensations. At his words I bring my gaze to his and suddenly I'm right there again.

I grip the barre and tighten my legs, determined not to burden him with my weight any longer. His fingers come to my most sensitive flesh again, and the barre creaks under his grip.

My clit quivers under his touch, still super sensitive.

He must feel it too, because he makes a V of his fingers and rubs the sides.

Holy shit. I'm on the precipice again. Two more swipes and I curl my torso forward with the ecstasy, shuddering all over.

Cam rams into me one last time. He brings both hands to the wood so we don't fall backwards on the hard floor, his arms quaking around me. He groans in my ear as he jerks and spasms inside me.

Finally, we are both spent, grinning at each other in the mirror like loons. At times like this, the rest of the world falls away, and I don't care about secrecy or casualness.

Chapter Twenty-Three

Cam

Home ice feels good under my blades. I've only lived in this city for three months and been playing on this ice for less than two, but the roar of the crowd and the sea of purple make it home. Not to mention the fact that once again, the ice seems a degree or two warmer. After spending some extra time stretching while the team goofs around and takes shots on the empty goal, I head to my post, surreptitiously checking the seats assigned to me.

Sweet. Christina and a woman with blonde hair peeking out from under a pom pom topped Tornadoes toque are already in place. She told me she was bringing her college pal Nicole, and admitted her friend wanted to meet the players afterward. I'd given up trying to get Christina to come out to Chasers after games, as she worried that it would give away we were doing more than dancing together. But thanks to Nicole, they're coming tonight and I'll get to meet her friend and have face-to-face time with Chris to absorb my post-game energy.

We're playing Ottawa tonight, and I focus on their two star players who I've been watching in game film the past few days. The rest of the team rides on their coattails (or sticks) as far as I can tell.

Sure enough, I field over forty shots on goal, most of which are by those two. Every time I block one, the crowd roars. I swear underneath the thunder, I can isolate Christina's voice cheering. But when the puck is in play, my eyes are on it.

Du Près scores in the second period, followed closely by one from Buzz, but in turn I miss one, the goal lamp blazing behind my head. However, we've shaken them, and they're on the defensive. The third period is full of sloppy passes and desperate, obvious shots on goal.

The Ottawa players keep aiming for my left shoulder. I guess some game film must have shown them that was my weakest point, which is something to check later and work on. But for now, it means they continue to be predictable and the last seven minutes fly by, punctuated by du Près scoring again. Mattie's on fire tonight.

With only seconds before the buzzer sounds, Saint has a clear shot on goal, but seems to randomly pass to du Près, who slaps a one timer between the Ottawa goalie's skate and the goal post. Hat trick! Our fans stomp their feet creating the thunder of a tornado. blink 182's "All the Small Things" blares as hats rain down on the ice.

After several minutes, they clear the ice of hats, all of which will be donated, and we play out the final seconds. The buzzer sounds with the puck down our end and du Près sprints toward me, hurtling us both backwards and dislodging the goal as Buzz and Saint and the rest of the guys join us. We're all laughing and hugging or at least I'm trying with my goalie gloves and pads.

We're only four rows below Christina. When he finally releases me to make our way off the ice, I glance back at Christina among the fans reveling in the win and du Près' hat trick. She gives me a subtle double fist pump at shoulder height and I raise my fist in answer, still grinning like a madman.

The locker room is typically post-win rowdy. By the time du Près comes in from the press room, Jack has champagne and is alternately spraying it on him and guzzling it. I shake my head. My roommate could not be more opposite to my approach, but he's a good guy and always upbeat.

Coach's post-game talk is short, and we're all headed to Chasers in no time. The roped off corner awaits us and a couple of the guys head over to Renec at the bar to get the first round. I spy a cinnamon-colored ponytail and veer off. Accepting congratulations and backslaps as I go, I nod and smile and make progress. When I'm a few feet away, Christina's friend, who is facing me, says something and gestures to me. Chris turns with a smile.

I beckon them, wanting to get out of the fray. She shakes her head and gestures at the bar, mimicking signing a tab, then holds up one finger. I point to the corner and she nods.

Nicole murmurs something to her and she blushes, making me wonder what she's told her friends.

I duck into the roped-off area and save them two seats with my suit jacket, taking the beer Jack points out from the end of the big booth he shares with five other players.

Du Près ambles over with his celebratory Wiser's 18-

year Canadian whisky, which he had charmed Renee into stocking for him. It had been a whole process, with him requesting Found North then contacting them directly when there were no distributors in Austin. Wiser 18 was his second choice when all that failed. I've tried both and can't tell the difference, but Canadians take their whisky—never spelled whiskey—seriously. He has a hat from the ice perched at an angle on his head, his souvenir from the game.

The women arrive and Mathieu perks up, arching a brow and sliding into another seat at the table. Introductions are made and Nicole shakes my hand with a smile before raving to Mattie about his performance.

Christina takes the opportunity to lean in, saying, "Thank you again for the tickets. I loved seeing all the action up close."

I grin, coasting on the euphoria of the win. "I can get you closer to some action in an hour or so if you want me to come home with you."

She rolls her eyes at me, but nods. A couple of the guys come by, surprised she's here.

Kyle is bouncing behind my chair, his voice coming over my head. "Ms. Donovan! My portfolio was up ten percent just in the last month. Do you think I can splurge on a Christmas gift for my parents?"

"I don't know, Kyle. What are we talking about? A weekend away, or a car? Or diamonds?" Christina asks with a smile.

"Ohh…now I don't know. Those all sound great." He's staring off into space when I turn to look at him.

I shake my head. "Pace yourself, rookie. Remember the goal is to save for…" I trail off and reword, as us hockey players never use the "i" or the "r" words in case they jinx us, "…the future."

Christina tells him she'll email him to set up a quick appointment to talk about it, reassuring him that she'll help him find something nice. It's another example of her going above and beyond her duties for the guys.

I squeeze her hand where it rests on the table, and she casts me a sharp glance before withdrawing it. Oops. Secret. Right.

Jack gets up for another drink and leans one hand on the table between Mattie and me. He does a chin lift at Christina and asks, "You're hanging with us after the games now, eh? Should we invite you to the team parties at our hou—ugh! Dude, what?"

I follow my jab in his side with a glare.

Christina answers in a mild voice. "My friend Nicole wanted to come."

"Oh yeah?" His grin is lecherous, as always, before he realizes Mattie has staked a claim, one hand on the back of Nicole's chair, as he leans in chatting her up. He turns back to me to ask, "Dude, I keep meaning to ask. You said your AHL buddies are coming to the Chicago game. Did you want my pair for any family members? Isn't your family from around there?"

Mattie lifts his head from his murmured conversation with Nicole to ask, "Are they?"

Ugh. Saint's advice about opening up resonates in my head. "They're from northern Indiana," I tell him before turning to Jack. "I doubt they'll be able to make it. Don't worry about it, but thanks."

"Cool. Just let me know if something changes."

I nod once, my jaw clenched.

Christina notices and asks in an undertone, "Are you still following them anonymously?" When I nod again, she asks, "But you're not ready to invite them?"

I shake my head.

"Okay," she drops it and skims a quick hand down the outside of my thigh under the table to show support. Holy crap, this woman gets me like no other. She accepts my fears about my family, my money, and my role on the team. She sees my weak underbelly and supports me. Only my mother ever did that.

Maybe if I understand why she doesn't want children, I can reconcile myself to that, or find another path. Dammit, there is still the optics of her being an owner of the team I want a very large contract from. Everything is working against us, but I'm falling for her so hard.

Wanting to avoid these dark thoughts, I relish my body's reaction to her hand on my thigh and focus on what I hope will be the next part of the evening. Finishing my beer, I ask, "Can we go? Or do you need to leave with Nicole?"

"I need to leave with Nicole, but—" she skims a hand down my thigh again—"she told me to make sure she left after an hour as she has an early morning. I'll meet you at my house in thirty."

Perfect. My preferred kind of celebration doesn't require alcohol.

* * * *

We have two more home games that week, splitting them with one win and one loss. For both, Christina sits in my seats. Once she brings her sister, and for the second, another friend who she tells me later is Lauren.

In between, we work on the new lifts with much of my time being spent on mastering a one-handed cartwheel. While my arm strength is more than adequate, Christina is a stickler for form. Of course, her touching me to direct my form leads to other things more often than not.

I also check in on my investments, given Kyle's excitement about his return. I log in to the investment account Christina set up weeks ago, eager for a similar return to Kyle's.

Instead, my portfolio is almost exactly equal to the amounts I've been funneling into it from each paycheck.

What the hell? She said she could outperform my savings account with a simple interest rate, but she's lost me money.

Luckily, I'm due at Christina's for our last practice session before I fly out tomorrow with the team. I bang on her door a little harder than normal before entering.

She's coming down the hall from the studio and bedroom and smiles, saying "Hi Ca—"

"What's up with my investments, Chris?"

Her chin retracts when I interrupt, but I don't have time for niceties when I'm losing money. "Those mutual funds you put my money in have decreased in value."

"Temporarily." She rolls her eyes and I nearly lose my shit. "Of all days for you to look at the market."

"I took your advice and didn't look. But Kyle's comment got me hoping."

"Oh. I didn't think about that. I'm sorry, Cam. I should have warned you. There's a little unrest in the market this week and next due to some economic indicators that are anticipated to be lower than previously expected. CPI…"

"You lost me at unrest." I make a slashing motion with my hand, then run it through my hair, trying not to lose my shit. I've lashed out at her once, and I never want to be dismissive like my father, but I'm upset and I need to understand. "But how was Kyle up ten percent then?"

She remains calm when I start to pace. "First, Kyle put more into investments I recommended that have a greater upside than interest on a savings account, even a high yield one. So they had time to grow before this week's volatility started. Second, if I looked this week, he might only be up five percent. I can't tell you if he is due to confidentiality, but it's why I urged him to be prudent on gift-giving this soon. By leaving more to grow, you'll achieve greater compounding growth in the long term."

"I can't *lose* money, Chris. This is exactly why I didn't want to put my money in risky stuff."

"Cam, if I may say, you make a—" she pauses and looks at the ceiling "—hundred times what you lost in every paycheck. This is a drop in the bucket, and it will smooth out by the end of the calendar year."

"So you're saying I'm overreacting?" I grit out.

"No." She sucks in a breath. "It can be scary to see red in an account. Believe me, I'm seeing a lot of it in our family's accounts, too, right now. But especially when you don't understand why something is fluctuating. I'm asking you to trust me for a little longer."

There's that word again. Maybe she and Saint are right and I have trust issues, especially where money is concerned after my father nearly prevented me from getting into this profession I love. "You have a much bigger nest egg to fall back on. I don't think it's the same."

"It's the same principle." Now her jaw is clenching.

She doesn't get it. "I don't know. I should probably

transfer it all into my interest-bearing account so I don't lose any more."

"It's your money. I'll do what you want. Look at it this way, though. When you applied to colleges, you weighed the risk—the application fee, the sense of loss—with the reward of going somewhere you were excited about. When you entered the draft your second year, you didn't know who would pick you up or if anyone would, but it was worth it to reach for your dream."

I smirk. "I got a scholarship to college and I was ranked pretty high in the draft."

"Well, that explains it. You've never had to risk, have you? I'm not saying it hasn't been hard work, but when you've put in the work, success has come to you. This is out of your control more, and it risks your hard work in a way."

Well, fuck. Now I'm a control freak as well as having trust issues. Whatever it is, I'm way out of my comfort zone. On the other hand, her words from our initial investment meeting come back. This is what she does, and I need to respect her expertise while getting out of my own way. Hurting her feelings is out of the question. Besides, she did guarantee my capital. I swallow.

Her lips are pressed together and there is a crease between her eyes, despite her continued outward calm.

Dammit, I've already hurt her. Looming end date or not, I *want* to trust her, and I have to start somewhere. "I'm sorry. You're right."

Surprise flashes across her face for an instant before a smile blooms. That's worth any losses I might incur.

* * * *

The team is in that lull between a light morning skate and heading back to the rink for warmups before the game. We went out to lunch in small groups based on what guys wanted to eat in Chicago—some have played here before in one capacity or another and have specific food memories they want to revisit.

I chose the group that was going to the place closest to the hotel so I can go back and rest. Jack is asleep with his phone on his chest on the other bed, but I can't settle. Between watching my sort-of-siblings on social media and the guys expecting them to come to my game, I'm antsy being this physically close to them.

I log into Instagram to pull up my stepmother's feed. She uses her married name—Dana Hill. I'm not surprised as my dad is not the kind of guy who would be happy with his wife keeping her own name. When her profile loads, I jackknife off the pillows to sit upright. A photo of her, teenaged Zoe, and six-year-old Robbie is posted. Both kids are wearing Tornadoes gear, although Zoe is smirking with her hand on the opened zipper of her jacket as though she unzipped it as the photo was taken. The image on the shirt under her jacket may or may not be a Chicago Icedogs logo, especially given that smirk. *Brat*. I'm smiling at my phone, though.

My father isn't in the photo but likely was the photographer. The caption under the image doesn't say either way. It reads, "Pulling the kids out one period early to head to see the @ChiIceDogs and @TxTornadoes play."

They're coming. They'll be here. Seeing me play. And for whatever reason, their mom has put them in Tornadoes apparel, despite the cult-like attitude of many Chicago sports fans.

The post is neutral about why they chose to come to this particular game. I doubt my father was the driver of this, so I guess that answers whether Dana knows about me or not. I assumed she either didn't know or wanted nothing to do with his old life, given the lack of an invitation to their wedding. But then she wouldn't bring her children to my game. I'm confused. And how the hell his other son ended up playing hockey is beyond my comprehension. Did the old man have a change of heart? And why is the new wife coming? It's not like she could have been a Tornadoes fan when he met her—we didn't exist.

Chicago is another team like Detroit, with a deep bench and an even deeper history in the NHL. They're one of the best teams in the league most years, including this one. Knowing my AHL friends will be here had me amped, but this new knowledge makes me nervous. Goalies can't afford to be nervous. I have to do something to shake this off.

If it was a home game, I could text Saylet to find out where their seats are, but she won't have access in another team's arena. Of course, if it was a home game, they wouldn't be attending, as they live in Indiana.

I'd already gotten permission to fly home separately from the team, on a commercial flight Sunday rather than tomorrow, because I wanted to support my AHL teammates. The fact that I check my brother's league schedule is simply a reflection of being so close to him. They have a home game tomorrow afternoon. I text my friend group, saying I might be late to their game tomorrow as something has come up, but we'll do drinks tonight after my game and tomorrow after theirs. I'll sleep on my early flight and hope that Coach will cut me some slack if we have practice Sunday afternoon.

I have no idea what prompts me to consider driving out to see my brother play hockey, or whether I'm prepared to have a conversation with him, Dana, or anyone else. I'm still antsy, and my thumbs return to my phone screen. I hit the call button for Christina.

It goes to voicemail. Damn.

"Hey, Dancer, it's me. I found out my family is coming to my game and I'm freaking out a little. Was hoping to catch you, but I'll figure it out. Hope you're having a good day."

Belatedly, I realize she might not be answering because she's still upset over my implied lack of trust. But here I am trusting her with my family turmoil. Hopefully, that'll help. Or do I look like I'm using her as a crutch? I need to stop and get out of my head. This is all making my anxiety worse, not better, and I need to be dialed in for tonight's game.

I go to the floor and move through some yoga flows, trying to find my Zen. It takes the edge off, and I replay game tape in my mind until my head is almost 100% back where it needs to be.

At the rink, we suit up and go out for warm-ups. The rest of the team starts without me as usual. As I side lunge, I watch the glass for kids in pom-pomed Tornadoes hats. When I don't see Robbie or Zoe, I drag in a long inhale and force myself to release all non-hockey thoughts on the exhale. I'm ready to kick some puppies in the form of ice mutts.

We hold our own through the first period, neither team scoring. They're pressing us hard, but my guys are fierce and I'm determined not to let a puck by me. In the second period, we score then they score almost immediately. That puck *flew*. I barely saw it, much less had time to react.

At the top of the third, they come barreling at me on all sides, but in their rush the puck gets passed behind the winger and my guys grab it. Saint and Buzz send it up on a breakaway, ensuring they're with it before the blue line. As much speed as they can get on the puck, the ice mutts are slow on their own acceleration. Maybe it's because they're an older team and can make up for it with how well they work together, but for whatever reason, they can't catch our first line. Buzz fakes a shot and passes to Saint, who lifts his stick for a one-timer, sending the puck right between the mutt goalie's legs for a five hole. The goal lamp lights!

Now if I can keep the speedy little disk out of my net for just under sixteen minutes, we're home free.

The final buzzer sounds and we've managed to win. Our team is ecstatic, celebrating on the ice, in the locker room and well into the night. My friends from Peoria get to experience how NHLers party after a win, which in all honesty is the same way AHLers party but with top shelf liquor and, at least at home, more women. To the entertainment of my past and current teammates, I stick to my usual one beer.

Jack is up and out early for the team flight. I have no idea how he can drink what he wants, eat crap food, get little sleep and still play as well as he does. I daren't try it. This is too important.

I roll out of bed an hour later, thanking my yesterday self for sticking to my guns on not drinking more. I scan @ProudINMama's feed for photos of the game and find a few. None have my father in them. Apparently, he's still boycotting "playing games." I laugh, picturing his face when he sees what Dana would have spent on tickets.

I have a voicemail from Christina from after the game. I hit play. "Cam! Congratulations! That was an awesome game. Apparently, you did indeed figure things out. Or maybe they should come to all your games?" Her tone is light. "Anyway, call me if you have time. Or I'll see you Sunday night."

Now that I've made the decision to do this, I'm on a mission. Besides, I'm not ready to contemplate my motivation too closely, much less explain it, so I don't respond to her message.

My rideshare takes me to a car rental place and I head east to Indiana, focusing on the logistics and then the directions. I don't allow myself to think too hard about what I'm doing.

Last night in the locker room, I borrowed Jack's baseball cap and Mattie's plain hoodie. The crazy Canadian wears that instead of a jacket half the time, but because team rules state we have to go home in suits and Austin's weather is still in the 70's most of the time, he allowed me to take it. This way, nothing I'm wearing has the Tornadoes logo.

I may want to see my half-brother on the ice, but I don't want to be recognized. I'm not ready for questions about why I'm in a town I haven't been back to in almost a decade. Because I was drafted, there's enough personal information about me out there that people could connect me to this kid. He shouldn't find out about me that way. That would be cruel. Damn, there's a Wiki page about me that lists my mother and father's names. They're public record so I can't ask them to take it down, but hopefully I'm new enough to the spotlight and Hill is a common enough last name that he doesn't go looking.

In case Zoe is there too, I'll have to be careful in the stands as I'm certain an angsty teen like her would choose to hide in a dark corner like I'll be doing.

The highway driving gives me too much time to think about my reasons for wanting to see Robbie's game. Dana's posts haven't mentioned what position he plays, but based on his helmet and stick, it's not goalie. Which is fine. I'm not looking for a mini-me. Hell, I'm still in shock that he's been allowed to play hockey after I went AWOL in my father's eyes. Do they even say AWOL anymore? The military probably uses a new acronym…

I shake my head at myself. I'm losing the thread.

More than his skill, I want to make sure he enjoys it. And his facial expressions when he talks, as I've only seen still pictures of him. And the sparkle in his eyes when he grins.

I want to know him. I nearly drive off the highway when that thought arrives. Shit.

My first inclination is to call Christina again to talk through this. She says we're a fling but she's always happy to help me work through emotions, whether about the team or my family. We fit together so well I wish the kids issue wasn't between us. Maybe we could be more. Even permanent. But my desire to know my brother and stepsister reinforces my craving for a family of my own. People who want me as much as I want them—forever. And Christina made it clear she isn't looking for forever.

My phone's GPS tells me my exit is next, and I push aside the deep thoughts to again focus on getting through this day. I'll think about the rest when I'm home. With or without my "fling" partner.

Chapter Twenty-Four

Christina

Cam is home! I shouldn't be this excited about a guy I'm in a situationship with, especially given his recent distrust about the investing strategy we'd agreed on, but I can't help it.

Cam

> On the ground at AUS.
> Checking on practice time.

> Yay! Welcome back! How was the trip? I was hoping you'd call on your drive to/from Peoria for your friends' game.

Nope. Keep it casual, Chris. I delete the last sentence of that before hitting send.

> Really good. It was great to hang with my OG friends. They of course made me buy dinner and drinks

> I hope you didn't whine, you big Grinch :)

> Hey :P

> Looks like I have practice in an hour. Just enough time to make it there - I was kind of hoping to skip it. I'm beat.

> Oh...

We'd talked about getting together tonight and I looked at it as our way of saying we missed each other while still giving the nod to keeping it casual. But his reaction is not what I'd want and given that I'm still prickly from the investment conversation, perhaps it's better not to interact when he's tired and jetlagged.

I finish my text.

> Oh...I understand. Why don't you catch up on some sleep tonight so you can be of more use to me later this week...

> For dancing of course ;)

> Of course :D That sounds good, thanks.

> Ping me when you know your schedule and we'll figure out studio sessions.

I stare at the last text, regretting it. Despite my efforts at self-editing, I can't help being needy. Thankfully, he seems too tired to notice or too polite to say anything.

> Will do. Thanks. Have a good night. Look forward to seeing you. Soon.

Those last two sentences ease my anxiety. Maybe he's a little eager, too.

Sure enough, he comes by the next night. He still seems tired as his mouth is drawn and his eyelids heavy.

"Hey, you all right?" I ask when he comes over to buss my lips with a kiss.

"Yeah."

His tone isn't tired, though. I've come to learn his emotional tells. It's his "I have something on my mind" voice.

"I made us dinner. Let's eat and talk and then we can get some dancing in if you're still up for it."

His leer is half-hearted. "I'm always up for dancing."

"Yes, I remember." My eyes glaze briefly, recalling our shadowed reflections at the barre, but neither of us pursues the idea.

"Whatdya make?"

"Oh, right. Sorry. A low-carb casserole with Italian seasoned ground turkey and a giant salad. It's keeping warm in the oven."

I pull the dish out and let it rest as I gather the salad, plates, and bowls. I dish twice as much for him as me, and we sit to eat. He fidgets with his silverware and napkin. When he does eat, it's with far less enthusiasm than normal.

I want to reach for his hand, but I don't know if I should do that, ask questions, or wait him out. Finally, I try, "Did you see your family at the game, then? How did it feel to have them there?"

"I didn't. It was a giant distraction and after I scanned the lower-level seats during practice, I had to put it aside."

"You don't think them being there helped you win?"

"I didn't win. We won as a team." He presses his lips together, unwilling to admit anything further.

I'm not sure what to say to that.

After a moment, he says to his plate, "I went to watch

my brother play on Saturday."

I blink in shock. No wonder he's off-kilter. "You did? Before or instead of your friends' game?"

"Before." He glances at me then away. "That's why I was so tired. I drove two and a half hours east to his practice, then three and a half west, then back to Chicago to catch my flight. And the guys partied both nights."

He may not be ready to rehash that field trip, but he's here now and talking. My curiosity prompts a jumble of questions in my head, but most importantly, I want to make sure he's okay. Trying to ease into it, I ask, "How was that?"

"Good. I mean, weird, but good. He's a defenseman." There is a trace of pride in his voice. "And he's good. I don't think he's as tall as I was at that age, but it's hard to tell from photos and with a bunch of kids on skates racing around."

"He has a bit of leeway, though, doesn't he? You're taller than average."

"Not by much. But who's to say he'll want to go pro anyway?"

That's a great point. A lot of guys, even fathers, would be pushing the kid to compete to the highest level. Cam, though, is already thinking like a supportive brother.

He continues, "Zoe was doing homework in the stands and I didn't see if Dana or my father were there."

"Did you talk to anyone?" I mean Zoe or Robbie, but I keep it generic. Also, I almost can't believe he avoided being recognized by the coaches, if not the kids.

"No. I borrowed a hat and a plain hoodie. No one knew who I was. Heck, I'm almost surprised they didn't call security on me."

I snort a laugh. "Oh boy. I can imagine the headlines now. Saylet might have killed you." I joke so he doesn't feel beholden to share more than he's comfortable with.

He snickers. "Right? At least I know you have bail money handy if I need it. I sometimes wonder if Jack would, even making what we do."

I keep my face neutral and remain silent. My consultations with the team members are all confidential. But Cam's mentioned Jack's financial support of his family, so I assume he's referring to that as much as his roommate's tendency to party.

Cam finally brings his gaze to mine. "It seems like they know about me, or why would Dana have put them in Tornadoes gear for our game—in Chicago, of all places?"

"She did?" He hadn't told me that.

Cam pulls out his phone and shows me the post. "Look at that. Although,"—he points to Zoe—"I swear that is an Ice Dog shirt under there. Freakin' smartass." His grin as he says it makes it clear that smartassery runs in the family.

"You said your father wasn't at Robbie's game. Did he come to Chicago?"

"I don't know, but I can't find any mention of him. He's not in any of their pictures, and the posts from the game itself look like they were taken from seat neighbors. In one, it shows someone sitting next to Dana, with the two boys on the aisle."

The man drove over five hours to see his little brother. It's proof that he wants a connection with them, so I push a little. "What do you want to do next? He wasn't there, and he's not tagged in her Instagram profile, so you have a path to talking with her without having to deal with him, if that's your concern."

"But," he says raggedly, "if they know about me and even came to a game, why haven't they reached out to me?"

There's an element of the abandoned teen in his voice and I want to hug him and reassure him. Instead, I say carefully, "They may know of your existence, but how can they understand why you aren't in touch with your dad? At best, they only have his version of the story. Putting myself in your stepmother's shoes, if my fiancé's son doesn't respond to calls or come to our wedding, I'd assume he doesn't want to be part of my family, maybe even that he resents me and my children. Yet here she is following you—for how long now?"

"A couple years ago."

"That's interesting timing. So it was when you went into the AHL?"

He nods. "I think so."

"And—" I draw out the word as I remember his brother is six—"around the time your brother started playing hockey."

"Yeah, but if she wanted a hockey connection for whatever reason, money for gear, or a word to get into a special program, why wouldn't she have messaged me?"

"What if it was just wanting a role model for her son? What if—" I raise my brows and give him a hard stare, "Your father's reaction to him playing hockey was the same or worse as he was to you? She could be wondering if there is a different side to the story she's been hearing all these years, but isn't sure how to connect."

He blinks at me. "I'd never thought about it like that."

"I'm not saying throw yourself out there and tell her

you want to be part of the family. But maybe a quick DM saying you saw they came to the game and if they're ever interested in another, you're happy to get them tickets…see how she responds."

He nods his head slowly. "I'll think about it."

"Now, are we dancing, or are we *dancing*?" I ask in a flirtatious voice, hoping levity will get him out of this maelstrom of doubt.

His grin is wide as he answers, "Yes to both, please."

* * * *

Greg is away on a business trip for one of our other family holdings, so Cam and I have more flexibility around the property.

He had a game yesterday, and I brought Maria with me for company, despite her lack of interest in hockey. Other than one game earlier in the season, Amy watches from the company box in order to network for the sake of the Tornadoes Foundation. Maria had an early morning at the café and had to head home right after the game, so I didn't have an excuse to go to Chasers.

The guys lost last night, and their after-game drinks were subdued, so Cam got to my house less than an hour after me. Lacking the adrenaline from a win, he was exhausted and we crashed.

Morning sex more than made up for it, though, so I made us breakfast and now we're lounging to digest before we start attempting cartwheels and spins in my studio.

Cam gestures to the stack of papers I cleared from my breakfast bar. "What's the current project?"

"Something to do with myself now I have you knuckleheads on the road to financial responsibility." I haven't shared my dream with anyone except Maria and Amy because they've both been advising me on it, and I'm scared that if it doesn't work I'll look like a failure. I'm not used to failing any more than Cam is, even if my risk tolerance is higher.

"Oh yeah?" He spies a brochure with a young ballerina and gestures. "Are you going to do more with Maria?"

"In a way."

He looks at me, clueing in on my prevarication, and arches a brow. "What were you saying last week about trust?"

I huff. Dammit, he's right. And part of me wants to share this with him, as I would a boyfriend. "Fine. It's a nonprofit organization to offer after-school dance programs for kids who otherwise couldn't afford it."

His eyes widen and his mouth curves into a smile. "Really? Dancer, that's great! Why wouldn't you be shouting it from the rooftops?"

"Because it's not ready quite yet. I'm only just now gauging interest from students and hiring instructors. And that will be a balancing act."

"Start with the most limited resource." At my stare, he shrugs. "What? I remember something like this from an entrepreneurial business class. I imagine it would be studio time. Well, or budget for instructors perhaps?"

"Interesting. I did that by the way, and your guess is wrong—as you know, budget isn't an issue." I slash my hand, ignoring the firming of his lips. He's going to need to get over his irritation at my bank balance; it's not something I can change. I tilt my head. Or perhaps he doesn't, as this is a short-term fling.

"Alright. Then studio space?"

"A little. Maria and I have worked out times that won't interfere with her classes and profits, and I have one other space with another dance friend so I can spread out over the city."

"What age group are you targeting?"

"I'm probably starting with middle school and high school, but I want to offer it to everyone eventually."

"Have you thought about mixing ages, and only offering beginner classes for the time being? You could do age buckets like they do in league hockey—5-8, under 12's, 12-15?"

"That sounds like excellent groupings for the second phase. Maybe I need to hear more how it works in hockey? It certainly would give me more flexibility in trying to get boys into classes for ballroom dances." I tilt my head, holding his gaze. "Thanks, Cam. I appreciate the ideas. Let me go back through things with this perspective and then I'd love to ask you some more questions if that's all right?"

"Of course." He patted his stomach. "Does that mean digestion time is over and I'm being put to work?"

"Yep. For the sake of the team's charitable efforts."

"I'm just full of charitable inclinations today."

Chapter Twenty-Five

Cam

I get home after dance practice to find a bunch of guys lounging by our pool. It's November, which in Austin means it could be 50 degrees or close to 80. Today is on the warm side.

I grab a seltzer water and throw myself into a lounger, still in my dance pants. Chris has been prodding me about messaging Dana, but I haven't gotten up the nerve yet. Nor have I raised the subject of having children with her. But I'm more confused than ever now she's told me about her passion project—involving kids.

Saint gestures at me. "Not what I'd choose for poolside apparel, but hey, you do you."

"Ha. I was practicing for the charity gig."

"With Christina?"

"Who else?" I frown at him.

"Defensive, much? How's the dancing going?"

"Really well. Y'all will get a show, so you better ante up for the Foundation." I smirk at him.

He looks me over, then narrows his eyes. "So I've noticed you don't hang with the other single players as much. Not interested in puck bunnies?"

That's an interesting segue. I review Christina's and my interactions in public. We haven't given anything away, so he must be fishing. I answer truthfully, "Nah. I want something real. Like you have."

A frown creases his brow for a second before he smooths it. "Marriage, huh? You're young for that."

"Not if you look at national averages. Anyway, what does age matter? It's finding the right person."

He nods, but counters with, "Just give it enough time to be sure they share the same long-term goals, they're not just right for right now."

"Well, yeah, but isn't the idea that you grow together?"

He slants me an exasperated look. "Yes, that's the *idea*. Reality is harder."

I frown. Saint is usually pretty mellow, but his tone is sharp. "You okay?"

"I'm fine." He waves a hand. "Just trying to impart wisdom from my advanced years."

I ask, "Do you want kids?"

His mouth twists. "Yes."

"Me too. But…" I try to phrase this without giving too much away. "This chick I was seeing doesn't want them. Full stop. But she's setting up a nonprofit centered around kids. It seems contradictory to me."

"My sister's a teacher, and she never wants kids. She wants to work with them, and mold them, and pass them along to others for nurturing long-term. Maybe that woman feels the same."

"Maybe. I just can't see it."

"Well, if you want them, it might be hard to understand her point of view. Anyway, that's a pretty big difference in goals. Sounds like it's not a good fit, so probably best that you stopped seeing her. Don't ignore the early warning signs about something that important."

His tone is dark, but his expression does not invite questions. There's something there, though, so I make a note to pay better attention to how he's doing. He watches over the whole team, but who watches over him?

"It sucks because she's such a great fit in every other way."

"You just switched to present tense. Are you still talking to her?"

I drop my head to stare at my drink can, rolling it in my hand. "Sort of."

He shakes his head. "You're setting yourself up for hurt, my man, but sometimes you young'uns have to learn the hard way. As long as you don't bring it to the ice, I'll let you figure it out. Remember, you can only control your priorities and dreams. The worst thing you could do is try to change someone else's."

The group starts dispersing as the sun has set and we have an early practice tomorrow.

As we stand, I say, "Thanks for listening. I hope you know it's not a one-way conversation. Any time you want someone to talk to, I'm happy to lend an ear."

He nods and knocks elbows as we take our empty cans inside.

After Jack and I scrabble together some supper, I head to my room and lie on my bed with noise-cancelling ear buds in. Jack's watching TV and my room is close enough I can hear it without them. Instead, I turn on mellow music and replay my conversation with Saint. His last words echo. If I want more with Christina, and I do, I'll have to take her as she is. Which means I'd have to reprioritize what I want in life, although I'm not sure she's really against having children, given her choice of charitable project.

* * * *

Tonight is a home game. As I skate onto the ice for warmups, I check my seats for Christina. She's already there, in a fuzzy Tornadoes-purple sweater. I'm not sure who's accompanying her tonight but that seat is empty right now. I tamp down the twinge of annoyance at her continued refusal to wear my jersey and focus on getting my head in the game.

The New Jersey Nightwings are in a rebuilding year, which is a nice way of saying they're one of the lowest ranked teams in the league. Sadly, they're not in our division so their poor performance doesn't help our ranking. But it does mean we're hoping for another W.

I center on their forwards' strategies as I go through my stretching routine. Widening my stance, I drop to my knees on the ice. Continuing to push out, my butt drops until the cold seeps through my layers of protective gear under my uniform. I know from doing this in front of the gym mirror that I'm only a couple inches off the ice. Keeping my upper legs perpendicular to my body, I stretch forward, laying my stomach on the rink until it's almost flat. I raise and lower my hips repeatedly so the muscles are warm and I can snap into a butterfly without risking a groin pull. Then I push out sideways off my skate edge, getting as low over my knee pad as possible in a side leg stretch. Finally, I do low forward lunges.

As I push up to skate toward the goal to field some shots, I can't resist glancing at Christina once more. She catches my eye and fans herself, and I laugh out loud, causing one of the opposing team to snap his head toward me and glare. Good. All the better if he thinks I'm laughing at him and it messes with his head.

Just to reinforce it, every time he comes near me, I snicker, chuckle, or otherwise fuck with him. The first time causes him to hit the post with his attempted shot. After that, he's mad. More missed shots and a missed pass keep me happy as we finish the first period with no points on the board from either team.

Buzz scores in the second period, proving his value as one of the team leaders, as he does every game. We head to the locker room with the score up 1-0, and we all know that means they'll come at us—at me—hard in the final twenty minutes.

This is our fourteenth game of the season. Shutouts happen on average about every twenty games, although a few goalies average as frequent as every six. I'd had a couple in the AHL, but the NHL is a whole new level of play. Plus, I'd heard one scout say that my low SA— shots against—meant I was untested, especially as I'd had a strong team in front of me. I didn't agree with that way of viewing it, and now I'm more determined than ever to prove any doubters wrong. As the third period creeps by, I up my concentration another notch.

Every goalie in every game wants a shutout and tries his damnedest for it. But we're a new team, with all new stats to create. And while we've made it to the third period once before with no goals against us, we hadn't made it to five minutes left. The whole team is vibrating, one eye on the clock and one on the puck.

As it passes behind me again and Jack takes control to get it out of our territory, I call to the team, "Focus.

Don't get cocky. One play at a time."

Determined to follow my own advice, I stop looking at the clock. The noise of the stadium recedes. It's me, the puck, and the other eleven players on the ice. I'm going to conquer this one, right here and right now.

They pull their goalie, upping the stakes.

An eon later, the time clock buzzes and I rise out of my crouch, stunned. My teammates come screaming at me down the ice, and I quickly move away from the goal so they don't ram my back against the frame. I did it. I just had my first shutout of my NHL career. I'm still silent, overwhelmed.

The noise of the crowd comes rushing back. Taking a deep breath that borders on a laugh, I grab Buzz and circle with him in a man hug, laughing outright now. We're tonight's stars. We each take a lap, our helmets pushed back on our heads, our sticks in the air. After he passes one section, a stuffed Tornadoes devil flies down on the ice in front of me. I slow and crouch to grab it. By the time I straighten, there are two more in front of me. I glance over where Buzz is now along the opposite side of the ice. There are none in front of him, and he turns, continuing his lap skating backwards, cheering me as well.

Holy crap, the fans are celebrating my shutout, even more than the win, by throwing stuffed mascots that they paid good money for.

Sure, this is the goalie equivalent of a hat trick, but still, between us being a new team, and Austin not really sure it's a hockey town, I never expected this. I scoop up as many as I can, a couple of the guys coming to help, before we head off the ice. The player I taunted glares at me.

Riding high, I head to the dressing room. Coach gives us the usual pep talk tempered by warnings not to get complacent, this team isn't like the ones going to the playoffs, keep our focus, blah blah blah. I can barely hear him until he says my name.

"What?"

"Saylet insisted. It's not usually a goalie thing but obviously tonight is different. You and Buzz are in the press room."

While the rest of the team heads to the showers, we go answer questions. Thankfully Saylet is there to coach us, because this is a first for me. I had maybe two post-game interviews in college, one after I went to Minnesota/Peoria in the first round of the draft, and then a couple local things after AHL games. But this could be on ESPN primetime. *Holy shit.*

They ask the usual reporter questions. How I feel. What was the difference tonight that enabled this to happen. We're both gracious to the other team and talk about how tight it was—and it was only 1-0 at the end, so it truly was close. When asked if we'd expected to score more, I joke, "I'm the goalie, I can't tell you what happens at the other end of the ice." But after the laughter subsides, I add, "Honestly? My guys wanted that as much as I did, so we were *all* playing defense those last five minutes. But we didn't need to score again to get the win, so I'm grateful to them for their efforts on my behalf."

On that note, Saylet shuts down further questions and I'm a free man so I head to the dressing room to shower and change.

There are still players greeting their families in the Tornadoes lounge as I walk through to get to my car, and

I pause in the doorway.

Saint and his wife seem to have left already, as they aren't there. Jack and Kyle are in a corner and gesture Buzz and me over when they see us.

My gaze makes a quick sweep of the room. When my shoulders drop, I realize I was hoping Christina would be there. I want to celebrate this milestone with her. We've drawn the lines around our relationship, though, and she has no reason to cross them.

A hand thumps my back, then tracks up to squeeze my shoulder as Greg comes into view at my side.

"Congratulations, Hill! I knew you had it in you. This, this is why we all wanted you. You were one of our first picks in our planning for the expansion draft. I'm so excited." And he is. He's bouncing on his toes, knowing not to say too much. Hockey players are suspicious and don't like to put voice to either their hopes or fears, but I can practically envision the Stanley Cup in a thought bubble over his head.

"Thank you, sir. I'm excited as well. But we're only fourteen games in, not even a quarter of the way through the season, so like Coach said, I'm trying to stay focused on the next game, the next win."

"The next shutout, eh?" He's giddy and won't be talked down. I shrug. I play for love of the game. He *built a team* for the love of the game. Who's to say he should temper his enthusiasm.

I blink as Greg's grin is so familiar I suddenly see him as Christina's brother rather than the team owner. I try to picture Christmas breakfast with him in the big house, golf in the off-season, or maybe a family vacation. I shake my head once and look at the suit that probably costs four times what mine did, despite both being bespoke. He is my boss's boss's boss first and foremost, and if he found out I was sleeping with his sister, I'd probably be playing for some local team in Alaska the next day.

This man controls everything I've always wanted—hockey, financial stability, and with the right contract, a place to stay and raise a family. If Christina wanted a family, it would be worth risking the rest and ensuring my stats are strong enough to play for another NHL team. But right now, I'm risking everything—and for what? A secret short-term casual relationship. And yet, as stupid as it is, I can't bring myself to stop wanting to celebrate this win and any others with her if she'll have me. Even though she's Greg's sister. As I head toward Jack and his threatening hold on a champagne bottle, I pull out my phone to see if Christina's texted me about a private celebration after.

Chapter Twenty-Six

Christina

Cam bounds into my house, hair wet, smelling like wine, and still revved from his shutout.

I've been pacing and tidying, unable to sit still despite the late hour from sheer excitement for him. Now he rushes to me and lifts me, spinning me around.

"Congratulations," I manage through breathless laughter. "But why are you wet and why do you smell like a wino?"

He shakes his head, sending droplets flying. "Someone decided it would be fun to celebrate with popping champagne. All over us."

"Let me guess. Your roommate?"

"Yep." He puts me down and shrugs, clearly uncaring about his suit right now. Skimming the jacket off his shoulders, he hangs it over a kitchen chair to dry. "My heart's still racing. I wasn't sure I was going to keep it locked down through the game. After, I was in shock for a couple minutes and since then I'm riding high. I shouldn't stay long because I have no idea how long it will take me to be able to sleep."

"Okay. We'll see." I slip off the robe I've been wearing to show his favorite baby doll nightie underneath. "I thought of one way you could burn some of that energy, if you're up for it?"

"God," his voice is a reverent whisper. "You're gorgeous in anything, Dancer. Damn if that doesn't give me at least a half dozen ideas. We can start with yours and go from there."

I squeak out a laugh as he grabs me again, carrying me down the short hall with his hands under my butt and my limbs wrapped around him.

Tossing me on the bed, he runs his hands from my shoulders over my breasts to my hips and then down my legs. Dragging them wide, he steps closer and unbuttons his shirt as he stares at me spread out, a feast for him.

His muscled chest and slabs of abs come into view and I salivate, wanting to taste him. His belt buckle jangles and my gaze goes to the big reveal coming, my desire to lick those muscles forgotten while I enjoy the view.

Hooking his thumbs in his boxer briefs, he is naked and crawls over me, kneeling between my legs.

I place a hand on his abdomen and the muscles flex under me, sending heat up my arm. "Hang on a minute. I want to enjoy the view."

"Later. I need to burn energy, remember?" he says with a grin. Breaking my hold, he leans in and takes one of the thin shoulder straps of my nightgown in his teeth and drags it down my arm until my breast pops free. His mouth and tongue are hot and wet, searing my sensitive flesh.

I arch up, but he pushes me back, going to my other shoulder and repeating the sequence.

His teeth hold my nipple, his tongue making fast flicks against it.

I writhe under him.

He takes advantage of my movements and skims the nightgown down and off me, releasing my breast to sweep the fabric off my legs. When he turns back, he takes a moment to admire me, and I've never felt so beautiful. Then he's in motion again.

I grab him as soon as he leans down to lick into my mouth. My back arches up to feel as much of his skin against mine as I can reach. When his cock brushes my damp folds, I sigh into his mouth. We're both eager to celebrate his victory, and my hand clenches on his hip to tug him closer, urging him to hurry.

Always considerate, he nudges against my opening, testing my readiness, as this is the shortest amount of time we've ever spent on foreplay. Bracing on one elbow, he grabs my knee to open me further and slides inside. Tearing his lips from mine, he groans in pleasure. "You're rushing me, but damn."

"We can try your ideas after this."

"If you insist." His hips begin a rhythmic glide in and out and I sigh against his cheek, running my hands along what I can reach of his broad back.

His hand lingers near my breast, my knee in the crook of his elbow, and he puts his fingers to good use, tweaking my nipple as he knows I like.

I'm in a fog of pleasure knowing how well he tends my goal. My body hasn't caught up, though. There is a bit less lubrication and a bit more friction. His speed is slow enough, I relax and enjoy his drugging kisses, his thumb across my hard tip, his strength holding himself over me.

He shifts his weight slightly, his hips thrusting at a different angle.

A dull pain erupts when he bottoms out and I tense.

He thrusts again, and it aches again. "Hey, are you all right? Did I hurt you?" I must have winced for him to notice.

"I—I don't know. I'm a little tender." My voice comes out shaky, but I don't want to ruin it for him. Tonight was a huge milestone for his career and this is supposed to be a celebration. Remembering my friends' advice regarding communication, I ask, "You're just so big. Can you not go quite so deep for a bit, please?"

"Sure." His movements get shallower, slower, but he's watching my face, and I can't get my brain out of worry mode. He, too, seems more concerned than aroused.

Great. I've killed our mood.

He withdraws. "Hey, I don't want to worry about hurting you. How about we try one of my ideas now?"

"If it's something that allows you to lay back and relax. This is supposed to be your night."

"Oh, trust me. It's my night. Getting to have you here like this is everything I want to celebrate." With that, he slides backwards off the bed to kneel, dragging me to him with his hands under my butt and then spreading me wide. Before I can form words to protest, his mouth is on me.

My thoughts are still half on concern about what that pain meant. But his tongue circling my clit is the best sort of distraction. Besides, I can't ask my doctor anything tonight. If this gorgeous man wants to find a different way to give me orgasms, who am I to deny him?

He adds one finger slowly, only going far enough to

flutter over my G-spot, and I'm lost. I stop thinking, but only after promising myself to return the favor when it's my turn.

* * * *

Cam has to leave at the crack of dawn to pack for tomorrow's away game.

I check Maria's recent texts to verify that she's on early at the café, so I throw on clothes and drive there. I'll drink tea until she can take a break.

As soon as her coworkers are caught up on the morning rush, she comes over. She knows this wide-eyed, hair up in a messy bun, yoga clothes look. She steps in to hug me before sliding into the chair across from me at the little corner table. "What's going on?"

"It's back."

She wags her head side to side, keeping her gaze on me. "It being…?"

"My condition."

"What makes you think that?"

"It hurt." I realize that may not be clear, so I lean in and hiss, "*sex* hurt."

"Oh no." Maria squeezes my hand on the table. "Tell me. How bad, what were you doing, how did Cam deal with it. Wait"—she tilts her head—"it *was* with Cam, right?"

I growl.

She laughs. "Okay, okay, just trying to get your shoulders to drop a bit."

"It wasn't cramping like last time. More of a dull ache. And it wasn't continuous."

She raises her brows, plants her elbow on the table, and plops her chin in her hand. "When did it hurt then?"

"When he went super deep."

"Fingers, cock, what?"

"Um, the second." I glance around. She's keeping her voice down, but still I worry. Not only is my family known to some extent in Austin, although my face less so than my brother's, but Cam certainly is.

"How's his size?"

"Maria! I'm not sharing that with you. Besides, I don't have that much to compare him to."

"Okay." She hesitates for a minute, then asks, "Just tell me, is he bigger than your BOB?"

I nod, my cheeks hot. I'm curious enough about why she's asking to capitulate on oversharing.

"What were you doing before that? Oh, and what position?"

"Missionary, which we haven't done a lot of because the doc said that was the most likely to hurt. But we were—ah, a little eager last night. So there wasn't as much activity before that."

She slaps her hand on the table lightly and sat back, folding her arms across her chest, grinning like Cheshire Cat.

"What?" There is nothing funny about my endometriosis being back.

"It's not back, sweetie. You're fine. I mean, call the doctor, of course, but you're okay."

I frown. "How do you know?"

"Cuz most women, the lucky ones, have had that once or twice."

"Have had *what*? Geez, cryptic much? Stop torturing me and tell me already." Even if she's telling me there's nothing to worry about, I'd feel more confident if I understand what she's talking about.

She grins and explains, "You didn't have enough warmup for a guy that big, and your vajajay wasn't as stretchy as it needed to be. He was just bumping you too hard."

No wonder she asked about his size. Could it be that simple? But, "Again, how do you know?"

"You said it yourself. It's a different pain than in the past, and it wasn't continuous, only when he went deep." She hisses a dramatic sigh and looks heavenward. "Ah, to have that happen again."

"You really think it's all right?"

"Ask your doc, she's great at responding in email within a day. But make sure you give her all the info you gave me." She uncrosses an arm to point a finger at me. "You didn't answer the most important question, though. What did he do? Did he notice at least?"

I describe his reaction and without giving details, add, "We both enjoyed the rest of the evening in turn."

She is gaping at me. "Dayum. Are you kidding? He not only notices, but stops what he's doing and gives you—" she leans in to hiss—"oral? You need to marry this guy or I will."

"What?! You know this is casual. He wants kids."

"Have you told him about the endo?"

"No. Why would I? It's *casual*."

"Because what if it isn't for him? And because of things like last night, although I'll admit he reacted better than I'd have bet any man would, even without knowing. And because I suspect you passed casual a month ago."

I glare at her, lips pressed flat. "It is, and I didn't. I appreciate the support, but please don't push the emotional stuff. I can't have kids and he wants them. This has to stay casual. Never mind the fact that he will be negotiating a new contract at the end of this season and dating an owner would be super messy. We're still ending it after the dances at the Holiday Ball."

That hurts to say, even to Maria. Dammit, she may be right. That doesn't mean I won't end it, though. And if he finds out I *can't* have kids, it won't be up to me.

Chapter Twenty-Seven

Cam

After a workout and a late morning skate, I shower and grab my phone from my locker to tell Chris I'm picking up tacos from her favorite place. I need a snack before we run through our dance routines at her home studio, but I would never assume that she'll feed me.

Out of habit, I open Instagram and scan my feed. Since I lurk under an alias and don't interact with other users, I'm shocked at the message notification.

Opening it, I gape.

@ProudINMama:

> Hi - I think this is Cameron Hill's account. If so, Zoe is coming to Austin in January to start deferred admission at UT Austin.

Apparently, my stepmother not only knows of my

existence, but suspects I've been following her and the kids on Instagram. But what the hell does she want? She doesn't ask me anything, even to confirm that it's me. She randomly throws this information at me, assuming I want to know. Fuck, I shouldn't have been such a chickenshit and avoided DM'ing her. Then I wouldn't have been caught by surprise.

My thoughts are whirling. Chris's intimation that I might be a bit of a control freak flits through. But there are more urgent matters to consider. Am I supposed to reply? What would I say?

I lean my elbows on my knees and stare at the screen. At least we don't have a game today. This would severely mess with my focus.

When Jack comes by and asks if I'm going to lunch with them, I snap out of it. Declining, I stand. I need to talk to Christina or Saint. They'll help me figure out what I should do. No, there is no "should." It comes down to what I want to do.

I drive over to Christina's, checking Instagram at every stoplight in case I've received any more DMs. I should have minded my own business and gotten on with my life.

I'm almost to her house when I remember I was supposed to pick up tacos, so I detour and grab those, ordering from the car then running in to pick them up. While Austonians are still adapting to hockey, today would be the day I get stopped by fans and I don't have the patience for it even though I usually plaster on my biggest smile and play the game. I head back to Christina's.

Two quick knocks on her front door and I'm striding inside.

She looks up with a grin from where she stands pouring waters for us at the kitchen bar, then tilts her head when she spies my frown.

I dump the takeout containers and lean over to give her a quick kiss. "I need your help, please. Look what I got today." It's already open on the screen when I unlock the phone and shove it toward her.

Her gaze flicks over the message and she blinks, then smiles as she hands it back. "Cam, this is awesome. She's reaching out. What are you going to say?"

"That's just it. I don't know. She doesn't ask me anything. She tosses that tidbit out there."

"Okay, sit and eat, and we'll talk about it," she says, scooping our food onto plates. She loves takeout, especially tacos, but hates eating out of takeout containers.

I sit, but I can't eat. I put my elbows on the counter and rest my head in my hands. "I should have DM'ed her. Then I could control the narrative."

Chris snorts. "Oh my gosh, this is family. I get that your dad sucks, but let's allow the jury to still be out on this woman you've never met. Besides, you wouldn't have been following them if you didn't want some connection."

"But why is she messaging me?"

"Maybe for the same reason I suggested you message her. Let's review. What do we know?" Chris looks around and grabs a pad and pen.

God, I love that analytical brain of hers when it goes into overdrive. Analytical Chris is hot. I want all of her from that brain to her always-sore dancer's feet. It hits me: this isn't casual anymore.

Unaware of my sudden distraction, she asks, "Dana's

aware you've been following her on Instagram, but she only reached out now. Why?"

"Because she wants something from me?" I half growl, half ask.

"I can think of some other reasons." At my questioning look, she cites, "She was trying to respect your privacy. She was as unsure of her reception as you have been of yours. Something changed in her relationship with your father. She only just figured out who you were, etc. My point is, now that her oldest child is coming to Austin for whatever reason, she decided it's worth trying to establish a connection. She may want to know someone is watching over her daughter—"

I growl, "Exactly."

She continues unphased. "Or she hopes you'll want to know Zoe will be here, since you've been lurking like a weirdo on Instagram. Half in the family, half out. Heck, one of them could have spied you at your brother's game. Which, by the way, is the same level of passive-aggressive contact you're frustrated with in her message. Maybe she's meeting like for like."

Perhaps I should have gone to Saint. But no, he'd have called me on my shit as much as Chris, even though he doesn't have as many details about my family situation. Dammit, I hate when she's right.

No I don't. Her perspective is clearer than mine, and I need that to figure out what I want. Saint's advice filters through my head. I don't share myself easily, which makes it hard for others to trust me. I've been doing the same thing with my stepmother.

"Cam? You okay?"

"Yeah. I think…I think I want to answer her. I don't know what to say."

She's nodding. "You have the first decision made. I figured you'd end up there, or you wouldn't have been following them to begin with. Now you have to decide what you want from the relationship. And if you want one with Dana or just Zoe for right now."

"I wish I knew where my father fit in with all this. Is he behind that message? Why wasn't he at my game with them or Robbie's practice?"

"Do you want to ask that?"

"Of course. But Saint's warning about establishing trust with my teammates comes to mind."

She hums in agreement, letting me work this out on my own.

"So what do I say?" I tug on my hair in frustration.

"Why not respond to what she said about Zoe for right now. A congratulations. An acknowledgment it's you. And, *if* you want to and feel ready, maybe an offer for Zoe to reach out if she needs anything when she's here?"

"Yeah. Something short for now, to ease into things. Alright, let me think about that and I'll send something later. Let's dance before our muscles go totally cold."

"You all right so soon after tacos?"

"I didn't even finish one, I was too distracted. You?"

"I'm good. We're just running through the routine at this point. We both know it and just need to keep it fresh."

My grin is wide and teasing. "More time for other stretching exercises afterwards, then."

* * * *

After practice and dinner at Christina's, I have to drive home. I was in such a rush to discuss my stepmother's message that I drove to her house.

I lie on the couch staring at Dana's DM for far longer than it should take a twenty-four-year-old to formulate a text message.

Finally, I go with something benign.

> It is. Thanks for coming to my game in Chicago, and tell Zoe congrats, but please leave her Chicago Icemutts shirt at home.

Within a few minutes, I get a response of laughing emojis.

Then,

Dana

> We're thinking of coming down to Austin for part of Thanksgiving weekend to see her dorm assignment and your Saturday game. I'm actually online right now trying to find the best seats available. (Zoe says if we're going to enemy territory, we better be able to see the whites of their eyes.)

Zoe cracks me up. But Dana's "we" was not defined. I debate how to ask without sounding like a dick, but I'm not offering to hook them up with tickets if my father is attending.

The devil in me rears its head. I smirk; it must be Zoe's influence. Why wouldn't I offer him the best seat in the house? He may not appreciate the skill or hard work it takes to play this game at the highest level, but he'll sure as fuck see the price of the ticket—about $200 a seat for what I'd be able to get through the org.

Not letting myself think about it any further, I type.

> I can get you tickets. How many do you want?

I hold my breath, my finger tapping the edge of the phone. Please say three, please say three. The app shows she's typing for what feels like eons. Finally it comes through.

> Cameron, I already think of you as family, but you don't need to do that. The kids want to see you play again, and I can make that happen.

> I don't mind. It's a perk with the job. Seriously. I like the idea of them being there.

Ugh. I'm rethinking the "them" as soon as I hit send. She's going to believe I have something against her, when it's more about not knowing if my father will be with them. I quickly send another message.

> How many? I can leave them at Will Call under your name.

> 3 please.

Yes!

> Send me your flight info when you get it and I'll see what else I can arrange.

Hopefully, she'll think I mean a stadium tour, but I'm still trying to suss out whether my father will be with them for the trip. If he isn't coming at all, I'm warming to the idea of meeting my siblings. And Dana seems cool.

I'm looking at hotels tomorrow, so if you can recommend one somewhere between the UT campus and the stadium that aren't full of rowdy students, I'd love the help. But you're new there, so don't worry about it if you don't know.

I don't, but I'll ask around. Oh, and I assume you do want seats where you see the whites of our eyes, rather than in a team box or something?

Ah, you're sweet. I'd love the wine and food in the box, I'm sure, but the kids want to be as close to the ice as possiblel

Hint - there's wine and food down there, too, if you don't want to deal with the concessions. Of course, I'm not sure the junk food will be up to Zoe's standards if it's delivered.

I get another laughing emoji again. Holy crap, I'm joking around with this woman I've never met who actually thought marrying my father was a good idea. I need to pace myself until I know what her long game is. If she's setting up for Zoe to live with me or for tuition money or something, I'm going to be pissed. I need to ease into all of this.

But this feels like a promising start of a relationship with my half-brother. Adding a stepsister and stepmother into the mix would be a bonus.

Chapter Twenty-Eight

Christina

I heat leftover Thai food and get settled for the warmups. Now that I've seen them up close from Cam's seats, pre-game stretching is my new favorite thing. And they're miked for TV now, so even though they're in Seattle, I get to hear the chirping between our team and with the opposition.

The home team players are in pigeon poses and squats on their half of the ice, while the Tornadoes circle and take practice shots on the open goal. The cameras pan to where the goalies go through their extreme side lunges and hump the ice. Cam is way flatter to the ice than the other netminder. The Seattle goalie gets up and skates to the boards and grabs a water bottle. He guzzles it like he's already worn out. Hopefully, that means a good game for us, even in Seattle's house.

The camera closes in on Cam as he does a quick scan of the crowd. He's already focused. I can almost see the game tape of the other team running through his mind. He'd told me about getting into it with his teammates early in the season when he sided with the coaches on their criticism of some plays. Saint had given him some pretty solid advice. As far as I can tell, he's kept quiet since then, trying to follow that guidance and build trust.

When Greg and I watched a game together, he mentioned that Coach Steele was impressed with Cam's remarks after the team reviewed the opponents' game tape. Saint's comments made sense, though. No one likes criticism, and his teammates need to understand he's trying to build them up, not tear them down.

The Tornadoes struggle in the first period, missing a couple easy shots. Cam manages to block every puck aimed at him, but when the cameras give a quick glimpse of the team on their way into the locker room, his face is tight. I recognize that look. Something is up that he believes is fixable.

I take a bite of panang curry chicken but it's cold. While I reheat my food, I decide I need wine for this game and open a malbec. On my way back from the microwave, the game comes back on the TV.

Victor Gauthier and Milo Petrvosky are headed to Cam in goal. Petrovsky struggled in the first period. The TV announcers drone on wondering what they're talking about, but I have a good guess.

Cam listens to Gauthier, then looks at Petrovsky. The second line winger nods and Cam's shoulders drop. Seems like they can live with criticism if it gets them wins. Cam then checks the camera and turns a few degrees away from it to say something to the other two. Damn, for an NHL rookie, he has a presence about him already.

Saylet only put him in the press room that one time after his shutout, and he told me after he'd been terrified, but he managed a few terse answers and otherwise stayed as quiet as the questions allowed, deferring to her guidance. On the ice, though, he's at home, a team leader. It's a shame goalies can't be captains, although he wouldn't be as a rookie anyway. As Lauren would say, he has captain energy. Well, she'd say big dick energy, but whatever. I'm borrowing it.

The second period starts with the second line on ice. Petrovsky must have said something to Coach so he could apply Cam's advice.

I eat two more bites of my spicy chicken curry but my stomach's in knots. It always is for our team. I was never this interested in Greg's games. Perhaps because they weren't at this level, and I didn't have money invested in them. I try to picture my concern if I hadn't spent the last two months dancing with the goalie. Nope, money wouldn't matter. Cam is the reason for this stress, especially in his position. Goals are the measurement of a win or loss and goalies bear the burden of both sides of that coin.

We get a shot on goal in the first two minutes, which is unusual against the Pikes, but it's blocked. Their goalie has five years in the NHL and his stats are better than Cam's. The teams race up and down the ice, jockeying for possession of the puck, with both defenses so fierce, neither gets a shot on goal.

Saint gets a penalty for interference, so dammit, they're on a penalty kill. I'm going to need more wine for this.

Two of their players break away from ours and race along the boards. I always expect that to split the goalie's focus, but Cam always says the puck is the only focus. The players' movements are peripheral so he can anticipate where it will go next.

The Pike left wing looks to his teammate. With our players closing in behind them, he twists his body a few inches as though to pass and—

Wham! His shot is aimed at Cam's right elbow. Cam blocks the puck, but it bounces back into play. Our team is already there and Jack flicks it around behind the net to where Kyle Scott is waiting to pass it forward.

The second period ends five minutes later with the score still 0-0 and I wilt back against the couch cushions. I get up and go to the kitchen to pour another glass of wine. Halfway back to the couch I turn around and grab the bottle, bringing it with me.

The third period starts with players on both sides fired up. Each team manages a goal within the first few minutes, keeping the game tied and pissing Cam off.

The clock counts down the last five minutes of the game with the score still 1-1. I reach for more wine but the bottle is empty. I'll regret that tomorrow, but I blink the thought away to avoid missing a second of play.

There is a tussle over the puck right in front of Cam, and a Pike drives his shoulder into Cam, whose face is dangerously close to that hit. I stand, waiting for the penalty whistle, but it doesn't come.

Cam doesn't let it bother him. His stick goes between the asshole's legs and flicks the puck out to Scott, who wings it forward to Buzz. How Buzz knew to stay further away from the action, I don't know. I guess Seattle had all their guys trying to press Cam to get another goal before the clock ran out, because Buzz almost strolls down with Jack at his shoulder protecting him. At the last second Buzz lifts his stick like he's going to take a slap shot on goal, then dekes toward the boards, the goalie's eyes following his stick for the second Jack needs.

The lamp lights! I'm standing, hands in the air like they kicked a field goal, yelling a long "ggooaall" like it was soccer. Wine trickles down my arm from the glass still in my hand as our guys play out the last twenty seconds of the game. The game clock hits zero and skate clad bodies flow over the boards celebrating victory. Cam, helmet shoved up on top of his head, skates over and offers one a hand, only to be yanked into a bear hug. I'm so happy for them I can't stand it.

As I step out from between the couch and the coffee table, I stagger. Glancing back at the panang chicken, I see that I've only eaten a third. No wonder I was mixing my sports celebrations. I clean myself and my house, make a piece of toast in the vain hope of soaking up some of the wine with carbs, and vow not to call Cam or to answer if he calls. I don't want to say something I shouldn't as my tongue is always looser when I've had a few drinks.

Lying in bed, I can't relax. If this is my level of excitement from watching (yeah, yeah, and the wine, stop harping, already), I can only imagine how hyped the guys are after a tight game. Wearing his jersey and knowing he'll be back tomorrow night doesn't help. I conjure his hockey stance without the clothes and pads. Mmm, that was his position for our barre sex.

I roll to my back, stripping off his jersey so I can pretend he's here with me. Laying it flat between my legs, I bend my knees and stroke myself. I grab my phone to find the photo album I've saved of candid shots of him on the ice.

Chapter Twenty-Nine

Cam

I've barely taken my leg pads off when my phone rings on the shelf in my open locker. When I grab it, Dancer's picture pops up on a video call. I quickly swipe to answer.

"Holy crap!" I fly up from the bench and spin, slamming my back against my cubby, almost squeezing myself into it. My adrenaline from our win is immediately channeled to another type of energy.

"Wha-? Hey lover," Chris's words are slower than normal. She's half-asleep, but she doesn't usually sleep naked. The phone keeps dipping to show a boob. "Great game tonight. You were amazing."

"Thanks…" I look around. The visitor locker room is older and cramped. The guys are rowdy from the win, so even with a third of them in the showers already, it's loud in here with celebrating. In addition to wanting to keep her identity and lack of dress private, I don't care to share my teammate's hairy asses with her. So I find my earbuds and connect them. I attempt nonchalance as I ask, "How's the jersey?"

She pans down her body. Scans. Her. Full. Front. My name is upside down between her legs. I swallow. I *really* wish I'd had time to remove my cup before this call.

Her hand enters the frame, sliding over her pouty pussy. Based on how swollen she is, it isn't the first swipe she's made. I have to lock my arm to stop my hand from shaking. "Chri—" I glance around and lower my voice, not using her name—"sweetheart, what are you doing?"

"Thinking of you. Thanks for calling me. It's nice knowing you were thinking of me, too."

Okay, based on a few slurs creeping into her words, I'm guessing she's had more wine than she should. I don't correct her about who called whom. The view is too good. I'm not going to spoil my own fun. Hell, I wish everyone would go shower so I can free my cramped dick and jerk myself off to this screen.

"What were you thinking of?"

"Positions where that goalie stance could work well."

Oh man. I'm never going to get into my stance again without a hard-on, no matter how focused on a game I might be. A dozen ways go through my head on how to put that to good use for when I see her next. "Hmm…like when we were at the barre?"

One of the guys calls out, "Which bar?"

I gulp and wave him off, pointing to the phone with my free hand that was clenching by my side trying not to grab my cock.

"Yeeaahh. A double plié," she says with a sigh. Her hand is still over her lower half. "And I thought maybe doggy style with me kneeling by the bed."

"Mmm, that's a good one." I lower my voice further given that the guys heard, "barre." Choosing my words carefully, I glance around the room. Jack is frowning at me, probably because I've never hovered with my butt almost stuffed into my locker, but otherwise the place is rowdy with celebration. "What about with me over you, you up on some pillows?"

"Yessss." Her hand is moving faster now.

"C, you're killing me here," I say with a groan. "Can you bring the phone back to your face?"

"Oh! Were you staring at me while I master-mastur-rubbed one out thinking of you? Perv," she says with a giggle. "How did you manage to do that?"

Drunk Dancer would be a lot of fun in person, I can tell. Or even on the phone if I was in a private room.

She continues to babble. "You sexy beast. How can you be so cute and young and innocent-looking, that dimple popping every time you smile. Then you get on the ice and into that crouch, and you're the fiercest warrior ever. It's a pussy-destroying combination, I tell you. Even before you showed me mad skills in bed."

I might be blushing in the middle of the locker room. Hopefully the guys will assume it's because I'm still in my pads and sweating.

"It's a shame this can't last after the holiday thing," Christina is saying, her words slowing.

"Why not?"

"Cuz—" she hiccups. "Cuz—I can't have babies." With that, she starts sobbing and hangs up.

What? She worded that differently than she had before. I swear she said she wasn't planning to have children or maybe that she didn't want them. Not that she couldn't have them.

No matter how many times I call her back, before and after I shower, she doesn't answer.

* * * *

Two more second line players come over to me at the bar under the cover of celebrating to ask for tips on things they could improve. Petrovsky already thanked me for the couple things I told him to try, and Buzz and Saint have both come by to bang on my shoulder and tell me I did good. One of them must have said something to these two.

I love that I seem to have conquered the trust barrier with these guys, but I can't enjoy the celebration of our win or my breakthrough. I'm concerned about Christina and losing my mind over her last statement.

Finally, I text Maria even though it's after midnight in Austin and she may have to open the café tomorrow. She has a key to Christina's house so she can swing by and check on her either tonight or tomorrow morning.

Telling myself I can't do anything more, I put the phone away and chill with the team.

Hours later, I lie in bed wide awake. Did she really mean she can't have children? If she can't have children, she may still want to have them by other means. If she doesn't plan to have children, I assume she's not interested in exploring those other options. However, until I understand where she is at, I can't assume anything.

Bottom line, does it make a difference to me? I want a family, children. Do they have to have my genetics? And what about my contract? Do I care anymore if I have a chance to be with her?

Right now I'm so confused I can't think straight

enough to answer that for myself.

The next afternoon, I get off the plane and throw my bag in Jack's car telling him I need to make a stop and to drop it in my room. Christina dislikes the noise in the office and she likes to do most of her work remotely so I'm guesstimating she'll be home. I head over there not caring about my car being in the driveway. Talking to her is more important right now than appearances.

Not wanting to invade her space after last night, I knock and wait.

Chris comes to the door in makeup and a pretty burnt orange sweater that clings in all the right places over dark skinny jeans. Her eyes widen and her cheeks flame when she sees me, but she steps aside and says, "Come in."

I hesitate, unsure about leaning in and kissing her like usual.

She ducks her head, stepping around me to close the door and walks over to the living room to sit in an oversized armchair.

Her choice of the single seater over the couch is loud and clear. I strip out of my suit jacket and throw it on the back of the sofa while perching on a cushion.

Her tone is half-hearted when she offers, "Can I get you anything to drink?"

I shake my head once. "Maybe later. I wanted to talk first."

"K."

I grin, hearing a trace of defensiveness in that one letter. "How do you feel?"

"About how you'd expect." She mock glares at me. "You outed me to Maria."

Chuckling, I say, "I wanted to ensure you were okay. I'm sure you both already have seen each other under the weather from partying too hard."

"Yeah, but not from sitting alone in my house watching my boyfr—dance partner play hockey."

Boyfriend? She's the one who always wanted this to be casual and secret. That word shouldn't feel as good as it does.

"Cam," she continues. "I'm sorry. I don't know who called who but I shouldn't have answered, should have hung up when I realized it connected, given the extra glass of wine I had. I was riding your win and got carried away."

"Hey, you can drunk dial me any time. I learned I *almost* fit into my locker last night, and the view was spectacular."

Her head dips again, bringing a curtain of hair to hide her face.

"Chris, do you remember the whole phone call?"

She nods, the curtain shimmering. Then she drags her gaze up to mine. "I'm sorry about that, too. I shouldn't have blurted it out like that. It never seemed the right time to tell you, especially when our…fling has the expiration date of the charity ball."

"You don't think it was important to tell me why you didn't plan to have kids?"

"What did it matter?" Her voice is sharp. "Would you not have respected a choice not to have children, but it's okay if it's only physical?"

"That's not fair. I've respected all your choices— secrecy, dance lifts, you name it. But it might have answered some questions I had, or maybe created new questions, I don't know." I grab my hair and tug on it, trying to find the right words. Saint's guidance comes back to me and now more than ever I get what he was saying about trust being vital beyond the rink. "It's your decision. I guess I'm hurt—you trust me in the studio to always catch you, but this feels like you didn't trust me with information."

"Because it wasn't relevant. We always had an end date, not only because you want kids and I will never have them, but also because Greg would have both our heads and you have a great future ahead of you if we don't let this get in the way."

"What if it didn't get in the way?" I spew, my thoughts unfiltered, possibly not even consciously configured until this minute. "What if we knew we wanted to be together? Wouldn't Greg and the organization respect that?"

"But we don't."

I suck in a breath. That hurts more than the lack of trust and even more than a direct hit from a puck travelling a hundred miles per hour.

Her eyes are huge and sad. It could be pity but I prefer to think it's mourning for what our relationship can't include. "Cam, I won't consider it because I would never want to stop you from having children and living your dream. You've been clear about what your goals are. You're a driven young man and will have huge successes and get everything you put your mind to."

I want a family, I'm clear on that. But I want Christina, too. It seems that I can't have both; however, I'm not yet ready to let her go. The Holiday Ball will be soon enough for that.

I stand and cross to her, capturing a hand to tug her up. Enveloping her in my arms, I round my shoulders over her as though to protect her from the world.

"I'm sorry about your health. I'd like to understand

that better, if and when you're ready. I'm…frustrated at you not sharing until now, but that's on me. I respect that it's your decision, and I get why you didn't tell me." It might kill me worrying about what condition it could be and how her ongoing health is impacted, but I'll respect her boundaries.

Her arms land on the middle of my back and she returns the hug. Her response is muffled by my dress shirt when it comes. "Thank you."

"What do you want to do now? Dance? Dinner? Neither?"

She lifts her head to meet my gaze. "Let me finish telling you about my condition. I hate talking about it so it would be harder to come back to it. Then, I might like to try out that position that drunk me thought up?"

I groan and release her, adjusting my hardening cock in my suit pants. "Tease."

Her grin is fleeting, but I'll take it. She seems a few degrees less forlorn, less hungover. Following me back to the couch, she sits with our knees touching, holding my hand.

She takes a steadying breath and says, "When I was dancing competitively, I started to gain weight without cause, sex became painful, and my energy level was all over the place, as were my menstrual cycles."

I nod, squeezing her hand.

"They discovered endometriosis. Have you heard of that?"

"Yes. A girlfriend in college had a friend who had it. My girlfriend borrowed the diagnosis when her parents found her birth control. I guess that helps manage it?" I find myself wishing I'd paid more attention. And hurting in empathy for past Chris, because part of why I've been struggling over her lack of trust these past few days is because of how in love with her I am. I have a new appreciation for why Petrovsky and the guys got defensive when I tried to improve their performance. Trust is essential in so many aspects and layers of life. And I can see how the parameters of our agreement precluded the need for this information. Regardless, I want to know *all* the things about her. I want baby pictures and home videos of dance recitals. She has found this incredible balance of supporting her family and following her dream, and it's freaking impressive. To say nothing of her graceful skill on the dance floor, her intelligence…

I tighten my grip on her hand and she wiggles her wrist. Loosening it, I refocus on the details she's sharing with me now.

She answers my question with, "If it's mild enough, or caught early enough. Mine required surgery, due to a cyst, and well other things that you don't need to know about now. It wasn't fun."

My brow furrows. "I don't remember a surgical scar?"

"It was laparoscopic. If you look closely at my belly button, you'll find it. But personally, I enjoy you spending your time on other areas." She smiles when I bark a laugh.

"Okay. I may need one detour, but I hear you. What did the surgery do?"

"For now, given my age and health, they wanted to see how my body would react to the surgery, so they removed the cysts and tissue deposits. They were able to save my ovaries, but if it comes back, I could need a hysterectomy. I'm on a pretty high dose of hormones to regulate that.”

“And the only way to have children is to go off the hormones,” I guess.

“Right. And possibly more surgery to clear the Fallopian tubes if there’s been any buildup. If you understood the amount of pain I was in by the time I was diagnosed, you’d understand why I can’t face that.”

I nod, still trying to process all this.

“I am sorry you had to go through that.”

“That’s why I eat healthy and rarely—last night aside—drink more than a glass of wine at a time. And why I drink more tea than coffee. The right diet helps manage my hormones. I also have to keep about ten more pounds on me than I did when I was dancing fulltime, but that’s not as much of a hardship.”

“I bet.” I snicker, but a new thought occurs to me, my heart pounding. “Wait, you were in pain the other night. Could it be back? Do we need to get you to a doctor?”

“Calm down,” she smiles as she brings my hand down from where it was thrashing. “I wondered that too. I checked with Mar—the doctor.”

“Why would you check with *Maria*?” I’m aghast that I wasn’t here but also that she’d assume Maria could help with a medical condition.

“Because she was there when it all went down the first time, and I was freaking out so I needed moral support. It was also before the doctor’s office opened.”

“Oh. So what did they say?”

Chris snorts.

I start to pull my hand out again, to do what, I’m not sure.

“They said it hurt because you’re so big. And I needed a bit more warmup time than we had patience for that night.”

“Oh.” I sigh in relief. Then a grin blooms on my face.

“That.” She points. “That is why I didn’t want to tell you. You’re so—so—”

“Cocky?” I ask.

We both nearly fall off the couch laughing before I pick her up and carry her to the bedroom.

Chapter Thirty

Christina

Who knew that sex is such a good hangover remedy?

After we tested his goalie stance against the bed and deemed it another successful position, Cam had to leave because his car was outside.

I slept like a baby, but now I'm back to wondering where we left things. I want to reconfirm with Cam that he's cool with us maintaining the status quo and then parting after the Holiday Ball.

After his practice and lunch with some of the guys, he comes to my house for the first dance session in almost a week.

Before we warm up, I ask him, "Now that you know my situation, do you understand the need for secrecy and a time limit?"

"Yes. I don't love it, but I agreed, and you're right, nothing has changed."

I need to hear him say it. "So we're good until the ball, and then dance sessions and…the rest will stop?"

"You crack me up. Sex. The word you're looking for is sex, Dancer." He's laughing, but sobers quickly. "I suppose, although if both of us decide to keep it going, I don't see why we couldn't."

"Because you need to free up your time to bond with your teammates and find a woman who can give you what you want." My heart clenches as I say those words.

He shrugs, the skin around his eyes looking pinched.

I give up. Whether he likes it or not, we're going our separate ways after the team party. I can't risk my heart beyond that, and if I keep spending time with him, I'm going to be a complete wreck when we do inevitably end things.

We run through the dances and the only glitch is still incorporating the consecutive cartwheels. Afterward, we spend a little time enjoying my playlist and freestyling West Coast swing, simply for the love of dance, until our dance goes horizontal as usual.

The following evening is a home game. I'm in his seats with Maria again. She finished her last class and closed the studio while I got to enjoy Cam getting down and dirty on the ice with spread legs during warmups. But by the start of the game, she was beside me, in full Tornadoes gear layered over her dance leotard and leggings.

We sip hot chocolate and lean forward on the edge of our seats as our team skates their asses off. The Vancouver Wolves score on Cam early, and he bangs his stick on the ice three times. He's told me he does that to shake off the score. A goalie has to stay calm even if he's down ten points, to focus on the puck, the sticks, and the direction of oncoming players' cores. That almost always tells you the direction they'll go or shoot.

We score and the stadium erupts. The Tornadoes are going to storm the opposition.

Cam lets another shot on goal in. Damn. Is this my fault somehow, a remnant of our conversation distracting him? Another reason I shouldn't have told him.

But no, Buzz swings in and puts his helmet next to Cam's, talking fast. Cam nods and I swear I hear him grunt. Buzz talks more and points to the player, and Cam replies. Petrovsky skates over and pats Cam on the back. I realize the same player, the one Buzz pointed at, scored on him both times. He needs the first period to be over so he can take a breath and analyze what he's missing in the guy's body language.

At the break, Maria goes to get her usual snack, a pretzel the size of her head, that I'll get approximately three bites of. Cam almost stomps to the locker room, but I'm confident he'll have his head on straight by the time he returns.

He does. No more points are let in during the second period and the Tornadoes torment the Wolves, keeping the puck in their zone for most of the time. We tie the score just before the end of the period.

In the third, the Vancouver player who scored both of their goals shouts to one of his teammates. As the puck hits his stick his smile splits his face, sure he'll be able to fake Cam out a third time.

Cam skates forward to the edge of the crease and faces off with him.

He's at war now, and I have no doubt he'll block every shot the guy makes. It helps that the winger is cocky, which means he won't pass it back to another teammate, trying for the hat trick instead.

The Wolves player takes his shot and Cam not only blocks it, he catches it in his glove, stopping play. After tossing the puck to the ref, he laughs at the disgruntled wingman and gestures. Tucking his stick under his arm, he pats his head then wags a hugely gloved finger at the guy to say, "no hat trick tonight."

The crowd goes wild as they all replicate the gesture. I'm laughing and doing it, too. The cameras pan the stadium before zeroing in on everyone in the owner's suite, including Greg, mimicking Cam as well. Both Cam and Greg will make ESPN tonight.

Unfortunately, the game finishes in a tie, so we're in sudden death overtime, our first as a team. Vancouver pulls the cocky winger, and the Tornadoes have Buzz, Saint, and Jack to protect Cam and bring the win home. Our theme song blasts as they get ready for the puck drop and then it's on.

Maria barely follows the rules, but even she's on the edge of her seat, fully invested in getting to a win. The five-minute period counts down. Cam makes two saves before the guys get the puck back into the other team's zone. They try once, twice, then come racing back toward Cam. I'm barely breathing and Maria is clutching my knee like a lifeline.

Jack wrestles it away before they can attempt a shot and passes it forward where Buzz hovers at the blue line. Immediately, he's off. Saint outpaces the other skaters, making it look effortless, and is there just in time for Buzz to attempt what looks like a missed shot on goal, overshooting it. Saint pushes off one last time and goes to his knee, catching the puck for a one-timer that flips up and over the goalie's stick and shoulder.

The goal horn blasts, and the crowd goes wild. Tornadoes pour over the boards onto the ice, on Saint as soon as he stands. Cam's helmet is up and his grin is huge, joining in the group hug before they head off the ice.

My heart is pounding. As Cam glances back, I pat my head and wave my finger and he laughs.

I almost wish I could go to Chasers tonight to celebrate with them. But he knows Maria starts work early most days, and she isn't enough of a fan to want to hang with the team at a bar, so we've already made plans for our own private celebration.

I'll have to be content with sex and secrecy, as that is what we agreed upon. If I have a momentary wish for more, I'll get over it. With only a month until the charity ball, I'll have to.

* * * *

Greg invited the whole Tornadoes organization to a catered Thanksgiving at our house. We had an away game on Wednesday, thankfully in Nashville so the guys could fly home late, and daytime home games on Friday and Saturday, so few players can get to their family and back in that window.

If anyone is in town, they're welcome to show up with their loved ones. We'll heat the pool and hot tub for the kids no matter what the weather. While it's a young team with only a handful children that I recall, several of the office staff have families.

Cam showed me his DM exchange with his stepmom, and I'm excited for him that they're coming in later this weekend. Too bad they couldn't have been here for today as well. It might have been a low-pressure way to meet the other team members.

Greg structured today as an open house, with a turkey dinner to be served at 4:00 p.m., but guests welcome from noon on. There are snacks and salads out on a buffet for early comers, and the back-office families arrive earlier than the players. Cam texted me that they landed after 1:00 a.m., so that doesn't surprise me.

The weather stays mild, in the seventies, and kids of all ages are splashing around in the pool. Some are playing made up games, while others call for their parents to watch them. I'm on lifeguard duty, drinking a Topo Chico for the time being, happy to take a role that enables me to sit down. Amy and I have tag teamed being on call in the kitchen for the caterers and directing guests to the bar or a large cooler for soft drinks.

The air shifts and my skin pebbles with awareness. Cam is here, although I can't see him with the sun reflecting off the windows.

Sure enough, two minutes later, Cam and Jack wander out with tall slim cans of Topo Chico in hand. Given the pool and family time, Greg had made the dress code uber-casual, and they're in board shorts and t-shirts, Jack's with the sleeves ripped out. Probably in case there are any single women here, so he can show off his guns.

Maria's family is out of state and given the costs and hours of her studio, she opted to join us here rather than spend the time and money to get home. Nicole is also coming, as she's not close to her family in the Panhandle, but Lauren and her sister drove to her family home in Clear Lake.

Jack says something to Cam, and they put their drinks on a side table, strip off their shirts, toe off their shoes, and make a run for the water. They're airborne, clutching their knees to their chests and yelling their heads off. The cannonballs spray everyone in the pool. Some droplets make it as far as my legs on a lounger along the side of the shallow end near my little house.

I roll my eyes at them. "No diving please."

"We didn't!" Jack gives me his cheesiest smile.

"Agreed. And that's all right, but I don't want anyone going in headfirst, as not everyone knows where it goes to shallow."

"Oh, right. Okay. More cannonballs, coming up!" He turns to a gaggle of older children. "Who's in? Christina will be judge."

Cam says, "I'll judge, too."

Jack shrugs. "Good. We can't have a *girl* judge, can we, guys?"

"Oh my god," I mutter. Then louder, "Do not encourage misogynistic behavior in young impressionable minds, Jack."

"Mis-what?" He plays dumb, then winks and gets the kids to sound off numbers for the spur-of-the-moment contest.

As Cam wades toward the steps in the shallow end, I point to a huge stack of towels. He shakes his head like a dog before toweling down, and I try not to pant. Behind my sunglasses, my gaze follows droplets of water down his sculpted abs to his waistband. I gulp some fizzy water, my mouth suddenly dry.

He throws himself down next to me with a quiet, "You look fantastic. You should always wear things that bare your middle and your legs."

My eyelet off-the-shoulder crop top in Tornadoes purple and black capris are my attempt to be festive and casual. "Thank you."

Just then Jack shouts, "Judges! Incoming."

After we declare one young girl a winner, I take her into the house for a cupcake from a hidden stash that's for after dinner. I return to find most of the kids in a water volleyball game with Cam and Jack as coaches.

Cam steps forward to lift a smaller boy up to spike the ball and Jack's team boos. Jack subs in for someone who went under and came up choking. Then Cam shadows a little girl in the back row, his huge wingspan allowing him to return balls that she wouldn't have reached.

Something in the region of my heart twists. Most twenty-four-year-old single guys wouldn't bother themselves with kids. Jack is an overgrown child himself, but the minute a couple of cute women walk in, he'll be out of the water shmoozing. Cam though is genuinely enjoying himself.

Knowing he wants kids is one thing; seeing how great he is with them is a whole new level. I long ago reconciled myself to not having children, but even before that, I'd never been as gung-ho as he is. Now I find myself wishing I could have them, so I could stay with him.

Alarm bells clang in my head, sounding remarkably like the buzzer signaling the end of a period. I cannot have children, not without a lot of pain and possibly surgery. Even then it's unlikely and I could end up needing a hysterectomy if the endometriosis returns. However, my need to review all that again is not what prompts the warning bells. I've fallen in love with Cam—with his powerful dance moves and guarantees he won't drop me, with that lopsided grin, dimple popping, with his consideration and gentlemanliness in and out of the bedroom, and with his mature life goals. And I'm only going to get more hurt if I spend more time with him. Better to break it now, with this evidence of his future in front of me.

Chapter Thirty-One

Cam

After a close game of coach-assisted kids' volleyball, I hop out of the pool and search for Christina.

She's not anywhere outside that I can see, so I head into the kitchen through the French doors.

Greg snags me there to talk football. The Detroit game highlights on the large screen TV are being reviewed by the same retired-players-turned-commentators who have been making the same tired jokes for years.

I ooh and ahh in the right places of the snippets of game plays and slip away as soon as I can. Maria and Chris are huddled by the bar.

Maria glances up as I stride toward them, and ushers Chris out a door on the other side of the room. As I reach the doorway, they head upstairs. The same upstairs which has been roped off for the party. I'd thought today would be the perfect guise to spend time together in public. But now with her hiding from a party she's sort of cohosting, I worry if something is wrong.

I circle, chatting to office staff and their families,

keeping an eye on the doors from the main hall where the stairs are. Although for all I know, this house has another staircase or three.

Something chimes to indicate dinner is being served. There's a huge buffet in the kitchen, and tables have been set up around the pool, complete with linens and pretty white folding chairs. This house could be a wedding venue, it's got so much space.

I linger, hoping to join the buffet line when Chris re-emerges, but no such luck. I grab food and join a few teammates. Only then do I see Chris and Maria helping themselves. They never come out, and when I go in later, they've disappeared once more from the areas of the house open to guests.

I talk football, hockey strategizing, and holidays with the back office employees with half my mind on why Chris disappeared without a word. I texted her before the meal, but when I check it every ten minutes, my phone remains silent and dark.

Finally, dessert has been served, parents have talked their children out of a second round in the pool, and football has ended. There are a handful of us lingering, finishing drinks and watching the post-game analysis.

I stand and head toward the hall to the bathroom. Checking to ensure no one is watching, I veer off toward the patio doors. All it takes is a dozen long strides to reach her cottage. Barely refraining from pounding on her door, I knock quietly and try the door. It's locked.

I turn back to look at the second floor, but Saint looms behind the patio doors. *Fuck.*

He frowns and steps outside. As he nears me, he asks, "Prancer, what the fuck are you doing?"

I'm in love, and I don't care if the whole world

knows. But we should have a conversation with Greg before anyone, and besides, I need to respect Christina's wishes for secrecy. I come up with an answer that is truthful but vague. "I was concerned about Christina. She sort of disappeared from the party."

"Dude, the owner's sister is not your concern, dance partner or not." He must see something on my face because he adds, "No. Please don't tell me she is the person you've been oh so casually seeing."

I swallow, managing to maintain eye contact, but I'm not going to lie to my captain.

He leans in and hiss-whispers, "What the fuck are you thinking, Prancer? Hell, she's a co-owner. You're fucking with your career, never mind your boss's boss's boss. What if I'd been Greg Donovan?"

"I'd have played it off as being her dance partner. You only guessed because of our prior conversation."

"Maybe, maybe not. He still wouldn't have been happy at one of his younger players sniffing around his sister, and then he'd end up watching you more closely and possibly having it weigh in on your contract negotiations. Jesus." He paces a few steps away, running his hand through his hair.

Turning back, he barks, "Let's go. You and I are going to a different place, even your house, and having a drink and talking about this. Or not talking. Either way, you're done here."

"No. I meant it. I'm worried about her."

"Then tell Mr. Donovan."

"Ha."

"Clearly not that worried about her, are you?" He arches a brow. "She's at her home, with her brother and sister on hand, and that dancer chick is still around, too.

She's got people to talk to if she wants."

I had ridden over with Jack, and he's still hanging around shmoozing with Greg, something I should have been doing but hadn't been able to concentrate on.

Knowing Saint is right, I put my head down and follow him back into what in a normal house would be the family room. Here, it's probably the media room or something. Or the ground floor media room. I shake my head and follow Saint's lead, thanking our host for opening his home to us and providing such delicious food.

In Saint's car, I stare out the window, trying not to stress about Christina's silence. He lets me stew until we're at my house, likely the best bet for a drink on a national holiday.

In an unspoken agreement, we grab a beer each and head out through the back door to lounge by the pool. Our relaxed poses counter the chaotic frenzy in my head.

"Talk to me, Prancer."

"She ca—doesn't plan to have children." Even wanting advice, I won't betray Christina's confidence. "I want a family. There's also a strict no-frat clause in our contracts, which she says Greg will expect her to abide by as well. So we planned to hang out until the charity ball then go our separate ways."

"And by hang out, you mean Netflix and chill or whatever you kids are saying these days?"

I roll my eyes at him. "Yes, Grandpa."

"That doesn't explain you risking your career because you're worried about her."

"I—" I clear my throat and glance away, then meet his eyes again "—may have caught feelings."

He takes his turn to roll his eyes. "Prancer," comes

out on a sigh.

"I know, I know."

"I'm not going to lecture you on shit that's already done. What do you expect to happen from here though? What do you want to happen?"

"I was hoping you could help me figure that out."

He barks a laugh. There is a strange bitter note in it, but my brain doesn't have the bandwidth to dissect that now.

"Listen, I need to share something else with you. I don't know if it's related, but here's the thing…" I tell him about Dana reaching out and my response and their visit tomorrow. "It's not the family I was aiming for, but maybe there's more than one way to have a family."

"Of course there is. But if you want children of your own and she does not, that's still an irreconcilable difference. There's more than one way to have children, too. Have you thought about that?"

"No, actually. It was always straightforward, and frankly more of a concept than a concrete plan, and this has thrown me for a loop. Imaginary families don't come with step-by-step instructions."

He chuckles with me, but then says, "You need to figure out what you really want. And of those things, which is most important and which you can and can't live without. But all that? It's only half the process. You'd still need to then discuss whatever you want with her and make sure she's on board."

I am nodding throughout his speech.

He stares at me hard and adds, "But for God's sake, do it more subtly than in the middle of a party hosted by her brother."

I give him a lopsided grin. "Alright. Sorry, Cap."

He heaves a deep sigh. "Now, if you'll excuse me, I have to get home. Jessica didn't come to the team party today because she's planning some cocktail thing this evening with a few friends of hers."

"Oh, I'm sorry to keep you."

He shakes his head in dismissal and waves as he heads to his car.

Chapter Thirty-Two

Christina

Last night, I derailed Thanksgiving by commandeering Maria to act as my therapist. I spewed out everything about Cam. Our conversations, Cam's family stuff, my confession, his reaction, and then seeing him play with the kids in the pool.

She was prepared to defend my honor when she heard his question about choice versus physical ability, but keenly pointed out that his trust issues with his family and his team also impact our relationship.

As the bestest best friend she always is, she was in my corner through the whole retelling. Then, playing her role to the hilt, she went downstairs and swiped a bottle of my favorite wine from the cellar, bypassing the stuff put out for guests. And we got drunk together. When I went to the bathroom early on, she hid my phone so there would be no drunk dialing. I've never been prone to that, but as she pointed out, I've never been in this situation before, either.

So now here I sit, phone in hand with a pounding hangover, trying to figure out what to say to Cam. I've been radio silent since his text yesterday during the party. More surprising, he has, too.

> Hey, sorry I didn't reply.

Lame. I delete and start over.

> Hey. We should talk.

Ugh. Trite, much? Backspace, backspace, backspace.

> Yesterday made me realize we're risking a lot. Maybe we should ease off sooner rather than later. The holiday ball is only a couple weeks away anyway.

Cam

> ...

>

> ...

> Sorry to sound so abrupt over text. You can call me if you want to talk, or I'll meet you somewhere.

> Coffee? The little place near me, so we're away from Tornadoes regulars?

> Sure. 30 min.

When I get a thumbs up, I pull a hoodie over my tank top and change my yoga pants for wide legged jeans.

Cam is in a dark corner when I arrive, facing away from as much of the cafe as he can. But I'll never not recognize those shoulders and that form. He has the posture of a dancer more than a hockey player, shoulders thrown back, chest out. Even with a cap on and his head lowered, he can't hide from me. My breath hitches at the idea of never dancing with him after this month, of never seeing those shoulders naked and looming over me. I picture a gorgeous pregnant wife across from him and press a fist to my sternum as though it can stop the resulting pain. Swallowing back the agony, I stiffen my spine and approach.

His face is tight, his mouth flat, and his eyes sad. There's a second drink cup across from the one in his hand, but he doesn't rise to greet me or lean in to brush my lips with his like he usually would.

I tilt the cup at him an inch. "Thanks."

He nods, gives me a minute to sip, and then asks, "What changed, Dancer? I thought we were riding this out until the ball at least."

"I"—I'm not ready to admit that I'm in love with him and being with him even in secret will hurt more every day when I know I can't have him.

"You said something about yesterday. Is it the fear of your brother catching us? I can be more careful—" he stops abruptly and grimaces, his hand tightening on the cardboard cup in it.

God, he's killing me. All the fears of abandonment rise in him again. The frustration that another person is walking away from him, even when he's practically begging me to stay. I thought I was prepared for this; I'd practiced in my cottage. But nothing could have prepared me to hurt him the way I'm doing now. Yet it'll only be worse in two weeks. Or however long he had in mind.

Finally, I shake my head. "It's not that. You're right, that hasn't changed. It's…me. I can't do it anymore. I don't want to sneak around any longer. We know the routines. We'll go over them that day before the ball and be fine." It's a terrible, thoroughly inadequate reason to stop suddenly, and we both know it. I try one more time. "It's important for you to be free to find the right person for your future."

"You're doing this for me?" He's incredulous. "I never asked you to do that. I want—"

Oh no. It sounds like it was more than casual for him, too. And now he's stopping himself from trying to talk me into continuing. Of course some of it is his pride, but more than that, why would he expect anyone to stay after his father walked away so easily?

Dammit, I hate myself right now. Feigning nonchalance, I say, "What is the difference between now and two weeks from now? We'd agreed the Holiday Ball was it."

His jaw muscle pops as he clenches his teeth. "I guess…I guess I wasn't ready quite yet."

My smile is faint. "I didn't think I was, either. It all became too much. I'm sorry. It's been fun. And I would like to try to be friends. I want to hear how things develop with your stepmom and siblings. Maybe meet Zoe in a couple months."

His jaw ticks again. "Maybe. I need a little time to get used to this."

"I really am sorry, Cam, but I can't figure another way. We'd only end up back in this place right before Christmas, which would be even more miserable."

"Right. I'm gonna go."

It takes everything in me not to reach across to hold his wrist and ask him to stay. But for what, so we can sit and mourn what we had that I'm forcing to end? This sucks. I nod.

He glances at me. "Are you still coming to the game tomorrow?"

I hadn't thought about that. It would be weird using his seats now, but I already asked Nicole to come. "Is that okay?"

"You mean to use my seats? Of course. They're yours through the holidays like we discussed. It might seem strange after that, and"—he swallows and tilts his head, his next words thoughtful—"I might want them for Zoe."

"Of course. Thank you." Geez, we're polite strangers

now.

"Bye, Dancer. Um, thanks? Ping me when you want to do a final run-through."

Tears sting my eyes, but I manage to blink through them until he's several steps away, striding out of the café in giant, graceful steps. He stops to hold the door for a lady coming in, and her gaze spans up and down him as she thanks him.

And then he's gone, invisible due to my tears.

Chapter Thirty-Three

Cam

I'm so nervous I almost don't have room for the heartache still piercing me from this morning's conversation. I didn't play in today's game so I spent far too long circling how I fell in love with someone who didn't want me—until I headed to the airport.

Dana, Zoe, and Robbie were able to book a flight that arrived when I could come get them after my early Friday game. So now I'm waiting here staring at the huge elaborately painted guitars on Austin-Bergstrom Airport's baggage claim carousels. I worry about recognizing these strangers who are family, as well as being distracted by someone recognizing me when they descend the escalator.

After I'd responded to Dana's text, things progressed quickly. Her plan was to bring Zoe and Robbie to Austin for a super quick trip the day after Thanksgiving, and wanted to take them to our Saturday game, after which they'd fly home late that night.

So here I lurk. I actually wouldn't mind being recognized and showing off for these people whose motives I still question. But then I think of the kids being put out there on social media, and the ramifications of my fame are still new enough that I don't know what effect that would have. Instead, I lean against the wall to mitigate my height, my hood up, and my face down toward my phone.

There they come. Dana appears serene, no eye flicks searching for me, no twitching hands about meeting me or bringing the kids all this way on her own. Damn. I'm reluctantly impressed.

I stride forward as they reach the bottom of the escalator and call their names.

Dana smiles and does a half wave as Robbie flies off the last step of the escalator toward me.

I crouch to greet him as he skids to a stop in front of me.

"Holy—" he glances back at his mother. "It's really you."

I grin. "In the flesh. And it's really you. You're a great hockey player."

"How do you know? If mom told you that, it doesn't count. She's kinda bi-bi-"

"Biased?"

"Yeah, that." He sighs.

"Nope. I saw you play." I'd already decided to come clean about this. I hoped my explanation for not introducing myself will hold up for both these kids.

Zoe and their mom have caught up to Robbie now and frown at me.

"The day after you guys came to my game in Chicago. I had a rental car to visit my teammates, but I wanted to see you skate like you watched me. So I drove out. Zoe was there, doing homework I think." I earn points for that, as she darts a "see, I told you" glance at her mother.

"Why didn't you come talk to me? Man, my friends would have *flipped*," Robbie says.

"Well, first, I didn't know you knew who I was. And second, your coaches would have flipped out with a strange adult coming in to try to talk to you. Safety first."

Dana nods and I hope I'm in the clear, until she says, "Or you could have reached out on Instagram."

Zoe snorts a laugh, muttering behind a fist, "She shoots, she scores."

I mock frown at her before standing to hold out my hand to Dana. "It's nice to meet you. Welcome to Austin."

I'd chosen my words carefully as I'm not entirely sure yet if it's nice to have them here. But she bats my hand away and steps in. "Nope. I'm a hugger, and we're family."

Then her arms are around me. I freeze for a second before loosely returning the hug.

I catch Zoe's expression over her mom's shoulder. She's still smirking at me. I glance around for phone cameras then stick my tongue out at her. She snorts.

"Do you have luggage?" I ask.

Dana shakes her head. "Just the roller bag and backpacks, since we're only here one night."

"Great. My car's this way." We'd agreed that they could use my car or rideshares for their short stay. I would catch a ride to the game with Jack.

At the hotel, Robbie says he wants to see my house so we all pile back into the car after I give Jack a heads up we're coming. The kids brought bathing suits in case the hotel had a pool, but overnight the fickle Austin weather has turned too cold even for Indiana natives.

We have dinner reservations in a couple of hours and I arranged a tour of the stadium, at least the parts that are open for the holiday weekend. In the meantime, Robbie is in the kitchen quizzing Jack on his reasons for becoming a defenseman, Zoe has her face pointed at her phone but I'm pretty sure she's listening to all of us, and Dana and I talk youth hockey.

She studiously does not bring up my father, and while I'm curious about her—and perhaps more importantly, Robbie's—experience with him, I don't want anyone to believe I care what he does or where he is, so I don't ask.

Dana excuses herself to use the bathroom and get a drink, and I look over to find Zoe staring at me with narrowed eyes.

I ask her, "Can I get you anything?"

She shakes her head, tilting it. "What's up with you and Frank?"

"Nothing." My voice is flat at the reference to my father.

"Why?"

"You should ask him that."

She glances away. Then turns back. "I'm asking you."

"I don't know what your family…dynamic…is like. Things may have changed, so I don't want to influence your relationships"—I circle a hand to include the three of them. "Suffice it to say, he and I didn't see eye to eye on the importance of hockey to me, or whether it could be a career."

Her brows raise. "And now you're laughing all the way to the bank, huh?"

Ah, the joys of a teen's unfiltered connection between brain and mouth. But I can't help it. I smirk and wink. "Something like that."

She laughs. No stifled snort, no half-smile or smirk. Outright laughter.

I'm enthralled. When she laughs, she's transformed into a beautiful young woman, rather than a bordering-on-sullen teen. Holy shit, the guys at UT are going to be all over her. Suddenly, it doesn't matter what any of their situations are with my father. I'm worried about my sister. "Hey. Before I forget, let me give you my number so you have it when you're here. If you need anything—*anything*—you call me. It'll be a safe space, no reporting back to Dana. You hear me?"

Her eyes widen. "Dude. You don't even know me."

"You heard your mama. We're family. And there's only one way to get to know you—to spend more time with you. Now gimme." I gesture for her phone.

She hands it over without a single snarky comment, a smile playing at the edges of her mouth.

We're back to staring at our phones in silence by the time Dana returns.

* * * *

Unsure of their tastes in food, I take my newfound family to Roaring Fork, reveling in the fact that I have relatives visiting like a fucking normal hockey player. The north location of the restaurant has a fantastic patio, but I've been warned repeatedly that the weather this time of year is uncertain, so I booked indoors. Given that it's now raining as well as cold, I'm glad I did.

Saylet sends us all an email and text reminding us that roads are slippery because the sun and heat bring the oil to the surface, and the wind through the underpasses means that rain might freeze on the bridges.

A couple of the guys joke on a group thread that she should realize almost every last one of us has spent more time driving in snow and ice in any given year than she's seen her whole life. Buzz shuts them down immediately, though, with a text reminding us to respect management and thank people when they're trying to help. He may not be our captain, but he's definitely a team leader, even at a relatively young age.

As we order, I spy a crab cake on the menu that Christina would love, and my breathing hitches. For the most part, traversing the stepping stones of getting to know these family members without twisting a metaphoric ankle has kept my mind off her for a few hours. I slept like crap last night unsure of how she was doing, so it was lucky that Murphy was on this afternoon's roster. I hope it's better tonight or my performance in tomorrow's game could be affected.

My lips twist at my thoughts, and I cover them with my napkin. There's no use wishing she was here to celebrate this relationship she helped me navigate. Even if we'd still been together, she'd never have come out to meet my family as my girlfriend. She was always cemented in it being casual. Now I know why, but I don't have to like it.

As the younger two argue over what dessert to share, Dana turns to me, twirling her wine glass. "We don't have to talk about him if you prefer, but I'd like to tell you one thing."

Clearly, "him" is my father. I grab my almost-empty beer and sit back silently.

Dana glances at me, her wine glass, the kids, then

back at me. Her voice is lower when she speaks. "We've been having issues since Robbie started hockey. He'd mentioned you when we married, but as a college kid. When Robbie wanted to play, though, your role in the AHL came out. He was—" she clears her throat.

"Dismissive?" I offer.

She nods and continues. "Anyway, when I looked you up, I was impressed. For someone to have a dream and then make it reality, to play—no, perform—at that level, is incredible. It's someone I want as a role model for my children."

I nearly choke on my own spit. With my beer empty, I reach for water, needing a minute. Robbie and Zoe are both silent now, staring at us.

"Thank you," I mumble into my water.

"I've moved out," Dana starts.

Zoe clears her throat.

"Excuse me, *we've* moved out," Dana smiles at her daughter. "I don't know what's going to happen, but I need you to understand that I wasn't fully aware of the divide between you. I should have been, and I'm sorry for not asking for more details sooner. But most of all, I—we—don't think like he does."

Both kids are staring at me intently.

I still have a lump in my throat from her words, and her last statements didn't help it. But nor do I want her to leave her husband over something that is ancient history. Can I ask that in front of the children? Zoe, maybe, but I'm not sure about Robbie. I dart a glance from Dana to him and back.

She smiles. "It's all right. You can say anything, although I prefer you edit your word choice for profanity."

Zoe smirks.

"I'm fine. I've moved on, and as you said, I'm living my dream. I hope the issues between him and me didn't cause your rift."

Zoe's eyebrows raise. I need to get better acquainted with this girl, so I can understand her reactions and facial expressions. I'd give a lot to know what's going through her head right now.

Dana responds, "That's kind of you. I honestly can't say if the knowledge of what he did in the past alone would have caused this, but when he started doing the same with Robbie, and even with Zoe given her choice of major—"

I glance at her.

"Art," she says with a wide grin.

Ah. Dear old dad must have loved that one. I snort a laugh.

Dana continues. "It showed a pattern of inflexibility, of lack of support of children's dreams. All of it reflects poorly on him as a father. I mean, look at your success. Even now, he still can't admit he's wrong. I want you in our lives and I want Zoe and Robbie to follow their dreams—as long as I'm not supporting them beyond university."

She slides a sly glance at the kids and they roll their eyes. Apparently, this part has been covered before. "We're still talking. If he can be more supportive, then great. Otherwise, he may end up lonely."

It's my turn to raise my brows. I consider her statements and mama bear tone, and something about her protectiveness of me, beyond that of Robbie, when she had never even met me, starts a bloom of warmth in my chest. While I'd always blamed my father for his shortsightedness about hockey, I had also taken his lack of love as a statement about me. For the first time, now someone else points out how wrong his actions were, the burden of feeling unlovable, of condemning myself for his abandonment, eases.

I swallow hard. It'd be just my luck to be caught on camera by a fan crying in a restaurant. "I agree. I don't want that for any of you, either. And I already know I want you all in my life."

It's Dana's turn to get misty, and being a woman, she allows the tears to form. "Thank you."

Zoe of course is a hardened case, and just grunts. "Yeah. Thanks."

"Cool! Does that mean you'll get us tickets to more games? And come to mine, and—" Robbie's voice is cut off by the rest of us laughing openly at his eagerness.

"Yeah, bud. That's what that means. And your sister will have family nearby when she comes to college."

Dana beams at that idea, and I yearn again for Christina to be here. If not for her help, I wouldn't have opened my heart to these people who don't seem to want anything more from me than me. Well, and a few tickets in the case of the six-year-old.

* * * *

Saturday morning Coach agrees to let me to bring Robbie to the morning skate. The defensive coach has a son Robbie's age and keeps him close, answering his unending stream of questions with a level of patience I wouldn't have expected, given how surly he is with our defensive line.

Dana and Zoe have arranged for a walkthrough of her dorm and hope to hang out in a café by campus to get a feel for student life. If Zoe was more outgoing, I'd have suggested she ask a few girls in the dorm for advice or tips, but perhaps Dana will do that. Hopefully, the teen will at least keep her phone tucked away.

Our skate is quick. After the tour I'd arranged, I bring Robbie back to the house to eat something and chill before the game. For better or worse, a young brother obsessed with hockey keeps my mind off Christina. Mostly. If she was here, she'd be giving me thumbs up at their enthusiasm and grinning when hugs are forthcoming. She'd be almost as happy as I am about the wonder of having a family again.

She's the one who chose to cut herself off, though. Okay, okay, cut herself off early. Part of me just wants to get to the Holiday Ball so I can see her, touch her, dance with her one last time. But then what? She's right. I want kids and she doesn't, or daren't. It's only been two days and I miss her more than I would have ever imagined. I never thought about what would happen after the holiday thing, because I assumed I'd convince her to stay with me. I knew I wanted long term even before I admitted to myself that I was in love with her. But her revelation about children has changed everything.

Except missing her. Whenever I've dated someone in the past who wasn't willing to move for hockey, start a family, or save rather than going on the next vacation or buying the next whatever-brand bag, I dropped her and moved on. I should be packed and out the door emotionally, ready to hang with Jack at Chasers and chase. Not puck bunnies, as I've never done that, but women.

Instead, I'm moping and barely managing not to text her details of my family's visit.

Crap. Being in love makes everything different. I couldn't envision our breakup after the party because I can't envision my future without her. I love her. I want to be with her forever, sliding takeout onto fine china and dancing as best we can when we're eighty. Well, she'd be eighty-six, ha.

Now what? I still want a family. I want to spend time with my children and offer them encouragement like I yearned for from my father. I want someone like Dana who takes the initiative to ensure her children's happiness, even when there are roadblocks. All of which I envisioned Christina doing until our last conversation.

Robbie tugs on my sleeve. He's been talking to me while I zoned out. Still reeling from searching for a way to make things work with Christina, I do my best to shove all thoughts of her out of my head and enjoy the time I have with him. While Dana says we're family and Zoe will be here, who's to say that they won't change their minds along the way, just as my father did? Even Robbie, who has a severe case of hero worship, will be easily distracted by other things when I'm out of sight, putting me out of mind.

A new resolve steals over me and I throw my shoulders back. Saint pointed out that I needed to establish trust with the team off the ice. I can do that with my family, too. I've already started. I'm not seventeen anymore. They'll have a harder time getting rid of me if they decide to. More, I need to learn to trust others, as he pointed out. Dana has given every indication that she chooses family over…whatever differences she and my father have.

As for Christina, she's super close to her family, to the extent of being in business together. And while her trust in sharing her illness was slower than I'd like, she did trust me with it, and had told me about her dream of a dance school for underprivileged kids before that. Now I need to have faith that her confidences are a result of deeper feelings that I can coax out to overcome her fears.

Saint also told me to figure out what I can't live without. I have a family. Here, in front of me, asking me to check his goalie stance for the dozenth time. There will be children in her dance school that I can mentor. What I need, what I can't live without, is Christina.

First, though, I need to refocus on hockey and win this afternoon's game in front of everyone I care about, and—hard as it is to fathom—who care about me.

The team isn't sure what to expect Saturday afternoon, given the nasty turn in weather Friday night. Texans aren't known for going out in inclement weather, particularly for a new sport in town. So while this is a holiday weekend, and today's and tomorrow's home games have been sold out since pre-season, we're cautious about hoping for a big turnout.

But when we skate out for warmups, the crowd is already sizeable. Kids line the glass to watch us and try to interact, way more than we're used to seeing at night games. Some hold signs. Robbie's wearing my number. Zoe hangs back, too cool to press against the boards. When I wave to Robbie, Buzz catches the gesture. He skates over, beckoning the guys. We all do a loop around our half of the ice, trailing a glove along it for the kids to high five. The Winnipeg Bucks see us and fall into step, both teams circling the rink.

I do everything I can to avoid looking at my seats to confirm if Christina is there already. But when we return to warmups, I can't resist showing off. As always, I start by ensuring I avoid the dreaded goalie injury, a groin pull. Just in case she's there, not that I'm thinking of her *at all*, I make sweet, sweet love to the ice in my hip stretches, rolling through the moves rather than fucking the ice like she says I do sometimes. As I head to the net, I force myself to put her and my newfound family out of my mind. My head needs to be one hundred percent in the game. Using every vestige of self-discipline that got me here, I revert to my normal routine, running the game tape through my head one more time.

As I weave through my teammates, the guys thump me on the back.

"Get 'em, Prancer."

"Thanks for the tips, man."

From Jack, "I got your back. I'm on #16 like white on rice."

We were all nervous about Winnipeg's first line winger, whose slapshot is vicious, the fastest in the league. In the spirit of trusting my team, I'd admitted my fears about stopping those while we analyzed the Bucks' game tape.

Their comments buoy me up, my blades barely skimming the ice, warmed by the acceptance and respect. Saint was right, I feel much more a part of a family now than I did at the start of the season. This sense of belonging might be addictive.

However, now's not the time for philosophical thoughts. I want to show a certain team owner my grit, determination, and competitiveness. Oh, and Greg, too.

For the next sixty minutes, I zero in on that black disk. #16 is in my peripheral vision, but Jack is there too, as promised. I'm on fire, determined to prove myself to Christina, my family, and the world.

An NHL game usually includes around thirty shots on goal. I hit thirty saves late in the second period before one slips by me. That stupid fast slapshot got me finally. #16 smirks, I glower, and the teams face off for another two minutes of play before the period ends.

In the locker room, we get a pep talk from Coach, and it turns out Saint is beating himself up for a missed shot on goal.

I tell him, "That was a legit good shot, just a better save. Sadly mine was the other way around. But I won't dwell on it if you don't. Let's go out there and finish this."

He nods, and we're back with a killer attitude. He doesn't make another shot, but Mattie does, and we finish the game with a win 2-1.

Chapter Thirty-Four

Christina

This game was torture. I'm also pretty sure Cam made sure it was extra painful with his warmups. Nicole, who accompanied me today, was swooning in her seat and fanning herself as I shushed her. She's all revved up to go to Chasers after the game again.

We took separate cars to the arena, so after the game she runs her car home and will meet me at the bar. I really don't want to sit at Chasers by myself waiting for her so I decide to kill the time by going to the owner's suite. Greg's not here, but Travis has just finished gladhanding with suits. Two businessmen brush by me with polite nods as they exit the room. They probably wouldn't have ignored me if they realized who I was. I'm so thankful I don't have to deal with the like of them in my day to day, unlike Travis who cultivates relationships with them.

He clearly hasn't seen me yet. He sets his drink down on the nearest available surface and heads to his laptop case. I take a deep breath, enjoying my calm. Up until this season, his mere presence has curled my lip in disdain—hidden, of course—before he even opened his mouth. Now, I feel nothing.

That's maybe a very tiny silver lining to the cloud of letting Cam go. I finally understand real love, and real loss. Travis is not worth my angst. I mean, away from his work, he's not a bad guy. The trick is getting him away from being "on" all the time.

I must make some movement, because he turns his head and says, "Chris. Good to see you. How are you?"

"I'm good, thanks." *Heartbroken, but otherwise fine.* "I was looking for Greg?"

"He beelined it to the friends and family lounge to congratulate the team."

Ugh. Seeing Cam there with his family will stab me in the heart all over again. But at least I'd fade into the crowd. And part of me wants to see Cam flush off a win, and to ensure things are going smoothly with his family members.

"Thanks Travis. See you around." I'm amazed at how relaxed I still am. Even a short courteous exchange like we just had would have had my shoulders around my ears afterward. I might still bristle if Amy is around, but that's sheer protectiveness. As for the rest, I wish him the best and don't regret anything. It all helped me appreciate Cam that much more, and he was worth waiting for.

Downstairs, the lounge holds several new faces, likely parents, siblings or other family in from out of town on a holiday weekend. Jack's parents live in Dallas and have come down for a few games, so I wave to them. They're in conversation with a woman a little younger than them. I recognize her and the teen and young boy hanging near her from Cam's Instagram feed.

I linger in a corner. Greg comes in from the direction

of the locker room. "What are you doing here?"

"Eh. Nicole is going to meet me at Chasers but not for half an hour, so I figured this has better food than the bar." I gesture to the buffet of snacks.

He nods, accepting my explanation at face value and leans in to kiss me. "I'm going to take off. Have a great time. Try not to get into trouble with Nicole."

I roll my eyes at him. "Go home, brother. You're not my keeper. I haven't called you for bail yet, have I? Besides, you wouldn't know where to find it, since I manage all your money."

He chuckles as he leaves.

I grab a Topo Chico off the end of the buffet. As I turn, I nearly bump into Cam's stepmom.

"Hi. Are you the owner's wife?" she asks.

I try not to be offended. It's a reasonable assumption, but my feminist side is irritated. "No. I'm one of the owners."

"Oh, I'm sorry. And the man that just left, he's another owner, right? The one who manages the day-to-day? I was looking at the website and only saw his photo."

"Yes, Greg is my brother, and I prefer to stay out of hockey management." I relent and hold out a hand. "I'm Christina."

"Nice to meet you, Christina. I'm Cameron Hill's stepmother. I brought his siblings here to see him play, as Zoe, my eldest, will attend UT in the spring."

"I went there as well and have fond memories. She picked an excellent school. What is she planning on studying?" I'm eager to learn more about these people connected to Cam and want to grill her for information. Or mandate that she never desert Cam after inserting herself into his life. And quiz her on what the ever-loving fuck her husband was thinking to walk away from such a wonderful son.

Before she can answer, the players start trickling into the lounge. Jack makes a beeline for his parents and hugs a man-child a few years younger than him, who must be his brother.

Dana sees her son edging toward the door to the hall and takes a step forward to rein him in.

Just then, Cam comes through the door and sweeps Robbie up onto his shoulders.

"You won! You won!" Robbie shouts, clutching his hair.

Cam winces, but doesn't let go, striding to Zoe. He stops at enough of a distance to satisfy a grumpy teen and asks, "What'd you think?"

"That #16 got one by you." She shrugs a shoulder.

"Thanks. I hadn't noticed." He laughs, and she lets a corner of her mouth turn up.

I'm staring, soaking every gesture, every syllable in.

Dana's voice reminds me she's still by my side. "He's amazing, isn't he?"

I flash her a glance. "The whole team is. Greg did an excellent job. I hope we can keep most of the team intact next year."

"Hmm." Her voice is noncommittal. "I'm bummed we have to leave. I would have liked to stay for another game. This energy is addictive. But Cam's driving us to the airport from here."

"I know," I say.

She shoots me a look, surprise turning to awareness. "It was great to meet you, Christina. I hope to see you again at a future game. Look out for our boy there, will

you?”
        If only I could.

Chapter Thirty-Five

Cam

In the car, Dana congratulates me on my win and thanks me again for the tickets. She adds, "We'll be back for sure, but only if it's not a problem to get the tickets. Please tell me they don't cost you face value."

I slant her a look. "They don't. You're welcome any time. Once I know my contract status for next year, I plan to buy a house, which would give me more room for guests."

She nods, ignoring or accepting the fact that I didn't outright say she'd be welcome there. I'm still afraid that all this is too good to be true, but I'm serious about my plan. I'm going to do my best to trust them and to prove myself trustworthy.

"I met one of the owners," Dana says casually.

I stiffen, and she notices, dropping her gaze to my hands clenched on the steering wheel. I do my best to loosen my grip and ask, "Greg?"

"No, Christina."

Damn. Something must have happened or she wouldn't be teasing the subject out like this. I glance in the mirror. The kids are sharing pictures on their phones, probably of the game or a few candids of the players from the lounge. I manage to stay unclenched and silent, hoping she'll drop it.

She doesn't. "You seemed to be important to her."

My heart twists in tandem with my lips. "Nope."

"That was a strong response." Dana's brows are raised when I glance at her. "Come on, Cam. There is clearly more than owner/player going on here."

"Not anymore," I mutter. There is silence in the backseat and the kids are staring wide-eyed at me in the mirror.

When my eyes meet Zoe's, she smirks. "Haven't you ever heard the saying, don't shit where you eat?"

"Zoe!" Dana scolds.

"Sorry, Mom. Don't *poop* where you eat." She's still smirking, the brat.

Thankfully, Robbie doesn't weigh in. He seems bored by the topic and goes back to his phone, humming to himself.

"It was casual." Great. Now I sound defensive to an eighteen-year-old.

"It didn't seem casual to her," Dana says quietly.

"Yeah, well, that's her problem. She's the one who broke it off."

"Do you know why?"

I glance back at Zoe. She's rapt. Oh well, I guess I'm sharing with the class. "I want children and she doesn't."

"If it was casual to her, that wouldn't matter, would it?"

My brain stutters as Dana's words register. She's right, damn it. Christina would have just ridden out the next month, getting the best sex of her life (per her; I'm not bragging), and prepping for our dances.

Zoe's voice breaks into my thoughts, sounding incredulous. "You want kids?"

"Yeah, I do. Why does that surprise you?"

"Cuz, you know." She flaps a hand. "Hot hockey player, twenty-four, making a mint. I'd expect all of you to be like Jack."

She's already seen to the core of my player roommate. Priceless.

"Plus," she continues. "After witnessing Mom's experiences with marriage, I sure as heck am not eager to think about it—sorry, Mom. I guess I assumed you'd feel the same."

"Here's another way to view it." I try to explain my thoughts. "Like you, I had one wonderful, supportive parent, so I know what that feels like to a kid. I want to recreate that for my own. I haven't had a family since my mom died when I was sixteen, and I'd like one."

Zoe is nodding.

Dana says, "You have one now. Families don't all have to be the same. No matter what Zoe believes, I wouldn't trade my relationships for anything because they gave me these kids. Now, I'm giving them to you to share, as well. Maybe that can be what family looks like, too." Dana's words match what I've been considering this weekend.

We're off the exit ramp to the airport and stopped at a light. I stare forward, not ready to meet her eyes as her words sink in. Swallowing, I manage, "Yeah, it can. Thank you."

She squeezes my arm. "You need to decide how flexible your view of family can be. And how flexible hers can be. And most of all, what you want more, should it come down to it."

Her words echo Saint's and reinforce my thoughts. I want Christina most of all.

Zoe is silent, eyes downcast, as we pull up to Departures. But when we all get out and I grab the roller bag from the trunk, she steps in first wrapping her arms around my waist. "Thank you, brother."

I hear the emphasis on the last word. She's reinforcing Dana's message about family. I choke and tighten my arms around her. "Thank you for coming." I glance up. "All of you."

Zoe steps back and nods to me once, allowing that half smile, half smirk to climb one side of her face. "I'll see you in January."

"I'll be here."

Robbie throws himself against my legs. "Please say you'll come to one of my games soon."

I laugh. "I'll check the schedule and do my best."

Dana tugs him away.

I don't wait. Stepping in, I wrap my arms around her. I bend my face to her hair and whisper. "Thank you. Thank you for giving me my family. For being my family."

"Absolutely. Don't be a stranger. Or a lurker on Instagram."

That lightens the mood enough that I can lift my head without embarrassing myself. "Text me when you get home please. And call me if anything goes wrong with the flight."

"Yeah, yeah, you said that already." Zoe is too cool for this and is already walking away as she tosses the words back.

Dana smiles and nods and grabs Robbie's hand.

I watch them until they are inside and lost in the crowd for the TSA check, feeling strangely bereft.

* * * *

She's not here tonight. The rink feels colder. Maybe it's from the high off Saturday's game and having my family here, but I suspect it's more Christina's absence.

I go through my warmups by rote, trying to concentrate on the game and the team we're facing. Try as I might, I can't find my Zen.

The game starts, and every shot on goal seems faster, sharper. I'm barely there in time to make the saves. Every reach feels slower, longer. Maybe the other team can sense it, or maybe the rest of my team is struggling with the fourth game in six days, because the pucks whizz at me more frequently. Eventually, one gets by me. I jab my stick at the ice three times, the only frustration I ever allow myself. We're down before the end of the first period in our own house.

As we head off for the first intermission, I glance over. My seats remain empty, mocking me with their folded silence.

When I'm struggling with focus, I channel the Vancouver goalie whose number I chose to wear, picturing his fantastic saves from the first night I saw him play. He was in the zone that night, his attention on the puck absolute. And nothing got by him. I vow the same for the next two periods.

But when I scrape onto the ice again, my gaze shoots to the stands. They're still empty, and my concentration is in tatters.

I let two more goals in that period. Thankfully, the rest of the Tornadoes have rallied and scored twice as well.

In the next intermission, Coach Steele stares at me hard. "What's up with you tonight, Hill?"

Ugh. We always know he's unhappy when he uses our real names rather than the nicknames we've garnered from the team. "Nothing. I'll do better."

Saint slants me a look.

"Do I need to put Murphy in?" Coach asks.

I hesitate for a micro-second. Dan's eyes pop wide before I crush his hopes by saying, "No, Coach. I got it."

Coach narrows his eyes at me.

Jack nudges my shoulder as he comes to stand next to me. "We got this, Coach."

"No more goals on us, eh?"

"Yes, sir." "No, sir." Jack's and my simultaneous responses are as snappy as if we were Marine recruits.

As I skate to the net, I keep my eyes riveted on it. "Empty. As you will be for the next twenty minutes. Empty."

Ignoring the thought that Christina's seat is also empty, I don't look up, around or down. Finally, my Zen is back. It's me and the little black disc, and I'm gonna win this round.

It's amazing what the threat of being replaced can do for one's concentration. At least in hockey.

A week later, we're back from another exhausting three-game road trip, this time looping up through two Canadian cities and down through New York. Canadian fans are a joy to play for. Sure, they're loyal to their teams, dedicated and knowledgeable. But unlike some Americans who go beyond loyal to rabid fandom, their expertise in good hockey shows. When a visiting team makes a particularly hard goal or save, there are as many cheers as boos. It's a more respectful ambiance in which to play.

It was also easier to stay in the zone without Christina's empty seat hovering in my peripheral vision. We split the trip with two wins and a loss. And partied like tourists in New York City after kicking some Banker ass. The puck bunnies sure didn't seem to care about their team losing, so I ended up bunking in with Saint while Kyle and Jack commandeered Jack's and my room to get their freak on.

Saint kept trying to catch my eye when we were winding down at the bar, so I hurried back and grabbed the bathroom first, feigning slumber by the time he finished preparing for bed.

Dana texts after each game, abandoning Instagram for direct communication after their visit. I've started looking forward to those messages as reassurance that people are watching and caring. I sit on the plane back to Austin wondering if these will taper off as the holidays approach and they get wrapped up in the world in front of them. Or maybe the texts will continue until she knows Zoe is safely settled here.

I remind myself that Dana chose me over my father in a way. Not everyone leaves.

But Christina did, and my chest aches every minute of every day from her departure. Perhaps more so as we get closer to the Holiday Ball. Dana's words resonate in my head again. What do I want most? I take out my phone and open it to the notepad app. I need to make a list of alternative versions of family. Then I can decide what I love the idea of, what I can live with, and what I can't live without.

The one thing I'm certain of is that Christina is on

top of the list. The question is whether she'll feel the same.

Chapter Thirty-Six

Christina

Meeting Cam's family was amazing and torture all wrapped together. Seeing him with his little brother reinforces my decision even as it tears me apart. His play with the kids at the Thanksgiving party was a knife to my heart; him with Robbie on his shoulders was the knife twisting. I'm eternally grateful he missed the after-game party at Chasers to drive them to the airport so I could fade into the background and be Nicole's wingman for a bit.

No breakup in my past has ever felt like this—not Travis nor anyone before him. This horrible well of darkness I want to crawl into is why I had my rules. Only date older guys, insist on casual, and verify that they aren't looking for a family. I got one out of three right with Cam, a failing grade. However, stupidity does not excuse my giant error in getting involved with him, and only exacerbates my frustration for catching feelings.

I've withdrawn to my pre-Cam anti-social self.

Thankfully, Maria found another instructor to join us, and I was able to shift my classes this week to her.

But the new teacher is a paid contractor whereas I still teach pro bono, which adds guilt to my pile of negative emotions.

I've spent far more hours than were needed staring at screens of stocks, bonds, real estate, and other investments. I've combed through all the players' holdings, sending them personalized notes on their success at saving. Well, all the players except one.

Unable to muster enthusiasm about my passion project, I cancel my weekly meeting with my sister about my nonprofit dance school.

My nights are spent guzzling wine and viewing hockey in grim silence.

Tonight, I've just finished pouring my first glass of wine and am hunkering down in front of the TV for the first Tornadoes game after a week on the road. A knock sounds at my door and makes my hand jerk. Wine sloshes over my glass onto my arm and I wipe it on my clothes. At some point I should return to normal five-ounce pours instead of filling the glass to the rim.

I get up, wine glass and all, to open the door. My brother stands there, his suit pants and dress shirt rumpled from the workday.

"Hey, I didn't make it to the arena because I was on calls until a few minutes ago, and I saw your light on. I thought you were going to games because you liked being close to the action." His words slow as his gaze roams over me.

I'm in my slouchiest stretched-out yoga pants and a loose t-shirt and hoodie. My unwashed hair is haphazardly tied back in a low ponytail, lank tendrils hanging by my face.

"Hey, are you okay? Are you sick or something?"

Being the obnoxious big brother that he is, he takes a step back.

I'm almost tempted to say yes, but I shake my head in the negative. "Just tired. It's been a long week."

"Really? You haven't been at the office at all. I thought you were taking it easy. You always say December is the worst month to mess with investments."

"Yeah, well, they still need to be overseen." My tone is sharper than the situation warrants.

He holds his hands up front of him in surrender. "Okay, okay, you're the expert. Come up and watch the game with me. The housekeeper made enough supper for both of us."

"I don't know." I'd prefer to continue to wallow and drink my wine in my cavern of despair.

"Come on." He gives my still-over-full wine glass a dubious look. "I have better wine up there, as you know."

"Nah, I steal most of my bottles from your cellar." I manage a half-smile.

"What? I never knew that. Dammit, I put some of those aside if I like the vintage, to try again in a year."

"Oops. Just mark them. I won't take those, then."

He grabs my wrist and drags me around the pool. "Come on. Game's about to start. But I'm going to quiz you during the commercial breaks about why you look so sad."

At least I managed to miss the warmups. That might have been too much nostalgia and Cam deliciousness for me to deal with. Thankfully, Greg will be so focused on the game and the team's stats and whether we'll make the playoffs that are still months and dozens of games away, to remember to ask me anything.

* * * *

As I'd expected, Amy calls the next day. "What's up? Greg says something is wrong. Is that why you canceled our meeting last week? I'm coming over."

I barely get out, "Okay," before she hangs up.

Ten minutes later she's letting herself into my house. Thankfully, I had showered earlier and had time to change into an outfit fit for human company, even if it was just jeans and a casual sweater.

Greg knocks and enters within a minute, and we're all standing in the entryway where my living room meets my hall.

"What are you doing here, Tattletale?"

"I told you last night, I'm concerned. My guess is you've got man troubles, so I thought Amy might be helpful."

"Ooo, I bet that hurt to say," she scoffs.

"You look better today, anyway," he says as he scans me.

"Yeah, well some people are courteous and call before they come." But something is distracting me from our usual sibling rivalry. "Wait, why did you think it's something to do with a guy?"

He grimaces at me. "You do realize we live on a gated property, right? The head of security brings two types of visitors to my attention—unidentified ones and repeats—even if they've been named by you or me."

"Oh." So much for secrecy. We'd have had more luck seeing if Jack could keep his mouth shut and spending time there.

He continues. "Really, Chris? Again? Perhaps you need to move away from here so you can date men unattached to our insular little world where they won't keep popping up in your life forever after."

"Oorr…she could pick one and stick with him," Amy adds with a grin.

"No frat policy aside, this could have a huge impact on his career." Greg folds his arms.

I hate when he does that. It's like he's trying to be parental. "No shit, Sherlock. He and I are both reasonably intelligent and had already figured that out for ourselves. Hence why we were keeping it secret and casual."

"Wait, were?" Amy asks. She turns to Greg and adds an aside. "Also, I'm pretty sure it wasn't casual for either of them."

He leans his head sideways and mutters, "Based on her appearance last night, it wasn't for her."

"Standing right here." My hands are on my hips, but they do this out of love.

We perch at the kitchen counter after I hand out Topo Chicos.

"So, as the cat is officially out of the bag, what happened with Prancer?" Amy spends so much time at the team offices, she thinks of all the players by their nicknames or their last names. I wonder if she remembers Cam's first name.

I give them the basics: we set it up as casual, agreeing to end it after the dances at the holiday event. Our conversations about kids, then my disease. Then, seeing him in the pool at Thanksgiving reminded me how unfair it was to him, so I ended it early.

"But you're still doing the fundraising dances, right?" she asks, alarm in her voice.

I grimace. "Thanks for the support, sis."

"I'm sorry, I'm sorry." She glances over at Greg. "This is why I said it's not casual."

"Yeah—" My throat clogs with tears, and I can't speak.

"Oh no! No, no, no. You pick the one guy who should be too young to worry about a relationship but who instead is looking for a family." Her shoulders drop on a sigh. Then she reaches out to hug me for an extended moment.

I cling to her while I regain my composure.

"I'm sorry, Chris. That sucks." Greg says, patting me on the arm.

"It does. Hockey does. Everything does right now."

They chuckle at my weak joke. Greg nods. "I bet."

"He's clearly a jerk. I mean, I know you wanted casual, but every guy should be head over heels for you, cuz yer awesome," Amy adds.

I admit, "It was mostly me driving the secret and casual, although he was concerned about his contract and violating team policy."

"Clearly that didn't deter either of you. It's like waving a red flag in front of a bull," Greg says through laughter.

"He's not a jerk. He's thoughtful. He was super careful about—about—"

"Sex?" Amy offers helpfully.

Greg cringes and says, "No details, please. You're my sister. But I'm glad he took care of you."

"Yes, especially when I told him about my condition. His family…" I stop myself. That's not my story to share. "Anyway, he loved my idea of the nonprofit dance lessons and even had a few suggestions."

She stares at me. "You told him about that?"

I shrug one shoulder.

"Huh." She looks down at the granite countertop,

tracing grains of stone with her fingernail. "I get this is hard for you, but I have to ask. Have you considered alternative routes to a family?"

I frown. *Alternative*…Oh, she means adoption and the like. Geez, I hadn't. "Not really. It all happened so fast and the pain was so extreme, and I knew I couldn't go through that again. So I totally shut down the idea of children."

"But I mean, you could adopt for instance. Surely your therapist talked to you about that?"

"I guess." I shrug again. "It was easier to not think about it. She had enough to do getting me back to being a functioning adult. And how many men are going to be open to adopting? They'll want their own genes."

"Not necessarily." Greg frowns.

I press my lips together, tilting my head at him. "Really? You don't care if your children, who will inherit everything you and the family before you have built, are yours genetically?"

"Honestly? I'm thirty-five and haven't managed to meet the right woman yet. I may not have children. But if I found my person and she couldn't biologically have children but wanted them, I'd be fine with alternate routes."

I think of Cam, so excited that his brother was following him into hockey. "A pro athlete would."

My sister plants a hand on her hip. "How do you know? Have you taken a poll? More importantly, have you asked the specific one you're worried about?"

Then again, Robbie is only his half-brother, and he's equally excited about Zoe coming to Austin, who shares no blood with him. I reply, "I hadn't considered children, so obviously I haven't asked."

"You should," Greg murmurs.

She tilts her head and sobers. Her voice goes quiet. "If it was important to you, I'd surrogate."

"Amy." I don't have the words to convey what that means to me, so I rush over and hug her. Squeezing her tight, I mumble into her hair. "Best sister ever."

"Only sister," she reminds me, but she is holding me just as close. "Ah, to clarify, you're still dancing at the ball, right?"

I release her and smack her arm. "Yes. We're still dancing, brat."

* * * *

I snag a high-top table in the wine bar and check my phone to see my friends' ETAs. Nicole can't make it again, but Lauren and Maria are en route.

Amy's words from this morning have interfered with my concentration all day. I'm glad I didn't have any contracts to review for our family holdings or I might have signed away a property or something. I'm still reeling from Amy's offer. She's always been the easygoing one in our family, the happiest and best adjusted. Maybe because she was the baby and Greg and I both doted on her. She's head of the Tornadoes Foundation for a reason—her giving nature. But this is a whole separate level of giving of her body, months of her time, health risks. I can't begin to imagine all the repercussions.

Everyone in the world of competitive dance was focused on their weight and shape. Most didn't get regular periods. Certainly, no one ever talked about wanting a family or bearing children. And I'd been young enough at nineteen to twenty-two that the whole thing had been in a hazy future.

When I was diagnosed, I'd been excited at the doctor's promise I didn't need a hysterectomy—this time—but devastated at the idea that going off birth control could trigger that need. Until then, I'd had a blurry vision of a husband and children one day, living near the big house where I grew up and expanding the Donovan clan. The doctor's warning that having children would be unlikely and if I did try, the idea of more pain caused me to cordon off the idea of babies. With the help of a therapist, I managed through my grief and closed the door on having a family of my own.

Afterwards, I was in UT with a bunch of teenagers, then here in a safe cocoon at my family home. I dated safe men, only ever short-term, and avoided all thoughts of relationships and children.

When he played in college, Greg had commented once that his hockey team was like a second family. Maybe that was part of why he pushed so hard to bring an NHL team to Austin. These women who I wait for are another version of a second family. It took this whole thing with Cam blowing up to get me to see this. I may need to consider returning to therapy given how much I bury the hard thoughts when left alone.

When Lauren and Maria arrive, I blurt out, "Would a pro athlete be open to adopting kids? Wouldn't he want his"—I do finger quotes--"'superior genetics' to continue on? Wouldn't they want perfection in a mate given their physical condition?"

They both stare at me wide-eyed, Lauren's purse is still in one hand while she's twisted in her seat to hang it from the back of her chair. Finally, she asks, "Uh, I thought you were doing a casual fling with Hill?"

Maria raises her brows at me knowingly.

"I was. We broke up."

"Why?"

"Because I saw how good he was with children and I fell in love with him and I needed to get out before it destroyed me." It all comes out in one breath.

"Okay, first, Imma need wine for this," Maria says, grabbing a menu. "And second—" she points it at me. "—back up and give us more details please."

I bring them up to speed. Maria knows a lot of it from taking me under her wing Thanksgiving Day, but none of us have ever thought about alternate paths to a family.

Lauren is indignant, pure feminist. "So now you're going to change your mind, your whole life path, because a hot guy wants mini-he's? What happened to my intelligent, independent friend?"

She doesn't want children and found solidarity in our life outlooks, so part of her statement comes from feeling defensive about her life choices if I change mine. So while her questions are harsh, I try to field them. "Not necessarily. I'm rattled. I hadn't given alternative paths to a family much consideration because it was easier to hide from my failing and date guys who didn't want kids."

"Ah ha!" Maria exclaims, a finger in the air like she's Sherlock Holmes or something. "You think of it as a failing."

"It is," I maintain.

"It's a failing of your body. My body failed at growing to a normal adult height—" Lauren and I both snicker and she mock-glares as she continues. "—but I don't consider myself a failure as a woman or feel like it's my fault."

"This is a little different."

"If Cam got cancer, would you say it was his fault?"

"No!" I retort. Holy smoke, I can't even contemplate that without shuddering in pain. "Of course not."

"What the hell is the difference?"

"My fault or not, it's not something others will want to take on. If I had cancer, I wouldn't be out dating, signing someone up to go through months of crap and potentially come out alone."

"I would," Lauren chimes in. "I'd be looking to get every ounce of fun along the way. And if a guy broke up with me because it was too hard, then he's not someone I'd want in my life anyway…" She slides a side glance at Maria and adds, "Giant schlong or not."

They crack up.

I shake my head and smile at their antics. "I'm never going to live that down, am I?"

"Nope," Maria says.

"You only told him a few days before Thanksgiving," Lauren says. "Then you have this wild over-reaction and break things off. Did you think to have a conversation with him?"

"No. I told you I had put the whole idea of children away."

"Well, if that fine ass couldn't bring you to at least consider other paths, there's something wrong with you," Maria says, shaking her head.

"That's part of it. He's a hot-as-hell pro hockey player who can have anyone he wants and doesn't need to settle for workarounds." I sigh. "It's not my story to share, but due to some stuff in his childhood, having his own family is important to him."

"Didn't Nicole say that family members came to the

game you and she attended?" Lauren is frowning.

"Well, yes…" Again, I don't want to give details Cam might not want me to share.

"Sounds like he has some family who support him, then."

"That's something of a new development," I hedge.

"Then maybe it allows *him* to rethink what a family looks like, too. If you have an actual conversation like adults in a relationship do, you can find a middle ground."

"Ugh. It was so much simpler to date older guys and not have to share my fai—" I change my word choice at Maria's glare—"condition and risk rejection."

"Yeah, but…" Lauren turns to Maria, then turns back and they say in unison, "giant cock."

Lauren relents and adds, "And clearly someone who cares about you and whom you care about."

There is that. We've agreed to practice one last time on the day of the ball. While that isn't conducive to introducing this conversation, I need to find a way. Although, Cam's been radio silent since the break-up, not sending a single text.

Chapter Thirty-Seven

Cam

Saint's words about there being more than one way to have a family gave me pause. But it wasn't until Dana and the kids showed me a practical application of that theory that I started to open my mind.

Now we're home again, and empty seats or not, I'm going to play my heart out. Earning a multi-year contract will give me the ability to keep Christina near her family. Because after a week of misery, I've figured out that *she* is my family. The rest we'll navigate together.

I need her sweet combination of hockey and dancing that matches mine. Her passion for investing to improve my passion for saving. And her interest in making the world a better place for children. She has simply chosen to go about it a different way.

Can I walk away from the idea of children? Not quite yet. But I'm certainly open to seeing how things go with my brother and sister, her dance school, and seeing if that fills my heart. And I sure as heck don't need biological children if it's going to threaten the health of the woman I love. I need to have a conversation with her to see if she's open to exploring possibilities together.

When I skate out to warm up for tonight's game, I send a side glance at her seats. My head snaps around to stare at them straight on. She's here.

She's here! I'm screaming in my head, ready to shimmy my hips to the music blaring overhead. I should do that after I warm my hips up though; if I pull something, the team will kill me.

Lauren is next to her, looking pissed. Does she not like hockey, or is that look for me?

I go to my knees on the ice, subtly pointing toward Chris rather than center ice like I normally do. As I stretch and undulate on the ice, my knees out and my legs at ninety degrees all flat against the ice, I sniff. I swear the ice smells better tonight, a hint of her vanilla and coconut scent mixing and making it a degree warmer, too. Yeah, yeah, if it was a degree warmer, it would be slushy and soupy. But it feels amazing.

I'm on fire throughout the game and crave a shutout again, even though we're only a third of the way through our season at twenty-seven games. It'd be highly unlikely for a rookie goalie to get two this soon in his career, but hey, a handful of goalies have had them in their first game so you never know.

However, the way to a shutout is not focusing on stats, Christina, contracts, or anything other than that puck.

As we re-enter the ice after the second intermission, the crowd chants, "Hill, Hill, Hill." They want a shutout as much as I do. My teammates join in as we fan out, quieter, but still supportive.

Jack comes by with a, "Let's fucking gooo!"

He'll do everything he can to get this for me as well.

We're up 1-0. The knowledge that letting a puck in would send us into overtime as well as killing the shutout is on all of our minds.

An impending loss is on the other team's mind as well, as they somehow speed up in this last period. Their key winger is out with an injury, though, and despite their speed, they can't get past me.

Just for good measure, Saint and du Près fake them out and the light at their net flashes a goal. Jack is practically dancing on his skates as he flies back toward me to set up for the faceoff. No one loves hockey quite like he does.

The crowd starts chanting. Usually they don't penetrate my sphere of concentration, but it's my name again. With the puck in the far end, I risk a glance at the clock. Twenty seconds left. My heart pounds, but I take a breath to regain my Zen, and block the crowd.

The puck whizzes my way, their players racing to get to the blue line before it does. The linesman raises his hand.

I don't move or wave it off.

The whistle blows. Icing. The penalty means a faceoff down their end, with seven seconds left.

Not daring another glance at the game clock, I count down in my head. Seven. Six. My team's battling to keep the puck in the other end. Five. Four. Three. Someone takes a slapshot toward my net and I brace, but it goes wide. Two. One. And the buzzer goes off. It's over. As I come forward, my teammates tackle me onto the ice. The crowd is thunderous, stomping their feet in time to our team song's bass.

My heart is full. Now if I can convince Christina to give me another chance, it'll stay that way.

* * * *

Dammit, I still haven't managed to talk to Christina and tonight is the Holiday Ball.

She texted me a couple days ago to congratulate me on the shutout. When I thanked her, she asked if we could talk, but our schedules didn't align. My agent had flown in to have dinner and discuss what I can get next year. And I had enough of a concern over a tight leg muscle that I scheduled extra physio sessions. If I pulled something dancing, the coaches would kill me. Those, the usual practices, and one more game made the past several days fly by.

Christina attended that game, too, which I took as a hopeful sign.

Now she's running late to Maria's studio, according to a frustrated text. *Trust me, I get it, sweetheart. I want to talk as much as you do.*

When she pulls up and gets out, another car arrives. A guy follows us inside, holding a suit bag over his shoulder.

I raise my brows. "What's this?" And who is the guy? I was hoping to talk to her before we practiced.

"This is Jules. I had a suit made for you, as I wasn't sure how stretchy yours are. We'd talked about costumes"—she corrects herself at my pressed lips. I don't like that word—"Excuse me, clothes, but we never did anything about them. It's a regular suit, just out of a fabric with more give, and the cut of the trousers is a bit looser. You can take the jacket off if you'd like. And the tie."

I'll reserve judgment until the guy unzips the bag.

"Huh." I admit to surprise—not out loud, of course. It's the darkest of charcoals, somewhere between a suit and a tux. It has the smooth look of a tux, rather than a wool suit texture, but it's not satiny or polyestery, which is what I'd told her I was worried about, given what I'd seen on the reality shows.

"Try it on, please. Your athletic shirt will have to do under the jacket for now," Jules says.

"Okay." Used to the locker room, I tug my track pants down.

Christina gasps and whirls.

He raises his brows.

I catch Christina's gaze in the mirrored wall she forgot to consider, and say, "Feeling shy, Dancer?"

She frowns and turns sideways. "Just trying to give you privacy."

If I'd wanted privacy, I would have adjourned to the bathroom off the studio, but I don't call her on it. If she doesn't want a fresh look, I'll assume her memory is good enough to keep her going, and my plan is to have her back in my life sooner rather than later.

The pants fit smoothly over my hockey thighs and ass and almost perfectly at my waist. I hadn't expected them to get that close.

The tailor is hemming and hawing and tugging various points.

"Will they stay up?" Christina asks.

"Yeah. Especially if I wear a belt." I glance sideways at Jules for confirmation.

He nods.

"Squat," Christina commands.

I lower slowly into a wide squat, trying not to remember other circumstances when I sank into this position with her in a dance studio. The trousers pull but stretch across my ass, groin, and thighs.

Christina swallows, her gaze on my crotch.

I smile. She does still like to look after all.

"I know you're not warm, but can you do a few stretches and then see how close you get to a split?"

"Sure."

"Just move slowly. Greg will have my head if you're hurt from this."

"Trust me, I know." I nod as I put a bent leg on the bar and do a standing pigeon, then rest an ankle on the bar and scootch my other foot back, leaning forward into my thigh. Not a single popped stitch or over-tight pull. "I gotta say, I'm sort of impressed with this fabric."

Jules grins. "Thank you. It was as much Christina's choice as mine, though."

I put the jacket on and raise my arms, considering a cartwheel in it, but there's no way I'm risking the suit for that. Nor would I be comfortable being that restricted. We decide that even if I keep the jacket for the first dance, it'll come off for the second.

Christina walks Jules out after I thank them both and returns with a garment bag over her arm. She checks her watch and squeaks, saying, "We have time for one run-through of both dances and then I have to go get ready. We'll talk tonight? I'll try to get there a little early."

I grit my teeth, trying to find patience. This dance is important, but our future happiness comes before everything else. Then again, maybe she's procrastinating. Or going to say things I don't want to hear. Perhaps it's better to wait. "No problem. I'd like to focus more on the first one. Then we can talk through the second one at the party if we need to?"

We'd decided along the way—with heavy influence from her sister Amy—that we'd do the first dance to earn the donations, promising the second, but save that until much later in the party. The more these whales drink, the bigger second checks they're likely to write.

After rehearsal, I head home and change. When I come out of my room, Jack and Buzz are dressed, but pre-gaming.

"Guys, it's a holiday party, but it's still a work function."

"Dude, you've been hanging around Saint too much. Chill. Have a beer."

"Dude," I retort. "I can't have a beer when I'm doing an exhibition dance with one of the owners."

Buzz points at me with one finger of the hand holding his beer. "Good point. Talk about a career limiting move, dropping the owner."

I stare at him. "Thanks for putting that out there. But there's no way in hell I'd ever drop a woman. Goalie reflexes, remember?"

I'd found a white dress shirt and emerald-green bow tie in the bag with a note that said, "Bow ties won't flap around as much while dancing. Trust me."

As we enter the iconic Austin hotel and climb to the ballroom, I'm suddenly nervous. Last time was just for fun, no one had any expectations except me. I felt bold. Strangely, the more I play, even as beautifully as this season is going, the more I stress about the outcome. My agent texted after the second shutout that unless I do something incredibly stupid, I can practically demand anything I want next year. If only it were that easy to negotiate for Christina's heart.

I'm glad we're doing the first dance before the dinner service, about an hour into the event. Most of the partygoers will have arrived and had their first drink by then—or in Jack's case, their second or third.

My shoulders are tight, even with the additional give in this jacket. I keep looking around for Christina. Finally, I see the back of her head, her hair pinned up with diamond-encrusted barrettes. I smile. I'll be hard-pressed to buy her jewelry when even my sizeable salary pales in comparison to her worth. But I also know she's not a big jewelry person. Between her focus on dance and her nonprofit, I'm not worried about finding gifts to suit her, just about gaining her love.

I start toward her and her shoulders come into view. She's wearing a halter-top dress the exact color of my bow tie. The skirt is longer than her norm but full, and I have no doubt she's tested its fit for our routine.

I bring my hand under her bent elbow and as she turns to me, I lean in. "I'm going to go loosen up."

"I reserved us a small room three doors down on the right. I'm going to the washroom then I'll meet you there."

As I start down the hall, Greg Donovan steps out behind me. "Hill, hold up a minute."

This has to happen now? But he's the owner, so I turn around and face him. His resemblance to Christina strikes me again, and I blink. "Of course, sir. How can I help you."

"You can be patient with my sister."

My eyes bug out of my head. I hoped she'd give me a heads up if she was going to out us to the guy who signs my contracts.

Greg chuckles at my expression. "Apparently, she didn't tell you. I admitted a few days ago that security informs me of repeat visitors. Especially those who don't come to the big house."

I deflate, closing my eyes for a second. "Sorry, sir."

"She explained most of it. And I likely have more backstory than you do. If I was concerned, I'd have said something to one or both of you. But you're a good guy. Strong player, not a bunny chaser, and you obviously have shared interests. Just be gentle with her."

I exhale a long breath of relief. That's a promise I can easily keep. "Always, sir."

"It seems we're close enough you should call me Greg, at least in private." He holds out a hand to shake.

I push a little, figuring it can't hurt to test when I have an advantage. Hockey players were never known for their shyness. "So a contract's looking good for next year?"

"If you're asking as my sister's boyfriend, abso-fucking-lutely. If your agent asks, I was never here. Nice try, though." He winks and strides back inside.

When I duck into our warmup room, Chris is pacing and checking her watch. "Where were you? I wanted to talk to you before we go out."

"Your brother stopped me."

Her eyes widen.

"You could have told me he knew. Anyway, I need to talk to you as well. But my right leg is still tight, I don't know how long our conversation needs, and we're due out there in fifteen minutes."

"Alright, then. Let's go out there and have some fun and raise some money."

Back in the ballroom, I signal the DJ and he clears the dance floor. We stay hand in hand by the door until the room darkens a degree and a spotlight comes to the empty hardwood. We stroll forward, take our bows, and find our starting positions.

The music starts, and she's in my arms again, where she belongs.

Chapter Thirty-Eight

Christina

It's all I can do to maintain the proper dance frame. I want to snuggle against Cam's chest once more and feel his arms wrap around me to hold me tight. Being this close but so far apart is torture. And the fact that most of our bodies will touch at some point during this dance? Sheer hell.

We fly through the song as the darkness around us helps me forget the onlookers. When he threads his hand through my legs to drape me over his shoulder, I get the same thrill I have every time since that first day in the studio. But now, every move is laden with emotion and history. We're in a cocoon we've created—of movement, respect, admiration, and at least on my part, love. Our feet and hands move seamlessly because we're so aware of one another. When he leads me through the hockey stick dance steps, we share a secret smile, remembering the first day we met.

I want to continue this layered interaction that is so personal and intimate forever. But the dance ends too soon. He spins me out, then in, then around so I'm behind him as he faces the crowd. While I only see broad shoulders, I can hear the murmurs and tinkles of glassware, and reality rushes in. On the final beat, in what is becoming a signature move in these dances, he drops into a split with my hand on his shoulder in a gender-reversed version of a typical ending pose.

His teammates are yelling and cheering and catcalling as I give him an assist to rise and bow. The lights come up and I swear they're ready to brush hundred-dollar bills off their palms. Amy is nearly drooling and Greg is giving us a standing ovation.

Cam turns to me with a huge grin, clearly pleased with his success. As he should be. After one last bow, we grab waters from the bar and walk out of the room to catch our breath. Then we'll walk through the next one while we're warm.

However, the emotions and connection of our dance added to my need to apologize and see if he's as interested as I am in continuing our relationship.

Ever the athlete, Cam's energy is riding high from his "win." He tugs me into the small room. The minute the door closes, he crowds me into the wall next to it. Nuzzling my neck where it's exposed by the clip holding my hair back, he whispers, "I missed you, Dancer."

We need to talk, but right now I savor being in his arms again clutching his shoulders. His muscles shift under my fingers as he slips one arm around my lower back and the other to the back of my neck, careful not to mess up my hair. His deodorant and laundry detergent smell are as familiar as my own perfume, and his strong arms make me feel safe, like everything will work out.

After another deep inhale, I respond, "I missed you, too. I'm sorry for ending things so abruptly at

Thanksgiving. I should have talked to you about my concerns rather than shutting down."

He raises his head and blinks at me, a smile starting to tease his lips upward. "Really?"

The icy fear that I might not be forgiven begins to thaw at that smile. Knowing his history, I'd wondered if he'd even listen. I'm willing to do what I need to earn his forgiveness and give us another chance. Still wrapped in his arms, I nod. "Really. When I was experiencing the worst of the pain all of my emotions got jumbled. Not being able to dance competitively. The surgery. I tied it all to not physically being able to have children and shut the whole subject down. It was all abstract anyway. This past week, my friends—and a call to my therapist—helped me figure out that I considered it a failing and I didn't want to admit that to anyone or be rejected because of it."

He tightens his hold around me then loosens to maintain eye contact. "There are always choices."

"I'm starting to see that. I'd never met someone who made me think about it again. In fact, I actively avoided men who might. Until you, you pushy goalie."

I poke him in the chest, but he captures my finger and raises it to his lips.

"Dancer, I don't want to keep doing what we were doing."

I gasp, pain knifing through me. I tug at my hand in his. I've admitted all this and now he doesn't want to be with me? He'd said he wanted to talk. I thought it was safe. In the next breath, I catch myself. It doesn't matter if it was safe or if he doesn't want me. I needed to do this for myself.

"I don't want to sneak around, and I don't want

casual. You met Dana briefly."

I stare at him, unsure where he is going with this.

"You left a strong impression. She gave me an earful about different sizes and shapes of families. As did Saint. Just like you had a unilateral view of having children, I had a myopic idea of how a family is formed."

Hope wars with fear again. I try to pull back, but the wall is behind me. When I drop my hands, he grabs them and holds them, holding my gaze. He looks so earnest but I don't dare trust that he means he wants more. I need to hear it. "If you don't want casual, and you do want kids, where does that leave us?"

"I want you to meet Dana and the kids. I want to look at houses with you, and dance with you, and have you manage my money without showing me all those risks you take so one day I can buy you a ring that will be in keeping with these." He touches my barrettes with a finger before reclaiming my hand, then continues. "I want to sit down and hash out what our family could look like. Because whatever else it looks like, it includes you. You are the first person I've thought of as family in nearly a decade."

I gasp and it comes out as a sob. My knees go weak, and I'm thankful he has me pinned against a wall. Tears leak out as I stare at him, this gorgeous perfect man who somehow wants me and my flaws. I sigh, releasing every hurt from the past. The pain and anxiety from dealing with a hidden chronic illness, Travis's deprecation of my dreams, and my unconscious mourning of my inability to bear children. All of it. I squeeze Cam's hands harder to draw on his strength, unable to form words to even check that this is real.

He bends slightly so we're face to face, an even

playing field—rink.

I want to touch his face, but I can't bring myself to ease my grip on his hands.

He says, "Dancer, I am in love with you, and you are the most important person in the world to me. I'll never let you fall—in dance or anything else. We can figure out the rest together."

My breath catches through my tears. I hadn't realized how badly I needed to hear those words. My knees choose then to give out. When I start to slide down the wall, he catches me and tugs me against him, exemplifying yet another thing I love about him. I'm sobbing, and petting him as he holds me, trying to smile, breathe and talk all at once through my tears.

Not understanding my garbled attempts at words, he looks at me in concern. "Hey, now. Are you all right? I can keep doing casual and secret if you're worried. I didn't mean to upset you. I'll keep trying to win you over if you're not ready."

I nod then shake my head against him.

He barks a laugh. "Sorry, what does that all mean?"

Finally, I pull myself together enough to tilt my head back. "I am completely in love with you, too, Cam. And yes, I won't let you fall either, and we'll figure it out together. But aren't you worried about your contract?"

"Didn't you just hear me? You're the most important thing to me. And anyway," he shrugs with a mischievous smile. "A little bird in the hallway said I was in the clear. Either way, I'm gonna continue to be the best damned goalie he's seen, so he won't be able to get rid of me."

* * * *

After some serious kissing, Cam puts his phone to

our next song and we step through the second dance without the full lifts. We contemplate skipping dinner to snog—a word I learned from Cam—in here, but we'll need energy for the second, sexier dance.

Tearing ourselves away, we return to our separate tables and try to eat, then return here to re-stretch.

In the ballroom, Cam sheds his suit jacket onto a random empty chairback and flings his bow tie over it. Him in an open-necked white dress shirt is like one of those TikToks where you know what muscles are under it, and they'll show in the next screenshot. I'm going to have a hard time not dirty dancing with him, never mind the room full of people.

At the end of the song currently playing, I signal to the DJ and Amy to clear the floor and announce us. Amy cajoles the crowd for donations per trick, hinting she hears there's more than one.

Jack calls, "I'm in for a grand for every time Cam's feet leave the floor."

I wonder if he has insider knowledge then laugh because it doesn't matter.

Either way, Amy is ecstatic when other players call out with their own over-the-top conditions.

I'm giddy from my conversation with Cam. My ebullience carries over into silliness, and I make a crying face at her, fists to my eyes, and she turns to the audience. "Wow, us Donovans are hurt. Must it always be about you hockey guys?" After the laughter dies down, she says, "I got you, Sis. A thousand for every trick Christina does."

I curtsy and nod to the DJ again. The room darkens and the spotlight returns.

The first notes of *Señorita* roll out. Where the first

dance was elegance, this is sex. It's designed as a reward for the earlier donations and a temptation all at once. Nothing could suit my mood better.

I'm already grinning as we start flowing with the music in a close hold wherever the steps allow.

Cam catches my leg after a small trick and places it on his shoulder, stepping back a few steps as he drags me on one foot across the floor. Wolf whistles sound out and the audience spurs me on again. Being in Cam's arms and knowing we'll raise a ton of money for a good cause elevates my mood and I'm floating.

I move into position for our assisted cartwheels and go up and over Cam's arm. My arms cross to grab his hands, and I cartwheel in front of him using only his arm strength and mine to keep me from falling headfirst.

The applause sounds subdued, as though they know there's more.

We turn and I stand perpendicular to Cam, in the position he had just been in, and using whatever power I have, hold his hand to help turn him through a one-handed cartwheel in front of me.

His teammates explode. Their cheers fill up the ballroom nearly drowning out the music.

We wrap with a flourish. Cam twirls me out and slides on his knees to my left leg where he hops up. But instead of taking his bow like we practiced, he tugs me in to face him and threads a hand through my hair under my ear.

Wide-eyed I stare at him, my arms coming to his shoulders.

Our breaths mingle and the ballroom fades away. He brings his other hand to my lower back and arches me into him as though he wants to be certain there's no mistaking his intentions. Leaning in, he tilts his head with a smile and whispers, "I love you, Dancer."

Our lips meet and I sense a shocked hush in the room. But I don't care what's going on out there.

In here, in this bubble where only Cam and I exist, there is mutual love and respect, and him showing me he means what he says—that I come first.

Chapter Thirty-Nine

Cam

Kissing Chris in the middle of the ballroom probably wasn't one of my smartest moves, but I don't care. I barely registered the team falling unusually silent. But once Greg Donovan stood and clapped for our performance while we were still kissing, the guys relaxed. The roof nearly came off with their stomping and hollering.

Chris drives us to her place after the ball to talk. I can't wait to park my car in the circular driveway, and leave it there all night, in the open, but Jack, Buzz, and I had rideshared to the event, so it has to wait.

Inside, I sober quickly. This conversation is far more important than my improved transportation options.

Chris offers me a drink, but both of us opt for water. We sit at the table so we can face each other comfortably and still hold hands. She seems nervous.

Trying to put her at ease, I lead with, "We don't have to work it all out tonight."

Her shoulders drop a little bit. "Thank you. I guess more than anything, I want to reset my own expectations, as you've been generous in your flexibility. We've been—excuse the pun—dancing around this for months, so now we're changing the rules, going public, without an end date, I'm a bit lost. In a good way, but still."

"That's cool. What would help you get more comfortable?" I hope my squeezing her hand reassures her.

"Again with the flexibility. Geez, this is like when we were supposed to be celebrating your first shutout, but I was the one that got oral."

"Will oral help? I'm happy to start with that?" I perk up, sitting forward. Mostly teasing.

"Sadly, no. Verbal, not oral. Two different things." She mock-shakes her head. Oh, Dancer has jokes now, too.

Keeping hold of her hand, I grab the other one that has been making flailing gestures as she talks. "Hey. This is you and me. No one else is in this relationship with us. And neither of us has been in a similar situation in our past. So we'll figure it out together, as we go. I meant what I said. You're mine and I'm yours. The rest is negotiable."

She blows out a breath, dropping her shoulders an inch. "I still don't know where to start."

"Come here." I stand and tug her up, then lead her to the couch. Sitting her at one end, I claim the other and grab her feet, placing them in my lap. "No one can stress out while getting a foot rub. I'm pretty sure it's physically impossible."

"I'm not sure I can be coherent while getting a foot rub, though." Her head rolls back as my thumbs dig into her arches.

"Here's what we'll do. I'll ask questions, and if you

can't answer I'll pause what I'm doing." I focus on her left foot first, using both hands to smooth the muscles below the ankle bone. "Any limitations on what you're comfortable doing short term as a couple? Being seen in public? Going out with the team after games? I need to give my agent a heads up because this'll be news, and there will be speculation about my contract, but other than that I want you with me as much of the time as you're willing."

Chris moans when I hit a tight spot. After a breath, she replies, "Depending on what your agent says, I don't have a problem being seen out and around. However, I'd like to play the 'hanging with the guys' part by ear, please. It might be hard for them to view me as your girlfriend."

My hands tighten on her foot at the word "girlfriend."

She flinches. "Ouch."

"Ohmigod, sorry, Chris." I forgot how sore the balls of her feet can get dancing in those crazy high heels.

"It's all right. Anyway, I don't want them to see me as an owner spying on their activities."

"Based on the couple times you've come out already, I don't think they do. Their financial advisor, maybe, but not an owner. Besides, at one time or another, some of those loons might need bail money."

She snorts. "Then an owner is the last person they'd want around. They'd be afraid it'll get back to Greg."

"Next subject. Houses."

She gestures for me to pause. "You've relaxed me enough you may need to pour me into bed, so I can wait on some of the subjects. For houses, suffice it to say I've been lazy, sponging off Greg with no house maintenance responsibilities, but I'm open on those. The most important thing is children, and I'm not sure where I'm at on that."

"Are you open to considering having some, if it doesn't include risking your health?"

"I'm open to *considering* considering having one or more."

I shake my head, chuckling. "What does that even mean?"

"I'm nervous to say I'm willing to think about it because you might take that as there is a definite path to us having kids, it's just a matter of which path. Whereas I'm not there yet."

"Ah. I understand. I would like to outline our options, because it might help you envision what might or might not work for you, but I'm not in a rush. I want to play a few more years of hockey before kids so I can retire and spend more time with them."

"Wow. You see yourself as a house husband after hockey? I could get on board with that." She grins. "But to answer your question, we can talk those through one day soon. What else?"

"Your legs are all I can think of at the moment. Can we table the rest for another day, while I trade in my verbal skills for my oral?"

"Yes, please."

I tug her toward me, positioning her legs on either side of me and she grins in anticipation. I'll never tire of making her smile.

When I stand with her straddling with me, she yelps.

I remind her, "I'll never drop you, Dancer. I love you."

Her responding, "I love you, too" is muffled by my lips slanting over hers as I head for the bedroom.

Cam

I've wracked my brain for a month about what to get a billionaire for her birthday. Google searches are not helpful on that front, even the few that don't assume the billionaire is male.

It's February, and we lead our division giving us a path to the playoffs. I'm more tired than I've ever been at this point in the season, but I'm revved about making the post-season our first year. Not to mention what that'll do for sponsorship opportunities. I've had some interesting requests from Arthur Murray and the like after the guys posted snapshots of our dances on Instagram, but my agent is holding out for the big bucks for hockey-relevant contracts like a sports drink.

Chris's birthday is in a few weeks and I'm still clueless. Her brother isn't much help, his budget is different. He got her a year's supply of her favorite wines delivered to her little house, so she'll stop raiding his wine closet. Checking to see if Chris is still in the bedroom, I start a new group text.

Birthday Phone-A-Friend

> Can y'all help please? What do I get Dancer for her birthday? I know I should know this, but I'm struggling

Mattie

> I kinda figured it would be a ring…?

I wish. I'm dying to get on a knee and promise her the rest of my life, and I am almost certain she'll have me. I'm still paying rent for my share of the rental with Jack, but I've moved all my stuff in to "the poolhouse" as we jokingly call it while we look for *our* house. Jack's jokes about me being the Donovans' pool boy are endless, but I don't care. I'd be her pool boy any time.

I keep my mail at the rental, though, just in case some reporter or rabid fan searches out my home address. Chris's idea, not mine. She's super protective of my reputation.

> No. She insisted we wait until after my next contract is signed, and my agent agreed with her. So after the season.

Mattie

Lingerie, then? Diamonds? Lingerie with diamonds?

Nicole

<rolling eyes emoji> Lingerie is a gift for himself. Maybe try something that SHE wants.

Yeah, but that's my question <smiling face>

Nicole

…I see your point. We all get girly things for each other, but that wouldn't be romantic enough.

How about a trip? But it would have to be after the post-season and I don't know how she feels about delayed gratification

Mattie

Then you're not doing something right <ROTFL emoji>

For birthday gifts! Sheesh!

Mattie

She's got that kick-ass dancer's bod – no offense intended – how about a boudoir photo shoot? That'd be for both of you <smiling devil emoji>

Nicole?

Ok, she must be busy. See what she thinks about that, the trip, and any other ideas you come up with?

Mattie

Me? She's the project manager

> Exactly. She'll manage you.
> <winking face>

Billie Eilish's *Birds of a Feather* starts, summoning me to the dance studio. Dancer loves this song and often plays it on repeat when we practice together. Sometimes we actually practice, and sometimes it's foreplay. Either works. My whole life feels like foreplay these days—pleasurable, fun, a little teasing, leading up to the big event that will be making her mine forever.

Sneak Peek at

Net Pucks and Chill

Nicole

When I'm an hour outside Austin, I punch in my friend Christina Donovan's number on my car's display. She made me promise to call when I got back from Christmas at my family's. We've been friends since attending UT together, although she's a few years older, so she knows how I feel about trips home, and she worries about me on the long drive. She's also a billionaire and part-owner of the new Austin NHL team, the Texas Tornadoes, so she has the resources to send help should I need it.

"Hey, are you home?" she asks.

"No, but I'm less than an hour out. I can almost see the skyline."

"How was it?"

"The same." I shrug even though she can't see it. "They barely sat down for the meal before they were out doing ranch chores again."

"I guess that's better than pestering you to help with them."

"True. What are you doing? I'm beat from almost

nine hours in the car, but I sure could use some company and a drink."

"Oh, uh, we were going to get Mattie from the airport in a bit."

Mathieu du Près is the most charming, beautiful man I've seen in a long time and an excellent hockey player to boot. I've met him a few times at after-game celebrations at the unofficial team hangout, Chasers. But the last thing I want to do is see him after three days with my family surrounded by two long days of driving. I'm not in a good state of mind, and I probably don't smell all that great, either.

I open my mouth to suggest Christina's boyfriend Cameron Hill, starting goalie for the Tornadoes, get his teammate while she comes and drinks with me, but Chris beats me there.

"We could swing by after we get him if you'd like? I'll order snacks for the guys and we'll bring the drinks. You don't have to do anything."

"You better give me time to shower if you're bringing a single guy to my place."

She laughs. "Ha! It's just Mattie." At my silence, she asks, "Nicole? Are you into Mattie?"

"First, I'd want to shower after this drive for anyone, probably even Cam now that I think about it. You're willing to deal with me with road grime, but there's no reason to subject others to it. Second, I'm pretty much into any hot single guy about now. It's been a long dry spell. But I also know my place in the world. I'm invisible to someone like him. He sees the exotic fun girls, the ones with legs for miles and honey blonde hair like you, or the spicy tiny dancers like Maria."

"Okay. I'm sorry. I know you're beat. We won't stay

long. But having the guys there could perk you up, or take the pressure off if you don't want to rehash your annoyance at your family just yet…?" She trails off, hopeful. "But I could come alone if you prefer."

It means a lot that she offers. Cam and she had a rocky few months as their secret, supposedly casual, relationship turned into real, long-term love. They've been fused at the hip—as much as hockey travel schedules allow—since then.

And now that I've wrangled the promise of shower time out of her, the eye candy that is Mattie and the tons of food that comprise hockey player "snacks" sound great.

"Bring 'em. Just no sooner than eight o'clock please."

"Perfect, he doesn't touch down until almost then and I'll order food to be delivered from the car. Love you!"

"Love you, too." But she's already gone, high on life and love. If I had her looks and money, I would be, too. But I'm the ugly duckling of the group. Not ugly, but not a beauty or unique like any of my close circle, either.

No matter. After this Christmas, I'm determined to start the New Year as the new me. I'm going to wear lower cut tops, push-up bras, more makeup, and flirt like mad. And I'll sleep with whoever strikes my fancy. I'm tired of holding out for someone who wants all of me, and I don't have time for a relationship until I finish my MBA anyway.

Mattie is the perfect practice target, even if he is beyond my reach.

Mathieu

As the plane touches down in Austin, Texas, I recall a similar flight only four months ago, when I started for the Texas Tornadoes. New city, new team. Again. You'd think I'd be used to it by now, having played for the Florida Fury before being nabbed by Greg Donovan in the expansion draft. And I am. We have the first two months of the season under our belt and there are some good guys on this team. Great players, too.

I also love that there are more single players like me. More opportunities to play. Every city has puck bunnies, but more importantly, my guys here are up for new adventures. If I feel like playing disc golf, I can call someone. If I want to go spelunking, there's someone up for it. And they don't have to check with their wife or girlfriend to know if they're available.

Austin isn't as hopping as Miami, but at least here less girls are looking for my paycheck as much as my body. And they're less plastic. People are also more active, which suits me, as I don't sit still well. They go out on a boat to kneeboard, or ski, or fish, rather than just be boat decorations that want you to "rub sunscreen everywhere."

Despite the ridiculous late December temperature of 18C, I'm surprised to find myself happy to be back in my new city. I'd bounced home for a day and a half, as we only had a three-day break and the weather for flights is unpredictable at this time of year.

Ottawa at Christmastime is amazing, although I might be biased. The Rideau Canal is decorated beautifully in readiness for when it opens to skaters next month. And my family home has all the best memories—handmade decorations from my sister's and my childhood art projects, silly holiday sweaters, all of it. Far more important, it has my family. My sister is finishing university this year, so we were both home for a couple weeks this summer. But winter is what Canada does best, and I've missed the colder temperatures and the snow almost as much as I missed my maman's cooking.

We've got practice tomorrow morning, then fly out to an away game followed by a home game on December 30, and another on New Year's Day.

Prancer and his owner-girlfriend (owner of the team, not him, although…) are supposed to pick me up tonight, and I'm starving, as I usually am, so I'm hoping they'll be up for a quick meal before dropping me at home.

I turn my phone on and it lights up. The team texts have been sparse as almost everyone was focused on family for the holiday, but they'll get going again as we all return.

I skim the ones waiting for me from Christina. Sweet! They're taking me with them to Nicole's apartment from the airport and Chris will ensure there are snacks.

I've met her friends a couple times, mostly at Chasers, our after-game go-to bar. The accountant one seems like a hardass, and the dancer is a firecracker. But the quiet one, Nicole, has promise. A no muss, no fuss interlude of fun until I'm bored. We had fun the couple times she came to Chasers, and the second time, she even sought me out.

Half a dozen puck bunnies did as well, and while their asses might have been a little tighter, and their hair a little silkier, I also like that I don't have to work as hard or worry about Nicole. She's not going to poke a hole in a condom, or hide a camera, or cling and try to keep me overnight.

* * *

Preorder Net Pucks and Chill now for $0.99

Want more hockey romance?
Get Emil Bergstrom's second chance love story when you sign up for my newsletter at
https://bookhip.com/TFJRZCH

Future Texas Tornado books will feature (in no particular order)
Jack
Buzz
Saint
Greg
Kyle
and others
(tell me which you want next when you sign up for my newsletter!)

Also by Debbie Charles

Second Chance Puck (exclusive newsletter novella)
Net Pucks and Chill
Spicy as Puck
Intentional Offside

For Love or Money (a spin-off novella)

Books written as Maggie Sims

The School of Enlightenment Series
Roslynn's Rebellion (prequel novella)
Sophia's Schooling (Book 1)
Penelope's Passion (Book 2)
Althea's Awakening (Book 3)
Beth's Behavior (Book 4)

Spin-offs
Helen's House
Ann's Angel (a Christmas short story)

The Control Series
Charlotte's Control
Lyon's Lover
Folly's Folly

Spin-offs
Duke's Diversion

Acknowledgements

I had a lot of help with this book, from a wide variety of sources, and I appreciate all of you. In particular, I want to note my inspiration, dance expert, hockey expert, and editing team.

Kate Meader, this whole story germinated from a one-line seed in **So Over You** when Isobel dismissed Vadim's future as a contestant on Dancing with the Stars. Thank you for the inspiration. I love all of your books, including the Chicago Rebels & Rookies series, and the hotter than fire Hot in Chicago series.

Justine Covington, was it luck or fate when you introduced yourself at a historical romance writers' conference and said you were pursuing ballroom dancing? Thank you for your guidance and review as a subject matter expert. All mistakes are my own, of course.

Below are also some YouTubers who broke down dance lifts and steps for me in a very beginner-friendly way, for those interested.

Stephen Meserve, my friend Julie mentioned your name and blog. I'm not sure she expected me to cold call you, but for someone who could not fathom the idea of hockey romance, you've been incredibly enthusiastic in helping me. I refer to you as my "hockey aficionado," and have refreshed my love of hockey watching Texas Stars games. I also appreciate your 100 Degree Hockey blog and book **We Win Here: The Definitive Essays You Need About The Texas Stars**. You have been patient, kind, and in general amazing, going above and beyond sharing your technical knowledge of all aspects of professional hockey to reading the hockey scenes for accuracy (or at least close). Did I mention patience? Thank you. All mistakes are my own, but there are far fewer thanks to you.

Julie Artz, you were a warm and helpful book coach early in

this process, extending your coaching to supplement my research on endometriosis, all of which was much appreciated.

Milly Bellegris, my editor extraordinaire of Gray Plume Editing, this manuscript needed extra love and attention from you. I feel like I might have taken advantage of your Canadian citizenship and love of hockey, and I am sincerely grateful for your efforts.

Last—but very definitely not least, Letty Bee. I don't know how to begin to thank you for giving the audiobook for this a shot. Whether you decide to publish it with me or not, your work and perfectionism are amazing, and I loved exploring this with you.

https://www.youtube.com/@bcdancepassion6922
https://www.youtube.com/@DanceInsanity

A lifelong romance reader, I cut my teeth on Johanna Lindsey, Jude Deveraux, and Kathleen Woodiwiss, along with Silhouette and Harlequin for palate cleansers.

Opting for a career that provided both a food and travel budget, I earned a BA, CPA, and MBA, and spent far too long being a corporate drone, then consulting other corporate drones.

Along the way, I was one of the few 1990s NBA season ticket holders never to see Michael Jordan play ('93-'94). I also attended a few NFL games, the Belmont Stakes, the NHL playoffs, the World Series, and managed to see more than twenty MLB parks, several of which have since been demolished. More recently, I've enjoyed the Texas Stars, the AHL affiliate of the Dallas Stars.

I have published a number of spicy Regency romances under the pen name Maggie Sims (www.maggiesims.com), along with hot hockey romances set in Austin as Debbie Charles, where I now live with my husband and three furbabies.